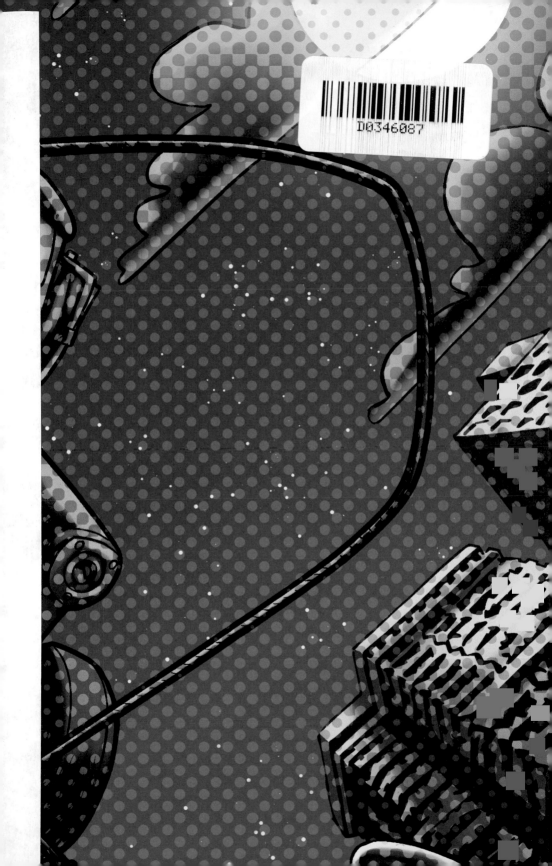

ADVENTURES OF TOW MATER

BASED ON THE CARS STORYBOOK "RUST BUCKET DERBY" BY CHUCK WILSON

WRITER:

Keith R.A. DeCandido

ART BY:

Travis Hill

Ross Richie - Chief Executive Officer
Mark Waid - Chief Creative Officer
Matt Gagnon - Editor-in-Chief
Adam Fortier - VP-New Business
Wes Harris - VP-Publishing
Lance Kreiter - VP-Licensing & Merchandising
Chip Mosher - Marketing Director
Bryce Carlson - Managing Editor
Ian Brill - Editor
Dafna Pleban - Editor
Christopher Burns - Editor
Christopher Meyer - Editor
Shannon Watters - Assistant Editor
Eric Harburn - Assistant Editor
Adam Staffaroni - Assistant Editor
Neil Loughrie - Publishing Coordinator
Brian Latimer - Lead Graphic Designer
Erika Terriquez - Graphic Designer
Stephanie Gonzaga - Graphic Designer
Travis Beaty - Traffic Coordinator
Ivan Salazar - Marketing Assistant
Brett Grinnell - Executive Assistant

For information regarding the CPSIA on this printed material, call: (203) 595-3636 and provide reference #EAST – 70597. A catalog record of this book is available from OCLC and from the BOOM! Studios website, www.boom-studios.com, on the Librarians Page.

BOOM! Studios, 6310 San Vicente Boulevard, Suite 107, Los Angeles, CA 90048-5457. Printed in USA. First Printing.
ISBN: 978-1-60886-607-6

Rust Bucket Derby

MUNICIPALE
10.99

COLORS BY:
Rachelle Rosenberg

LETTERS:
Deron Bennett

COVER BY:
Allen Gladfelter

DESIGNER:
Erika Terriquez

ASSISTANT EDITOR:
Jason Long

EDITOR:
Christopher Meyer

SPECIAL THANKS:
Jesse Post, Steve Behling,
Rob Tokar, Bryce VanKooten and
Kelly Bonbright

Chapter One

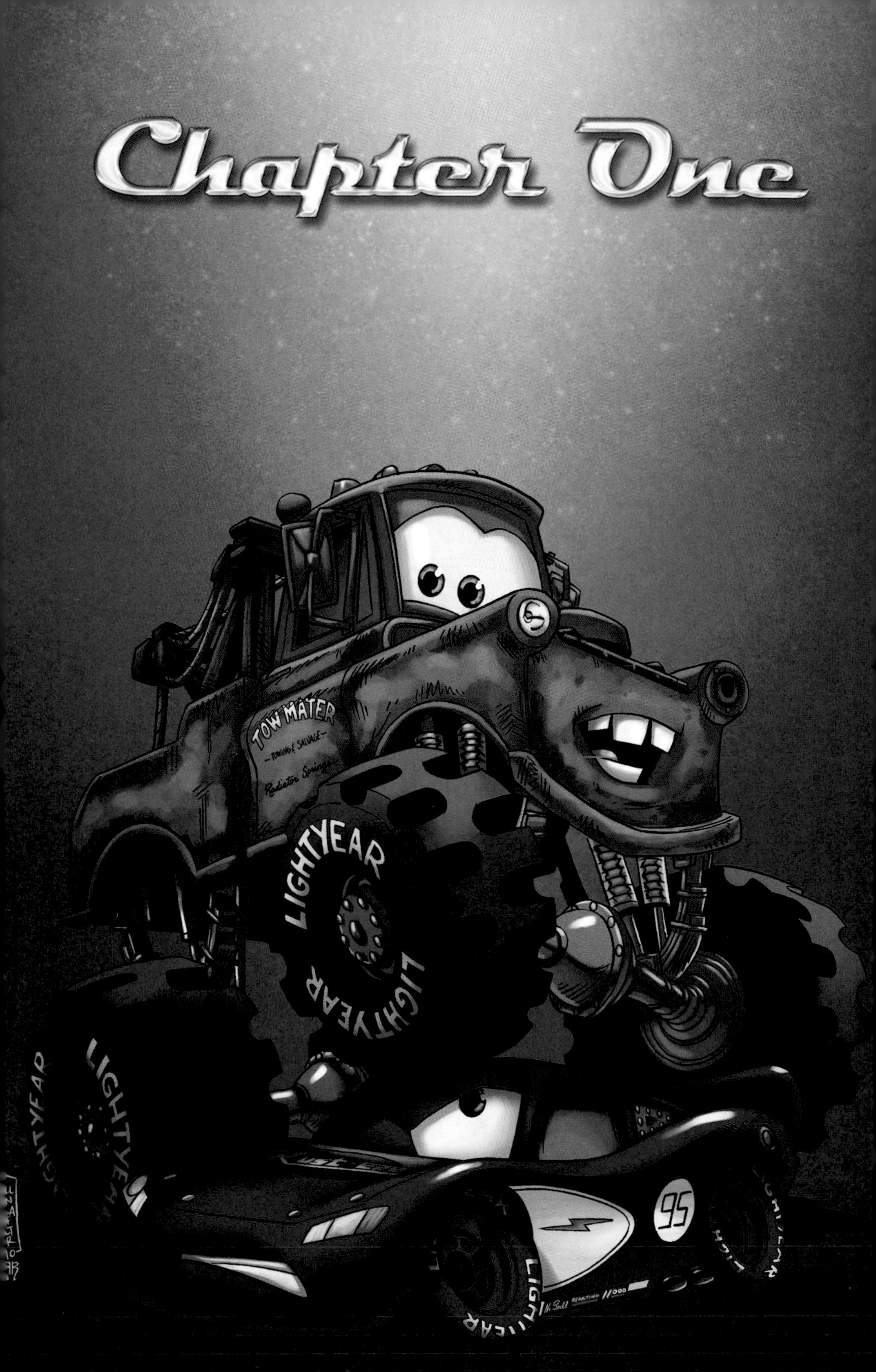
TOW MATER
TOWING & SALVAGE
LIGHTYEAR
LIGHTYEAR
95

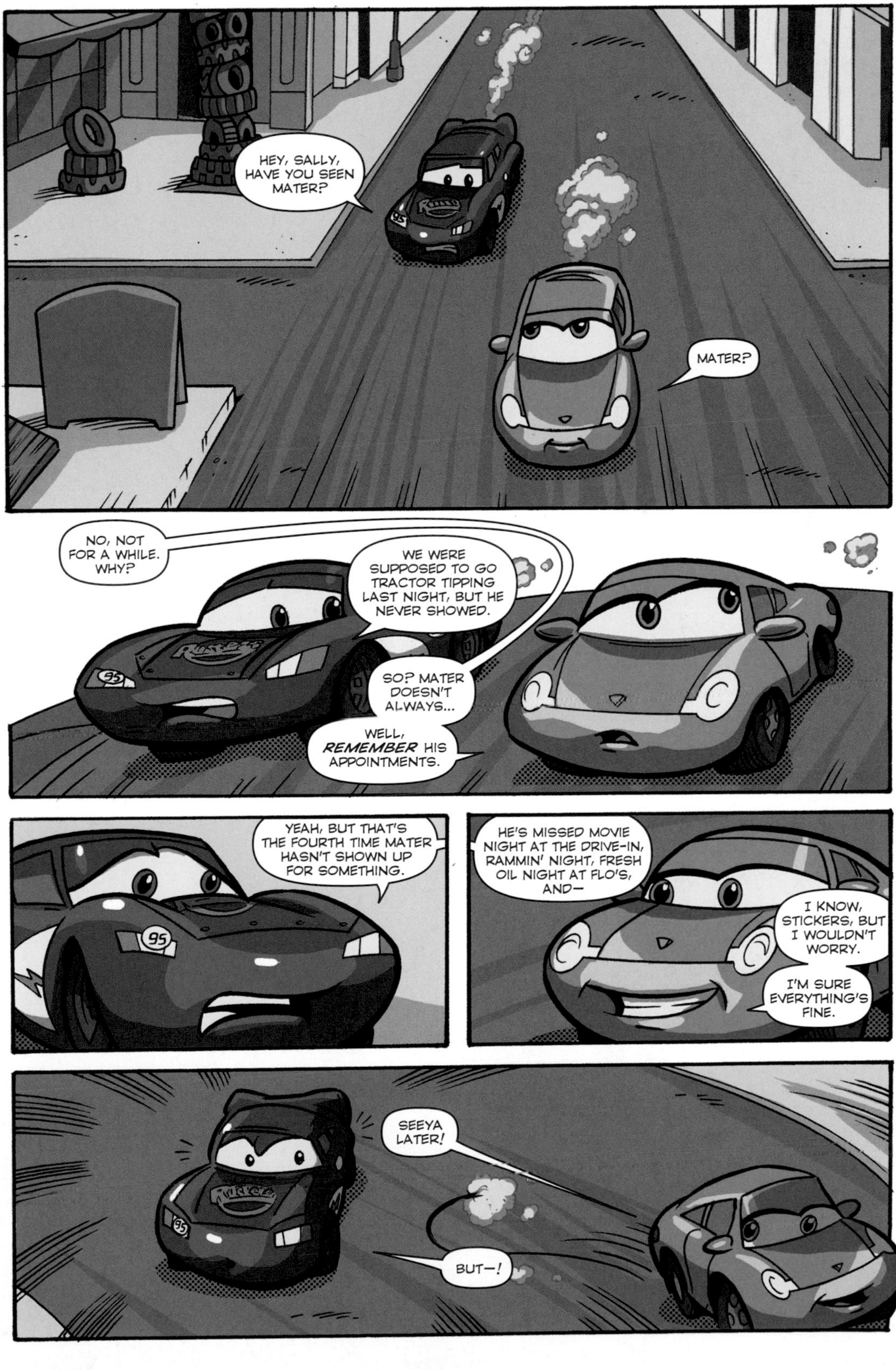
HEY, SALLY, HAVE YOU SEEN MATER?
MATER?
NO, NOT FOR A WHILE. WHY?
WE WERE SUPPOSED TO GO TRACTOR TIPPING LAST NIGHT, BUT HE NEVER SHOWED.
SO? MATER DOESN'T ALWAYS...
WELL, REMEMBER HIS APPOINTMENTS.
YEAH, BUT THAT'S THE FOURTH TIME MATER HASN'T SHOWN UP FOR SOMETHING.
HE'S MISSED MOVIE NIGHT AT THE DRIVE-IN, RAMMIN' NIGHT, FRESH OIL NIGHT AT FLO'S, AND—
I KNOW, STICKERS, BUT I WOULDN'T WORRY.
I'M SURE EVERYTHING'S FINE.
SEEYA LATER!
BUT—!

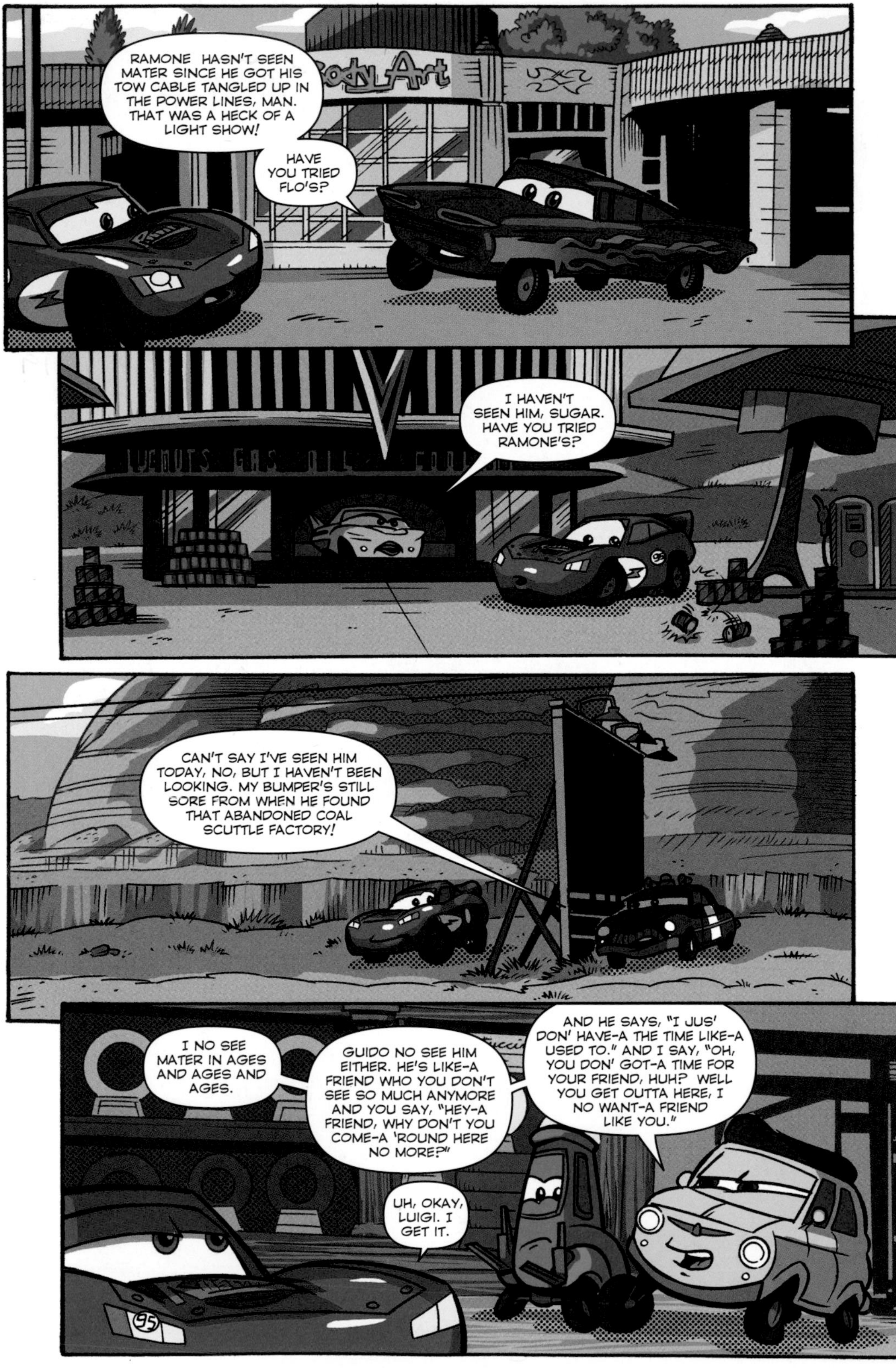
RAMONE HASN'T SEEN MATER SINCE HE GOT HIS TOW CABLE TANGLED UP IN THE POWER LINES, MAN. THAT WAS A HECK OF A LIGHT SHOW!
HAVE YOU TRIED FLO'S?
I HAVEN'T SEEN HIM, SUGAR. HAVE YOU TRIED RAMONE'S?
CAN'T SAY I'VE SEEN HIM TODAY, NO, BUT I HAVEN'T BEEN LOOKING. MY BUMPER'S STILL SORE FROM WHEN HE FOUND THAT ABANDONED COAL SCUTTLE FACTORY!
I NO SEE MATER IN AGES AND AGES AND AGES.
GUIDO NO SEE HIM EITHER. HE'S LIKE-A FRIEND WHO YOU DON'T SEE SO MUCH ANYMORE AND YOU SAY, "HEY-A FRIEND, WHY DON'T YOU COME-A 'ROUND HERE NO MORE?"
AND HE SAYS, "I JUS' DON' HAVE-A THE TIME LIKE-A USED TO." AND I SAY, "OH, YOU DON' GOT-A TIME FOR YOUR FRIEND, HUH? WELL YOU GET OUTTA HERE, I NO WANT-A FRIEND LIKE YOU."
UH, OKAY, LUIGI. I GET IT.

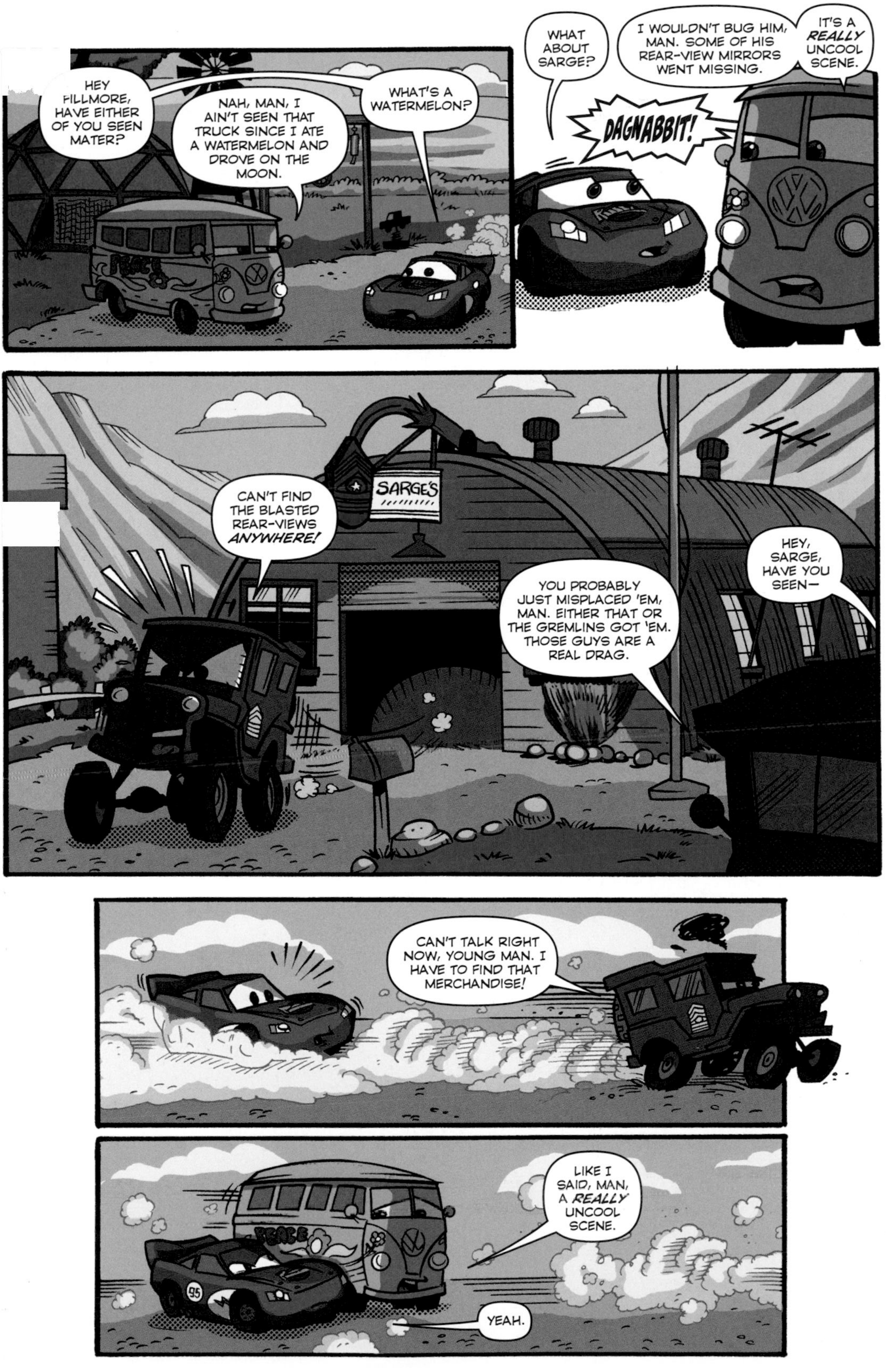
HEY FILLMORE, HAVE EITHER OF YOU SEEN MATER?
NAH, MAN, I AIN'T SEEN THAT TRUCK SINCE I ATE A WATERMELON AND DROVE ON THE MOON.
WHAT'S A WATERMELON?
WHAT ABOUT SARGE?
I WOULDN'T BUG HIM, MAN. SOME OF HIS REAR-VIEW MIRRORS WENT MISSING.
IT'S A *REALLY* UNCOOL SCENE.
DAGNABBIT!
SARGE'S
CAN'T FIND THE BLASTED REAR-VIEWS *ANYWHERE!*
YOU PROBABLY JUST MISPLACED 'EM, MAN. EITHER THAT OR THE GREMLINS GOT 'EM. THOSE GUYS ARE A REAL DRAG.
HEY, SARGE, HAVE YOU SEEN—
CAN'T TALK RIGHT NOW, YOUNG MAN. I HAVE TO FIND THAT MERCHANDISE!
LIKE I SAID, MAN, A *REALLY* UNCOOL SCENE.
YEAH.

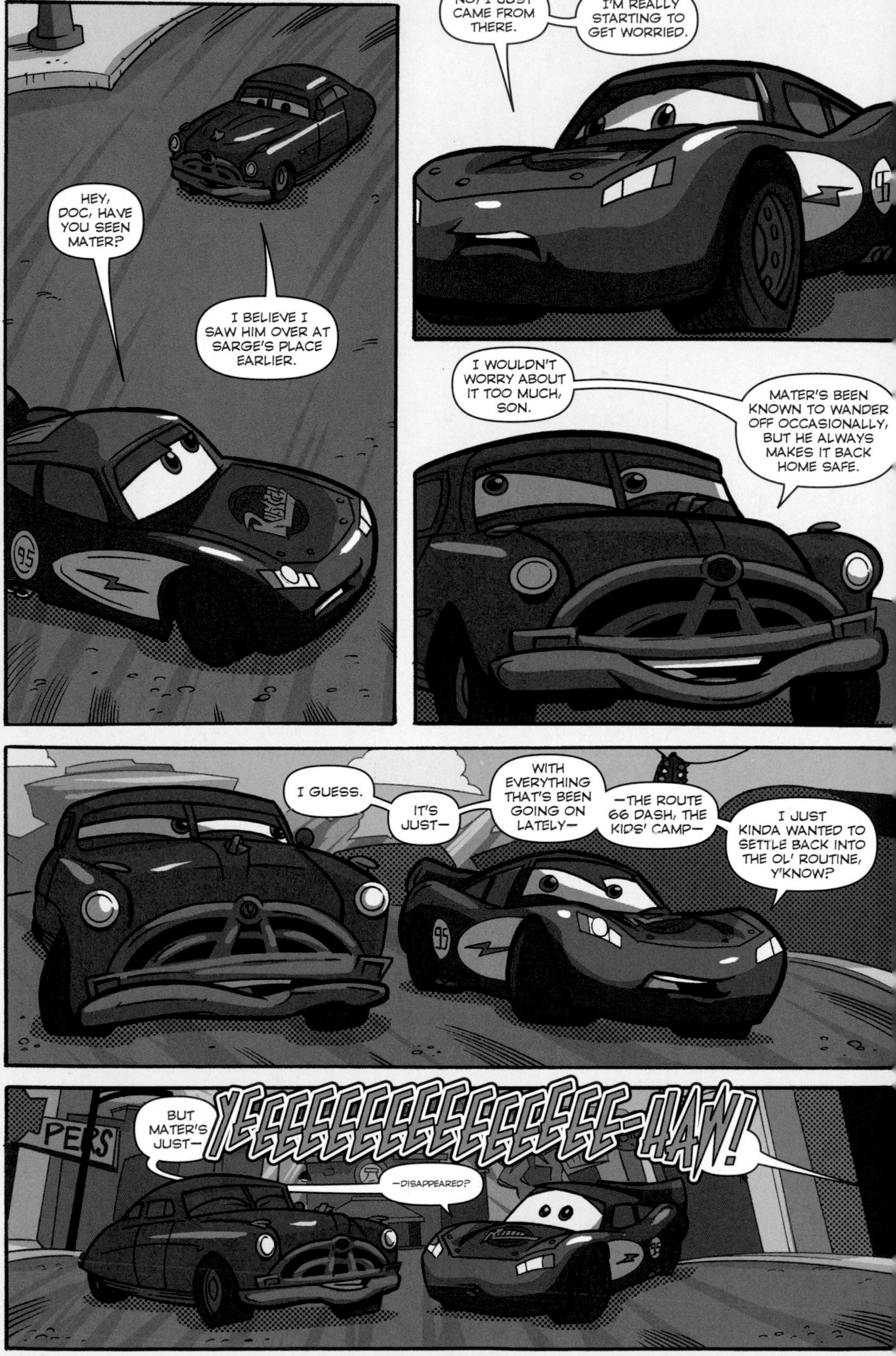

HEY, DOC, HAVE YOU SEEN MATER?
I BELIEVE I SAW HIM OVER AT SARGE'S PLACE EARLIER.
NO, I JUST CAME FROM THERE.
I'M REALLY STARTING TO GET WORRIED.
I WOULDN'T WORRY ABOUT IT TOO MUCH, SON.
MATER'S BEEN KNOWN TO WANDER OFF OCCASIONALLY, BUT HE ALWAYS MAKES IT BACK HOME SAFE.
I GUESS.
IT'S JUST—
WITH EVERYTHING THAT'S BEEN GOING ON LATELY—
—THE ROUTE 66 DASH, THE KIDS' CAMP—
I JUST KINDA WANTED TO SETTLE BACK INTO THE OL' ROUTINE, Y'KNOW?
BUT MATER'S JUST—
YEEEEEEEEEEEEEEEEE-HAW!
—DISAPPEARED?

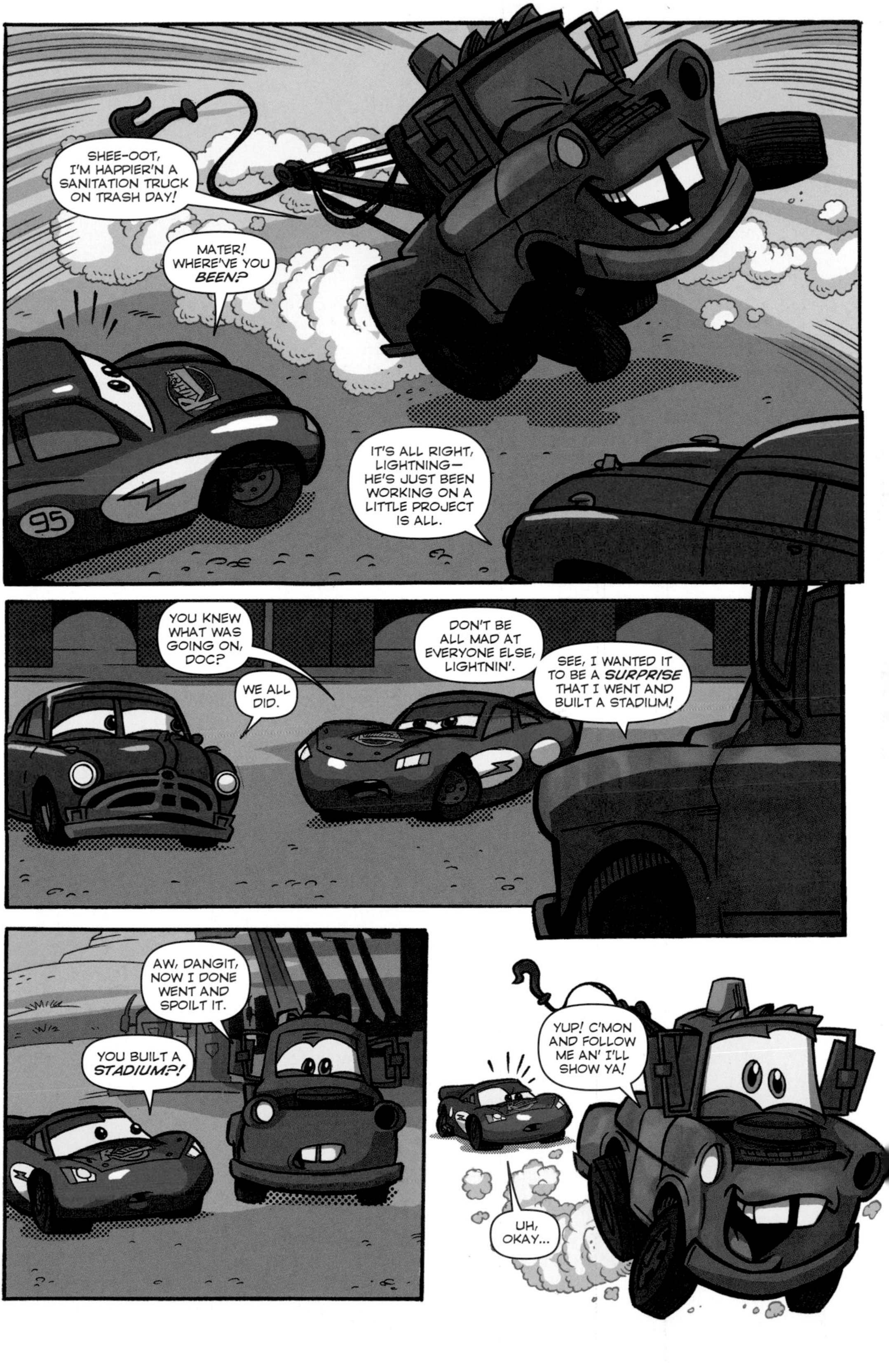

SHEE-OOT, I'M HAPPIER'N A SANITATION TRUCK ON TRASH DAY!
MATER! WHERE'VE YOU BEEN?
IT'S ALL RIGHT, LIGHTNING— HE'S JUST BEEN WORKING ON A LITTLE PROJECT IS ALL.
YOU KNEW WHAT WAS GOING ON, DOC?
WE ALL DID.
DON'T BE ALL MAD AT EVERYONE ELSE, LIGHTNIN'.
SEE, I WANTED IT TO BE A SURPRISE THAT I WENT AND BUILT A STADIUM!
AW, DANGIT, NOW I DONE WENT AND SPOILT IT.
YOU BUILT A STADIUM?!
YUP! C'MON AND FOLLOW ME AN' I'LL SHOW YA!
UH, OKAY...

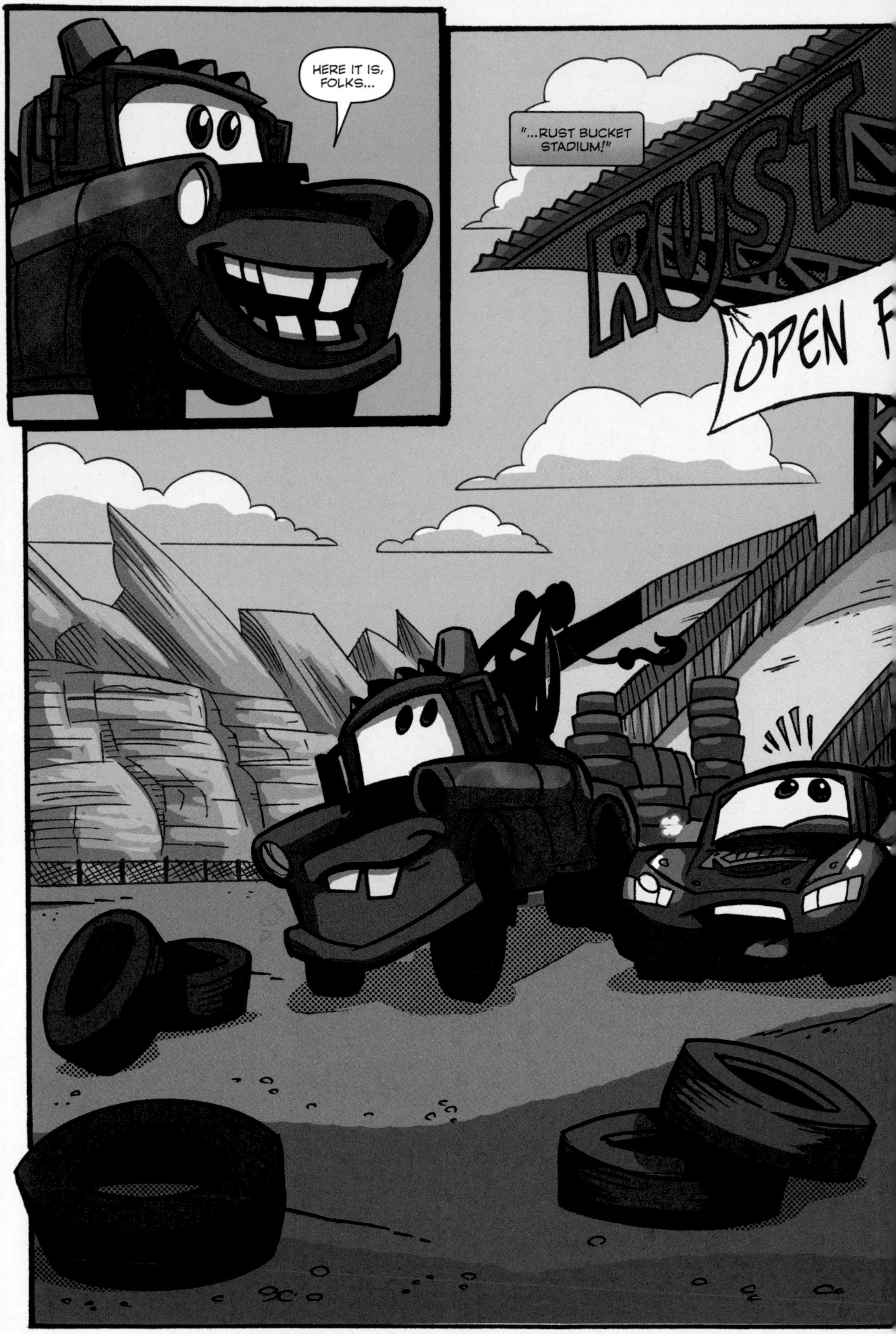
HERE IT IS, FOLKS...
"...RUST BUCKET STADIUM!"
RUST
OPEN F

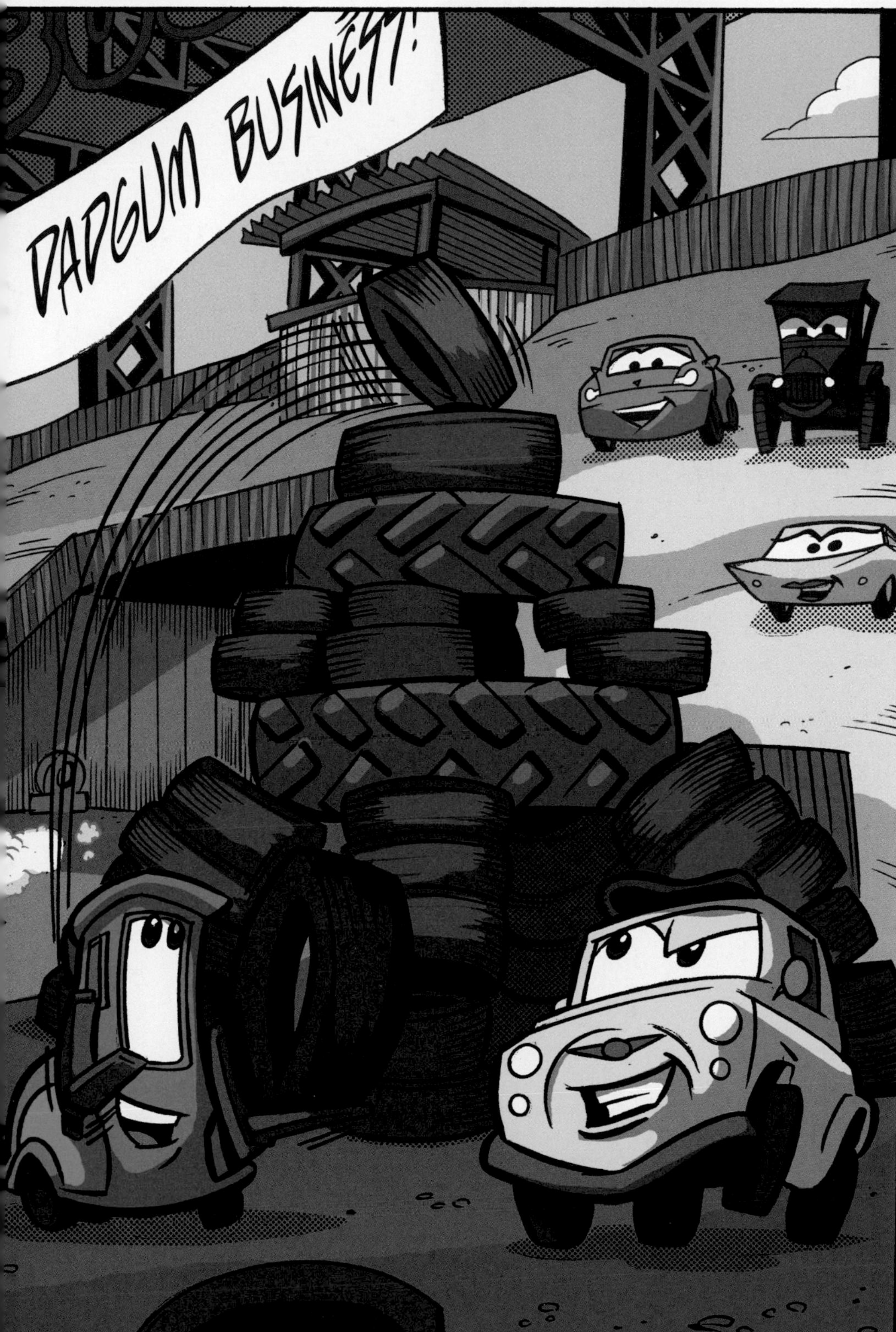
DADGUM BUSINESS!

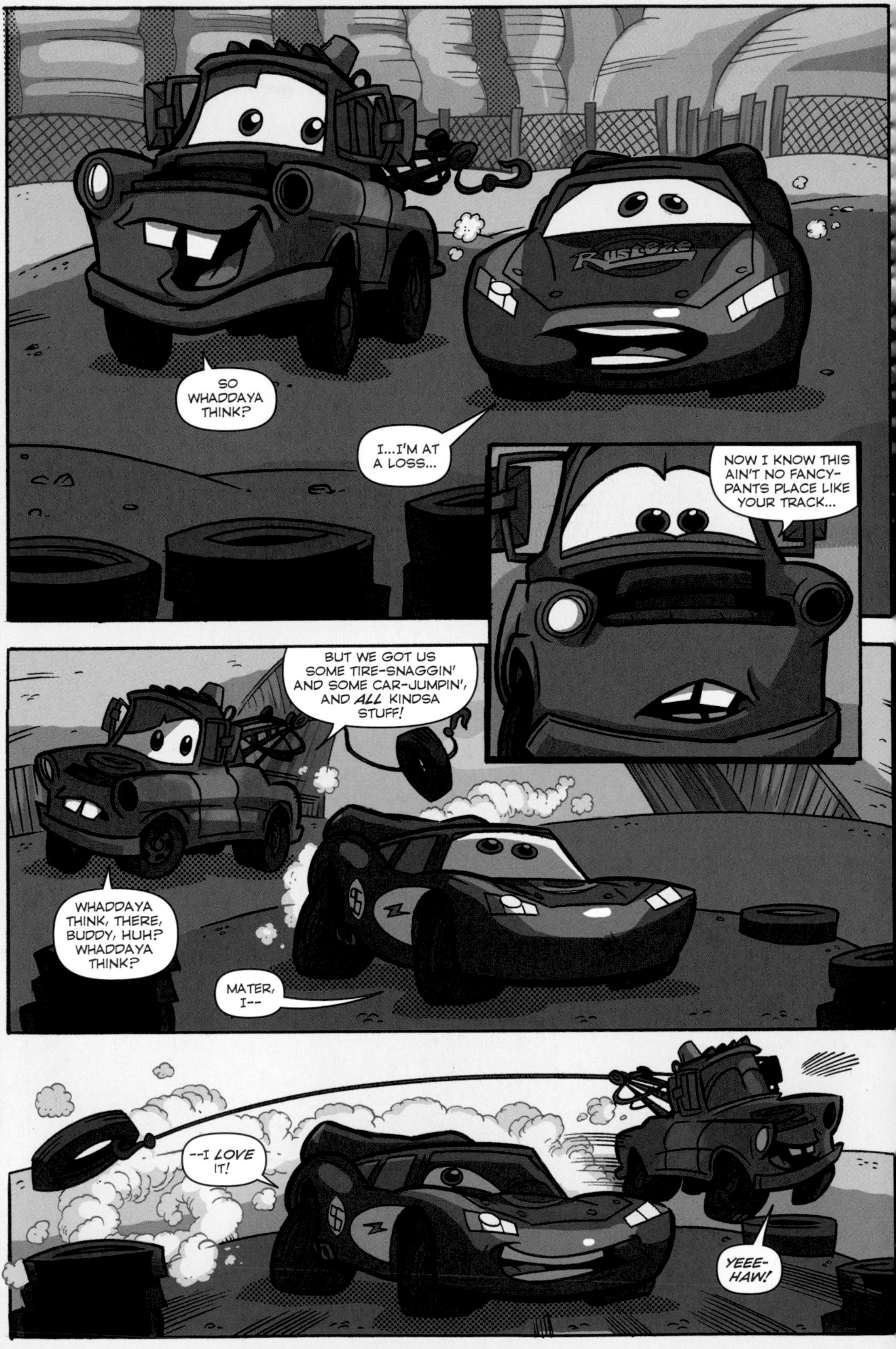
SO WHADDAYA THINK?
I...I'M AT A LOSS...
NOW I KNOW THIS AIN'T NO FANCY-PANTS PLACE LIKE YOUR TRACK...
BUT WE GOT US SOME TIRE-SNAGGIN' AND SOME CAR-JUMPIN', AND ALL KINDSA STUFF!
WHADDAYA THINK, THERE, BUDDY, HUH? WHADDAYA THINK?
MATER, I--
--I LOVE IT!
YEEE-HAW!

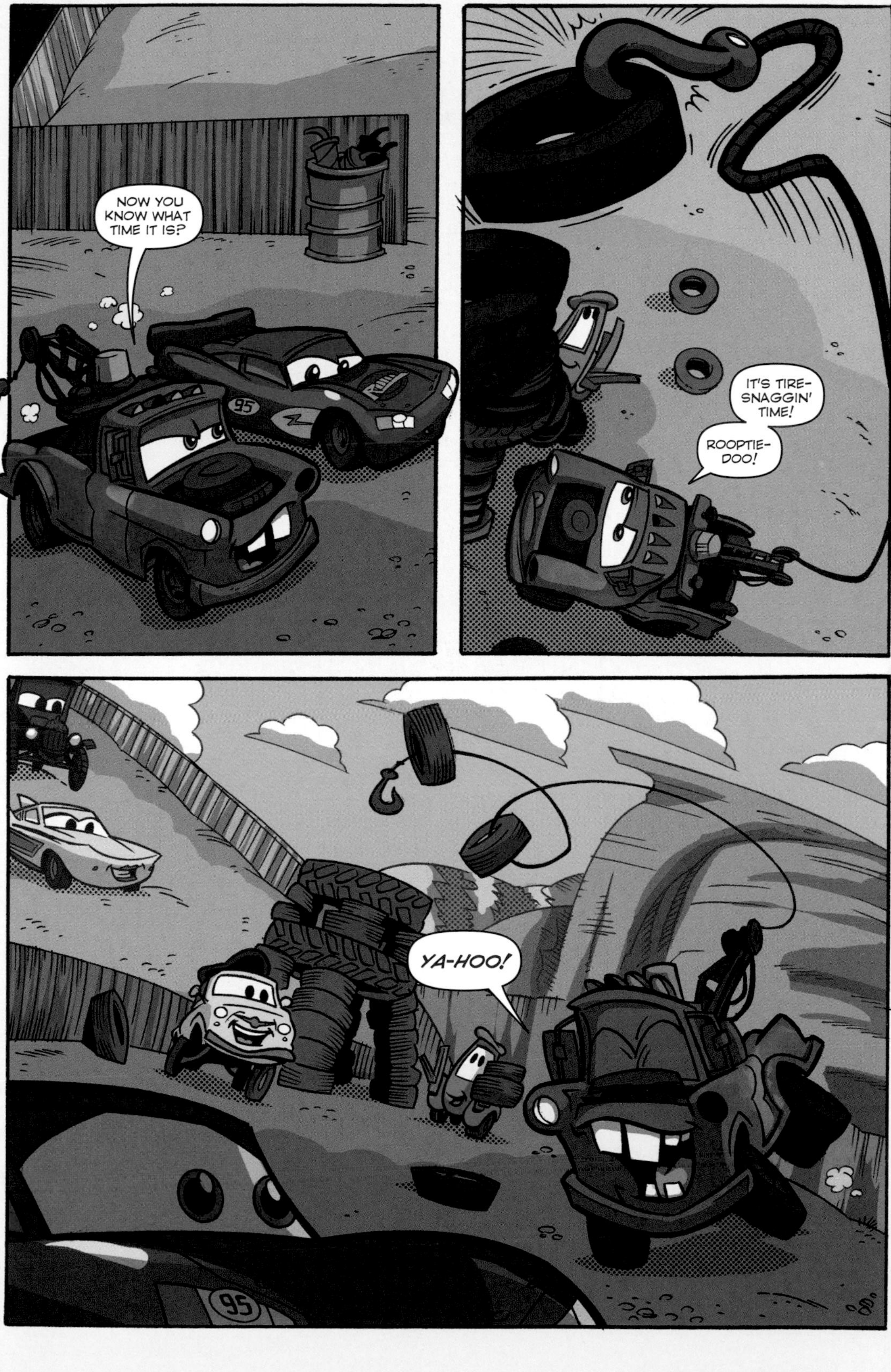
NOW YOU KNOW WHAT TIME IT IS?
IT'S TIRE-SNAGGIN' TIME!
ROOPTIE-DOO!
YA-HOO!

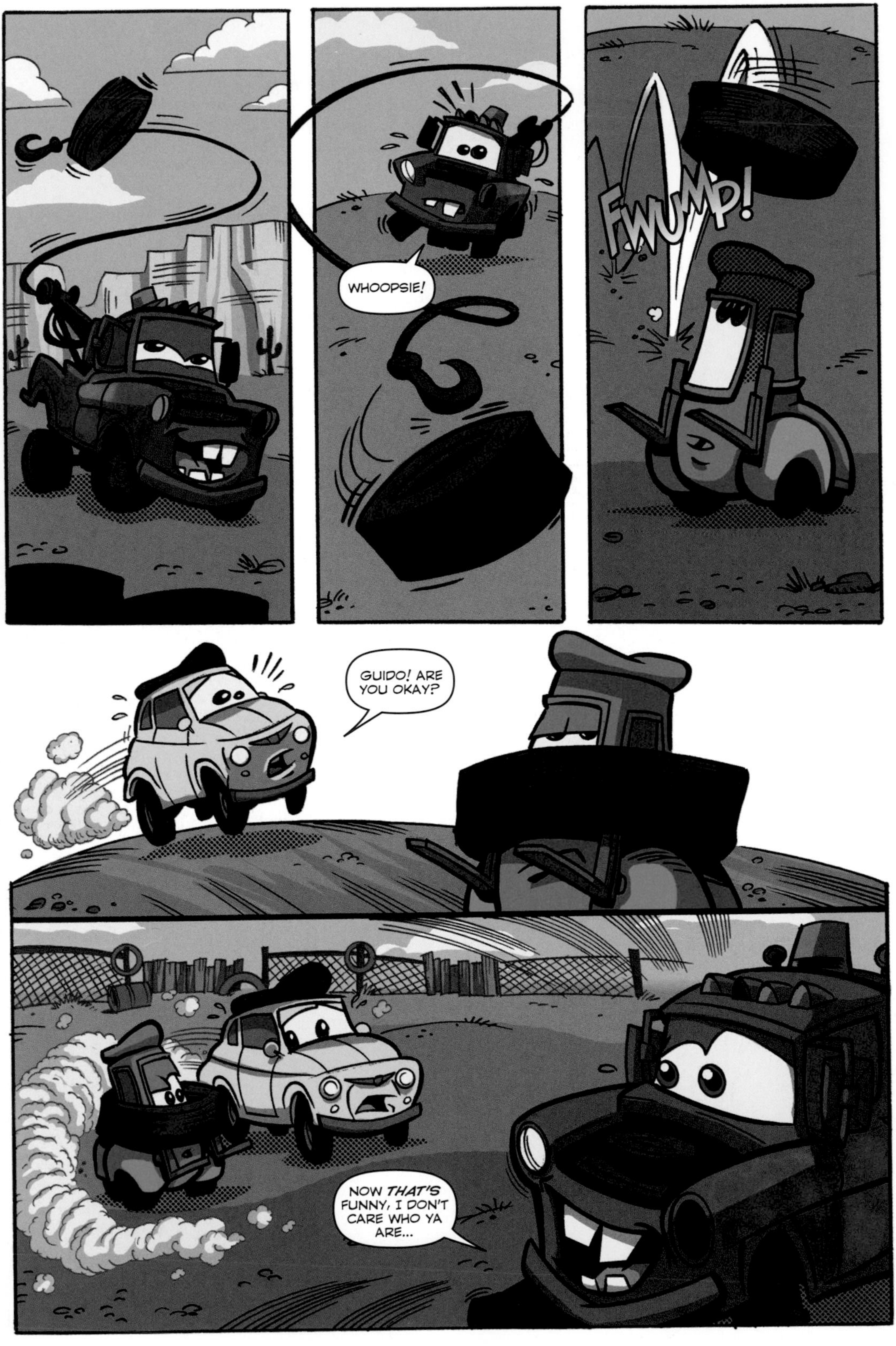
WHOOPSIE!
FWUMP!
GUIDO! ARE YOU OKAY?
NOW THAT'S FUNNY, I DON'T CARE WHO YA ARE...

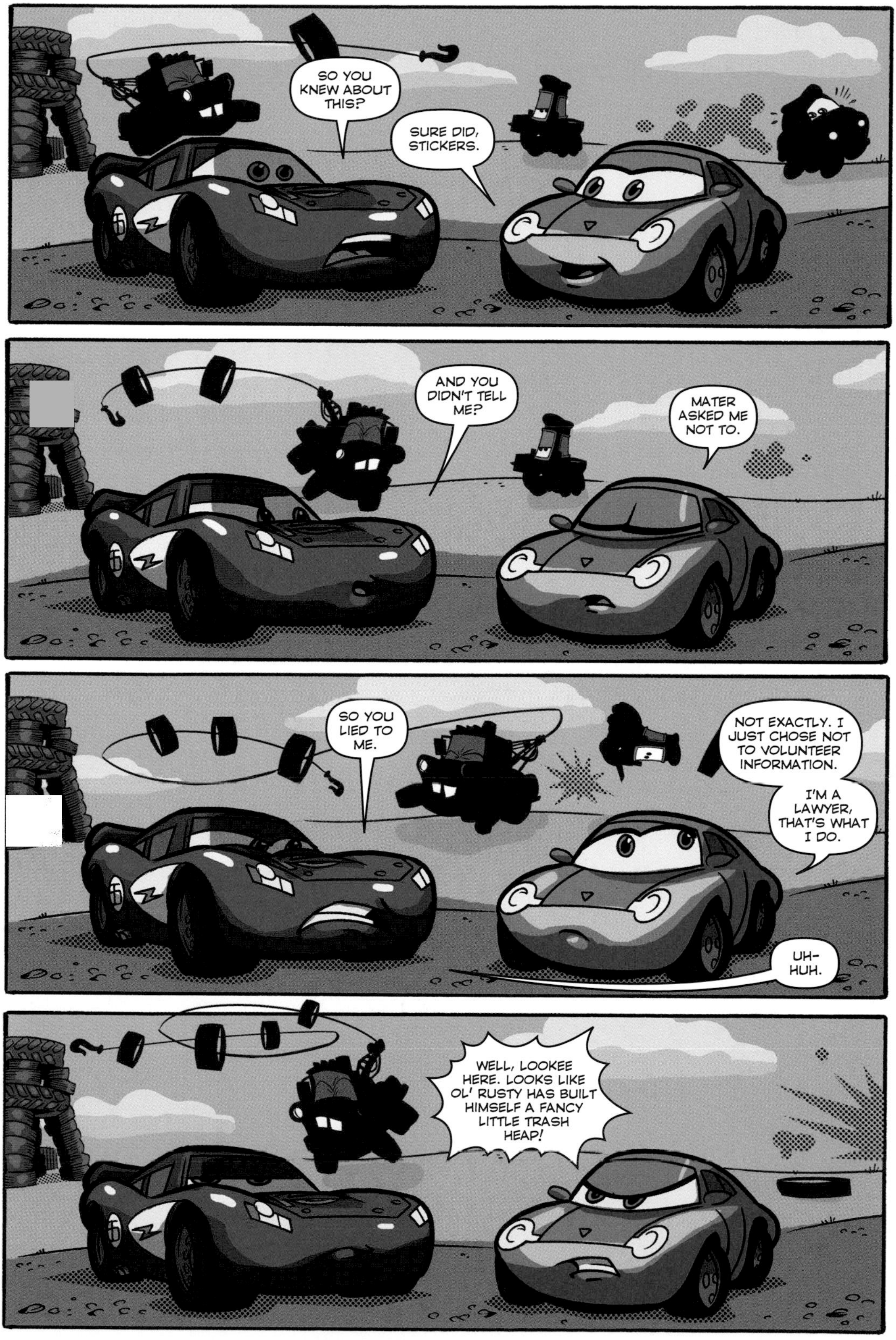
SO YOU KNEW ABOUT THIS?
SURE DID, STICKERS.
AND YOU DIDN'T TELL ME?
MATER ASKED ME NOT TO.
SO YOU LIED TO ME.
NOT EXACTLY. I JUST CHOSE NOT TO VOLUNTEER INFORMATION.
I'M A LAWYER, THAT'S WHAT I DO.
UH-HUH.
WELL, LOOKEE HERE. LOOKS LIKE OL' RUSTY HAS BUILT HIMSELF A FANCY LITTLE TRASH HEAP!

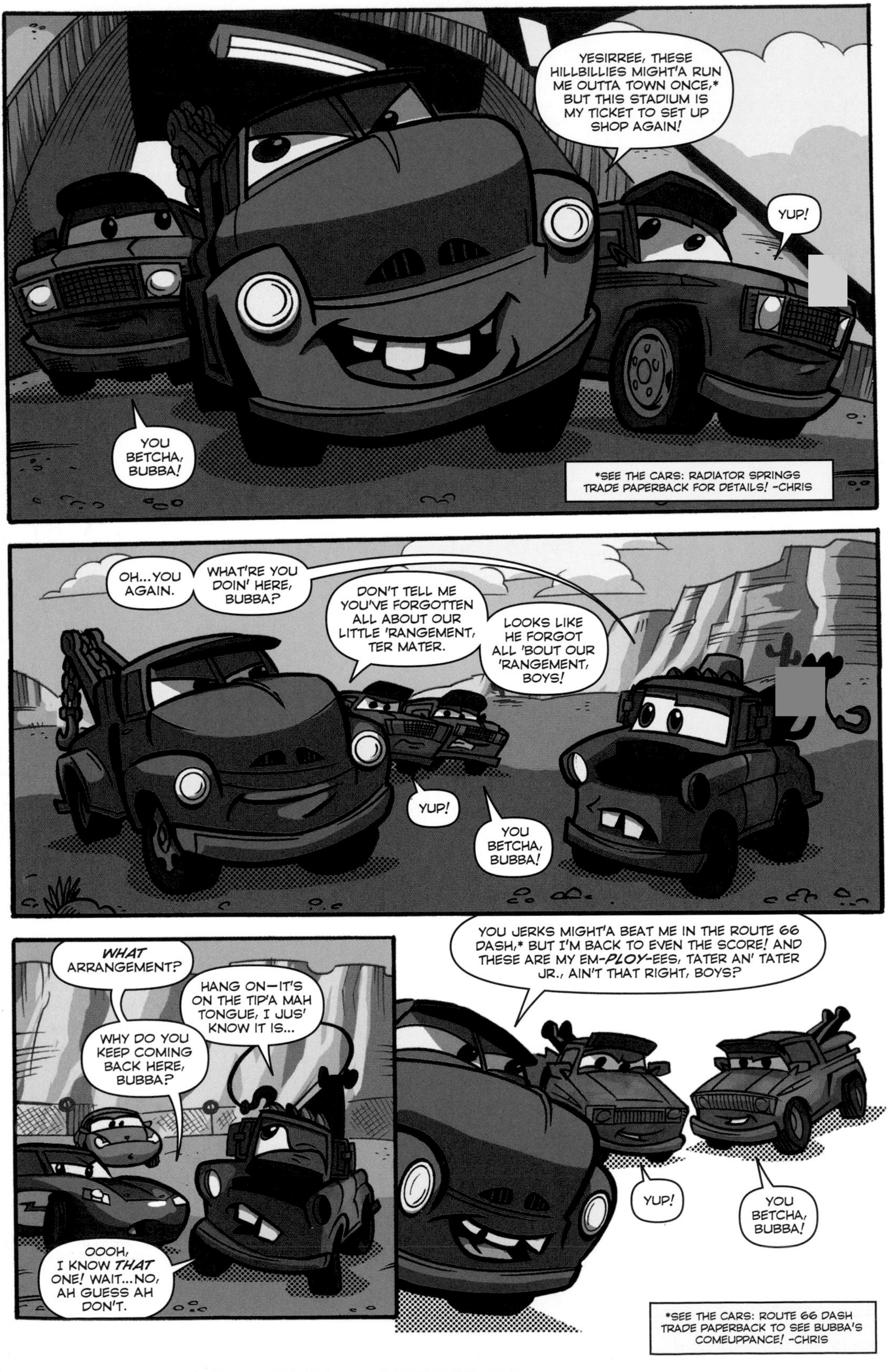
YESIRREE, THESE HILLBILLIES MIGHT'A RUN ME OUTTA TOWN ONCE,* BUT THIS STADIUM IS MY TICKET TO SET UP SHOP AGAIN!
YUP!
YOU BETCHA, BUBBA!
*SEE THE CARS: RADIATOR SPRINGS TRADE PAPERBACK FOR DETAILS! -CHRIS
OH...YOU AGAIN.
WHAT'RE YOU DOIN' HERE, BUBBA?
DON'T TELL ME YOU'VE FORGOTTEN ALL ABOUT OUR LITTLE 'RANGEMENT, TER MATER.
LOOKS LIKE HE FORGOT ALL 'BOUT OUR 'RANGEMENT, BOYS!
YUP!
YOU BETCHA, BUBBA!
WHAT ARRANGEMENT?
HANG ON—IT'S ON THE TIP'A MAH TONGUE, I JUS' KNOW IT IS...
WHY DO YOU KEEP COMING BACK HERE, BUBBA?
OOOH, I KNOW THAT ONE! WAIT...NO, AH GUESS AH DON'T.
YOU JERKS MIGHT'A BEAT ME IN THE ROUTE 66 DASH,* BUT I'M BACK TO EVEN THE SCORE! AND THESE ARE MY EM-PLOY-EES, TATER AN' TATER JR., AIN'T THAT RIGHT, BOYS?
YUP!
YOU BETCHA, BUBBA!
*SEE THE CARS: ROUTE 66 DASH TRADE PAPERBACK TO SEE BUBBA'S COMEUPPANCE! -CHRIS

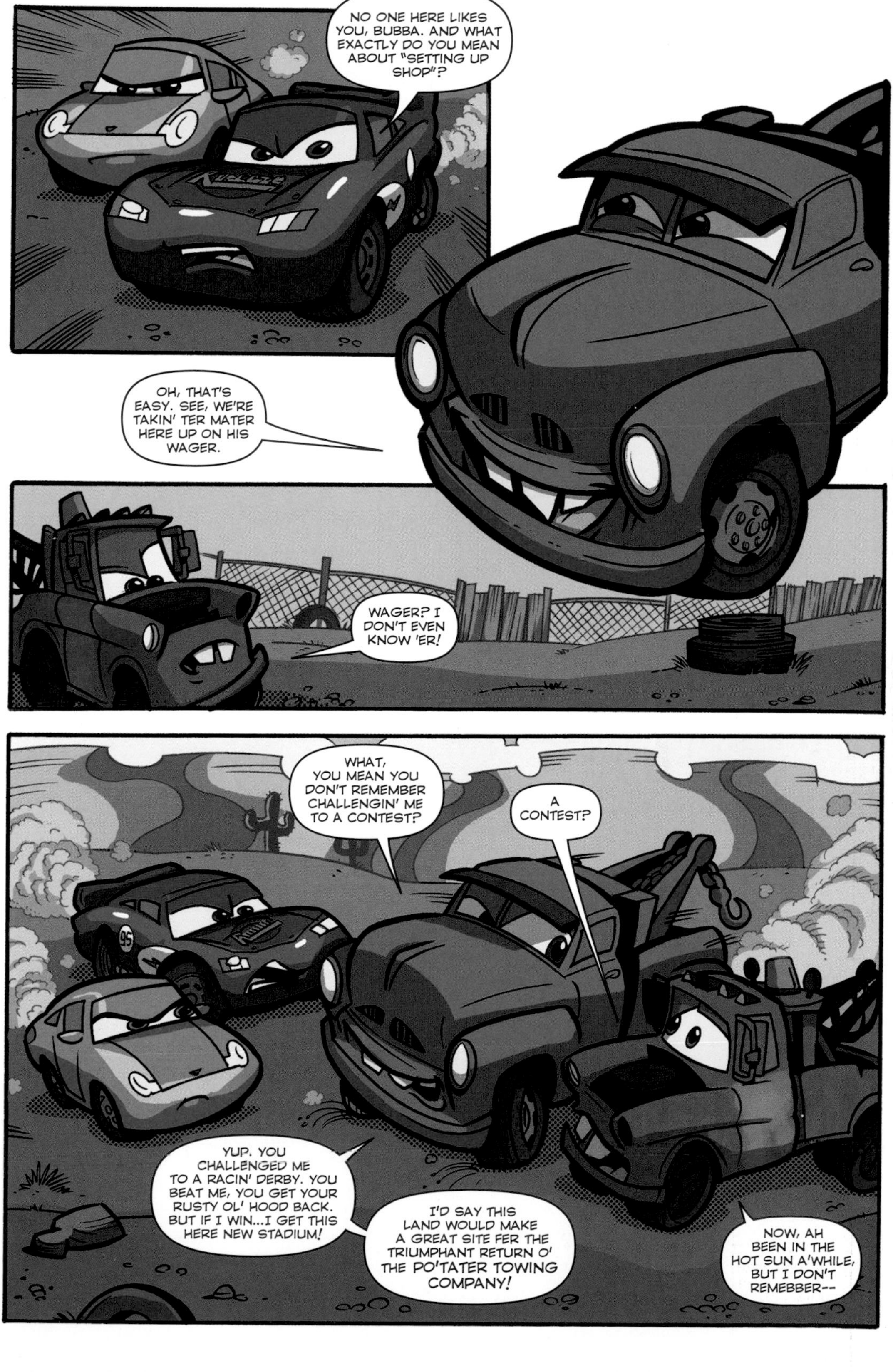
NO ONE HERE LIKES YOU, BUBBA. AND WHAT EXACTLY DO YOU MEAN ABOUT "SETTING UP SHOP"?
OH, THAT'S EASY. SEE, WE'RE TAKIN' TER MATER HERE UP ON HIS WAGER.
WAGER? I DON'T EVEN KNOW 'ER!
WHAT, YOU MEAN YOU DON'T REMEMBER CHALLENGIN' ME TO A CONTEST?
A CONTEST?
YUP. YOU CHALLENGED ME TO A RACIN' DERBY. YOU BEAT ME, YOU GET YOUR RUSTY OL' HOOD BACK. BUT IF I WIN...I GET THIS HERE NEW STADIUM!
I'D SAY THIS LAND WOULD MAKE A GREAT SITE FER THE TRIUMPHANT RETURN O' THE PO'TATER TOWING COMPANY!
NOW, AH BEEN IN THE HOT SUN A'WHILE, BUT I DON'T REMEBBER--

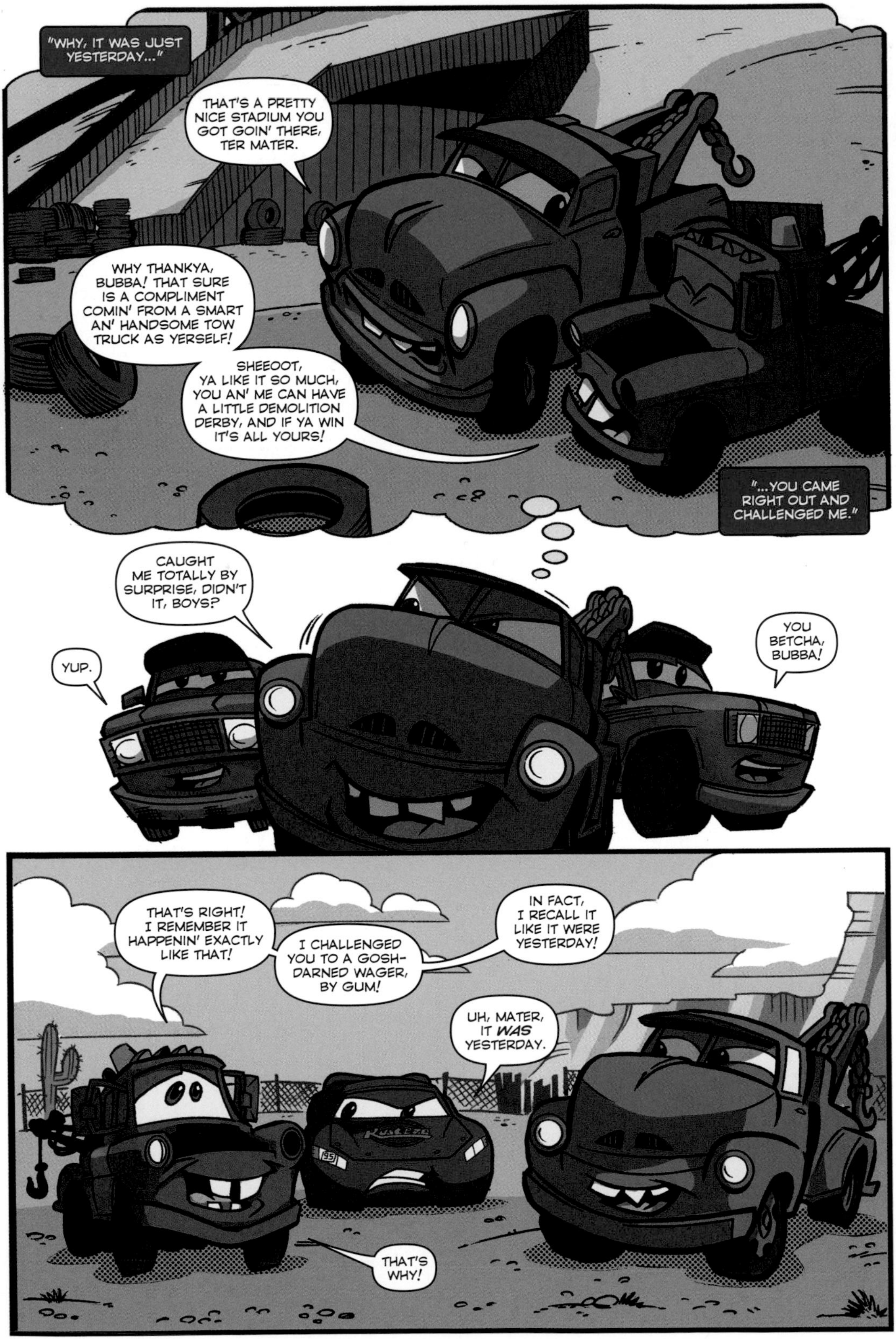
"WHY, IT WAS JUST YESTERDAY..."
THAT'S A PRETTY NICE STADIUM YOU GOT GOIN' THERE, TER MATER.
WHY THANKYA, BUBBA! THAT SURE IS A COMPLIMENT COMIN' FROM A SMART AN' HANDSOME TOW TRUCK AS YERSELF!
SHEEOOT, YA LIKE IT SO MUCH, YOU AN' ME CAN HAVE A LITTLE DEMOLITION DERBY, AND IF YA WIN IT'S ALL YOURS!
"...YOU CAME RIGHT OUT AND CHALLENGED ME."
CAUGHT ME TOTALLY BY SURPRISE, DIDN'T IT, BOYS?
YUP.
YOU BETCHA, BUBBA!
THAT'S RIGHT! I REMEMBER IT HAPPENIN' EXACTLY LIKE THAT!
I CHALLENGED YOU TO A GOSH-DARNED WAGER, BY GUM!
IN FACT, I RECALL IT LIKE IT WERE YESTERDAY!
UH, MATER, IT WAS YESTERDAY.
THAT'S WHY!

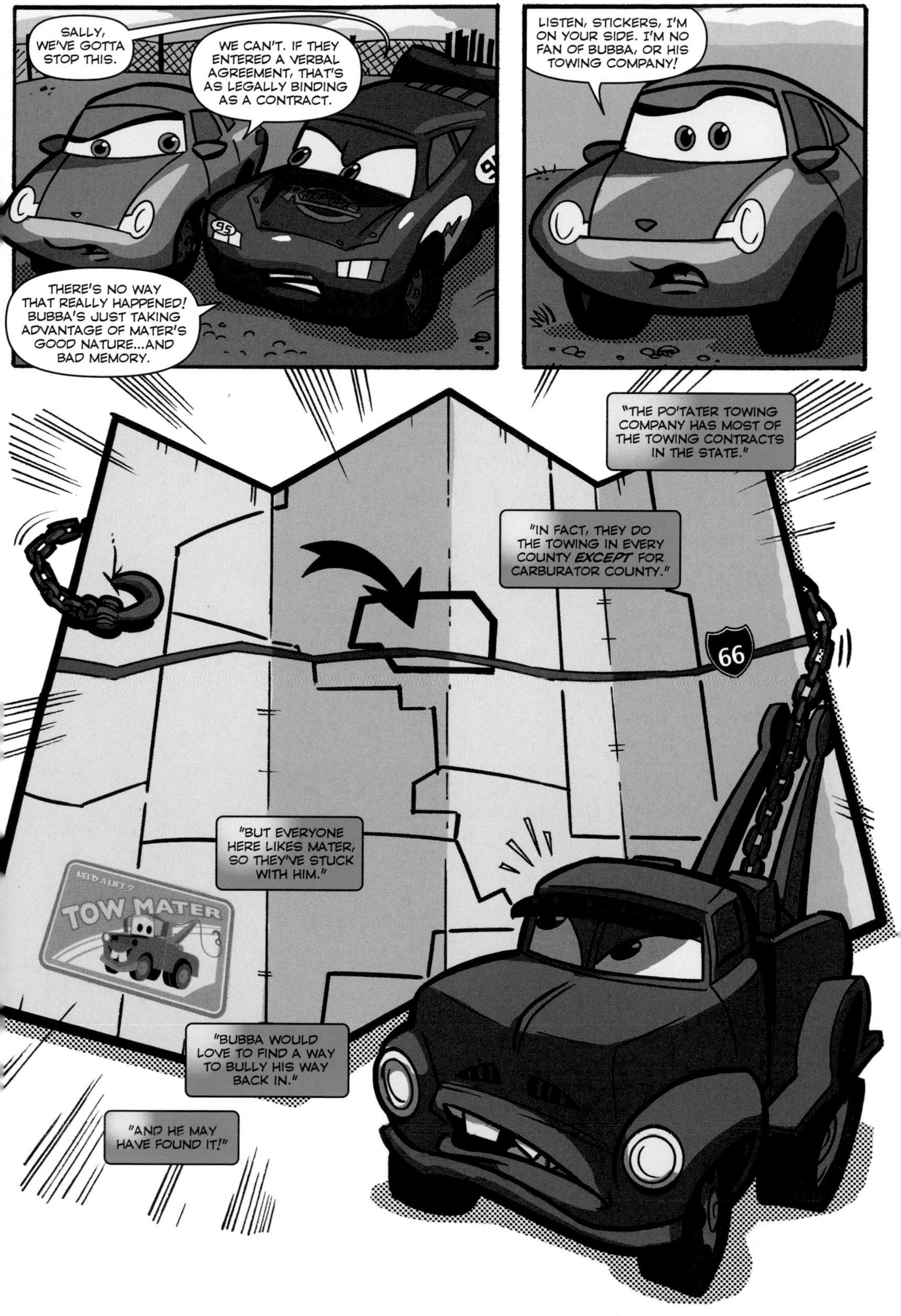
SALLY, WE'VE GOTTA STOP THIS.
WE CAN'T. IF THEY ENTERED A VERBAL AGREEMENT, THAT'S AS LEGALLY BINDING AS A CONTRACT.
THERE'S NO WAY THAT REALLY HAPPENED! BUBBA'S JUST TAKING ADVANTAGE OF MATER'S GOOD NATURE...AND BAD MEMORY.
LISTEN, STICKERS, I'M ON YOUR SIDE. I'M NO FAN OF BUBBA, OR HIS TOWING COMPANY!
"THE PO'TATER TOWING COMPANY HAS MOST OF THE TOWING CONTRACTS IN THE STATE."
"IN FACT, THEY DO THE TOWING IN EVERY COUNTY *EXCEPT* FOR CARBURATOR COUNTY."
66
"BUT EVERYONE HERE LIKES MATER, SO THEY'VE STUCK WITH HIM."
NEED A LIFT?
TOW MATER
"BUBBA WOULD LOVE TO FIND A WAY TO BULLY HIS WAY BACK IN."
"AND HE MAY HAVE FOUND IT!"

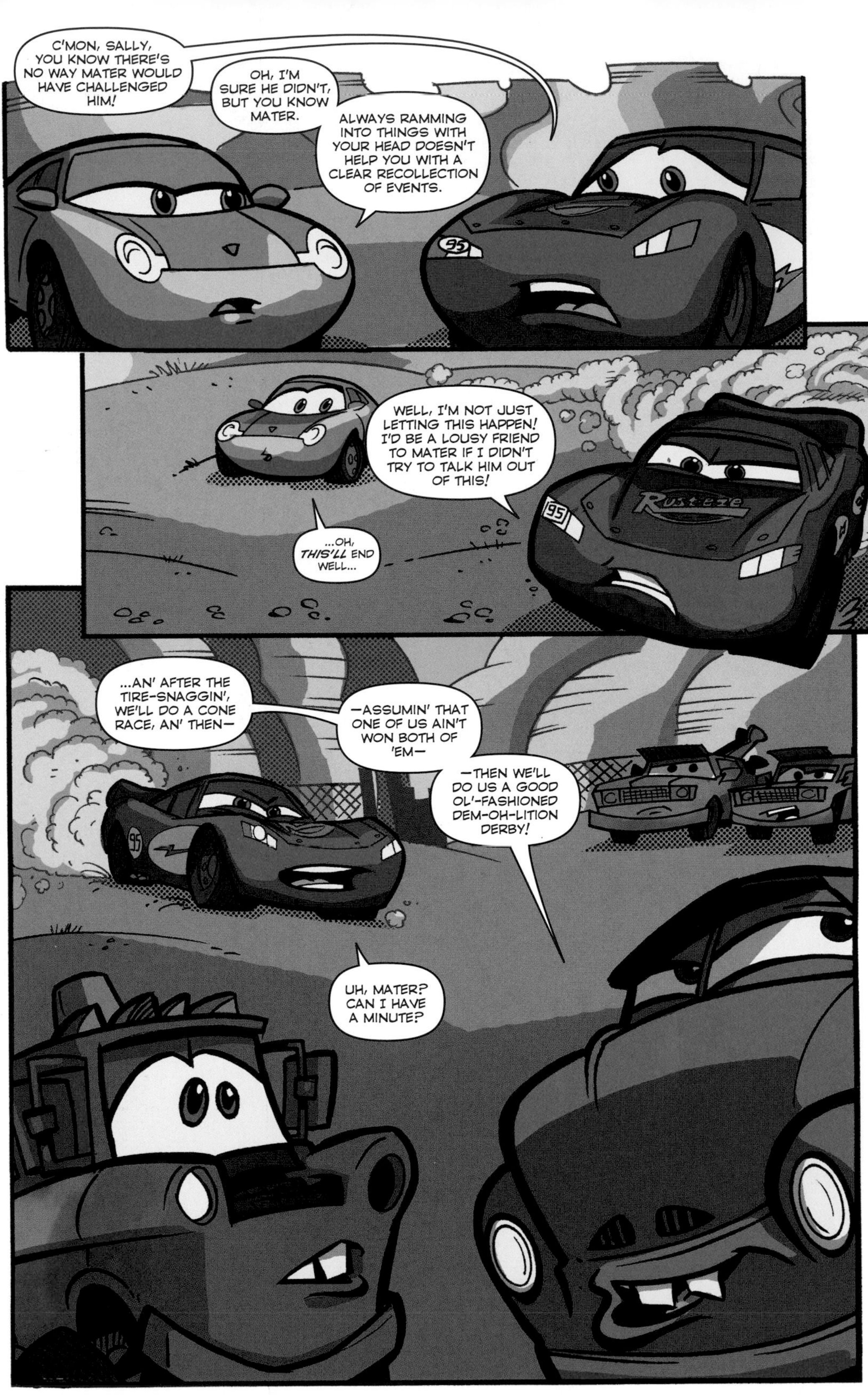
C'MON, SALLY, YOU KNOW THERE'S NO WAY MATER WOULD HAVE CHALLENGED HIM!
OH, I'M SURE HE DIDN'T, BUT YOU KNOW MATER.
ALWAYS RAMMING INTO THINGS WITH YOUR HEAD DOESN'T HELP YOU WITH A CLEAR RECOLLECTION OF EVENTS.
WELL, I'M NOT JUST LETTING THIS HAPPEN! I'D BE A LOUSY FRIEND TO MATER IF I DIDN'T TRY TO TALK HIM OUT OF THIS!
...OH, *THIS'LL* END WELL...
RUST-EZE
...AN' AFTER THE TIRE-SNAGGIN', WE'LL DO A CONE RACE, AN' THEN—
—ASSUMIN' THAT ONE OF US AIN'T WON BOTH OF 'EM—
—THEN WE'LL DO US A GOOD OL'-FASHIONED DEM-OH-LITION DERBY!
UH, MATER? CAN I HAVE A MINUTE?

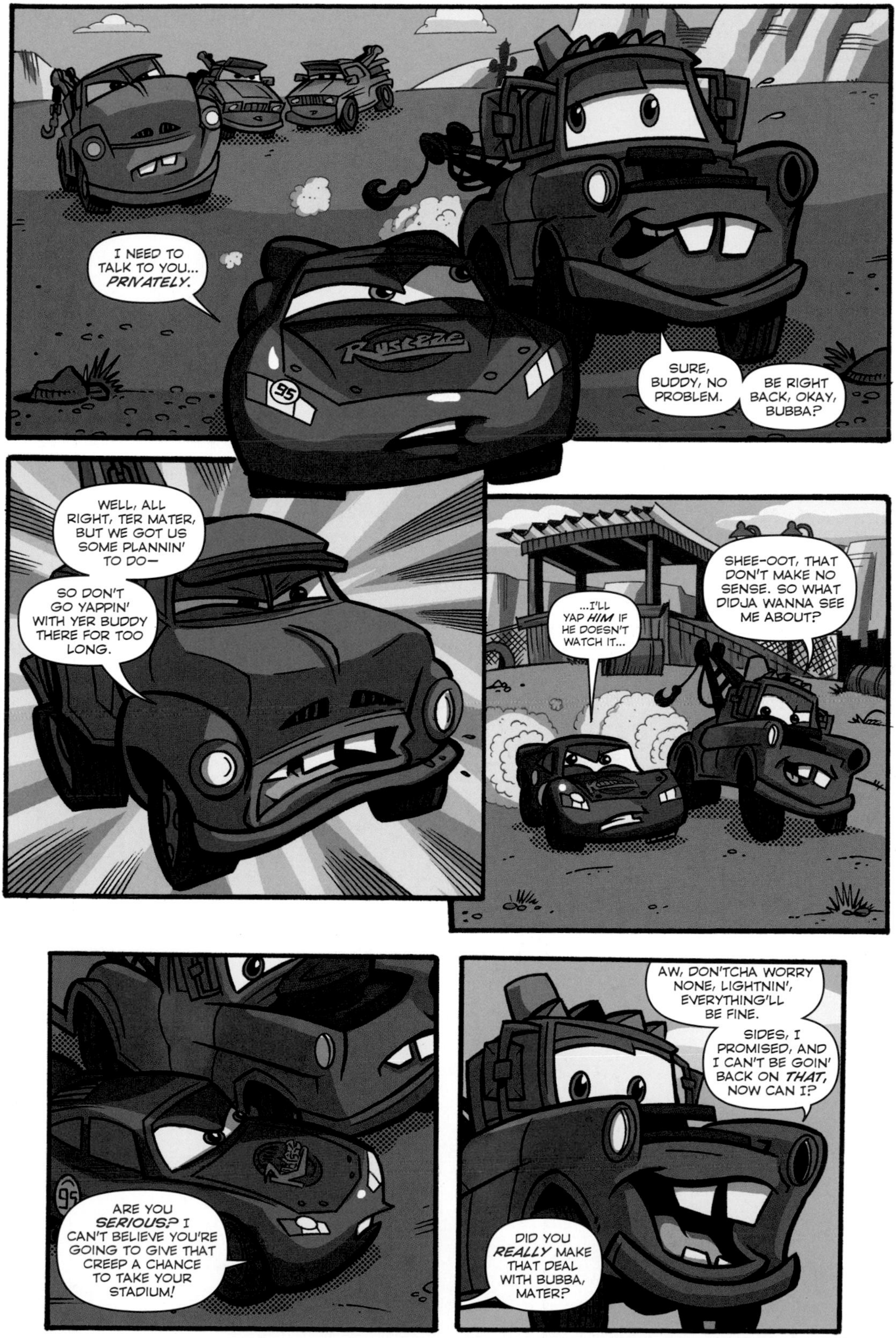
I NEED TO TALK TO YOU... PRIVATELY.
SURE, BUDDY, NO PROBLEM.
BE RIGHT BACK, OKAY, BUBBA?
WELL, ALL RIGHT, TER MATER, BUT WE GOT US SOME PLANNIN' TO DO—
SO DON'T GO YAPPIN' WITH YER BUDDY THERE FOR TOO LONG.
...I'LL YAP HIM IF HE DOESN'T WATCH IT...
SHEE-OOT, THAT DON'T MAKE NO SENSE. SO WHAT DIDJA WANNA SEE ME ABOUT?
ARE YOU SERIOUS? I CAN'T BELIEVE YOU'RE GOING TO GIVE THAT CREEP A CHANCE TO TAKE YOUR STADIUM!
DID YOU REALLY MAKE THAT DEAL WITH BUBBA, MATER?
AW, DON'TCHA WORRY NONE, LIGHTNIN', EVERYTHING'LL BE FINE.
SIDES, I PROMISED, AND I CAN'T BE GOIN' BACK ON THAT, NOW CAN I?

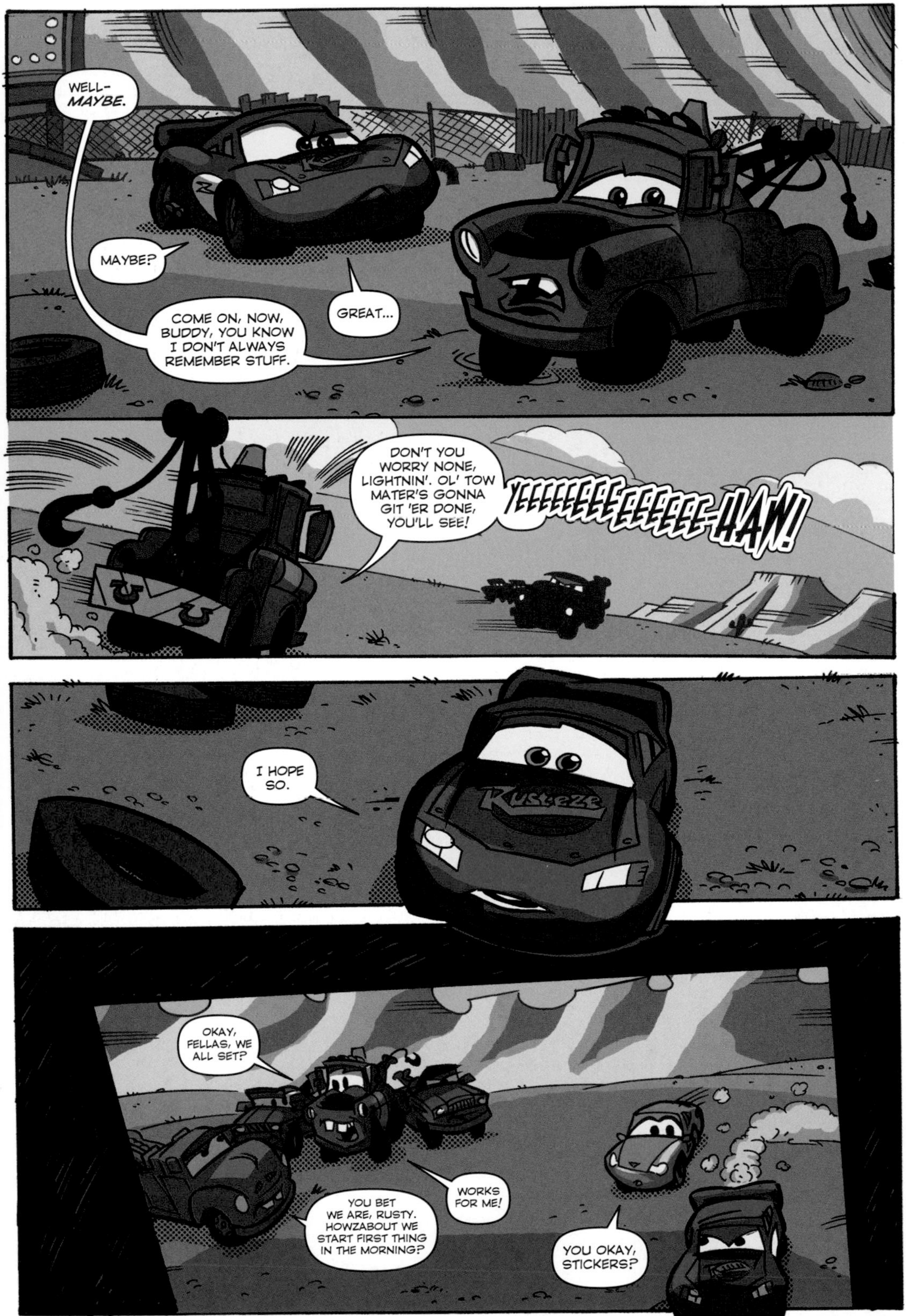
WELL- MAYBE.
MAYBE?
GREAT...
COME ON, NOW, BUDDY, YOU KNOW I DON'T ALWAYS REMEMBER STUFF.
DON'T YOU WORRY NONE, LIGHTNIN'. OL' TOW MATER'S GONNA GIT 'ER DONE, YOU'LL SEE!
YEEEEEEEEEEEEEE-HAW!
I HOPE SO.
OKAY, FELLAS, WE ALL SET?
WORKS FOR ME!
YOU BET WE ARE, RUSTY. HOWZABOUT WE START FIRST THING IN THE MORNING?
YOU OKAY, STICKERS?

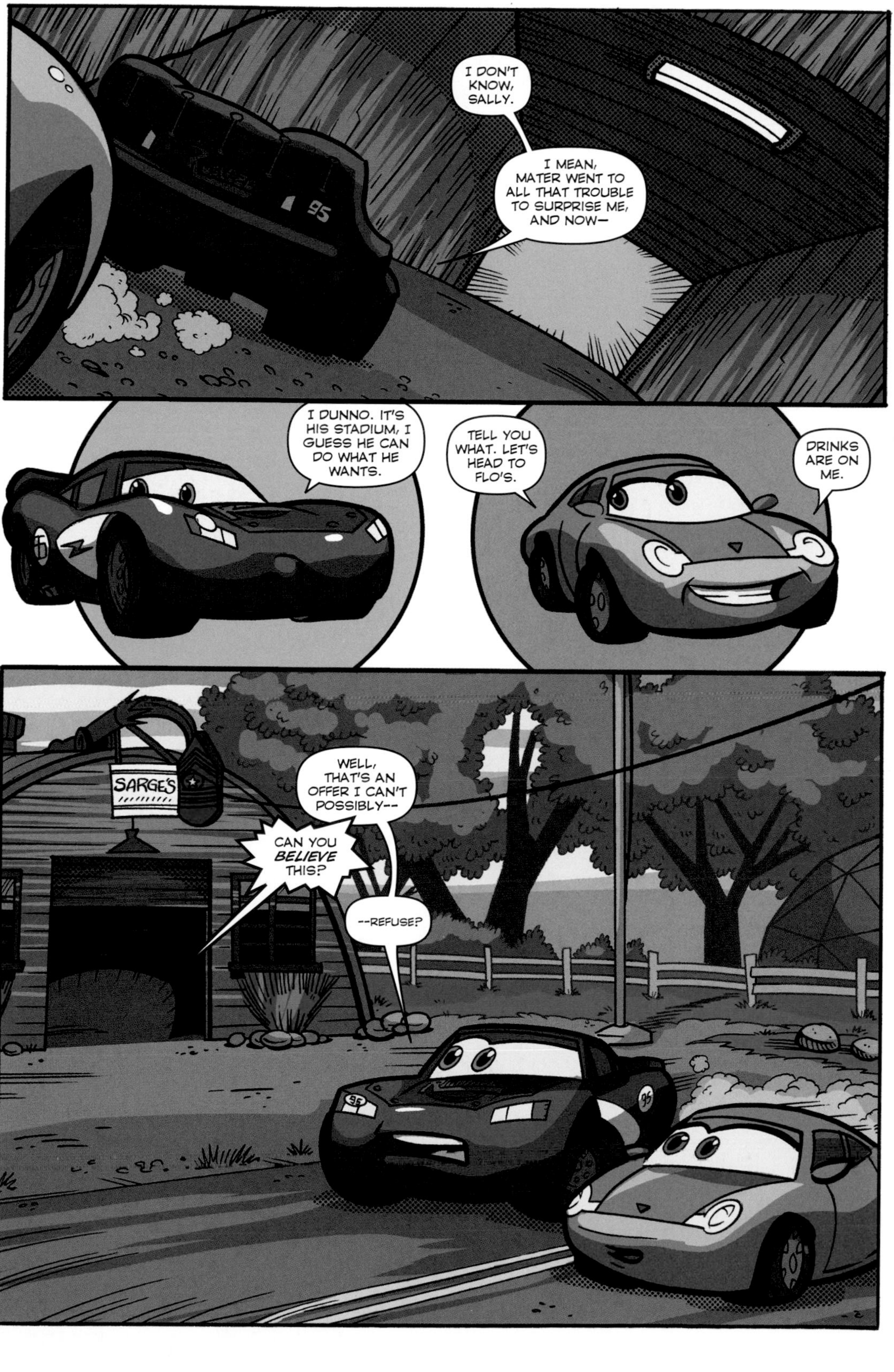

I DON'T KNOW, SALLY.
I MEAN, MATER WENT TO ALL THAT TROUBLE TO SURPRISE ME, AND NOW—
I DUNNO. IT'S HIS STADIUM, I GUESS HE CAN DO WHAT HE WANTS.
TELL YOU WHAT. LET'S HEAD TO FLO'S.
DRINKS ARE ON ME.
SARGE'S
WELL, THAT'S AN OFFER I CAN'T POSSIBLY--
CAN YOU *BELIEVE* THIS?
--REFUSE?

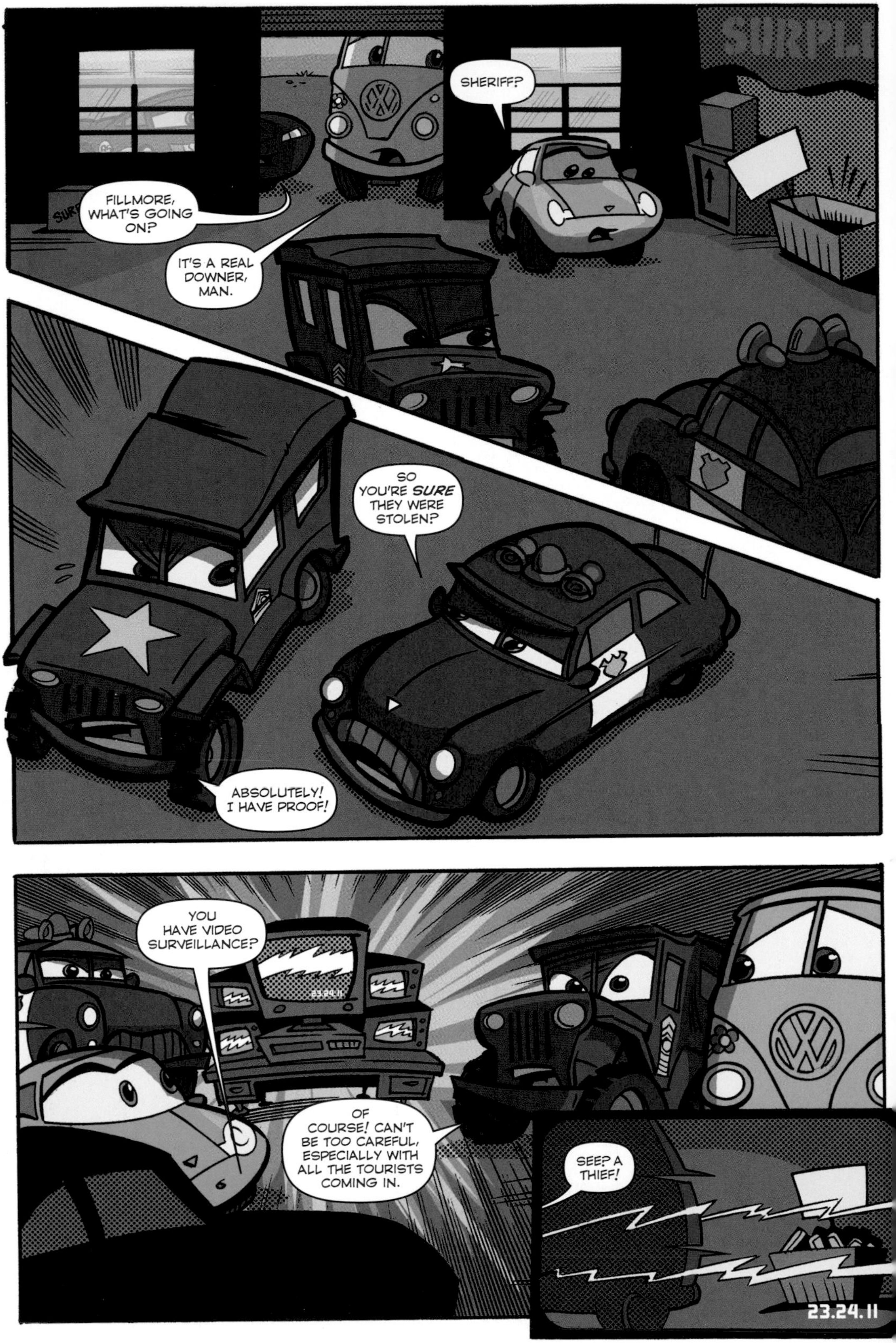
SURPL
SHERIFF?
FILLMORE, WHAT'S GOING ON?
IT'S A REAL DOWNER, MAN.
SO YOU'RE *SURE* THEY WERE STOLEN?
ABSOLUTELY! I HAVE PROOF!
YOU HAVE VIDEO SURVEILLANCE?
OF COURSE! CAN'T BE TOO CAREFUL, ESPECIALLY WITH ALL THE TOURISTS COMING IN.
SEE? A THIEF!
23.24.11

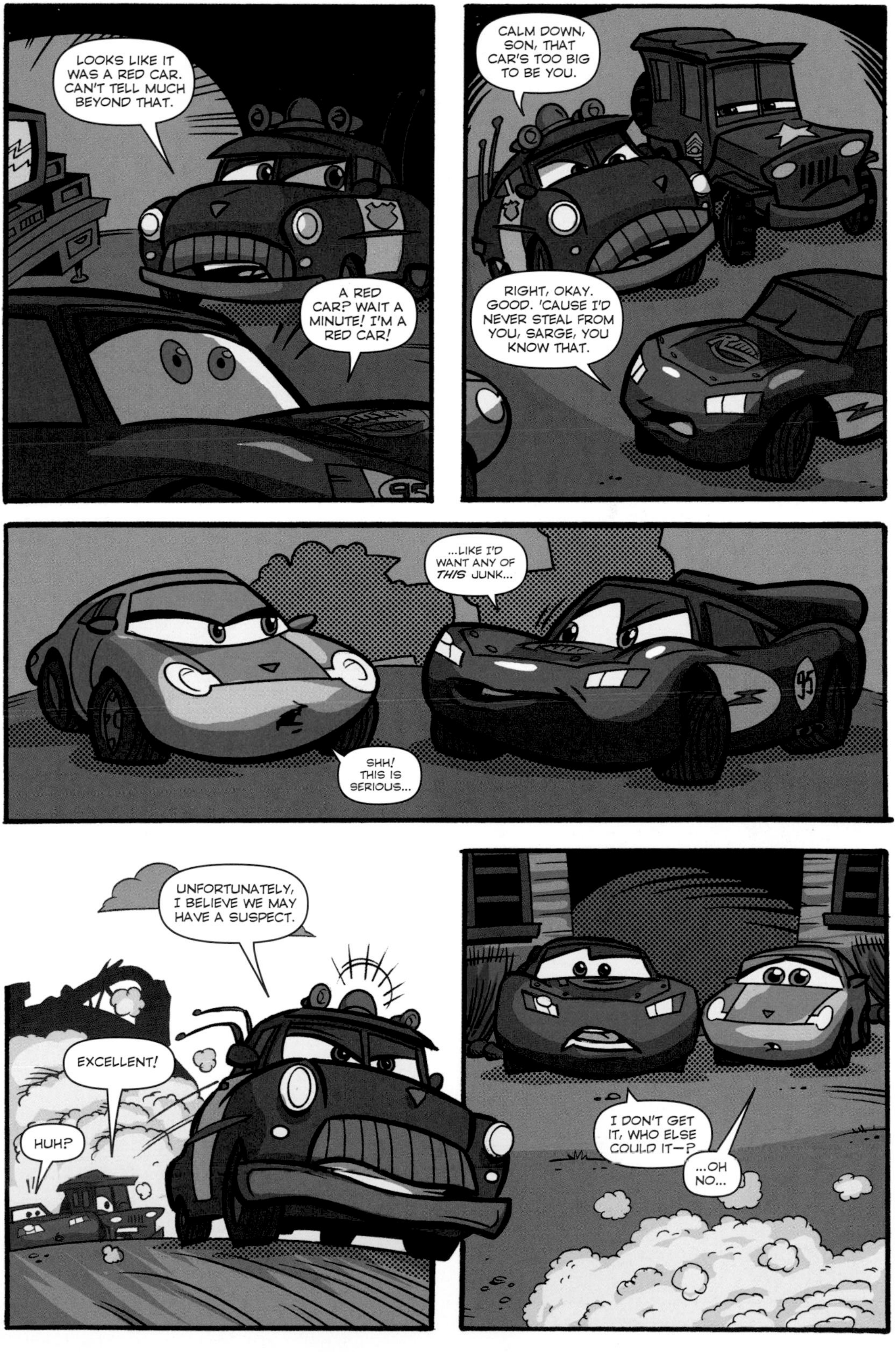
LOOKS LIKE IT WAS A RED CAR. CAN'T TELL MUCH BEYOND THAT.
A RED CAR? WAIT A MINUTE! I'M A RED CAR!
CALM DOWN, SON, THAT CAR'S TOO BIG TO BE YOU.
RIGHT, OKAY. GOOD. 'CAUSE I'D NEVER STEAL FROM YOU, SARGE, YOU KNOW THAT.
...LIKE I'D WANT ANY OF THIS JUNK...
SHH! THIS IS SERIOUS...
UNFORTUNATELY, I BELIEVE WE MAY HAVE A SUSPECT.
EXCELLENT!
HUH?
I DON'T GET IT, WHO ELSE COULD IT—?
...OH NO...

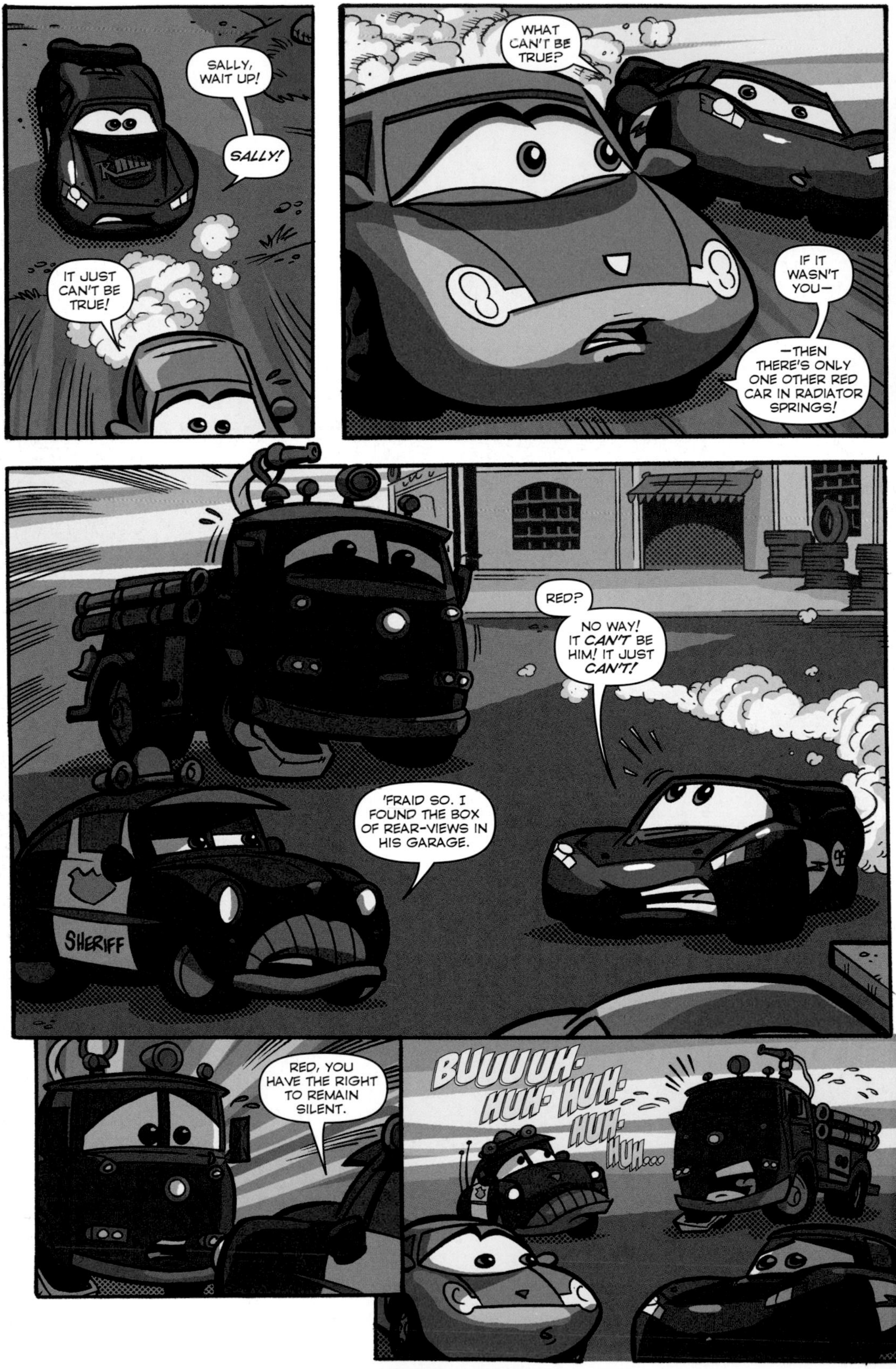
SALLY, WAIT UP!
SALLY!
IT JUST CAN'T BE TRUE!
WHAT CAN'T BE TRUE?
IF IT WASN'T YOU—
—THEN THERE'S ONLY ONE OTHER RED CAR IN RADIATOR SPRINGS!
RED?
NO WAY! IT CAN'T BE HIM! IT JUST CAN'T!
'FRAID SO. I FOUND THE BOX OF REAR-VIEWS IN HIS GARAGE.
SHERIFF
RED, YOU HAVE THE RIGHT TO REMAIN SILENT.
BUUUUH-HUH-HUH-HUH-HUH...

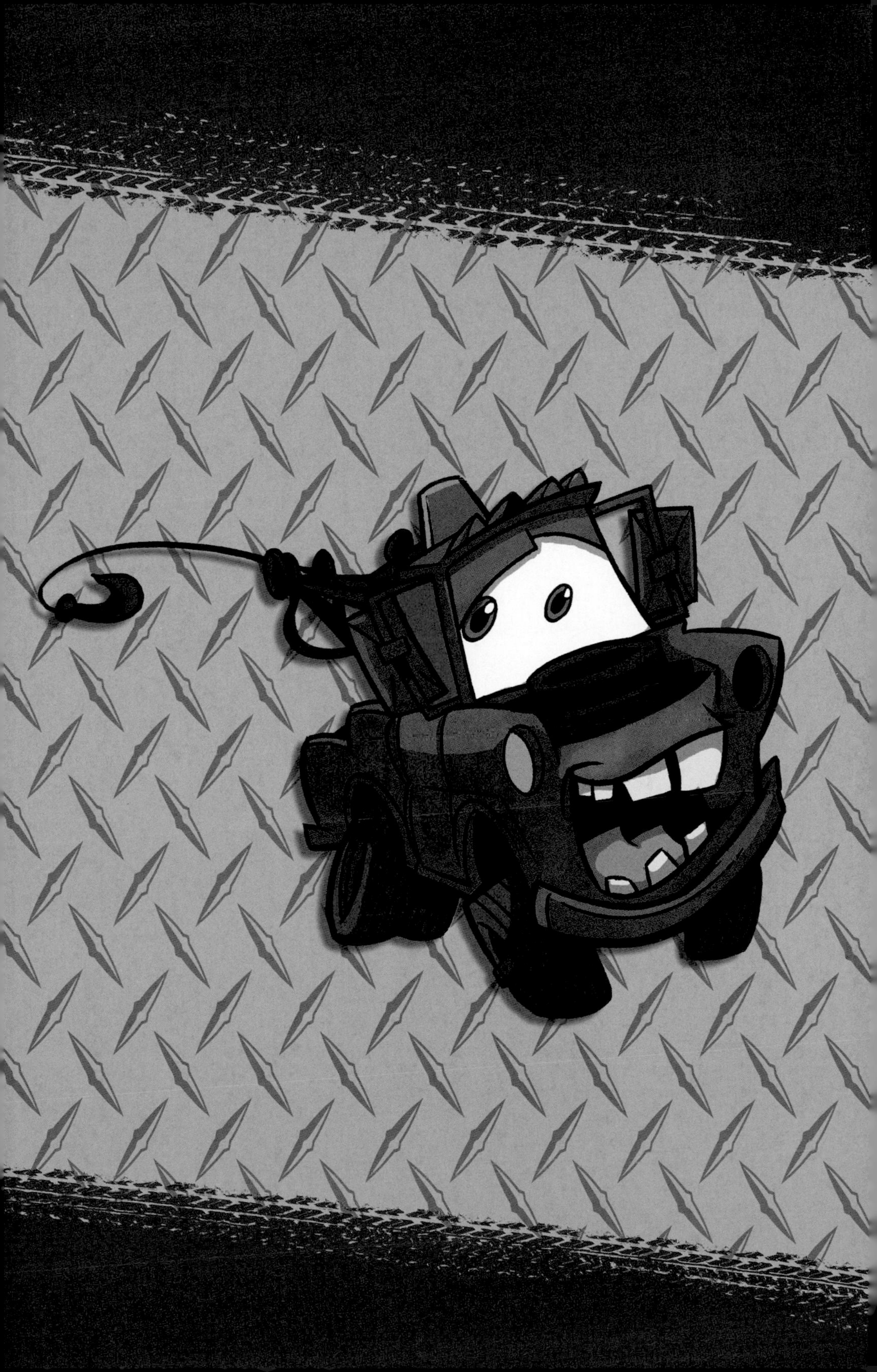

Chapter Two

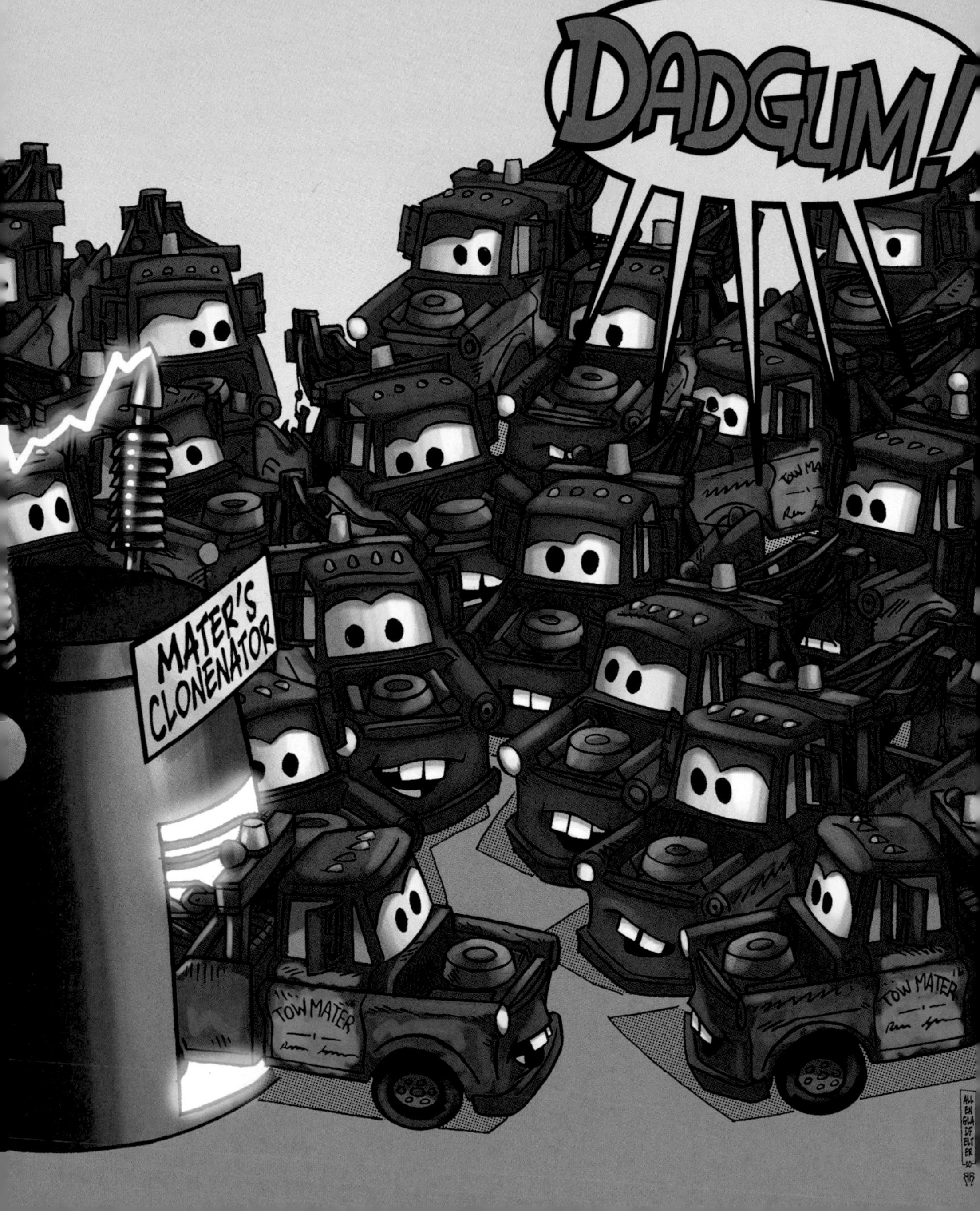
DADGUM!
MATER'S CLONENATOR
TOW MATER
TOW MATER
TOW MATER

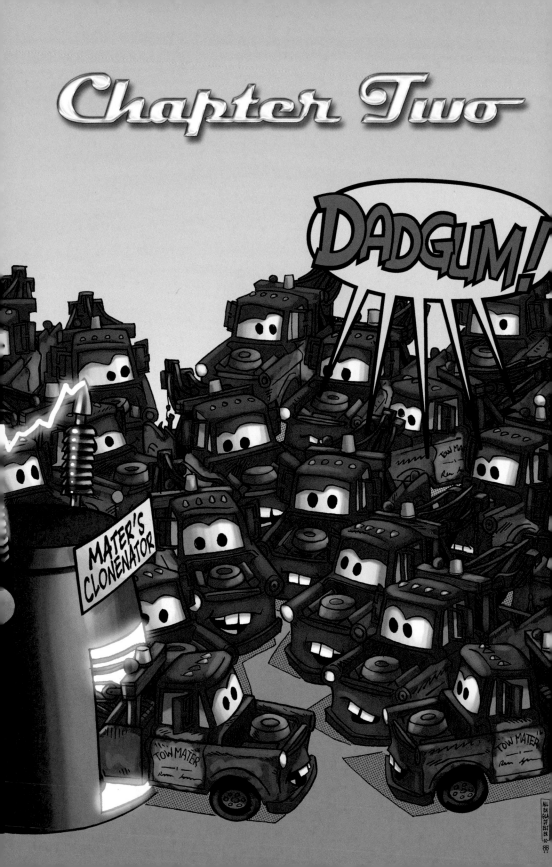

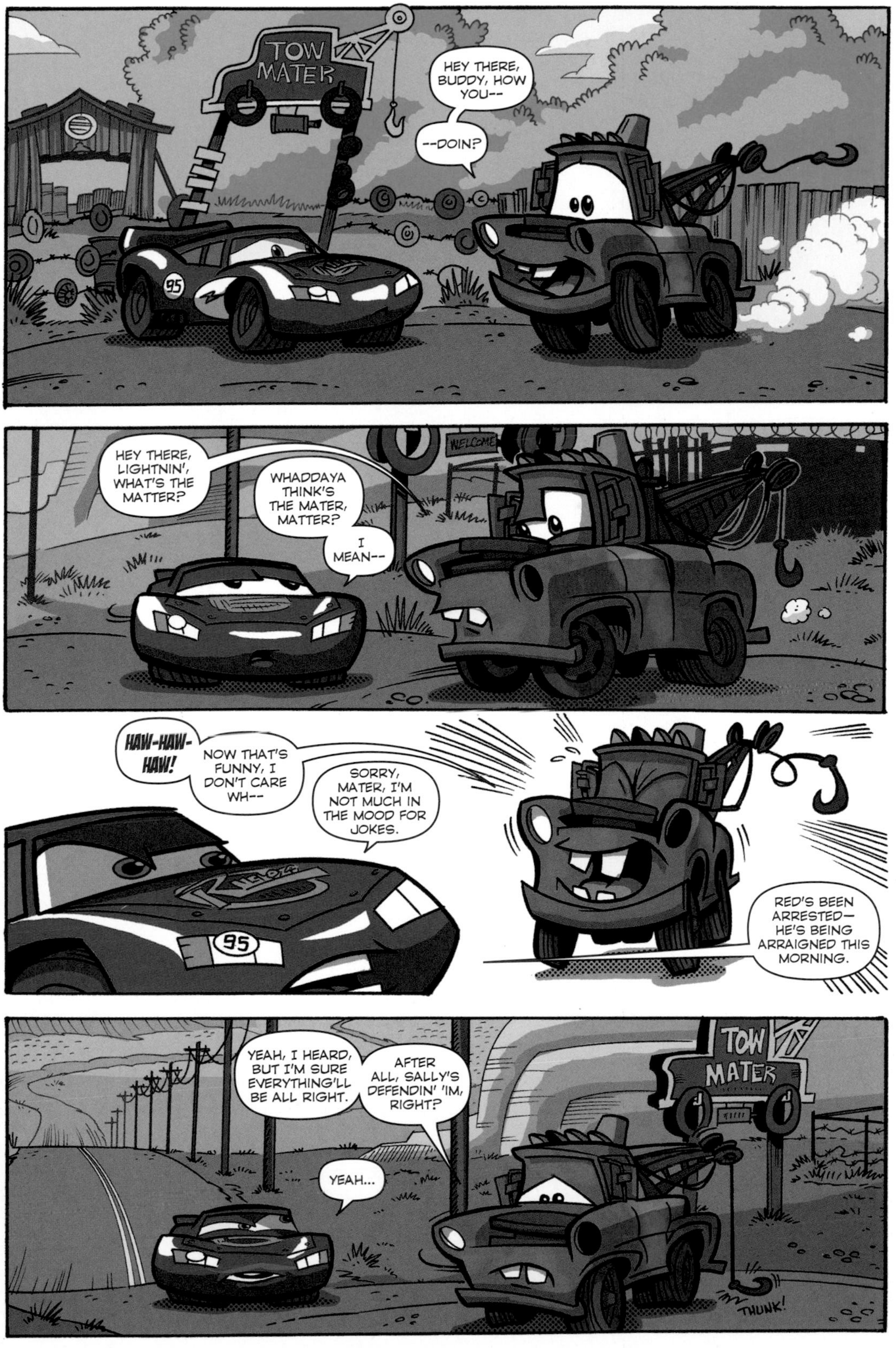
TOW MATER
HEY THERE, BUDDY, HOW YOU--
--DOIN?
WELCOME
HEY THERE, LIGHTNIN', WHAT'S THE MATTER?
WHADDAYA THINK'S THE MATER, MATTER?
I MEAN--
HAW-HAW-HAW!
NOW THAT'S FUNNY, I DON'T CARE WH--
SORRY, MATER, I'M NOT MUCH IN THE MOOD FOR JOKES.
95
RED'S BEEN ARRESTED—HE'S BEING ARRAIGNED THIS MORNING.
TOW MATER
YEAH, I HEARD, BUT I'M SURE EVERYTHING'LL BE ALL RIGHT.
AFTER ALL, SALLY'S DEFENDIN' 'IM, RIGHT?
YEAH...
THUNK!

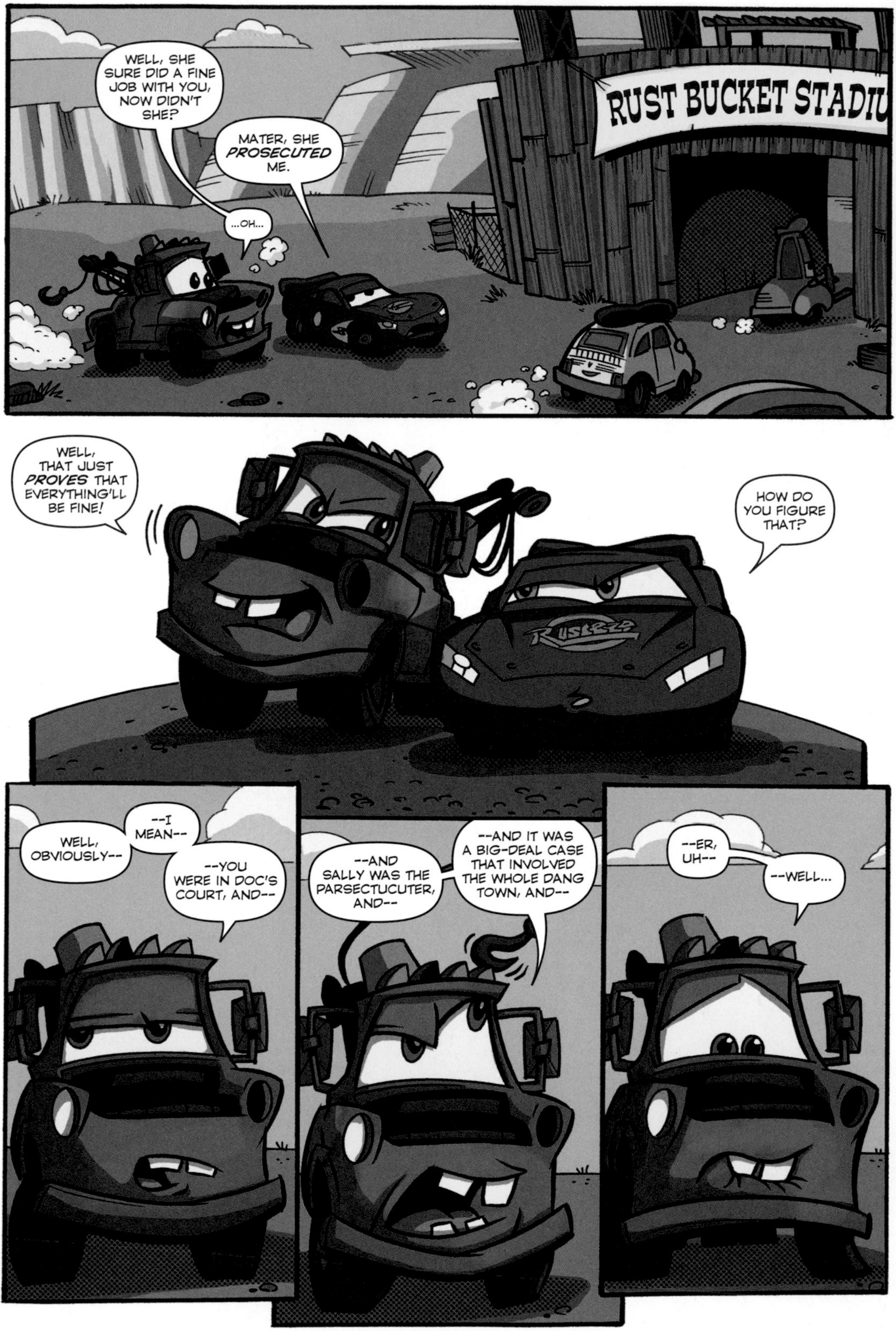
RUST BUCKET STADIU
WELL, SHE SURE DID A FINE JOB WITH YOU, NOW DIDN'T SHE?
MATER, SHE *PROSECUTED* ME.
...OH...
WELL, THAT JUST *PROVES* THAT EVERYTHING'LL BE FINE!
HOW DO YOU FIGURE THAT?
WELL, OBVIOUSLY--
--I MEAN--
--YOU WERE IN DOC'S COURT, AND--
--AND SALLY WAS THE PARSECTUCUTER, AND--
--AND IT WAS A BIG-DEAL CASE THAT INVOLVED THE WHOLE DANG TOWN, AND--
--ER, UH--
--WELL...

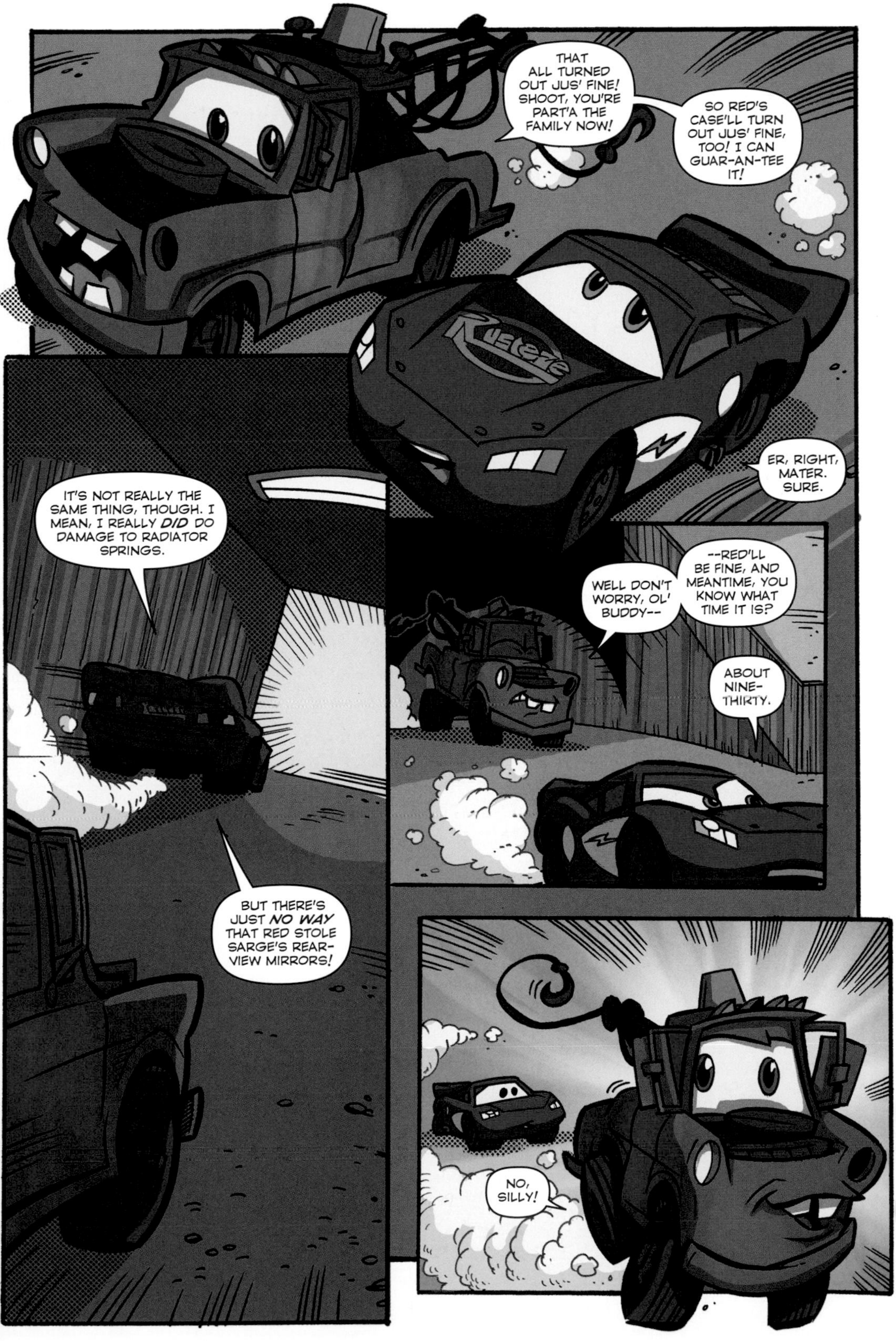
THAT ALL TURNED OUT JUS' FINE! SHOOT, YOU'RE PART'A THE FAMILY NOW!
SO RED'S CASE'LL TURN OUT JUS' FINE, TOO! I CAN GUAR-AN-TEE IT!
ER, RIGHT, MATER. SURE.
IT'S NOT REALLY THE SAME THING, THOUGH. I MEAN, I REALLY *DID* DO DAMAGE TO RADIATOR SPRINGS.
BUT THERE'S JUST ***NO WAY*** THAT RED STOLE SARGE'S REAR-VIEW MIRRORS!
WELL DON'T WORRY, OL' BUDDY--
--RED'LL BE FINE, AND MEANTIME, YOU KNOW WHAT TIME IT IS?
ABOUT NINE-THIRTY.
NO, SILLY!

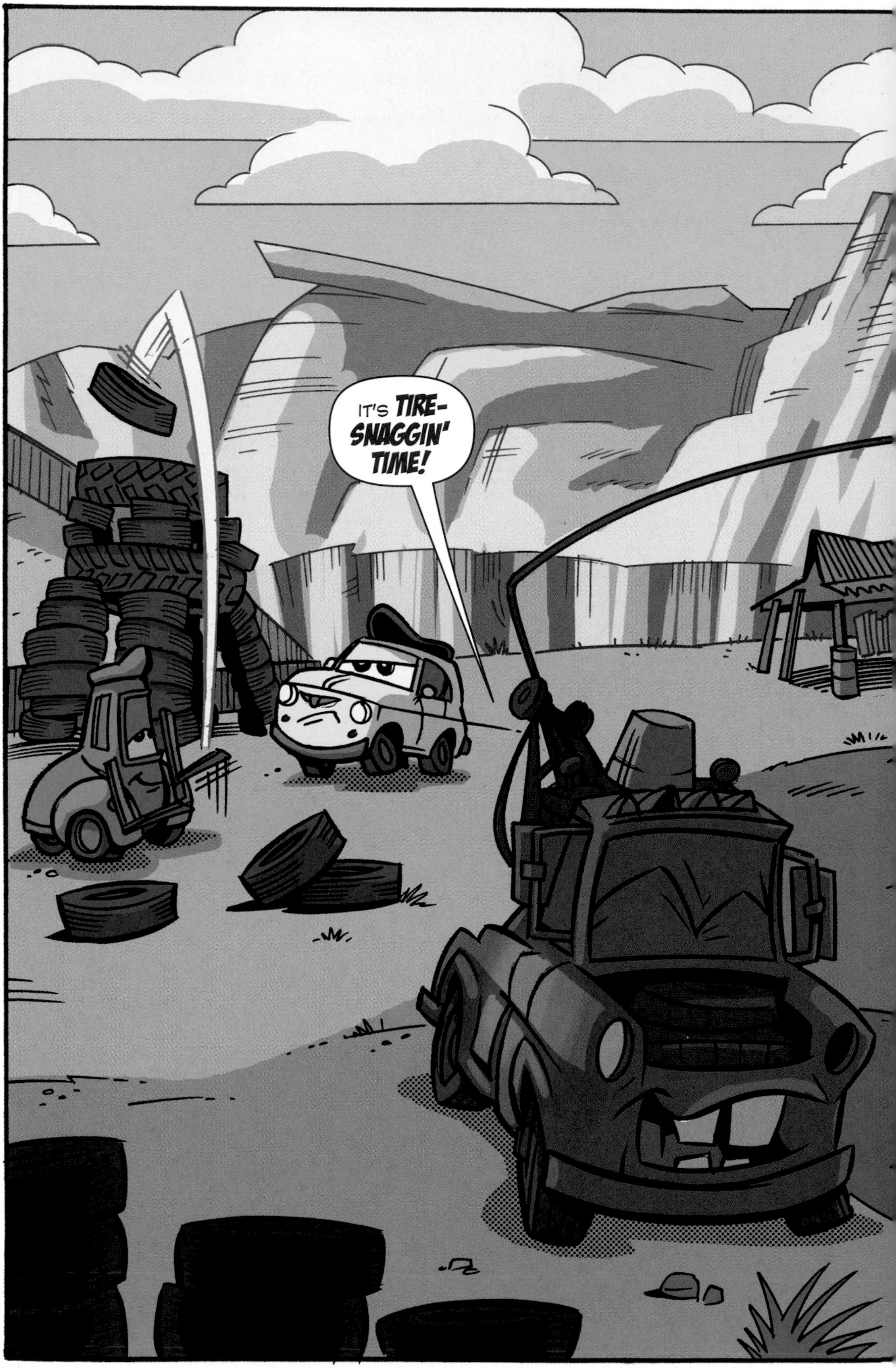
IT'S TIRE-SNAGGIN' TIME!

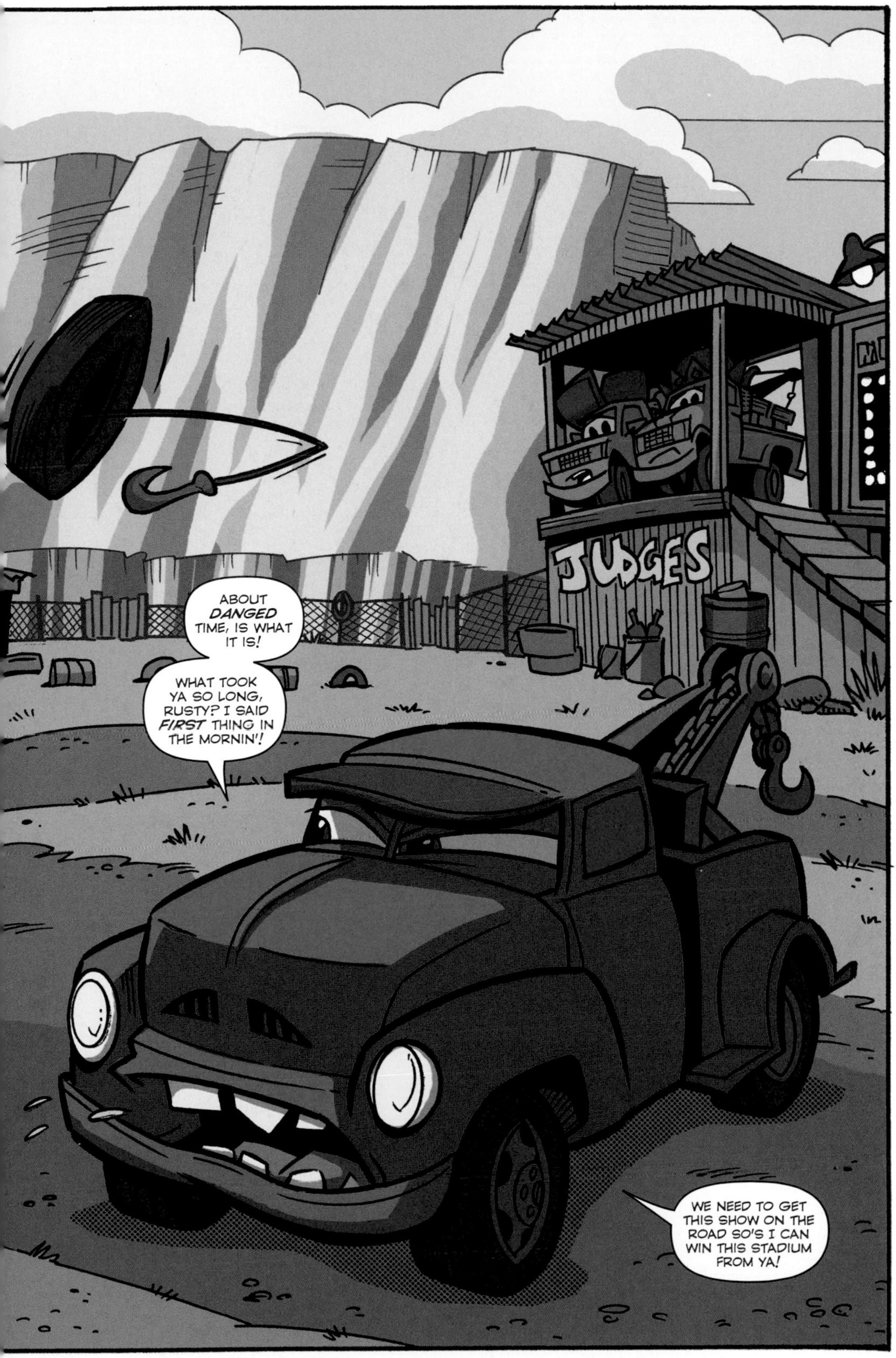
JUDGES
ABOUT DANGED TIME, IS WHAT IT IS!
WHAT TOOK YA SO LONG, RUSTY? I SAID FIRST THING IN THE MORNIN'!
WE NEED TO GET THIS SHOW ON THE ROAD SO'S I CAN WIN THIS STADIUM FROM YA!

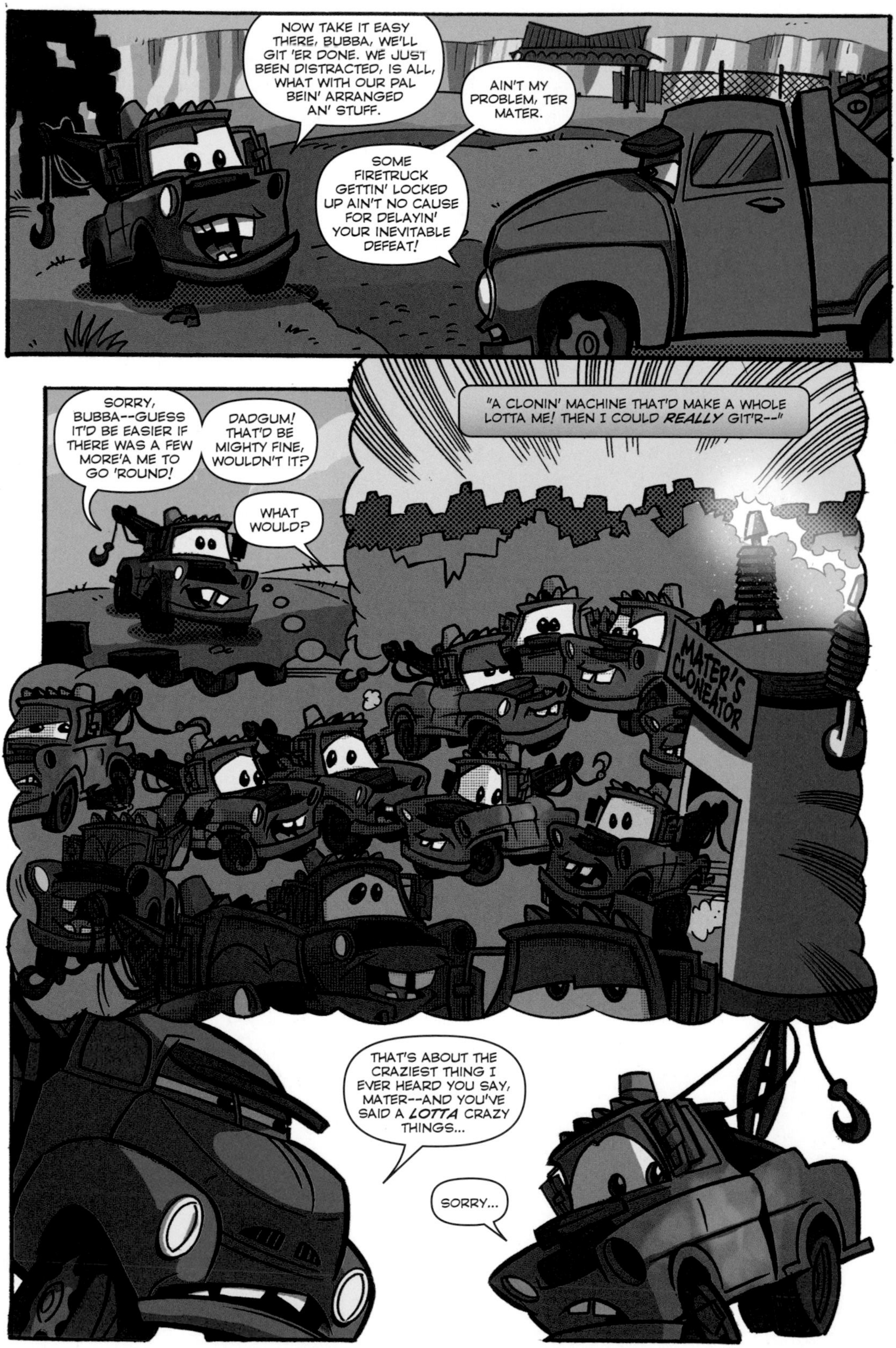
NOW TAKE IT EASY THERE, BUBBA, WE'LL GIT 'ER DONE. WE JUST BEEN DISTRACTED, IS ALL, WHAT WITH OUR PAL BEIN' ARRANGED AN' STUFF.
AIN'T MY PROBLEM, TER MATER.
SOME FIRETRUCK GETTIN' LOCKED UP AIN'T NO CAUSE FOR DELAYIN' YOUR INEVITABLE DEFEAT!
SORRY, BUBBA--GUESS IT'D BE EASIER IF THERE WAS A FEW MORE'A ME TO GO 'ROUND!
DADGUM! THAT'D BE MIGHTY FINE, WOULDN'T IT?
WHAT WOULD?
"A CLONIN' MACHINE THAT'D MAKE A WHOLE LOTTA ME! THEN I COULD REALLY GIT'R--"
MATER'S CLONEATOR
THAT'S ABOUT THE CRAZIEST THING I EVER HEARD YOU SAY, MATER--AND YOU'VE SAID A LOTTA CRAZY THINGS...
SORRY...

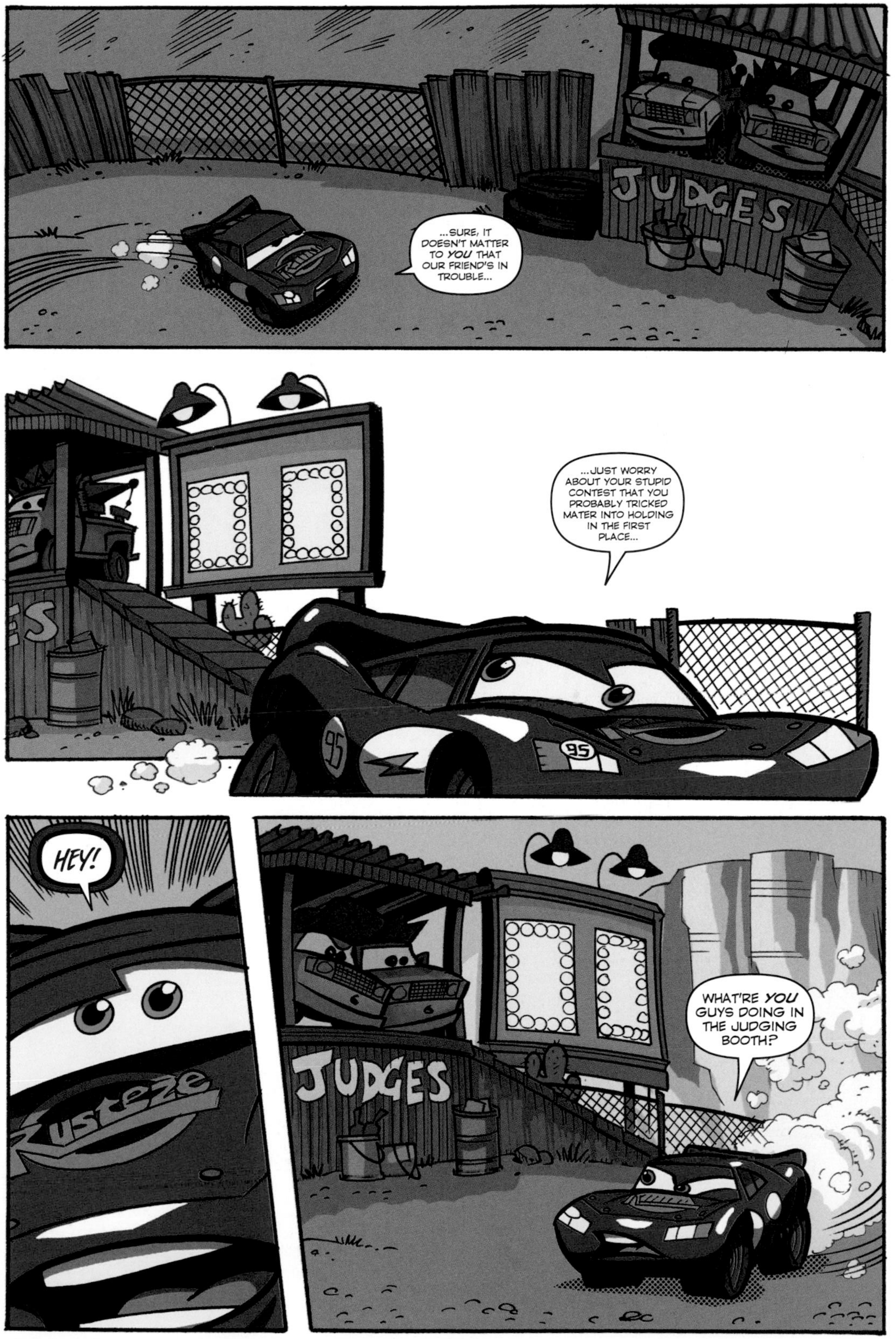
...SURE, IT DOESN'T MATTER TO *YOU* THAT OUR FRIEND'S IN TROUBLE...
...JUST WORRY ABOUT YOUR STUPID CONTEST THAT YOU PROBABLY TRICKED MATER INTO HOLDING IN THE FIRST PLACE...
HEY!
WHAT'RE *YOU* GUYS DOING IN THE JUDGING BOOTH?
JUDGES
JUDGES
Rusteze

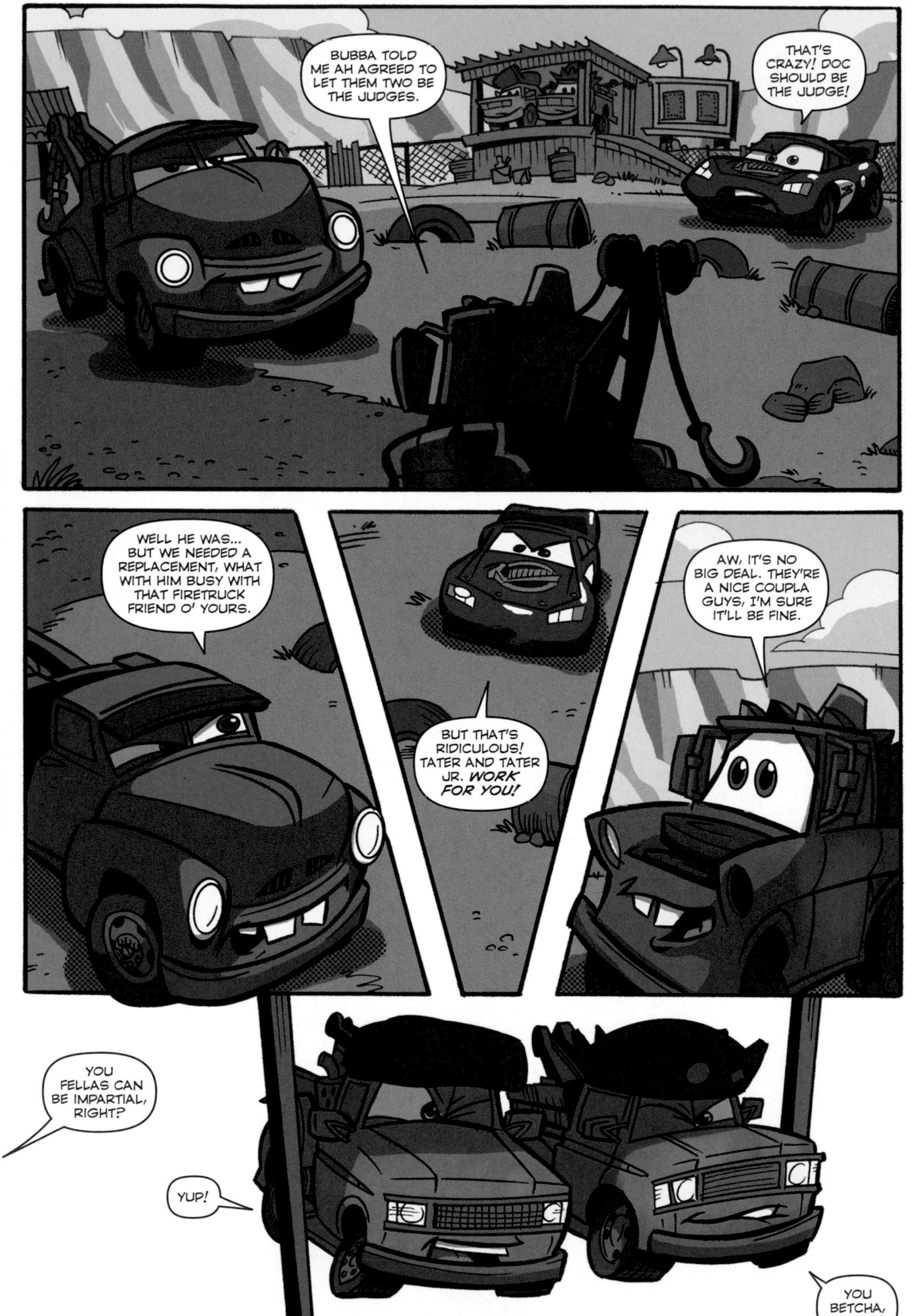
BUBBA TOLD ME AH AGREED TO LET THEM TWO BE THE JUDGES.
THAT'S CRAZY! DOC SHOULD BE THE JUDGE!
WELL HE WAS... BUT WE NEEDED A REPLACEMENT, WHAT WITH HIM BUSY WITH THAT FIRETRUCK FRIEND O' YOURS.
BUT THAT'S RIDICULOUS! TATER AND TATER JR. WORK FOR YOU!
AW, IT'S NO BIG DEAL. THEY'RE A NICE COUPLA GUYS, I'M SURE IT'LL BE FINE.
YOU FELLAS CAN BE IMPARTIAL, RIGHT?
YUP!
YOU BETCHA, BUBBA!

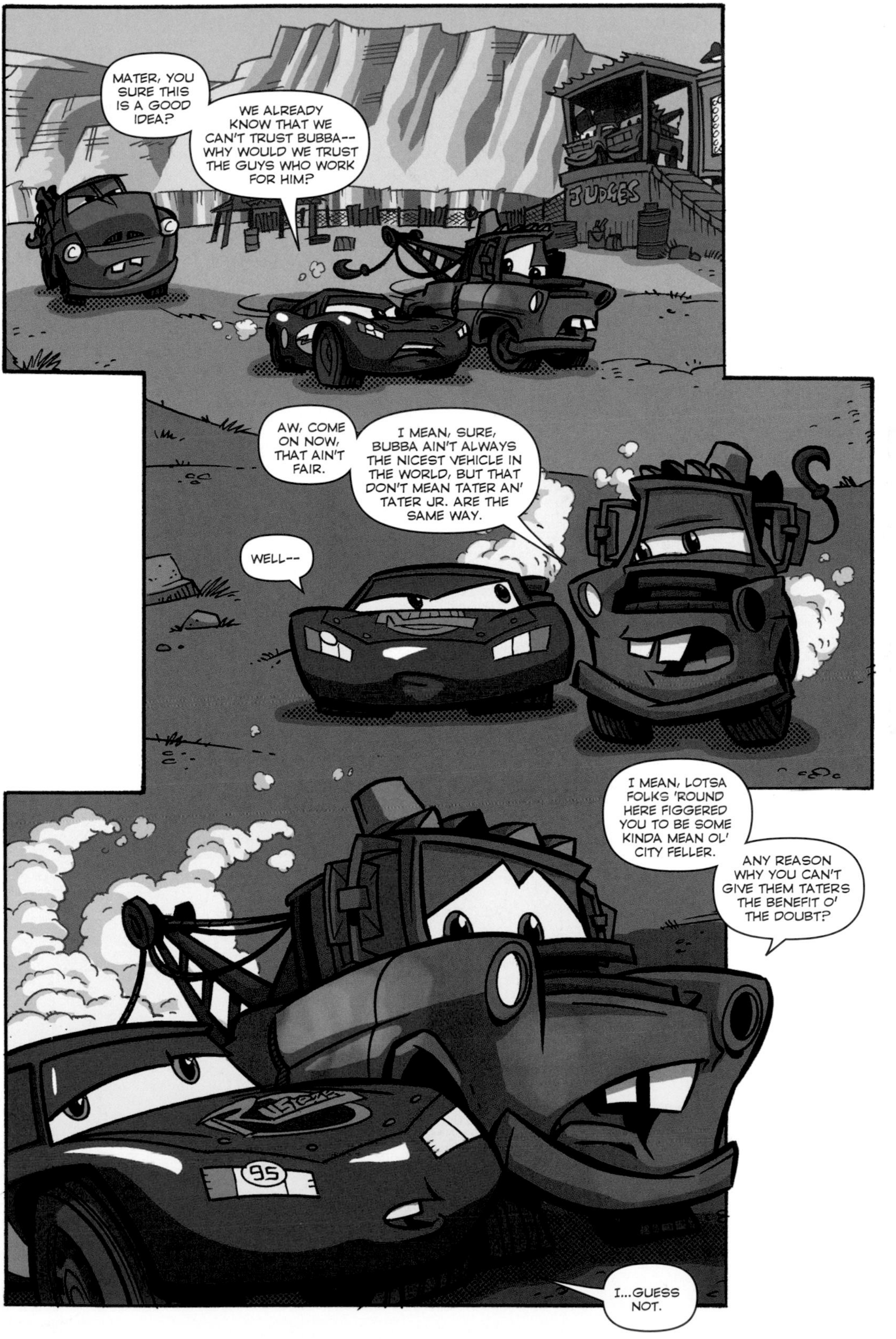
MATER, YOU SURE THIS IS A GOOD IDEA?
WE ALREADY KNOW THAT WE CAN'T TRUST BUBBA-- WHY WOULD WE TRUST THE GUYS WHO WORK FOR HIM?
JUDGES
AW, COME ON NOW, THAT AIN'T FAIR.
I MEAN, SURE, BUBBA AIN'T ALWAYS THE NICEST VEHICLE IN THE WORLD, BUT THAT DON'T MEAN TATER AN' TATER JR. ARE THE SAME WAY.
WELL--
I MEAN, LOTSA FOLKS 'ROUND HERE FIGGERED YOU TO BE SOME KINDA MEAN OL' CITY FELLER.
ANY REASON WHY YOU CAN'T GIVE THEM TATERS THE BENEFIT O' THE DOUBT?
95
I...GUESS NOT.

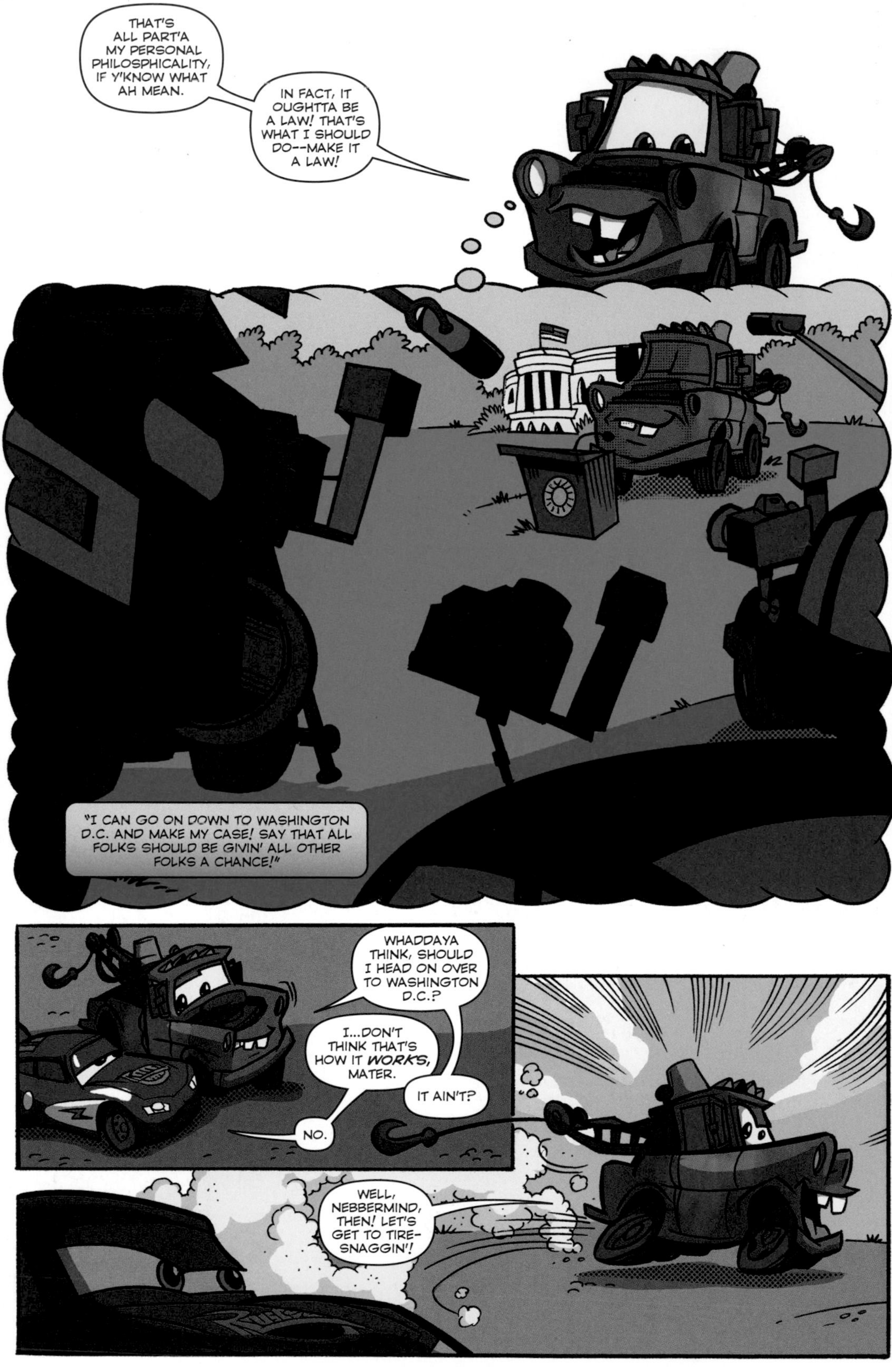
THAT'S ALL PART'A MY PERSONAL PHILOSPHICALITY, IF Y'KNOW WHAT AH MEAN.
IN FACT, IT OUGHTTA BE A LAW! THAT'S WHAT I SHOULD DO--MAKE IT A LAW!
"I CAN GO ON DOWN TO WASHINGTON D.C. AND MAKE MY CASE! SAY THAT ALL FOLKS SHOULD BE GIVIN' ALL OTHER FOLKS A CHANCE!"
WHADDAYA THINK, SHOULD I HEAD ON OVER TO WASHINGTON D.C.?
I...DON'T THINK THAT'S HOW IT *WORKS*, MATER.
IT AIN'T?
NO.
WELL, NEBBERMIND, THEN! LET'S GET TO TIRE-SNAGGIN'!

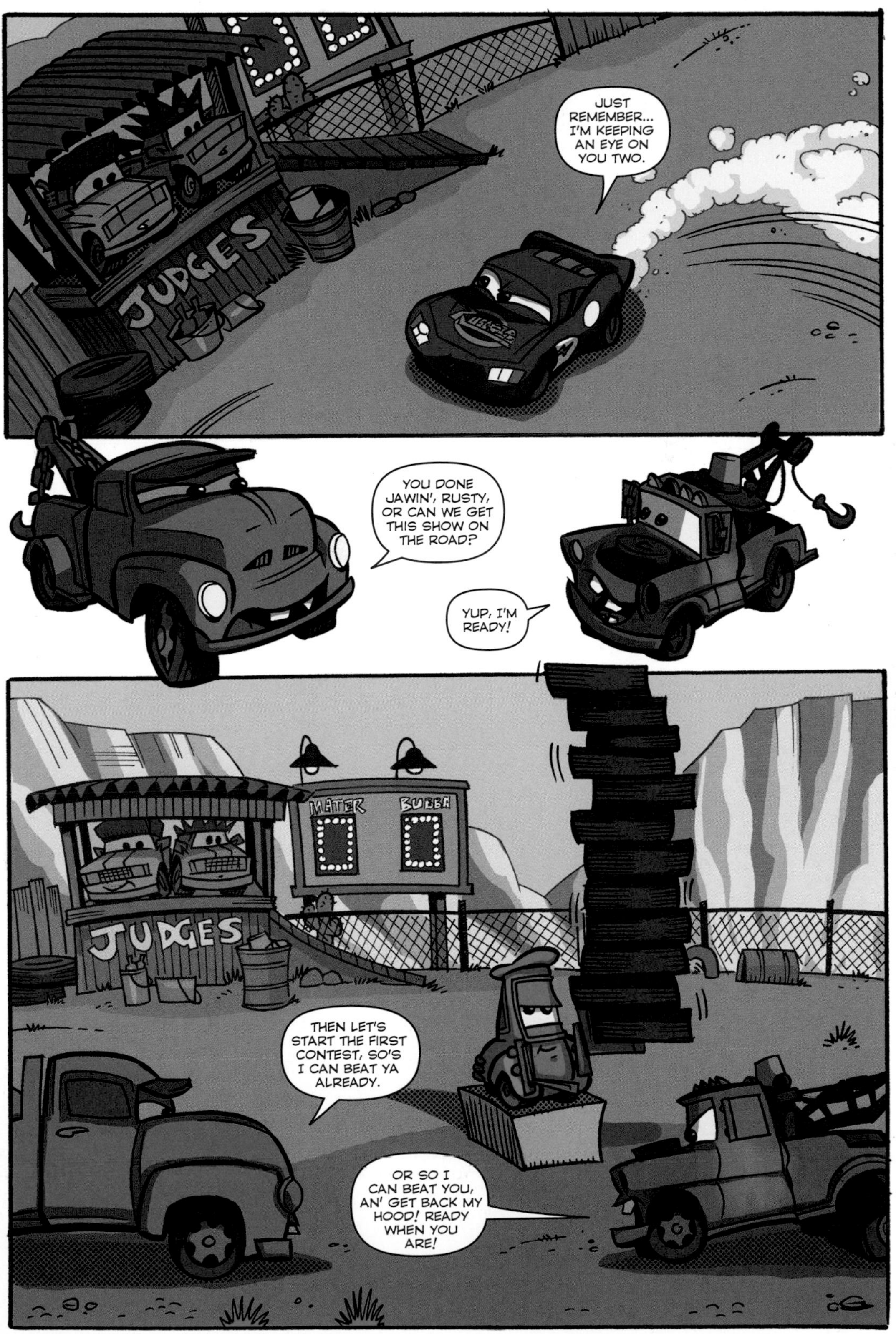
JUST REMEMBER... I'M KEEPING AN EYE ON YOU TWO.
JUDGES
YOU DONE JAWIN', RUSTY, OR CAN WE GET THIS SHOW ON THE ROAD?
YUP, I'M READY!
MATER
BUBBA
JUDGES
THEN LET'S START THE FIRST CONTEST, SO'S I CAN BEAT YA ALREADY.
OR SO I CAN BEAT YOU, AN' GET BACK MY HOOD! READY WHEN YOU ARE!

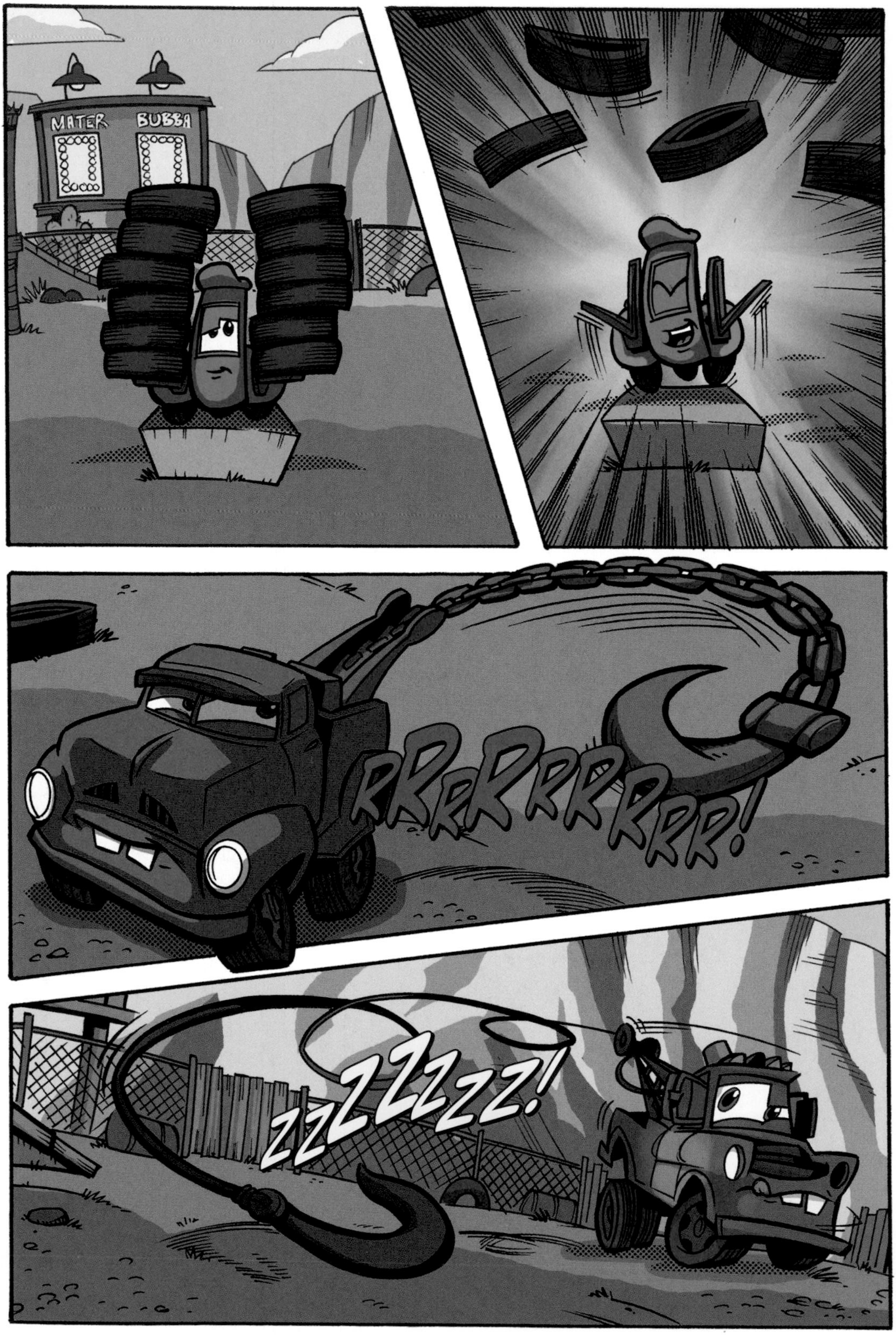
MATER
BUBBA
RRRRRRRRRRRR!
zzZZZZZZ!

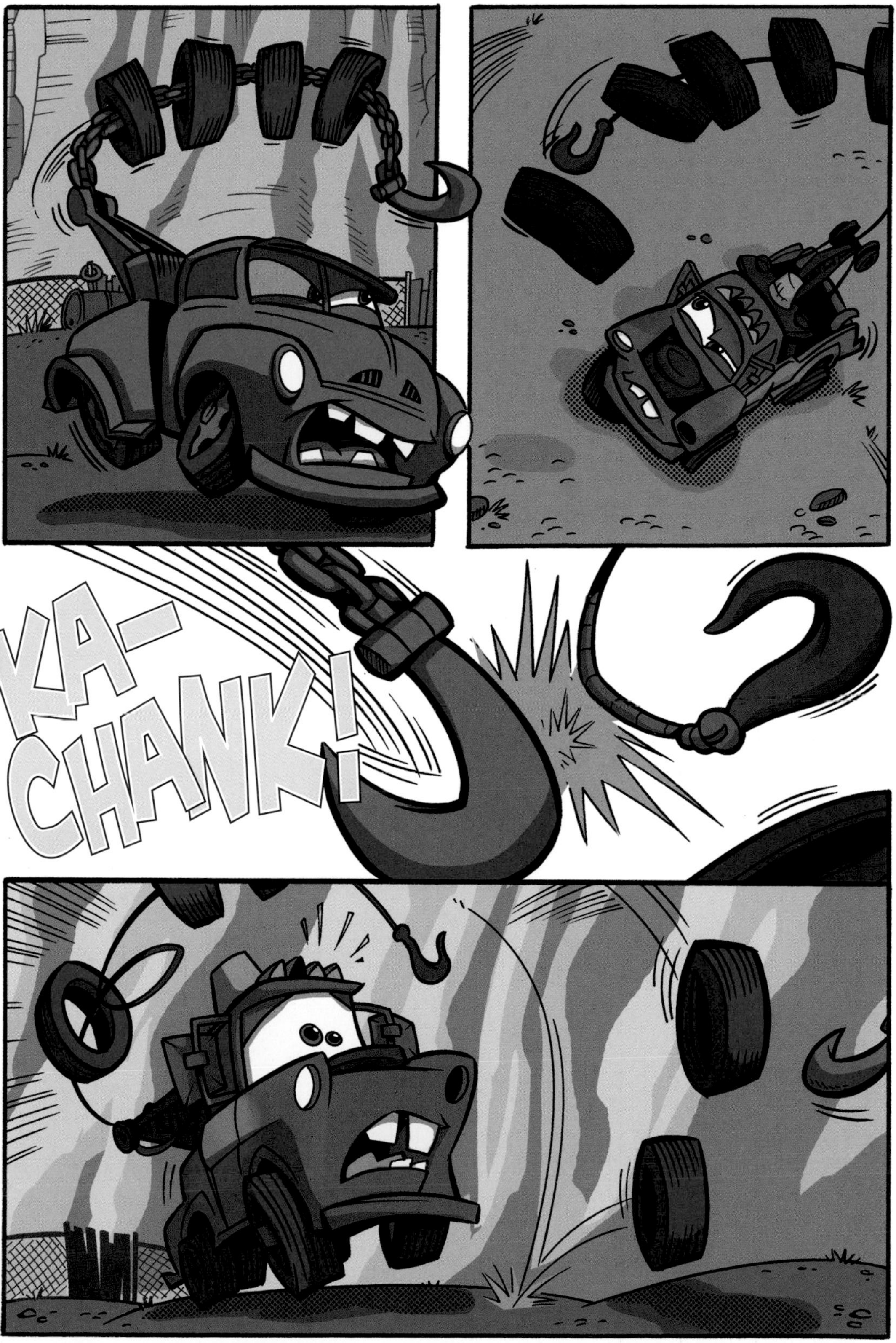
KA-CHANK!

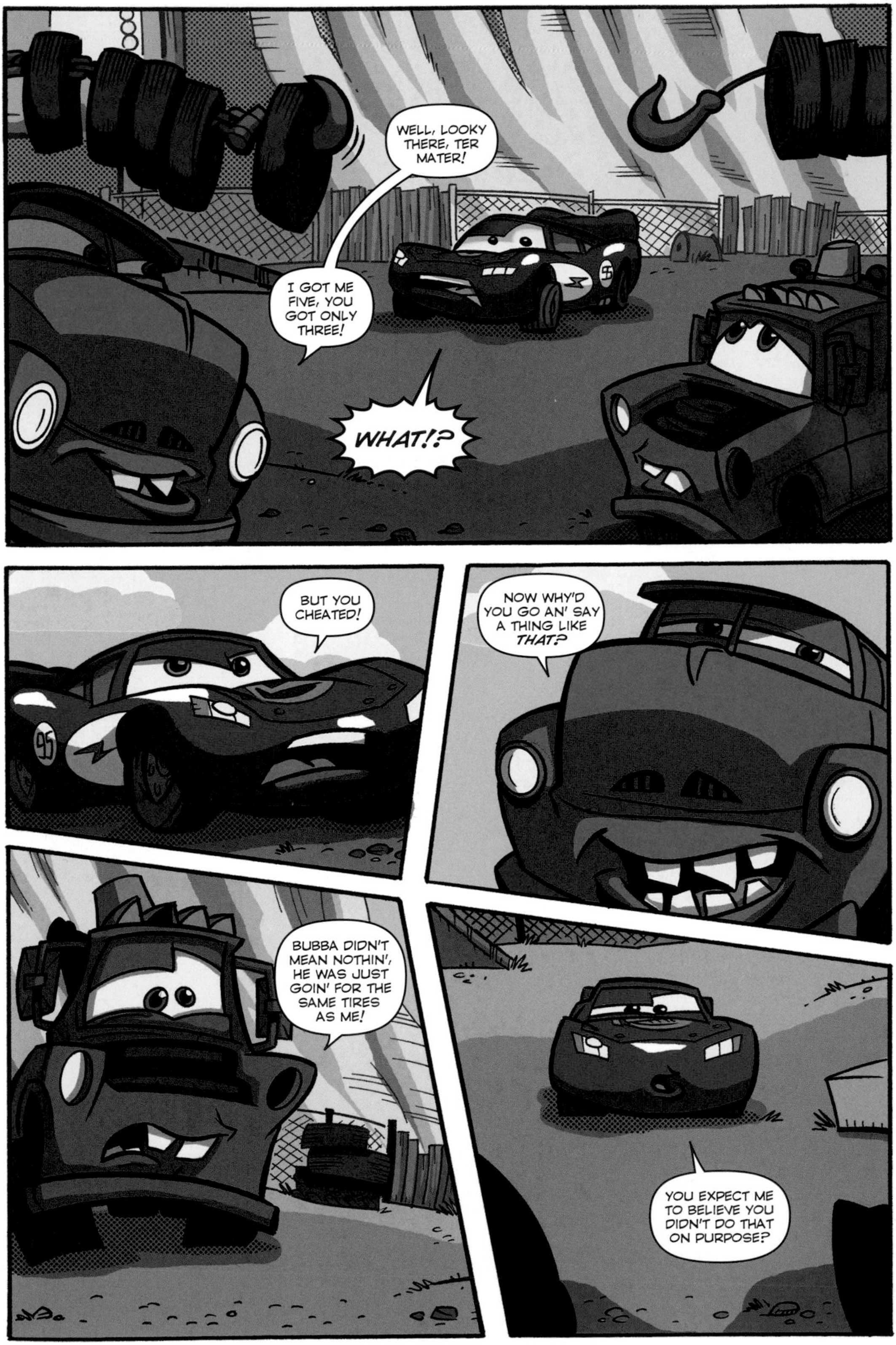

WELL, LOOKY THERE, TER MATER!
I GOT ME FIVE, YOU GOT ONLY THREE!
WHAT!?
BUT YOU CHEATED!
NOW WHY'D YOU GO AN' SAY A THING LIKE THAT?
BUBBA DIDN'T MEAN NOTHIN', HE WAS JUST GOIN' FOR THE SAME TIRES AS ME!
YOU EXPECT ME TO BELIEVE YOU DIDN'T DO THAT ON PURPOSE?

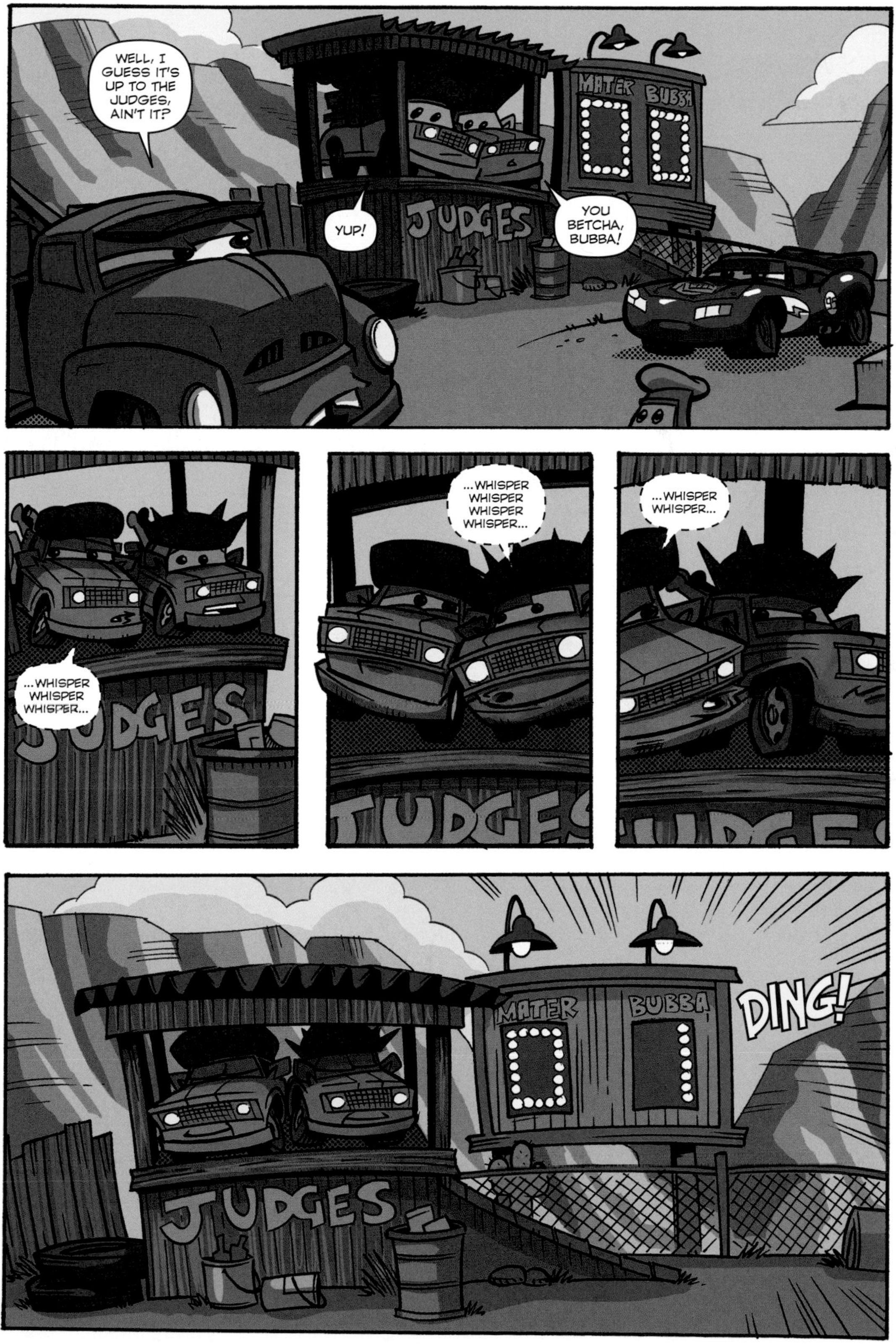
WELL, I GUESS IT'S UP TO THE JUDGES, AIN'T IT?
MATER
BUBBA
JUDGES
YUP!
YOU BETCHA, BUBBA!
...WHISPER WHISPER WHISPER...
...WHISPER WHISPER WHISPER WHISPER...
...WHISPER WHISPER...
MATER
BUBBA
JUDGES
DING!

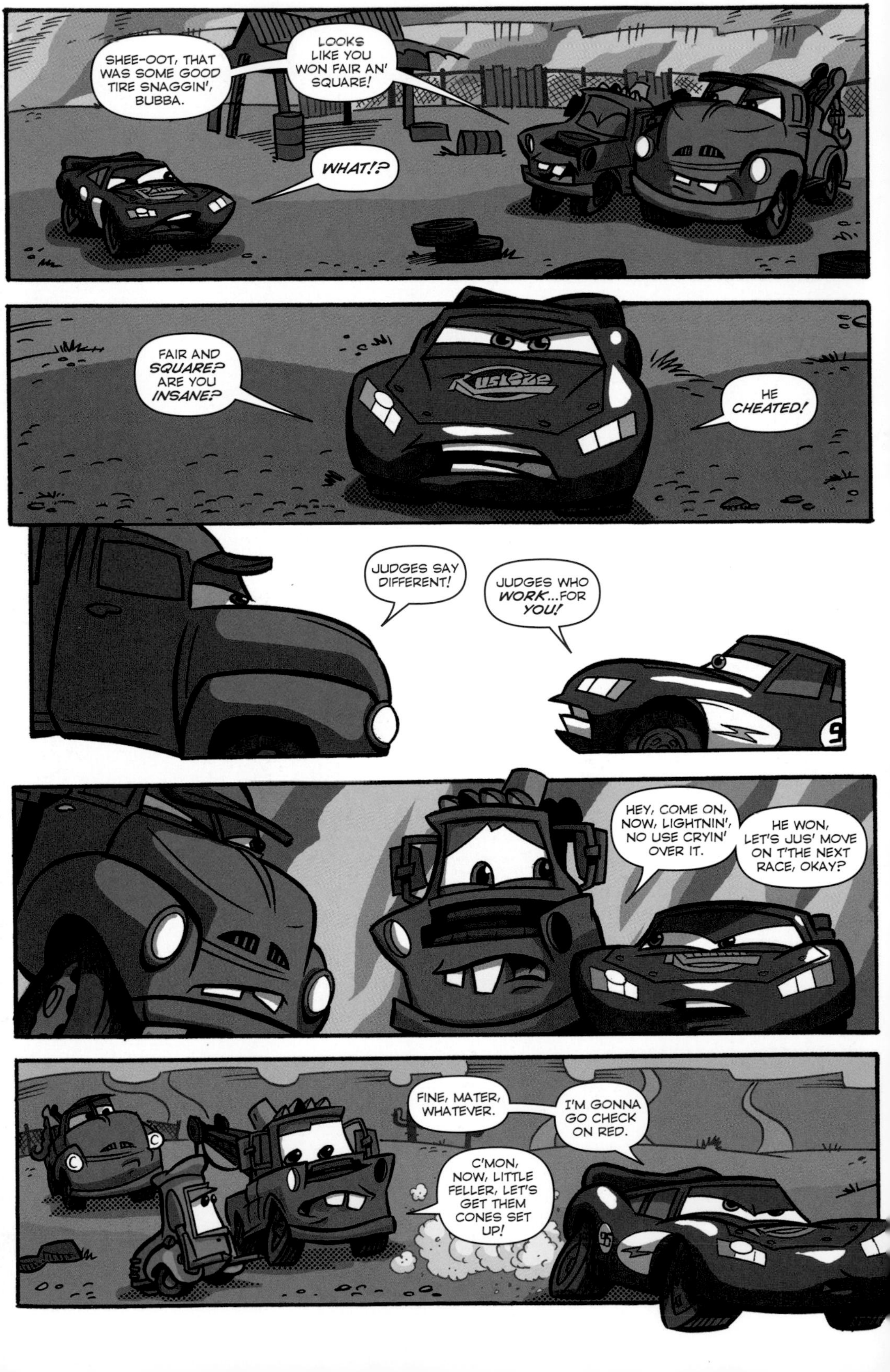
SHEE-OOT, THAT WAS SOME GOOD TIRE SNAGGIN', BUBBA.
LOOKS LIKE YOU WON FAIR AN' SQUARE!
WHAT!?
FAIR AND SQUARE? ARE YOU INSANE?
HE CHEATED!
JUDGES SAY DIFFERENT!
JUDGES WHO WORK...FOR YOU!
HEY, COME ON, NOW, LIGHTNIN', NO USE CRYIN' OVER IT.
HE WON, LET'S JUS' MOVE ON T'THE NEXT RACE, OKAY?
FINE, MATER, WHATEVER.
I'M GONNA GO CHECK ON RED.
C'MON, NOW, LITTLE FELLER, LET'S GET THEM CONES SET UP!

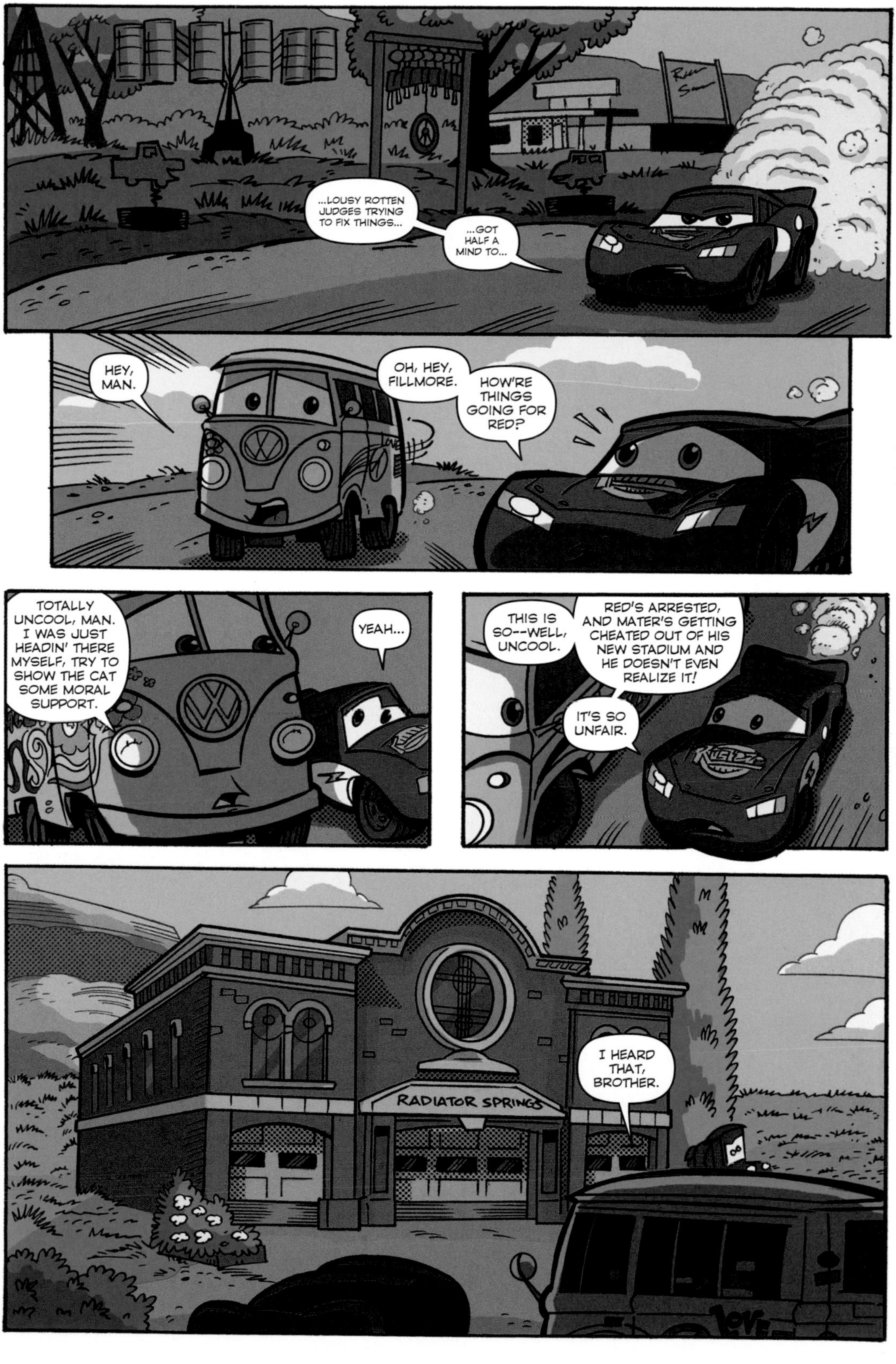
...LOUSY ROTTEN JUDGES TRYING TO FIX THINGS...
...GOT HALF A MIND TO...
HEY, MAN.
OH, HEY, FILLMORE.
HOW'RE THINGS GOING FOR RED?
TOTALLY UNCOOL, MAN. I WAS JUST HEADIN' THERE MYSELF, TRY TO SHOW THE CAT SOME MORAL SUPPORT.
YEAH...
THIS IS SO--WELL, UNCOOL.
RED'S ARRESTED, AND MATER'S GETTING CHEATED OUT OF HIS NEW STADIUM AND HE DOESN'T EVEN REALIZE IT!
IT'S SO UNFAIR.
RADIATOR SPRINGS
I HEARD THAT, BROTHER.

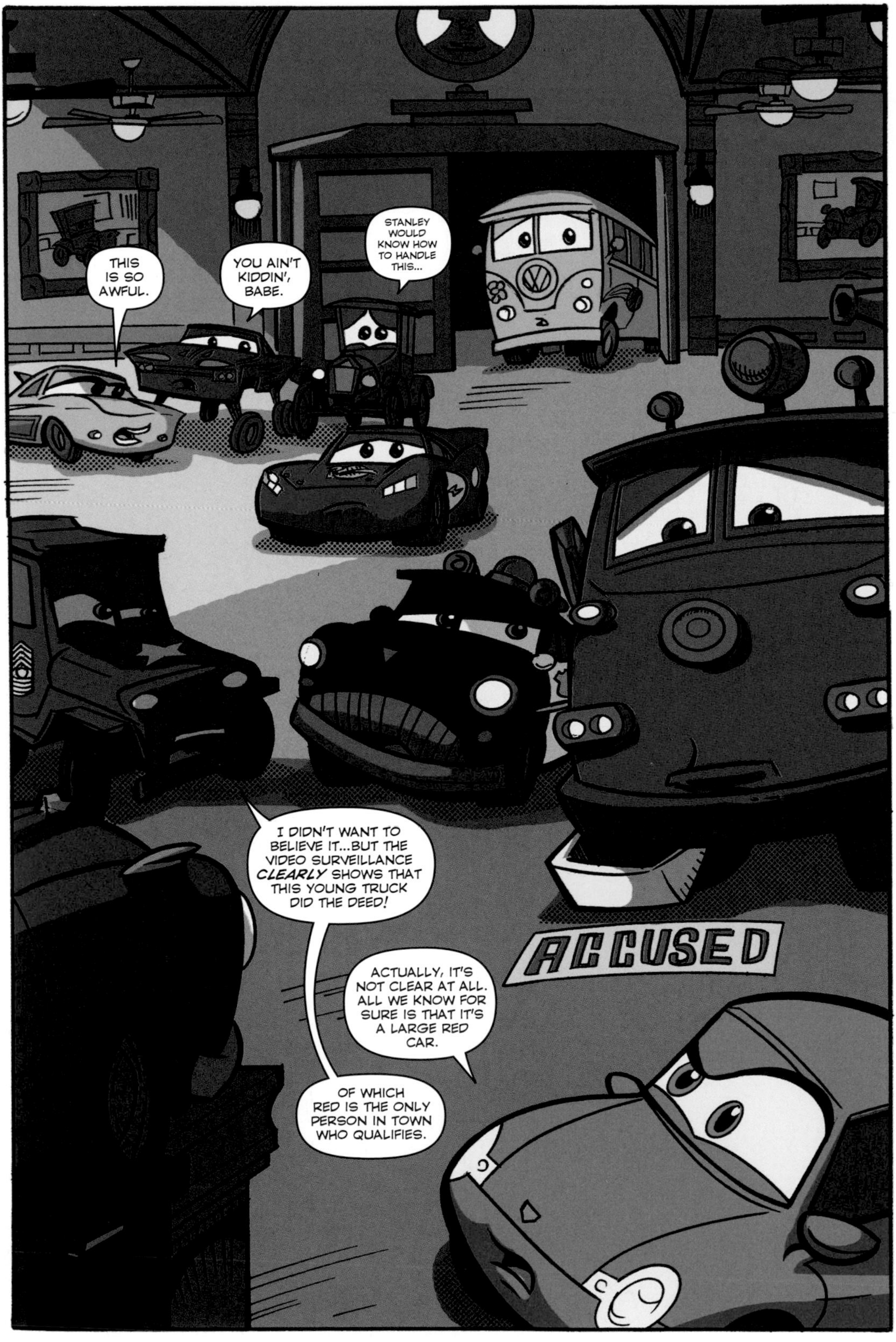
THIS IS SO AWFUL.
YOU AIN'T KIDDIN', BABE.
STANLEY WOULD KNOW HOW TO HANDLE THIS...
I DIDN'T WANT TO BELIEVE IT...BUT THE VIDEO SURVEILLANCE *CLEARLY* SHOWS THAT THIS YOUNG TRUCK DID THE DEED!
ACCUSED
ACTUALLY, IT'S NOT CLEAR AT ALL. ALL WE KNOW FOR SURE IS THAT IT'S A LARGE RED CAR.
OF WHICH RED IS THE ONLY PERSON IN TOWN WHO QUALIFIES.

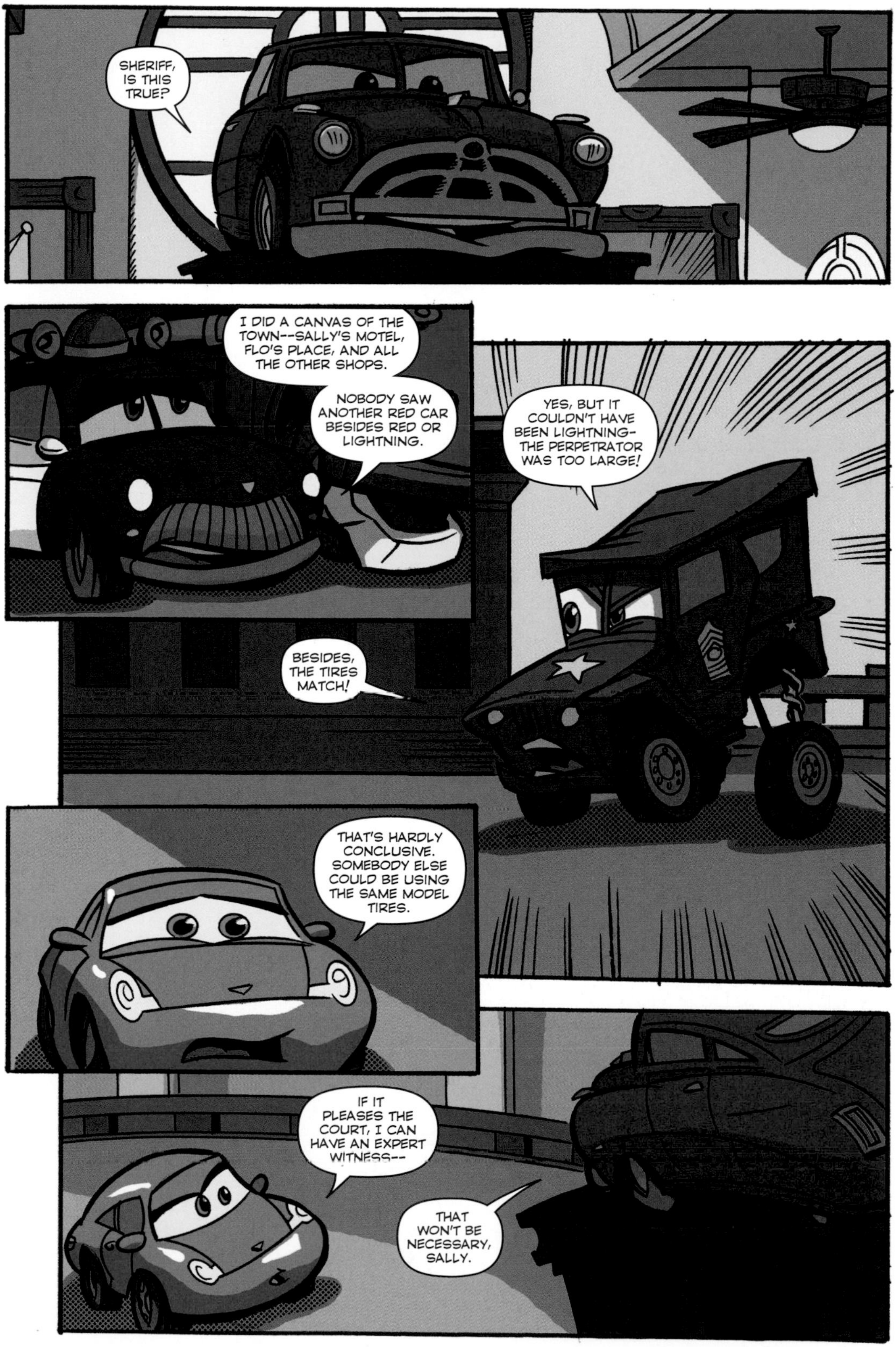
SHERIFF, IS THIS TRUE?
I DID A CANVAS OF THE TOWN--SALLY'S MOTEL, FLO'S PLACE, AND ALL THE OTHER SHOPS.
NOBODY SAW ANOTHER RED CAR BESIDES RED OR LIGHTNING.
YES, BUT IT COULDN'T HAVE BEEN LIGHTNING- THE PERPETRATOR WAS TOO LARGE!
BESIDES, THE TIRES MATCH!
THAT'S HARDLY CONCLUSIVE. SOMEBODY ELSE COULD BE USING THE SAME MODEL TIRES.
IF IT PLEASES THE COURT, I CAN HAVE AN EXPERT WITNESS--
THAT WON'T BE NECESSARY, SALLY.

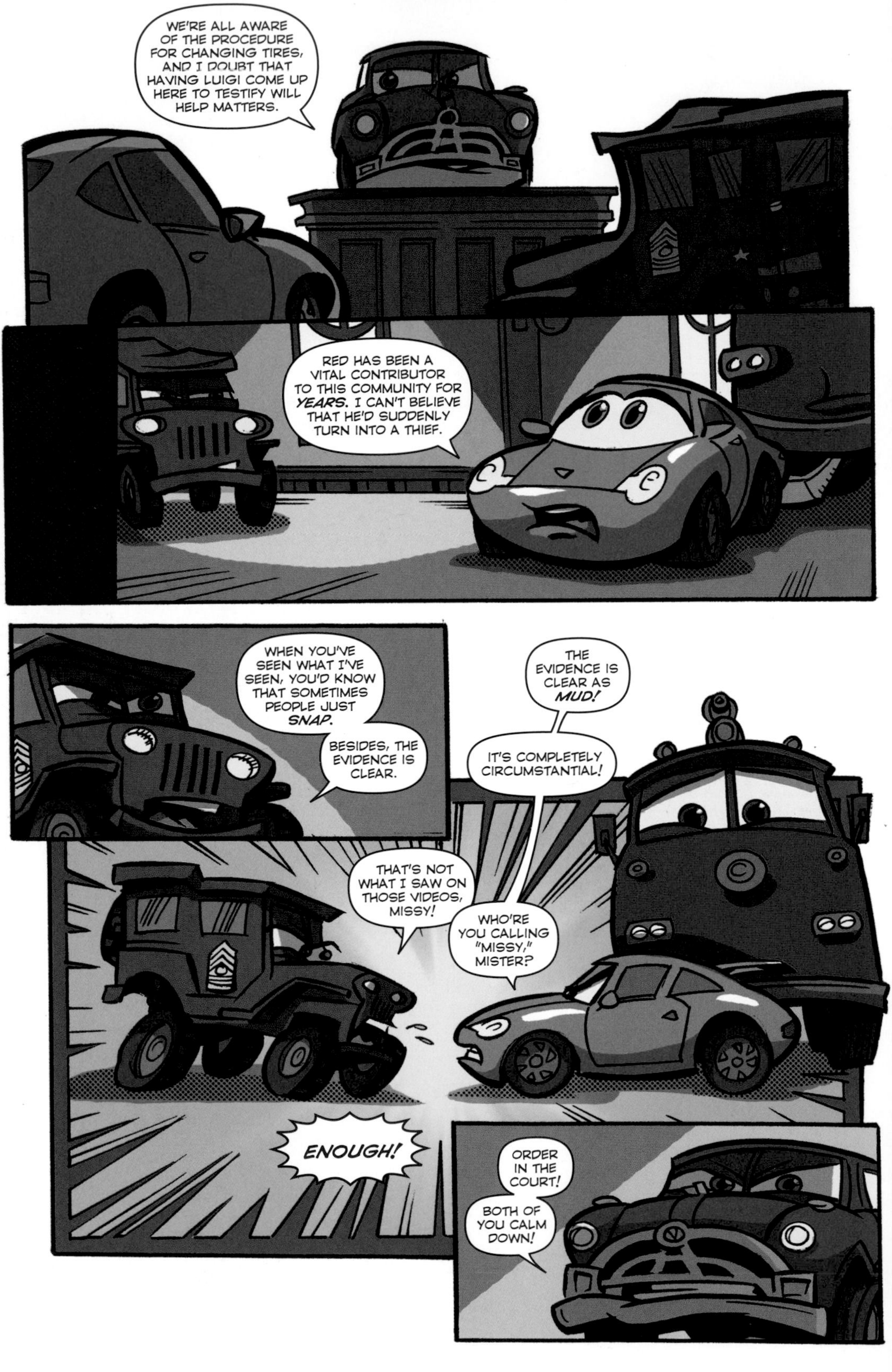

WE'RE ALL AWARE OF THE PROCEDURE FOR CHANGING TIRES, AND I DOUBT THAT HAVING LUIGI COME UP HERE TO TESTIFY WILL HELP MATTERS.
RED HAS BEEN A VITAL CONTRIBUTOR TO THIS COMMUNITY FOR *YEARS*. I CAN'T BELIEVE THAT HE'D SUDDENLY TURN INTO A THIEF.
WHEN YOU'VE SEEN WHAT I'VE SEEN, YOU'D KNOW THAT SOMETIMES PEOPLE JUST *SNAP*.
BESIDES, THE EVIDENCE IS CLEAR.
THE EVIDENCE IS CLEAR AS *MUD!*
IT'S COMPLETELY CIRCUMSTANTIAL!
THAT'S NOT WHAT I SAW ON THOSE VIDEOS, MISSY!
WHO'RE YOU CALLING "MISSY," MISTER?
ENOUGH!
ORDER IN THE COURT!
BOTH OF YOU CALM DOWN!

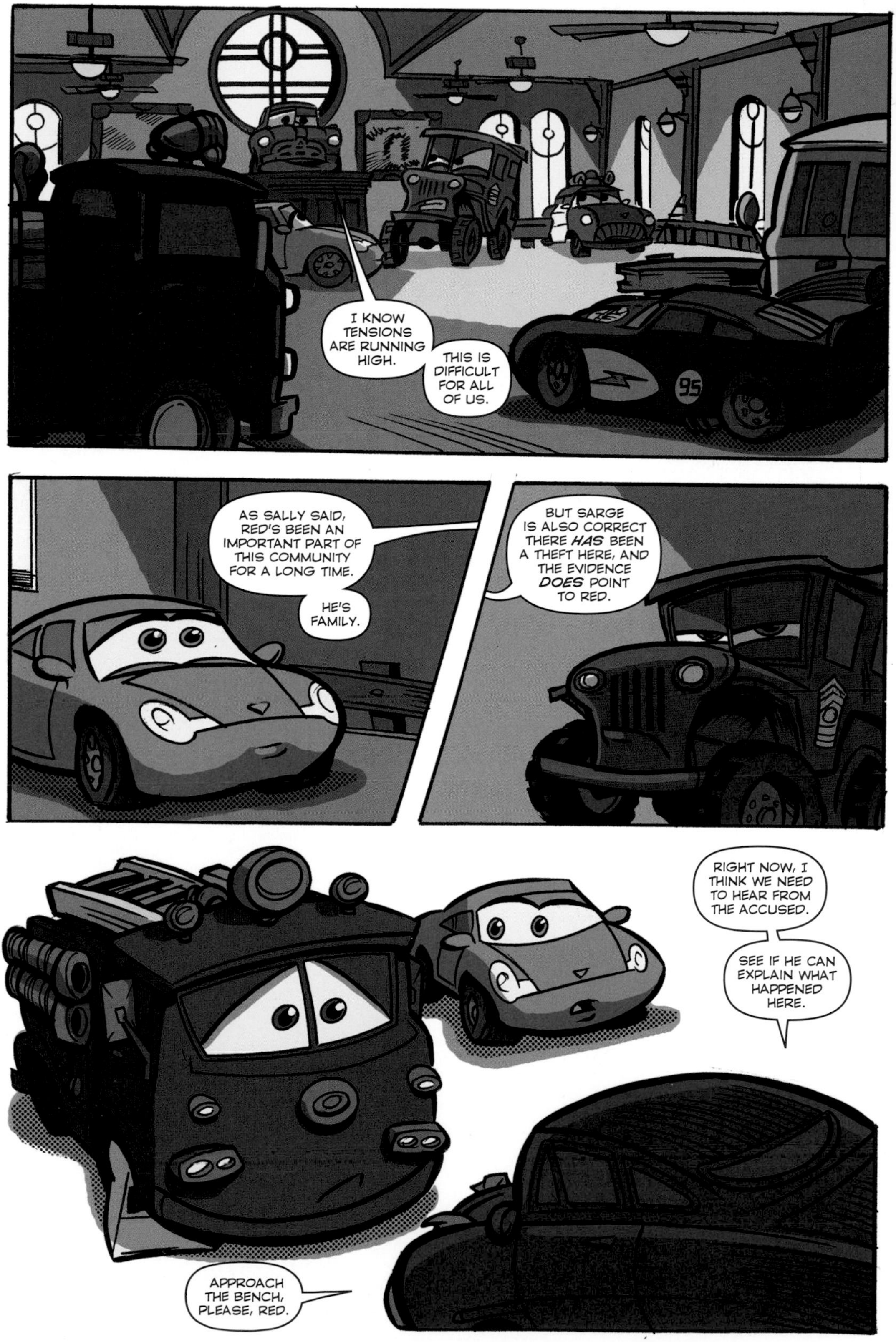
I KNOW TENSIONS ARE RUNNING HIGH.
THIS IS DIFFICULT FOR ALL OF US.
AS SALLY SAID, RED'S BEEN AN IMPORTANT PART OF THIS COMMUNITY FOR A LONG TIME.
HE'S FAMILY.
BUT SARGE IS ALSO CORRECT THERE *HAS* BEEN A THEFT HERE, AND THE EVIDENCE *DOES* POINT TO RED.
RIGHT NOW, I THINK WE NEED TO HEAR FROM THE ACCUSED.
SEE IF HE CAN EXPLAIN WHAT HAPPENED HERE.
APPROACH THE BENCH, PLEASE, RED.
95

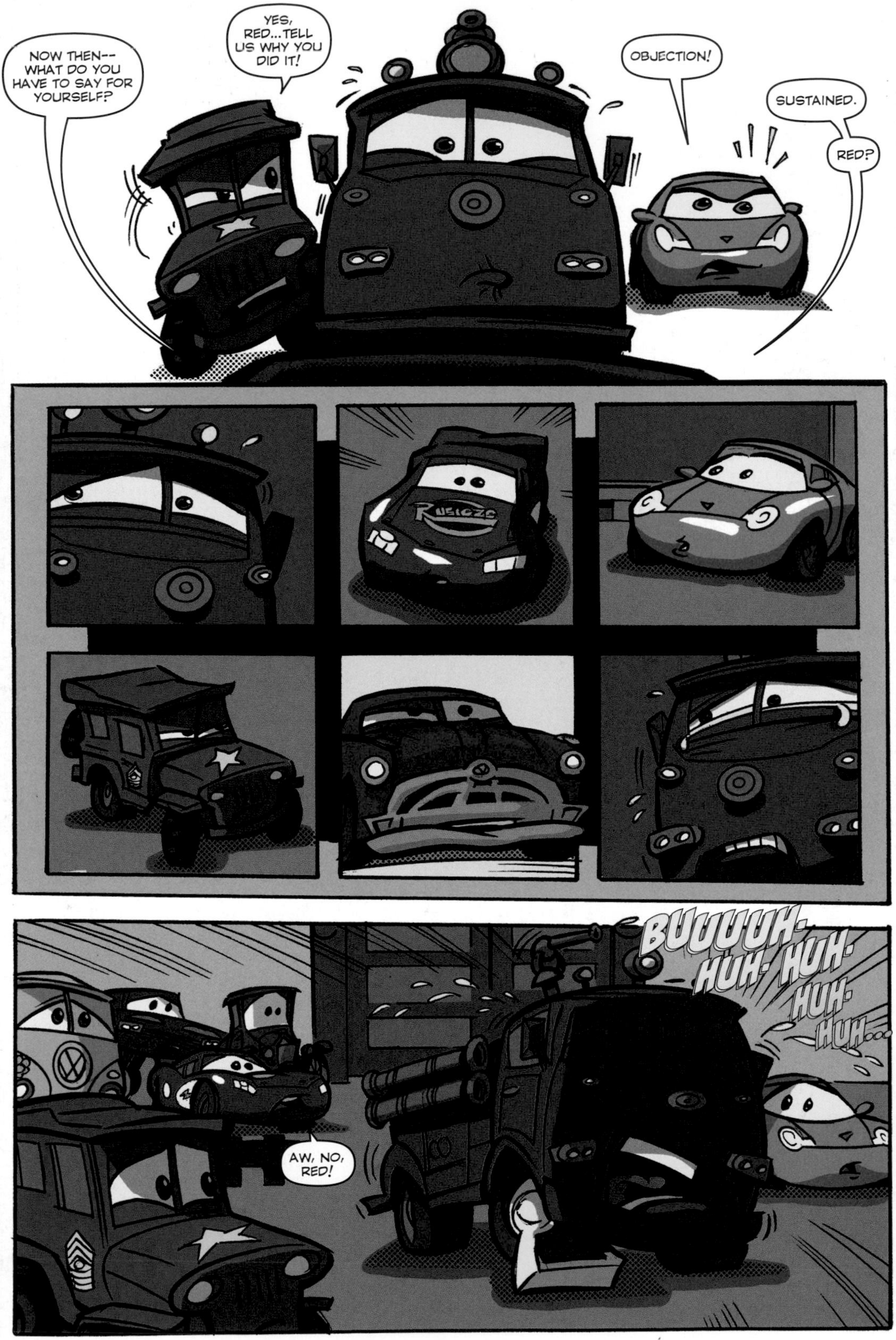
NOW THEN-- WHAT DO YOU HAVE TO SAY FOR YOURSELF?
YES, RED...TELL US WHY YOU DID IT!
OBJECTION!
SUSTAINED.
RED?
BUUUUH-HUH-HUH-HUH-HUH...
AW, NO, RED!

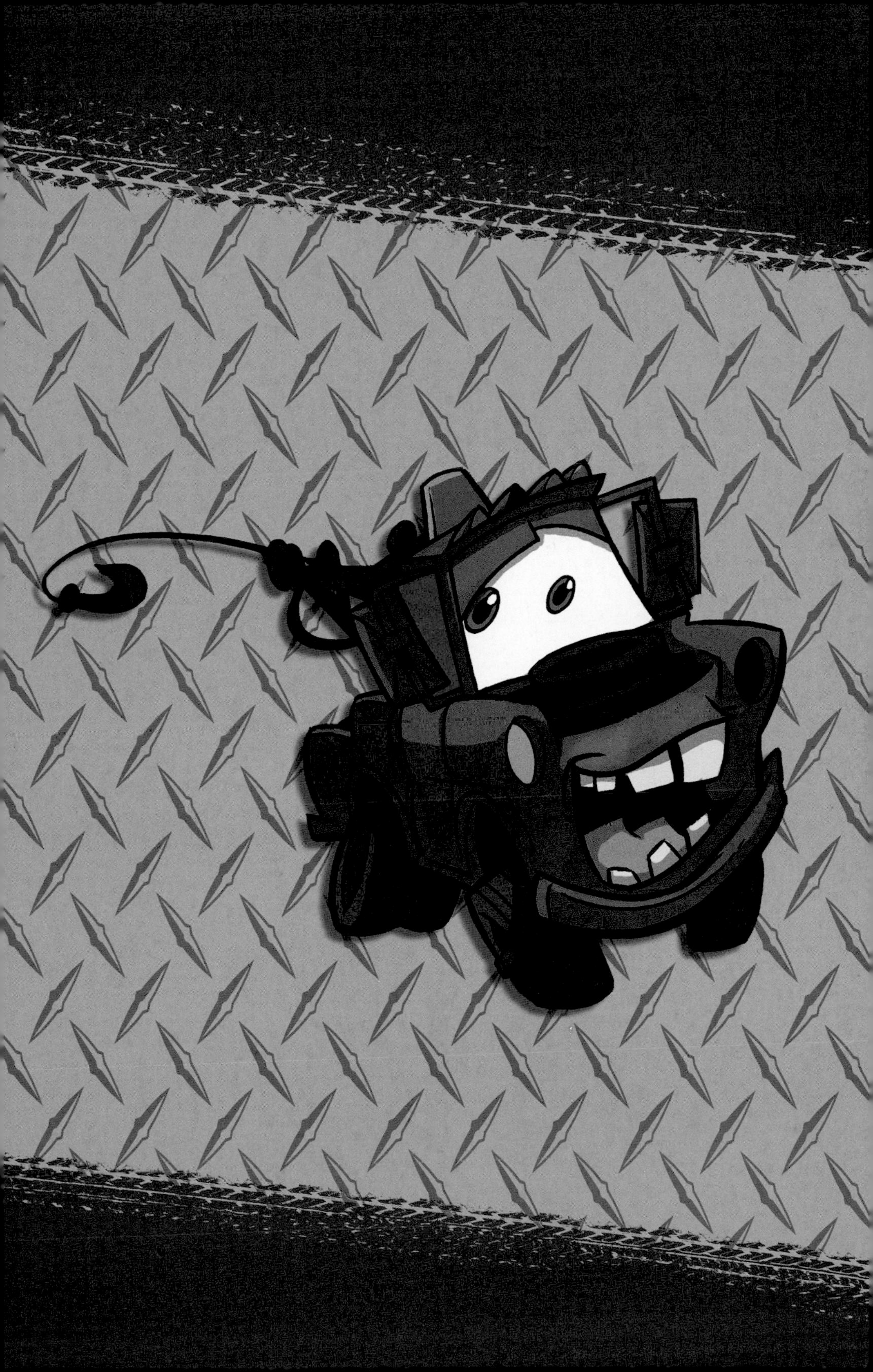

Chapter Three

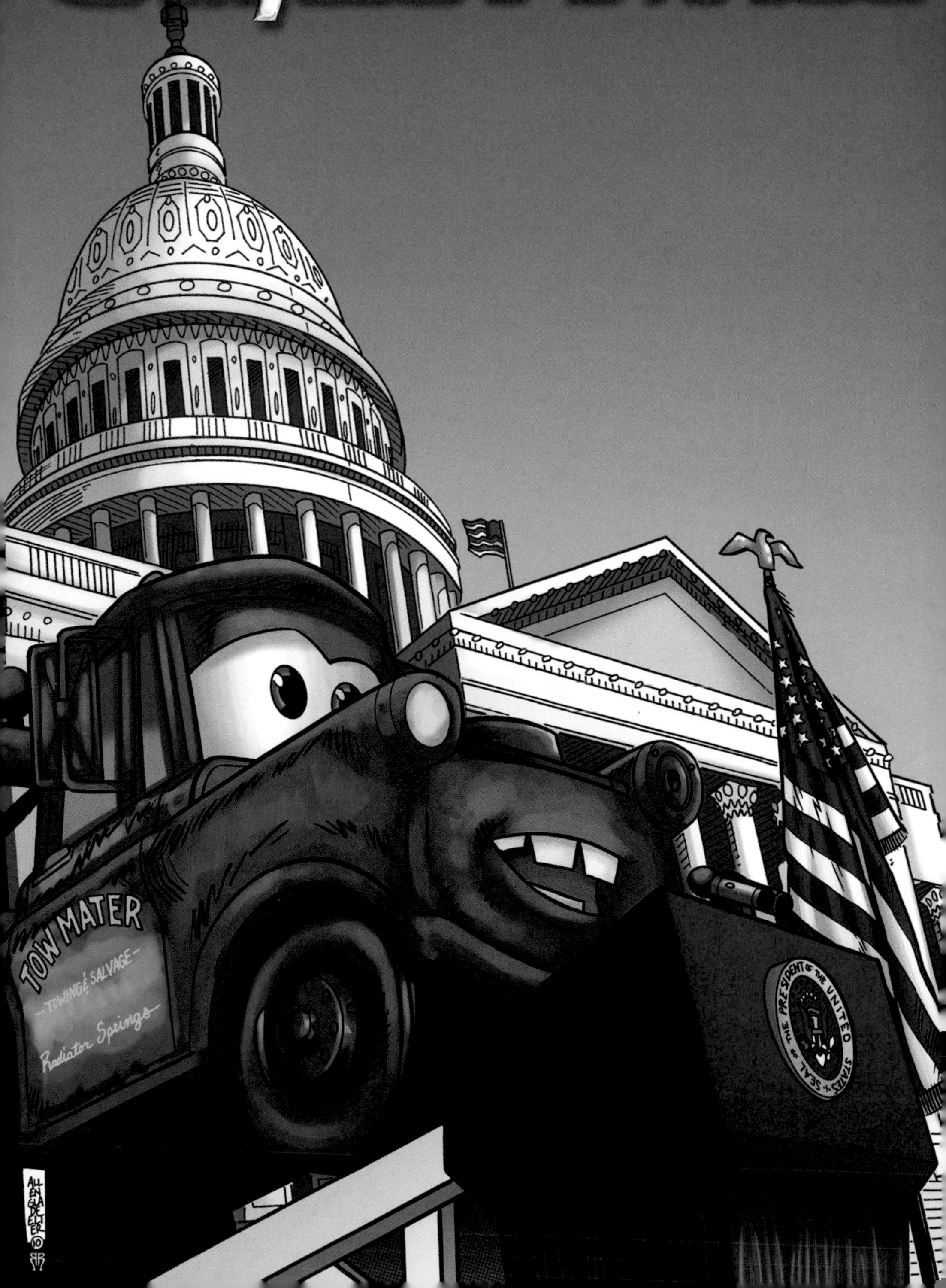
TOW MATER
TOWING & SALVAGE
Radiator Springs
SEAL OF THE PRESIDENT OF THE UNITED STATES

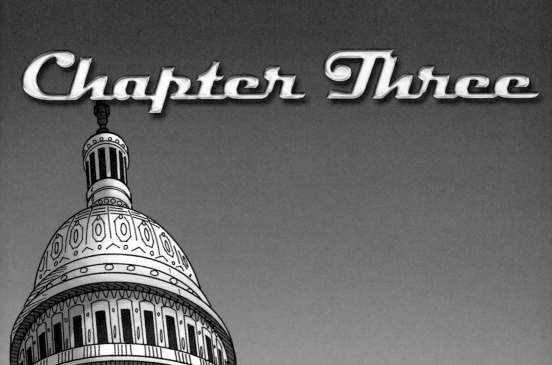

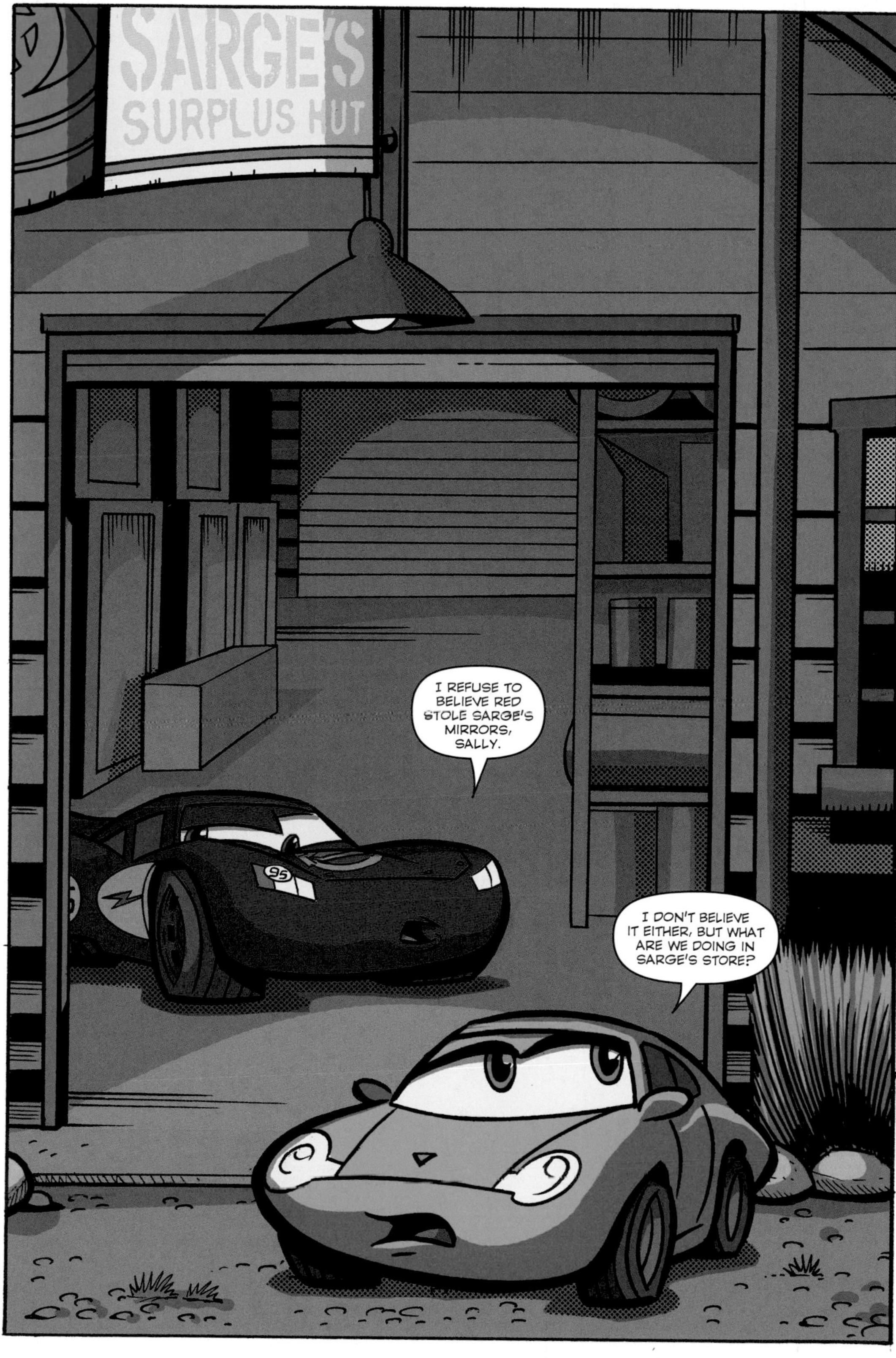
SARGE'S
SURPLUS HUT
I REFUSE TO BELIEVE RED STOLE SARGE'S MIRRORS, SALLY.
I DON'T BELIEVE IT EITHER, BUT WHAT ARE WE DOING IN SARGE'S STORE?

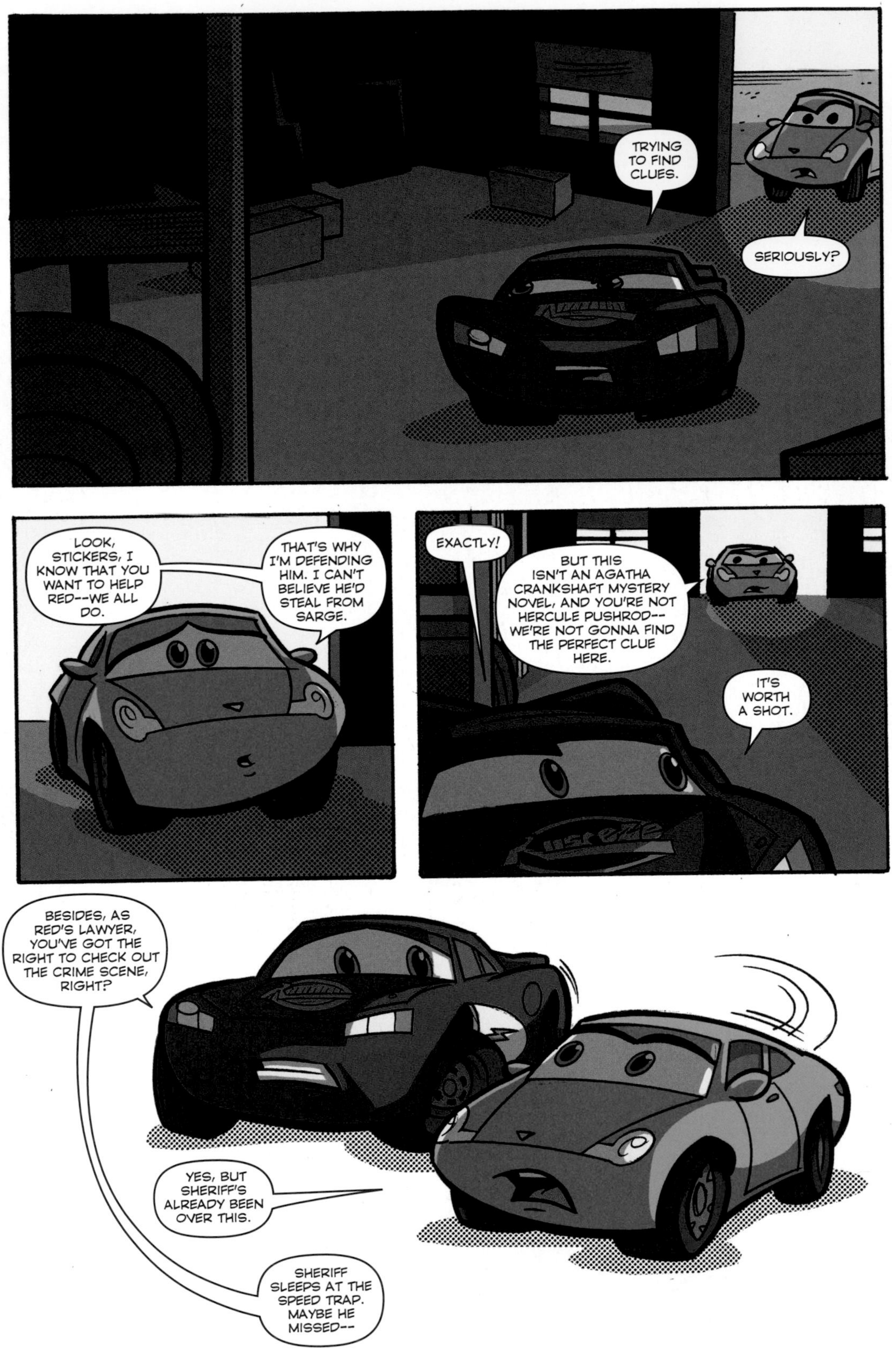

TRYING TO FIND CLUES.
SERIOUSLY?
LOOK, STICKERS, I KNOW THAT YOU WANT TO HELP RED--WE ALL DO.
THAT'S WHY I'M DEFENDING HIM. I CAN'T BELIEVE HE'D STEAL FROM SARGE.
EXACTLY!
BUT THIS ISN'T AN AGATHA CRANKSHAFT MYSTERY NOVEL, AND YOU'RE NOT HERCULE PUSHROD--WE'RE NOT GONNA FIND THE PERFECT CLUE HERE.
IT'S WORTH A SHOT.
BESIDES, AS RED'S LAWYER, YOU'VE GOT THE RIGHT TO CHECK OUT THE CRIME SCENE, RIGHT?
YES, BUT SHERIFF'S ALREADY BEEN OVER THIS.
SHERIFF SLEEPS AT THE SPEED TRAP. MAYBE HE MISSED--

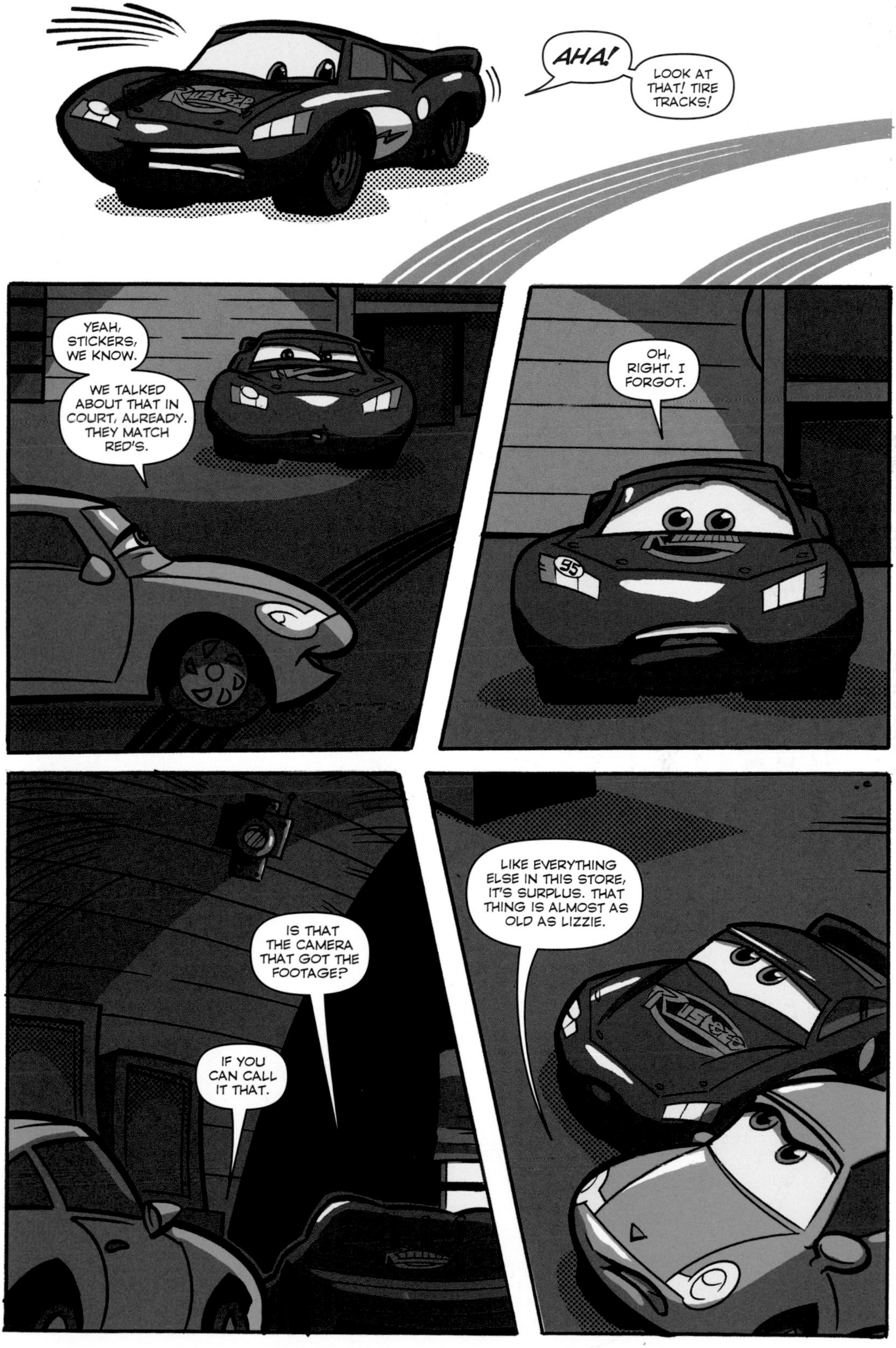
AHA!
LOOK AT THAT! TIRE TRACKS!
YEAH, STICKERS, WE KNOW.
WE TALKED ABOUT THAT IN COURT, ALREADY. THEY MATCH RED'S.
OH, RIGHT. I FORGOT.
IS THAT THE CAMERA THAT GOT THE FOOTAGE?
IF YOU CAN CALL IT THAT.
LIKE EVERYTHING ELSE IN THIS STORE, IT'S SURPLUS. THAT THING IS ALMOST AS OLD AS LIZZIE.

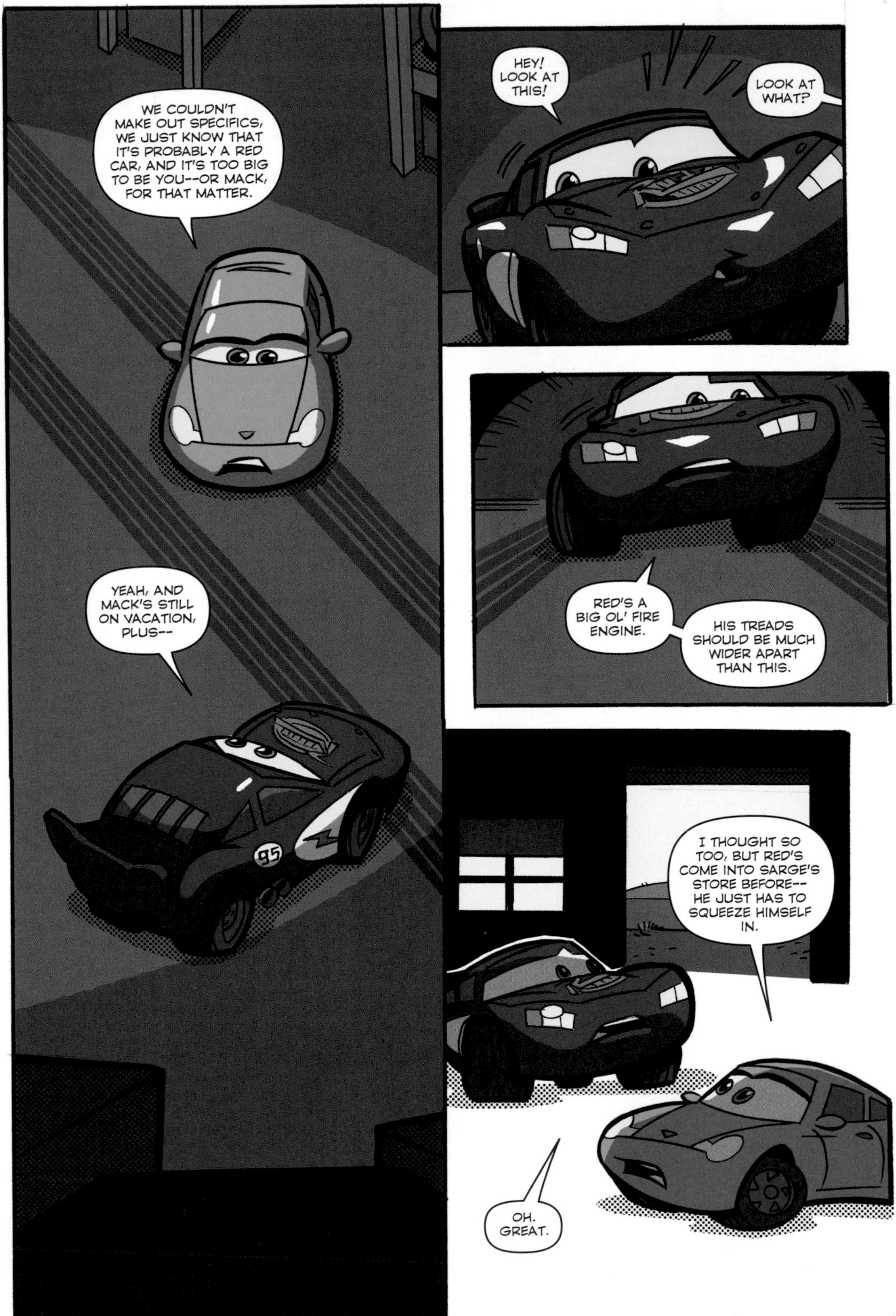
WE COULDN'T MAKE OUT SPECIFICS, WE JUST KNOW THAT IT'S PROBABLY A RED CAR, AND IT'S TOO BIG TO BE YOU--OR MACK, FOR THAT MATTER.
YEAH, AND MACK'S STILL ON VACATION, PLUS--
HEY! LOOK AT THIS!
LOOK AT WHAT?
RED'S A BIG OL' FIRE ENGINE.
HIS TREADS SHOULD BE MUCH WIDER APART THAN THIS.
I THOUGHT SO TOO, BUT RED'S COME INTO SARGE'S STORE BEFORE-- HE JUST HAS TO SQUEEZE HIMSELF IN.
OH. GREAT.

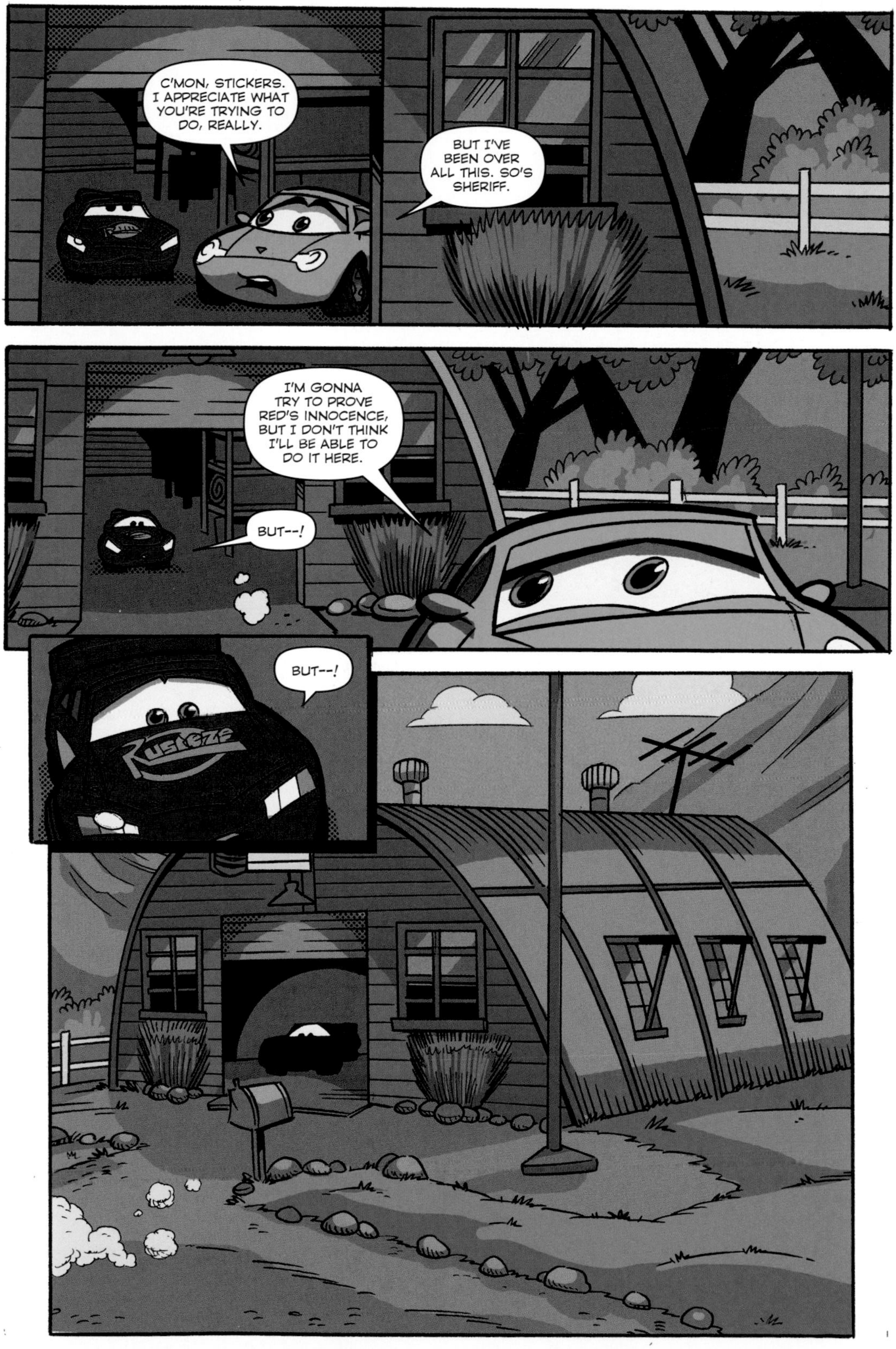
C'MON, STICKERS. I APPRECIATE WHAT YOU'RE TRYING TO DO, REALLY.
BUT I'VE BEEN OVER ALL THIS. SO'S SHERIFF.
I'M GONNA TRY TO PROVE RED'S INNOCENCE, BUT I DON'T THINK I'LL BE ABLE TO DO IT HERE.
BUT--!
BUT--!
RUST-EZE

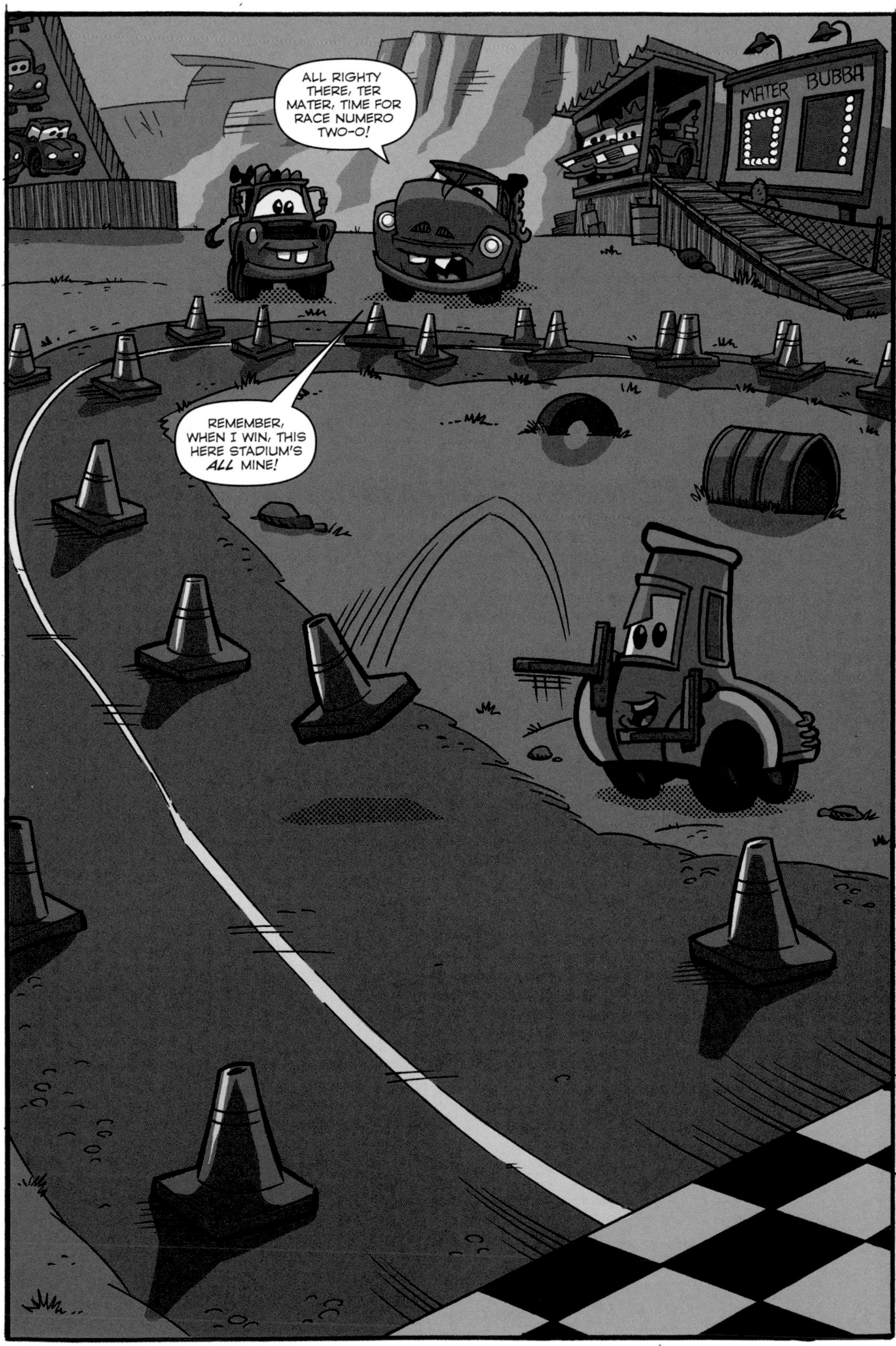

ALL RIGHTY THERE, TER MATER, TIME FOR RACE NUMERO TWO-O!
REMEMBER, WHEN I WIN, THIS HERE STADIUM'S *ALL* MINE!
MATER
BUBBA

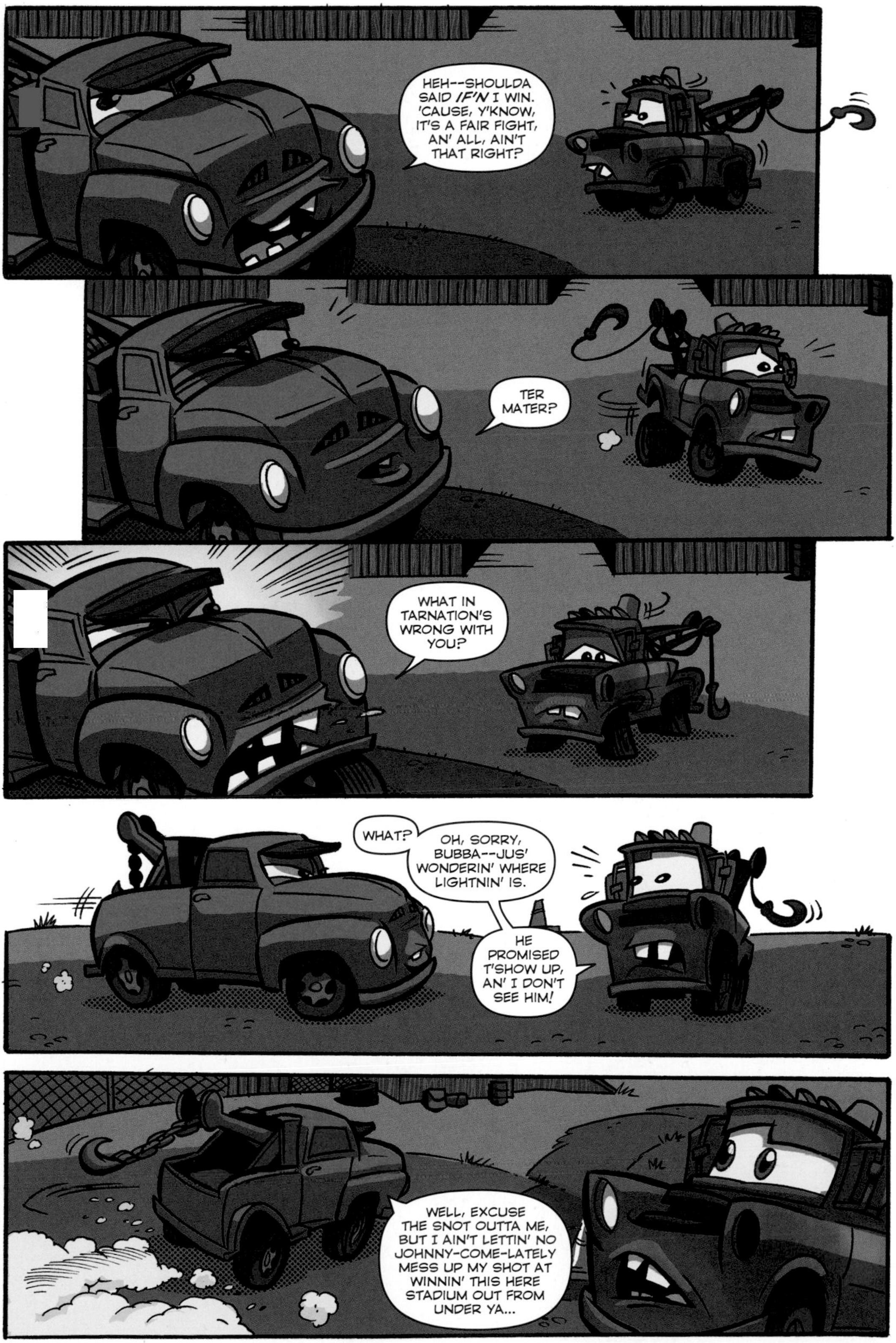
HEH--SHOULDA SAID IF'N I WIN. 'CAUSE, Y'KNOW, IT'S A FAIR FIGHT, AN' ALL, AIN'T THAT RIGHT?
TER MATER?
WHAT IN TARNATION'S WRONG WITH YOU?
WHAT?
OH, SORRY, BUBBA--JUS' WONDERIN' WHERE LIGHTNIN' IS.
HE PROMISED T'SHOW UP, AN' I DON'T SEE HIM!
WELL, EXCUSE THE SNOT OUTTA ME, BUT I AIN'T LETTIN' NO JOHNNY-COME-LATELY MESS UP MY SHOT AT WINNIN' THIS HERE STADIUM OUT FROM UNDER YA...

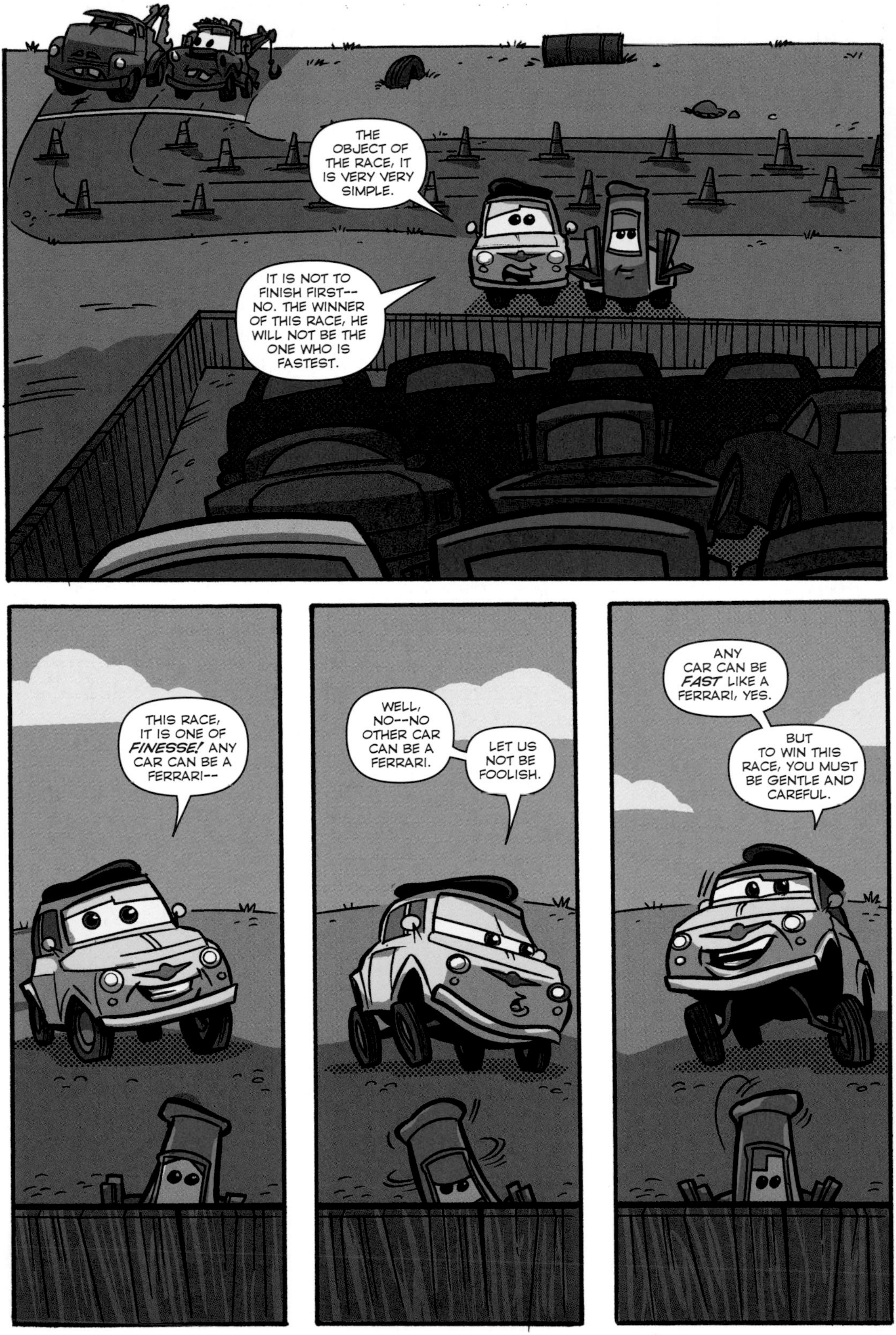
THE OBJECT OF THE RACE, IT IS VERY VERY SIMPLE.
IT IS NOT TO FINISH FIRST-- NO. THE WINNER OF THIS RACE, HE WILL NOT BE THE ONE WHO IS FASTEST.
THIS RACE, IT IS ONE OF *FINESSE!* ANY CAR CAN BE A FERRARI--
WELL, NO--NO OTHER CAR CAN BE A FERRARI.
LET US NOT BE FOOLISH.
ANY CAR CAN BE *FAST* LIKE A FERRARI, YES.
BUT TO WIN THIS RACE, YOU MUST BE GENTLE AND CAREFUL.

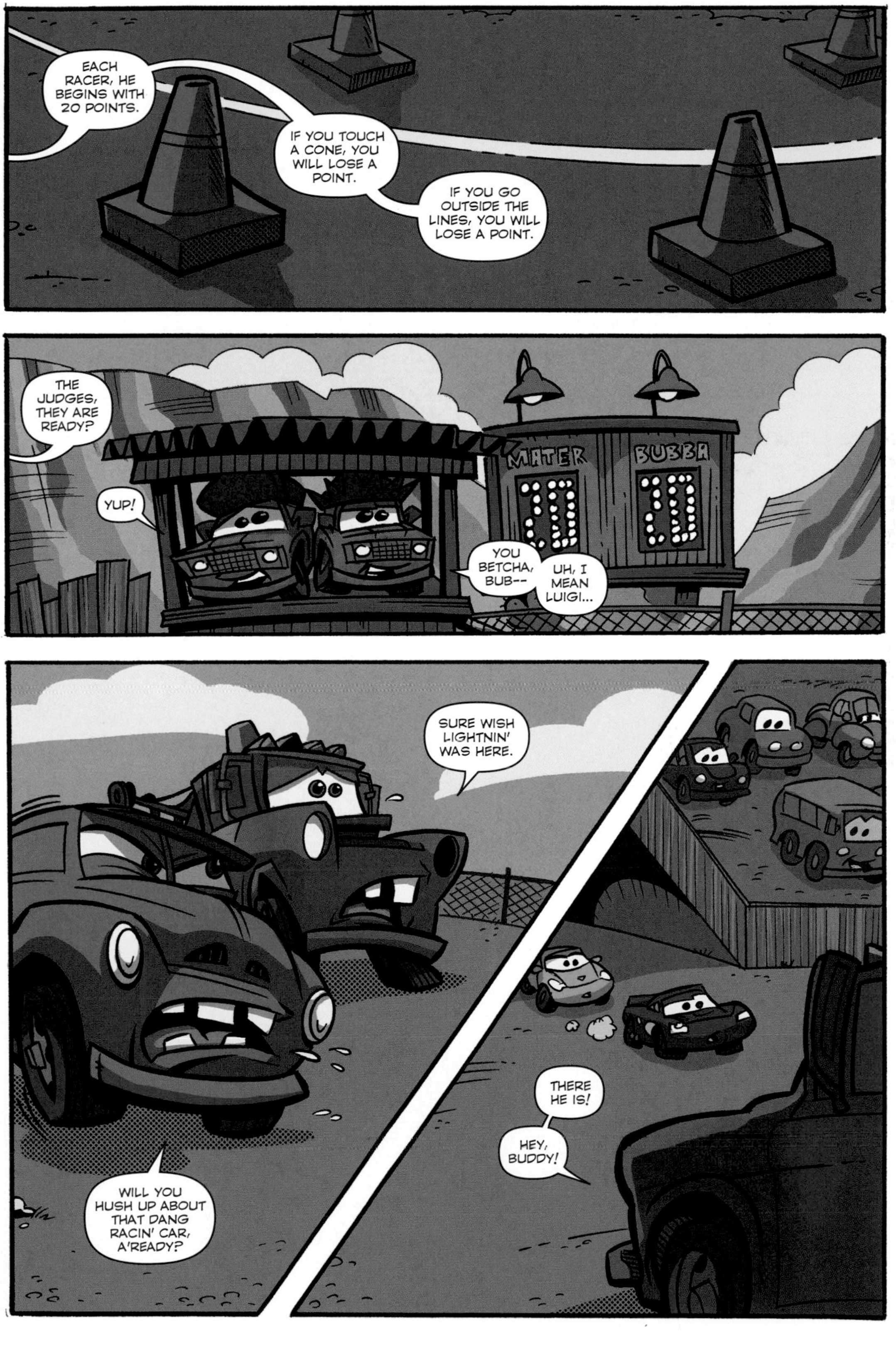
EACH RACER, HE BEGINS WITH 20 POINTS.
IF YOU TOUCH A CONE, YOU WILL LOSE A POINT.
IF YOU GO OUTSIDE THE LINES, YOU WILL LOSE A POINT.
THE JUDGES, THEY ARE READY?
YUP!
MATER
BUBBA
20
20
YOU BETCHA, BUB--
UH, I MEAN LUIGI...
SURE WISH LIGHTNIN' WAS HERE.
WILL YOU HUSH UP ABOUT THAT DANG RACIN' CAR, A'READY?
THERE HE IS!
HEY, BUDDY!

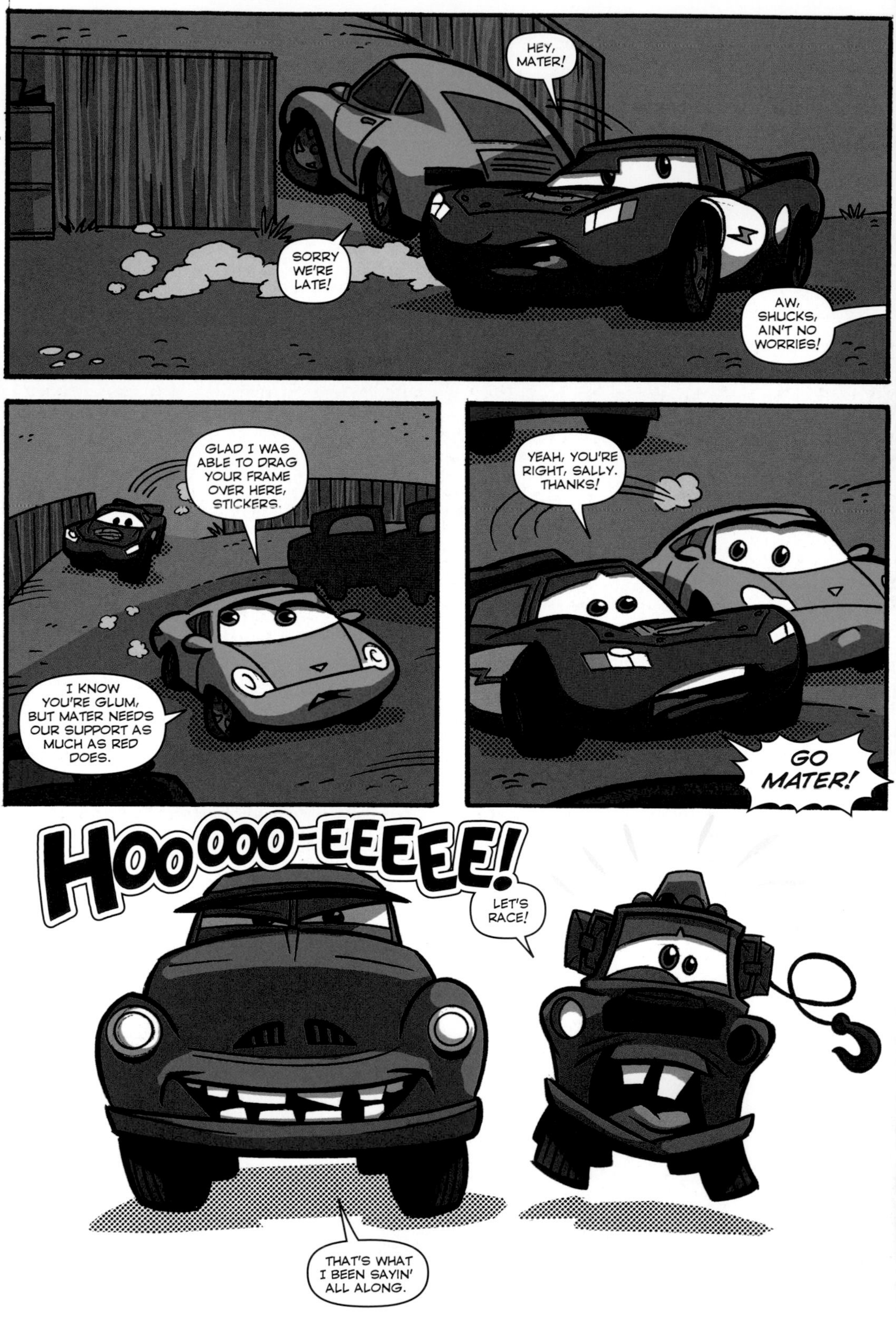
HEY, MATER!
SORRY WE'RE LATE!
AW, SHUCKS, AIN'T NO WORRIES!
GLAD I WAS ABLE TO DRAG YOUR FRAME OVER HERE, STICKERS.
I KNOW YOU'RE GLUM, BUT MATER NEEDS OUR SUPPORT AS MUCH AS RED DOES.
YEAH, YOU'RE RIGHT, SALLY. THANKS!
GO MATER!
HOOOOO-EEEEE!
LET'S RACE!
THAT'S WHAT I BEEN SAYIN' ALL ALONG.

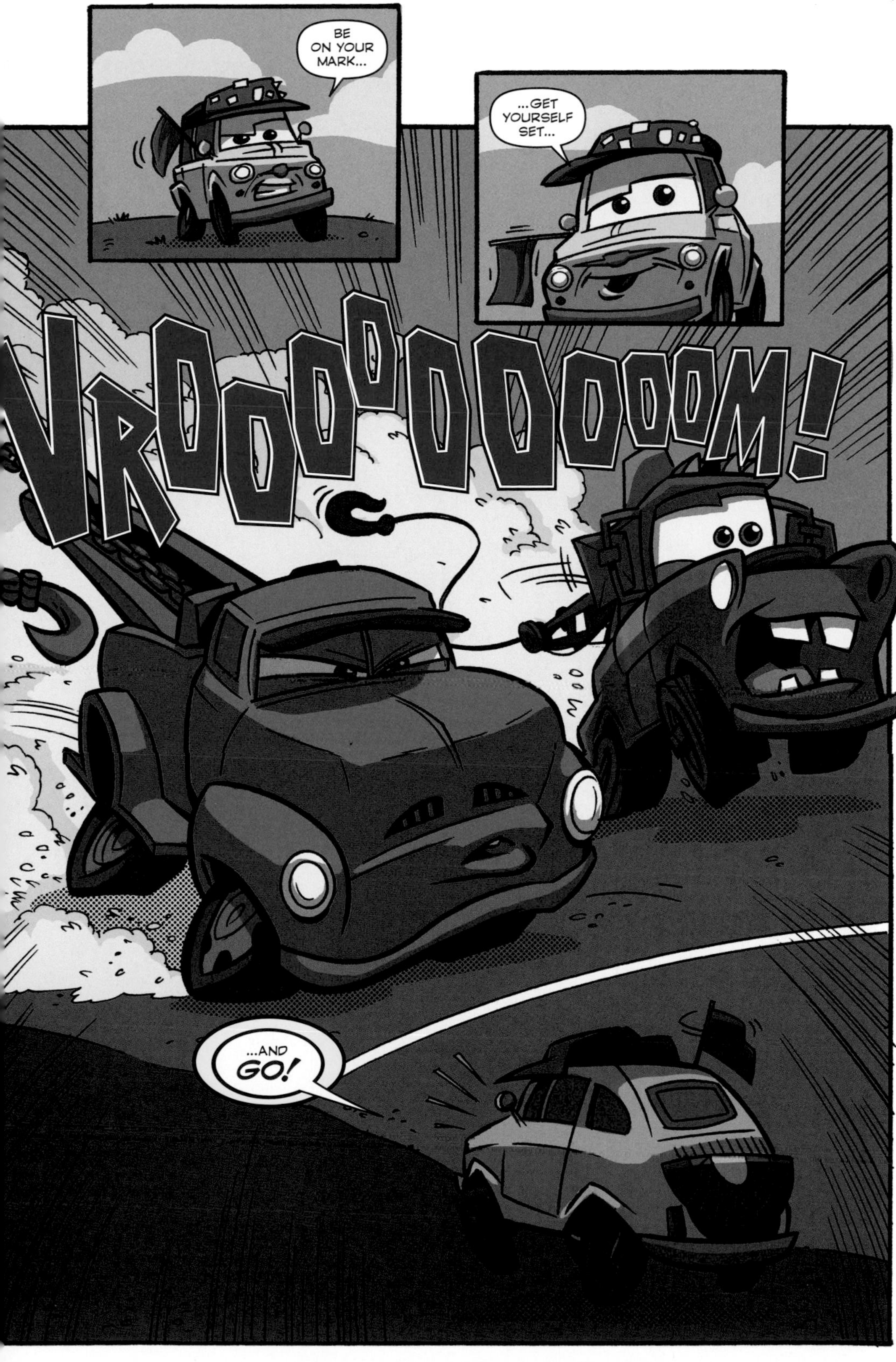
BE ON YOUR MARK...
...GET YOURSELF SET...
VROOOOOOOOOOM!
...AND GO!

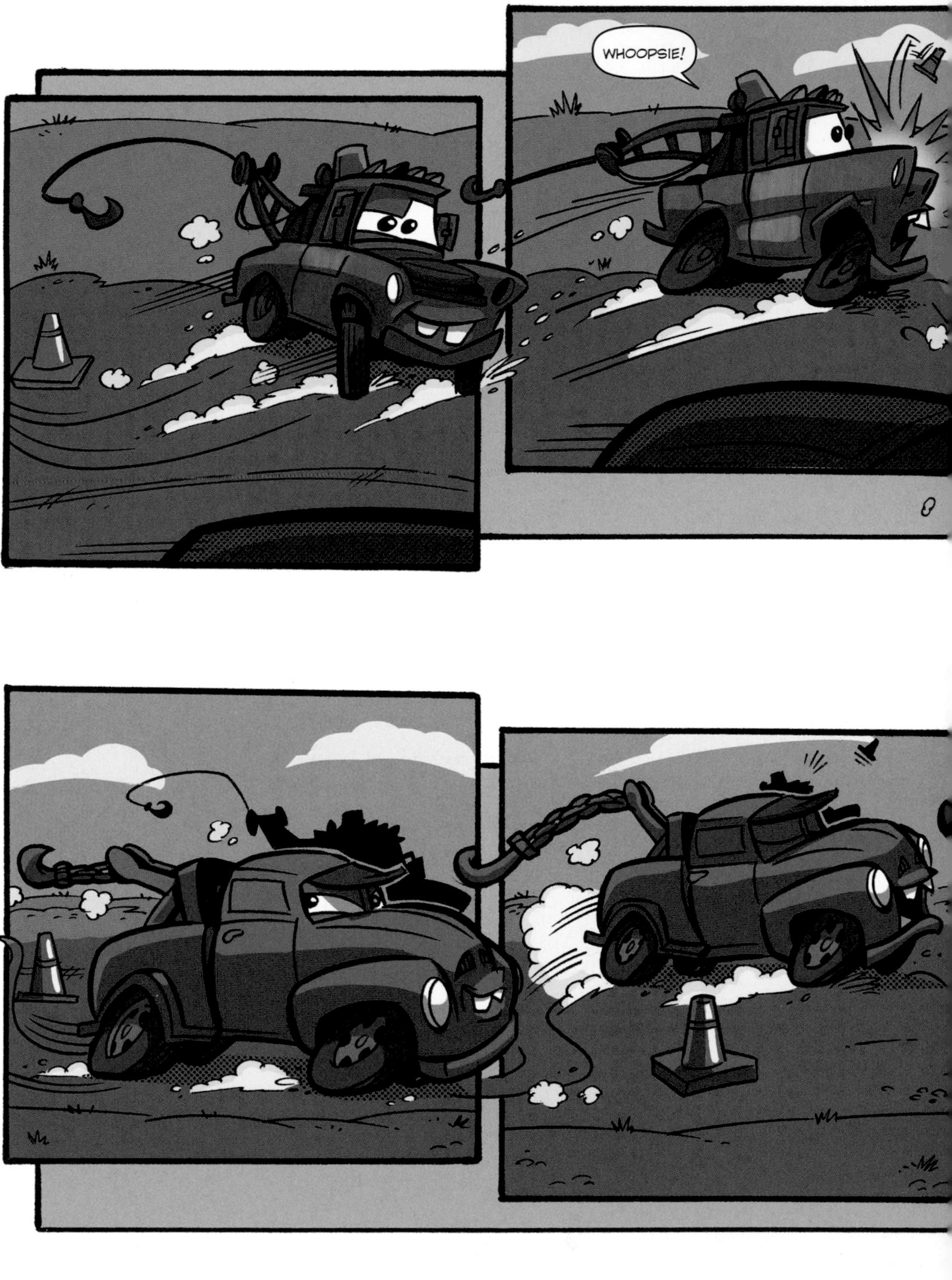

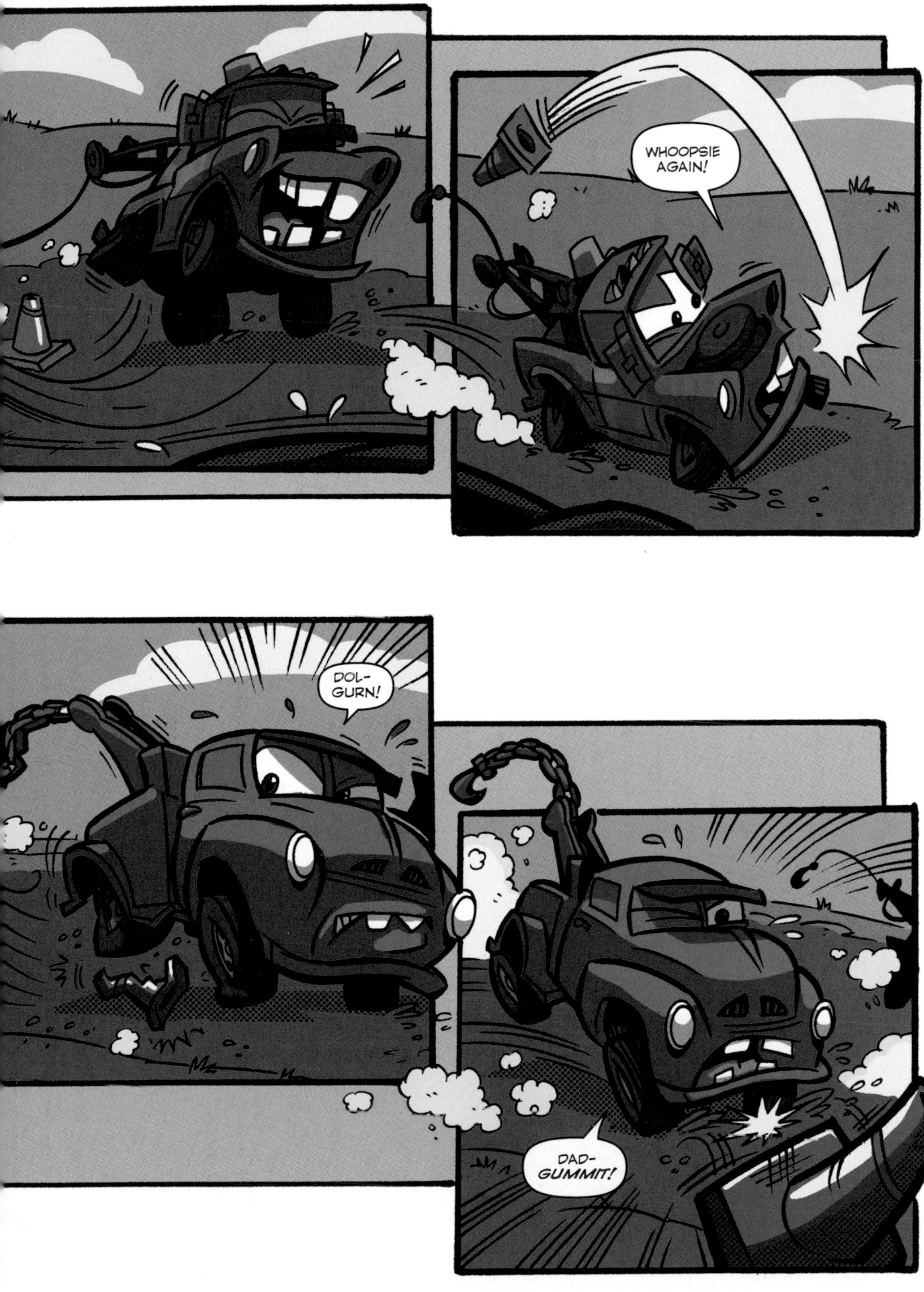
WHOOPSIE AGAIN!
DOL-GURN!
DAD-GUMMIT!

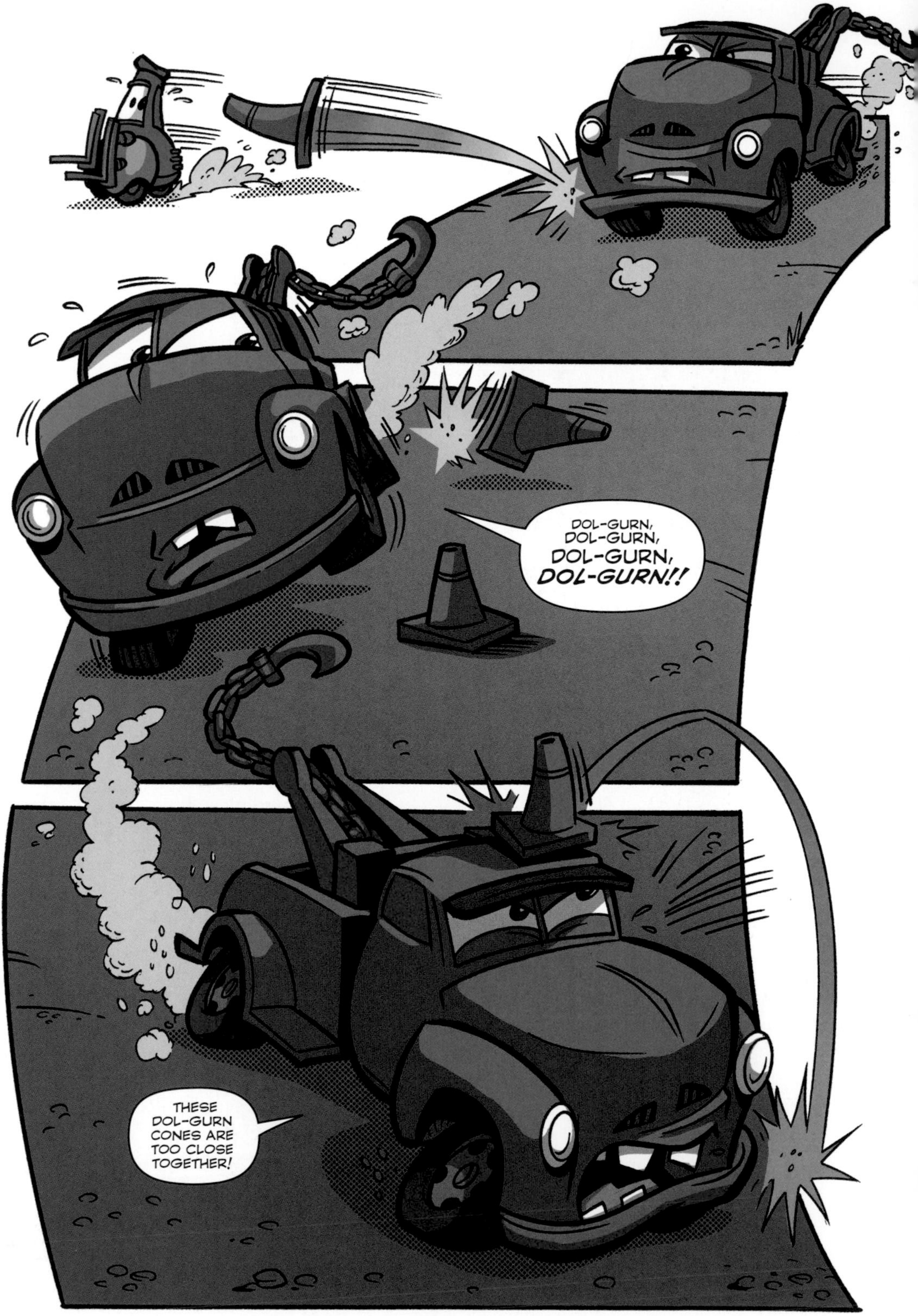
DOL-GURN, DOL-GURN, DOL-GURN, DOL-GURN!!
THESE DOL-GURN CONES ARE TOO CLOSE TOGETHER!

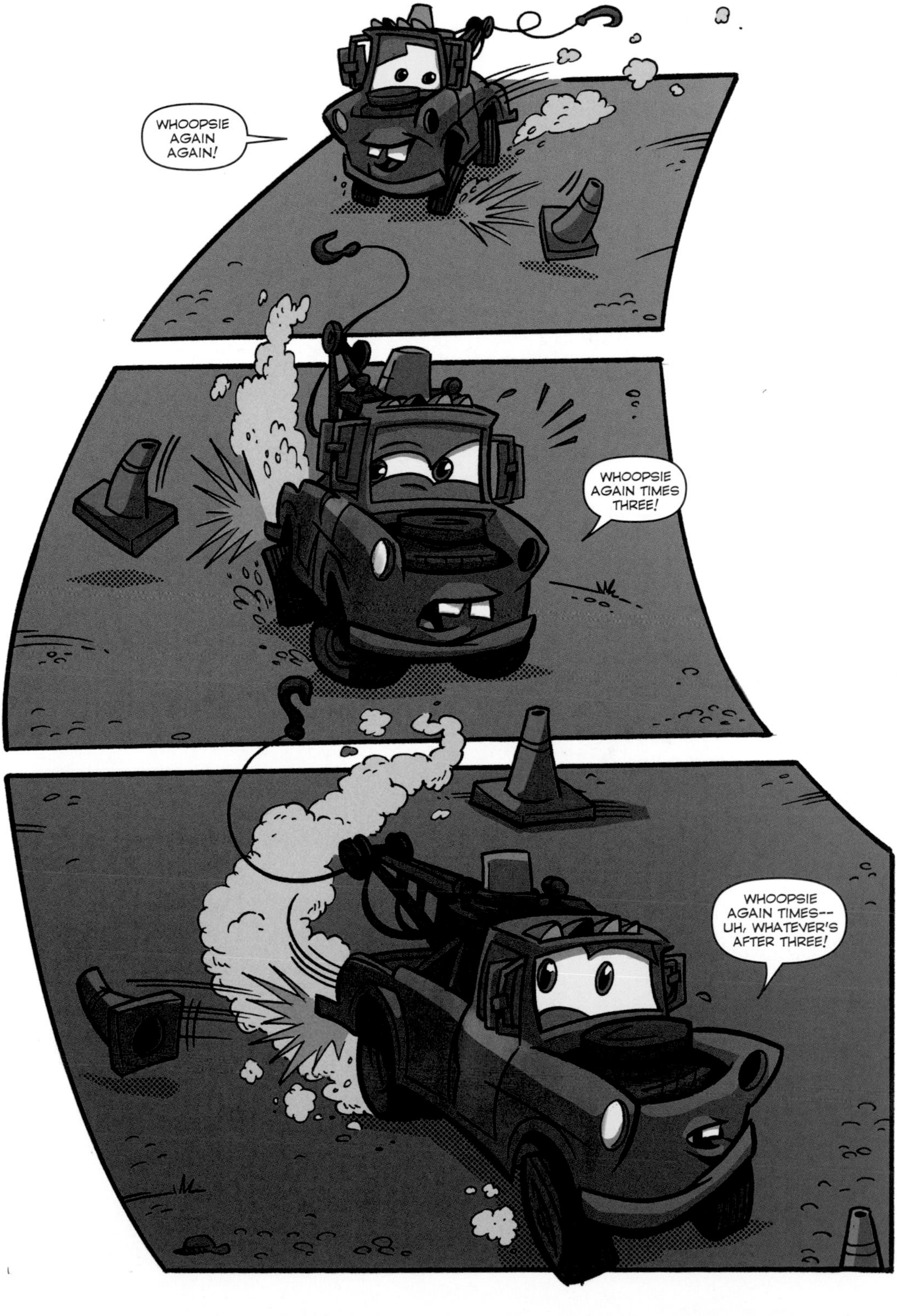
WHOOPSIE AGAIN AGAIN!
WHOOPSIE AGAIN TIMES THREE!
WHOOPSIE AGAIN TIMES-- UH, WHATEVER'S AFTER THREE!

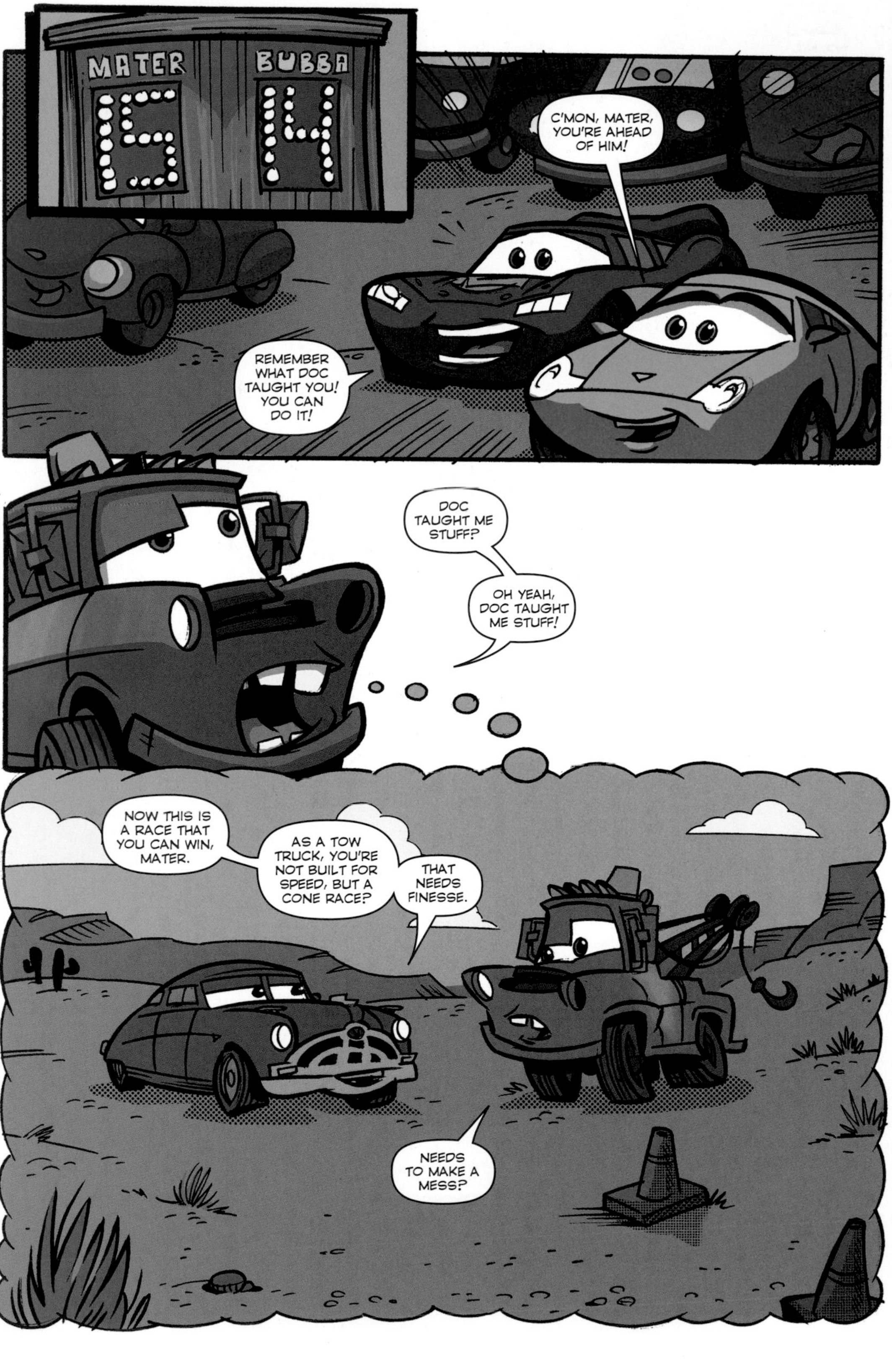
MATER
BUBBA
15
14
C'MON, MATER, YOU'RE AHEAD OF HIM!
REMEMBER WHAT DOC TAUGHT YOU! YOU CAN DO IT!
DOC TAUGHT ME STUFF?
OH YEAH, DOC TAUGHT ME STUFF!
NOW THIS IS A RACE THAT YOU CAN WIN, MATER.
AS A TOW TRUCK, YOU'RE NOT BUILT FOR SPEED, BUT A CONE RACE?
THAT NEEDS FINESSE.
NEEDS TO MAKE A MESS?

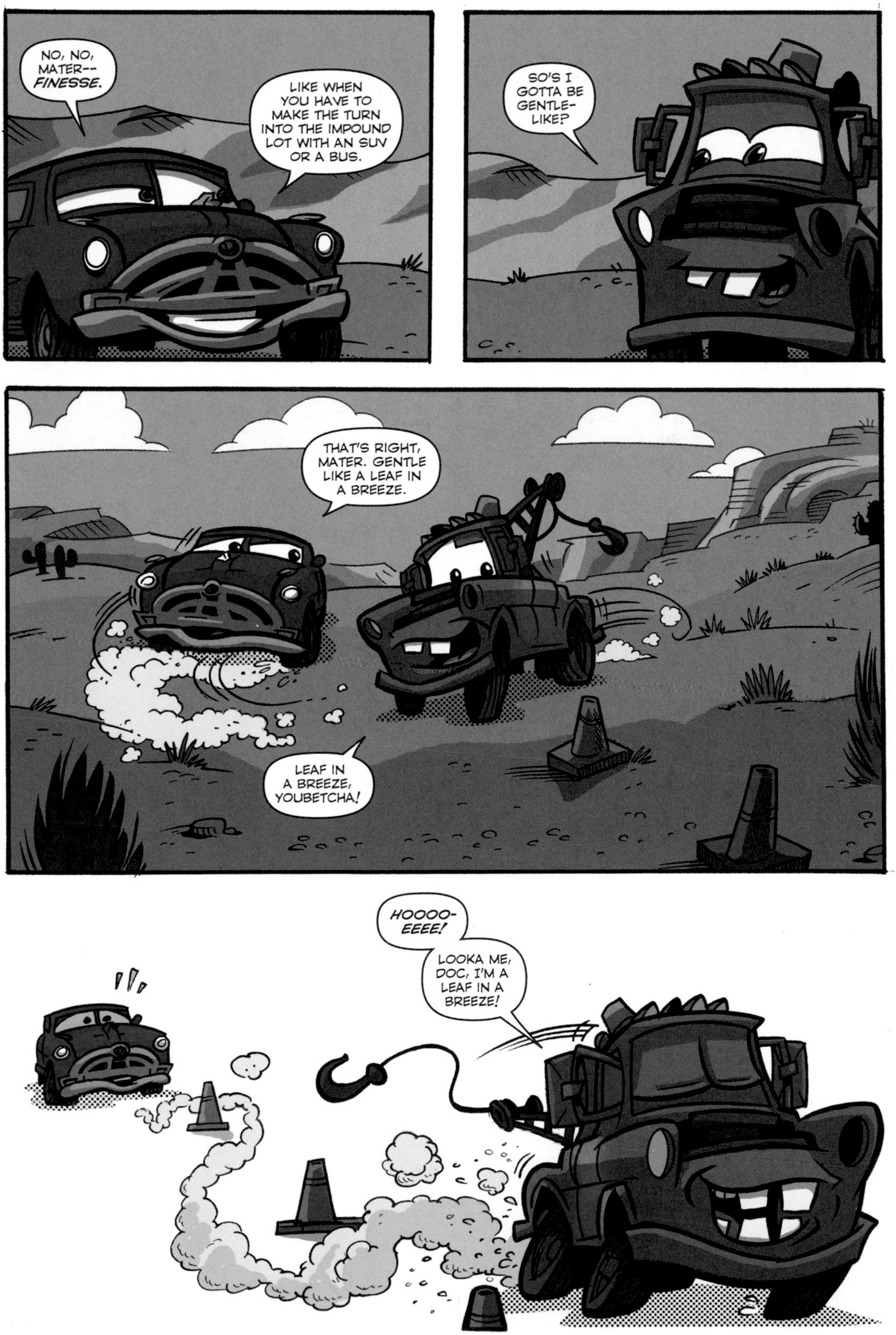
NO, NO, MATER-- FINESSE.
LIKE WHEN YOU HAVE TO MAKE THE TURN INTO THE IMPOUND LOT WITH AN SUV OR A BUS.
SO'S I GOTTA BE GENTLE-LIKE?
THAT'S RIGHT, MATER. GENTLE LIKE A LEAF IN A BREEZE.
LEAF IN A BREEZE, YOUBETCHA!
HOOOO-EEEE!
LOOKA ME, DOC, I'M A LEAF IN A BREEZE!

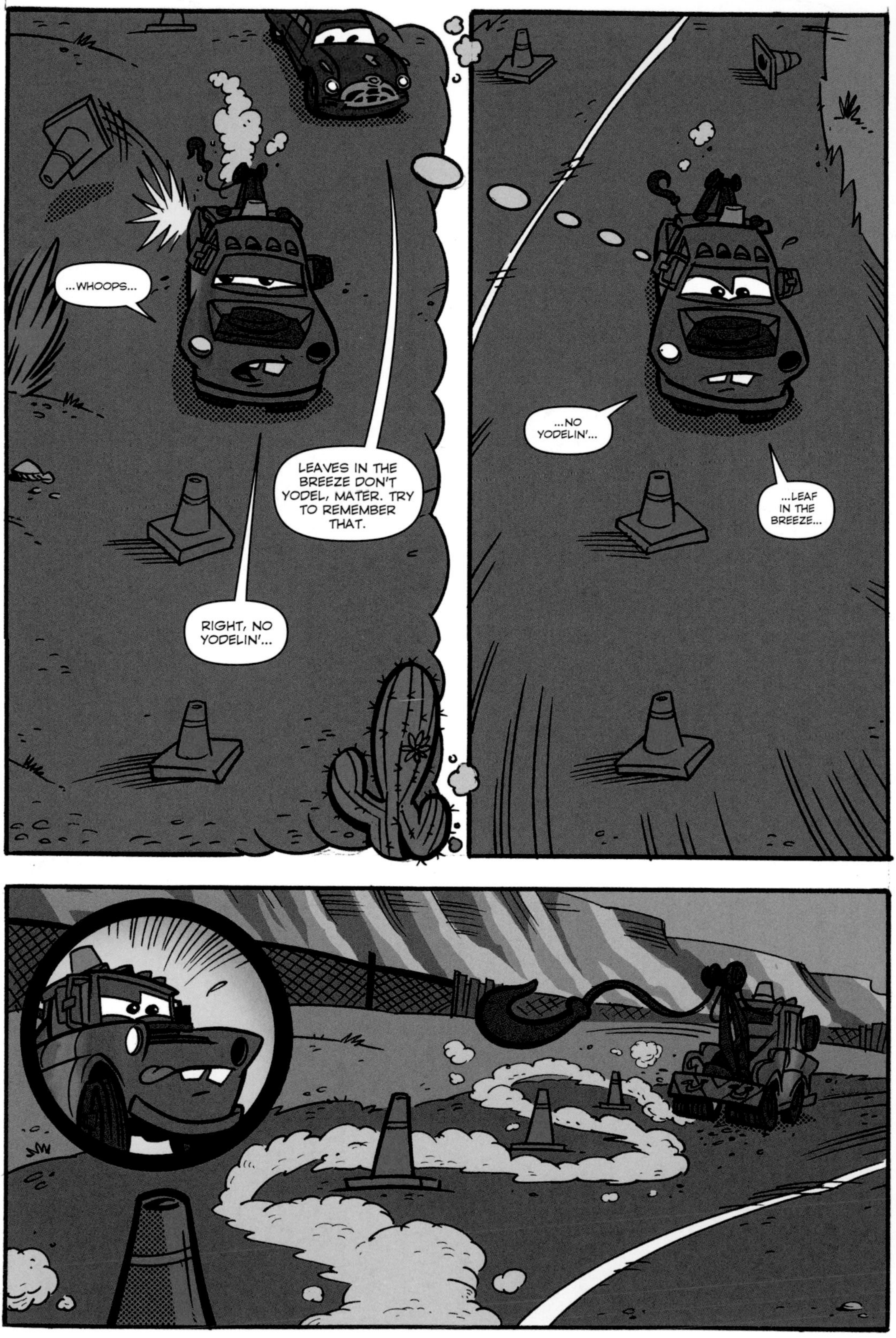
...WHOOPS...
LEAVES IN THE BREEZE DON'T YODEL, MATER. TRY TO REMEMBER THAT.
RIGHT, NO YODELIN'...
...NO YODELIN'...
...LEAF IN THE BREEZE...

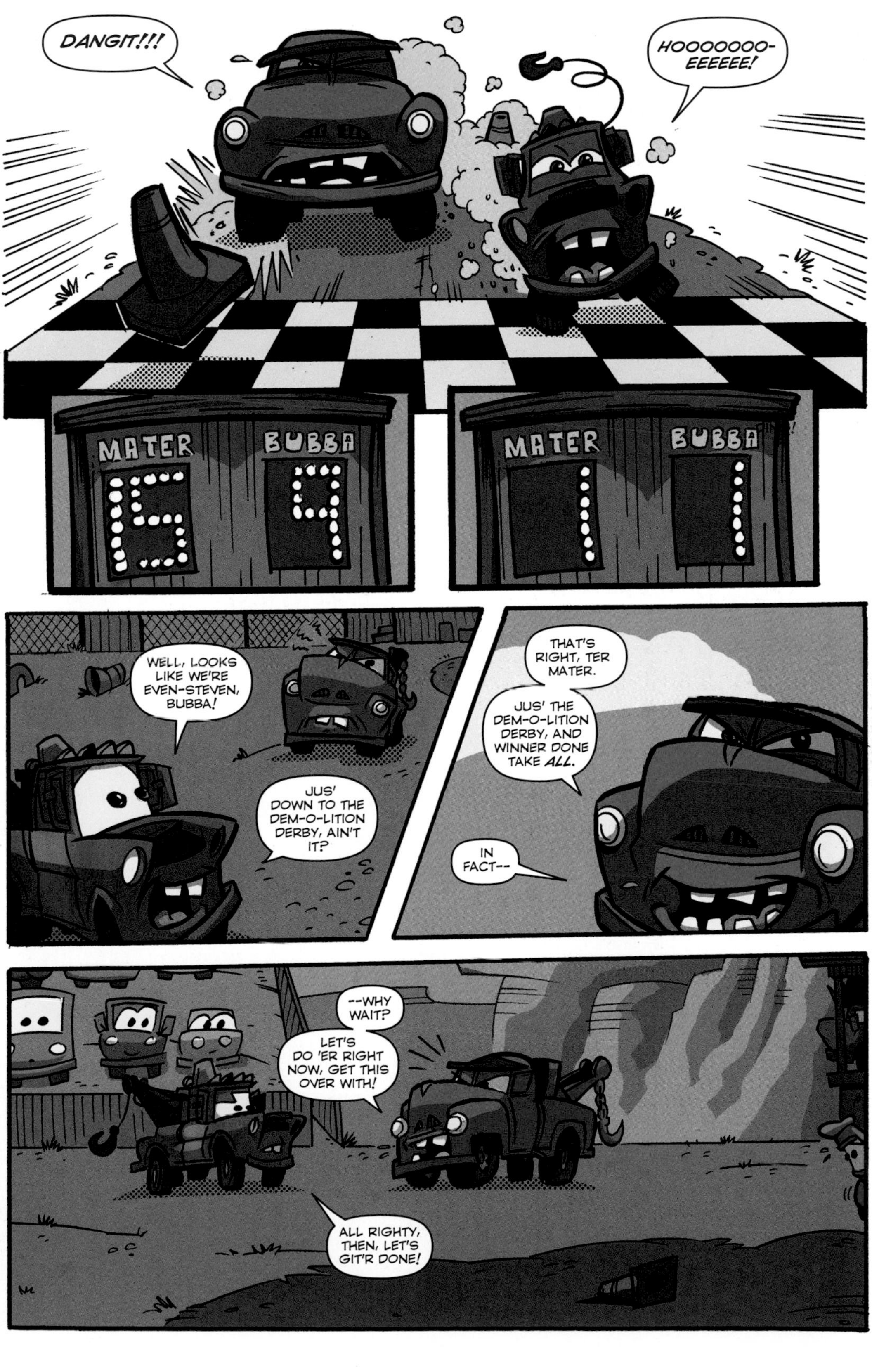
DANGIT!!!
HOOOOOOO-EEEEEE!
MATER
BUBBA
MATER
BUBBA
WELL, LOOKS LIKE WE'RE EVEN-STEVEN, BUBBA!
JUS' DOWN TO THE DEM-O-LITION DERBY, AIN'T IT?
THAT'S RIGHT, TER MATER.
JUS' THE DEM-O-LITION DERBY, AND WINNER DONE TAKE ALL.
IN FACT--
--WHY WAIT?
LET'S DO 'ER RIGHT NOW, GET THIS OVER WITH!
ALL RIGHTY, THEN, LET'S GIT'R DONE!

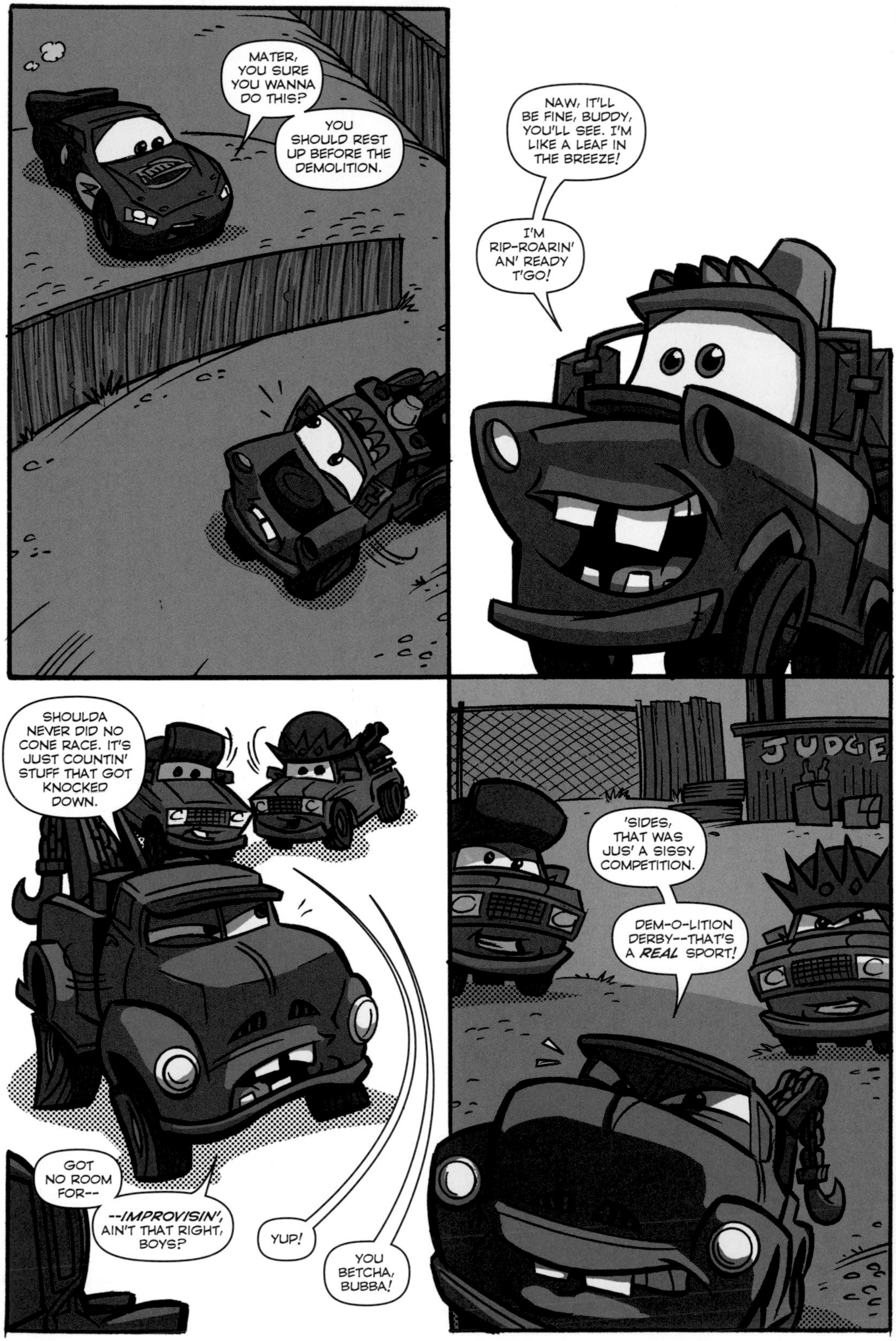
MATER, YOU SURE YOU WANNA DO THIS?
YOU SHOULD REST UP BEFORE THE DEMOLITION.
NAW, IT'LL BE FINE, BUDDY, YOU'LL SEE. I'M LIKE A LEAF IN THE BREEZE!
I'M RIP-ROARIN' AN' READY T'GO!
SHOULDA NEVER DID NO CONE RACE. IT'S JUST COUNTIN' STUFF THAT GOT KNOCKED DOWN.
GOT NO ROOM FOR--
--*IMPROVISIN'*, AIN'T THAT RIGHT, BOYS?
YUP!
YOU BETCHA, BUBBA!
JUDGE
'SIDES, THAT WAS JUS' A SISSY COMPETITION.
DEM-O-LITION DERBY--THAT'S A *REAL* SPORT!

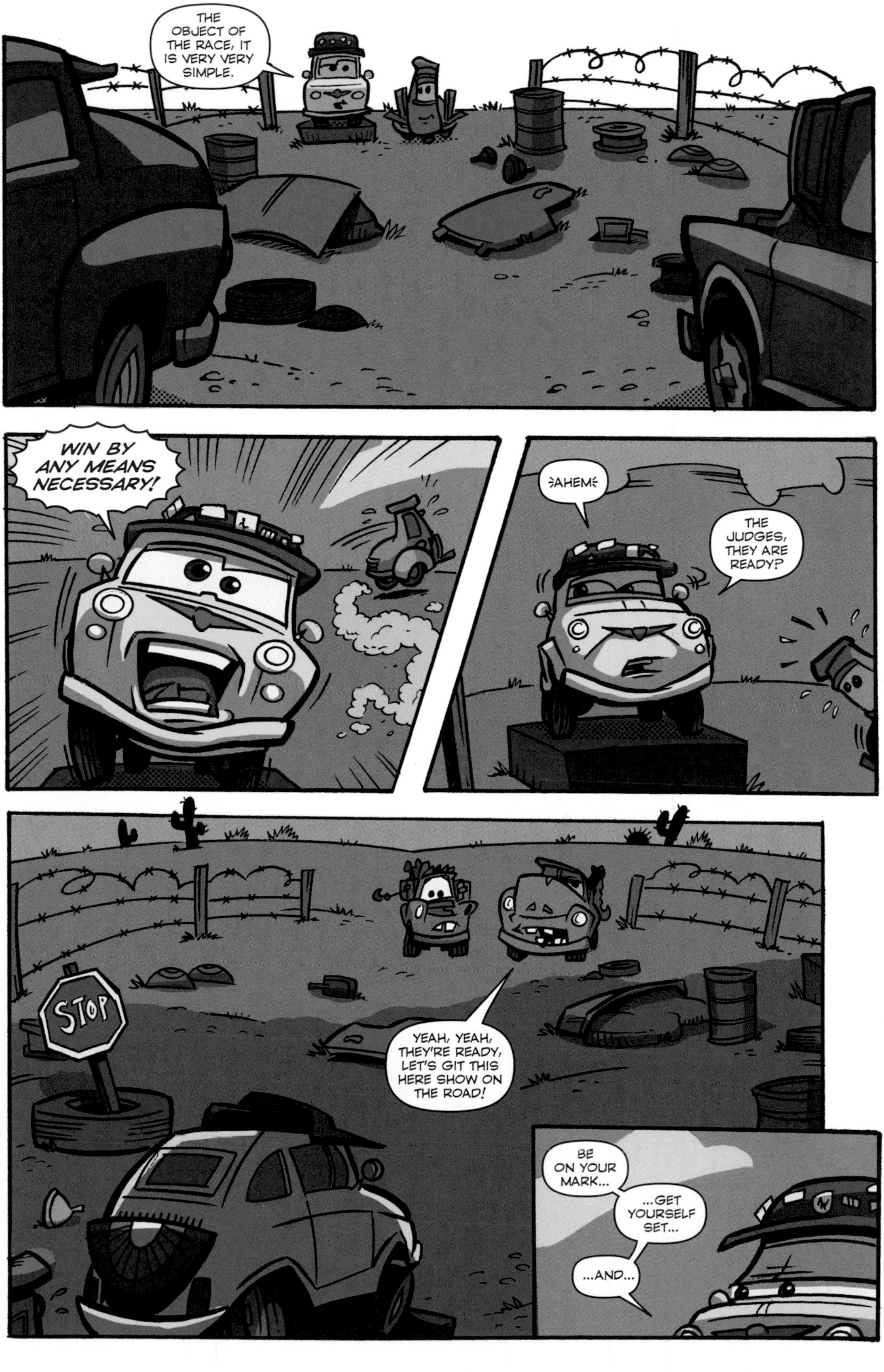
THE OBJECT OF THE RACE, IT IS VERY VERY SIMPLE.
WIN BY ANY MEANS NECESSARY!
AHEM
THE JUDGES, THEY ARE READY?
STOP
YEAH, YEAH, THEY'RE READY, LET'S GIT THIS HERE SHOW ON THE ROAD!
BE ON YOUR MARK...
...GET YOURSELF SET...
...AND...

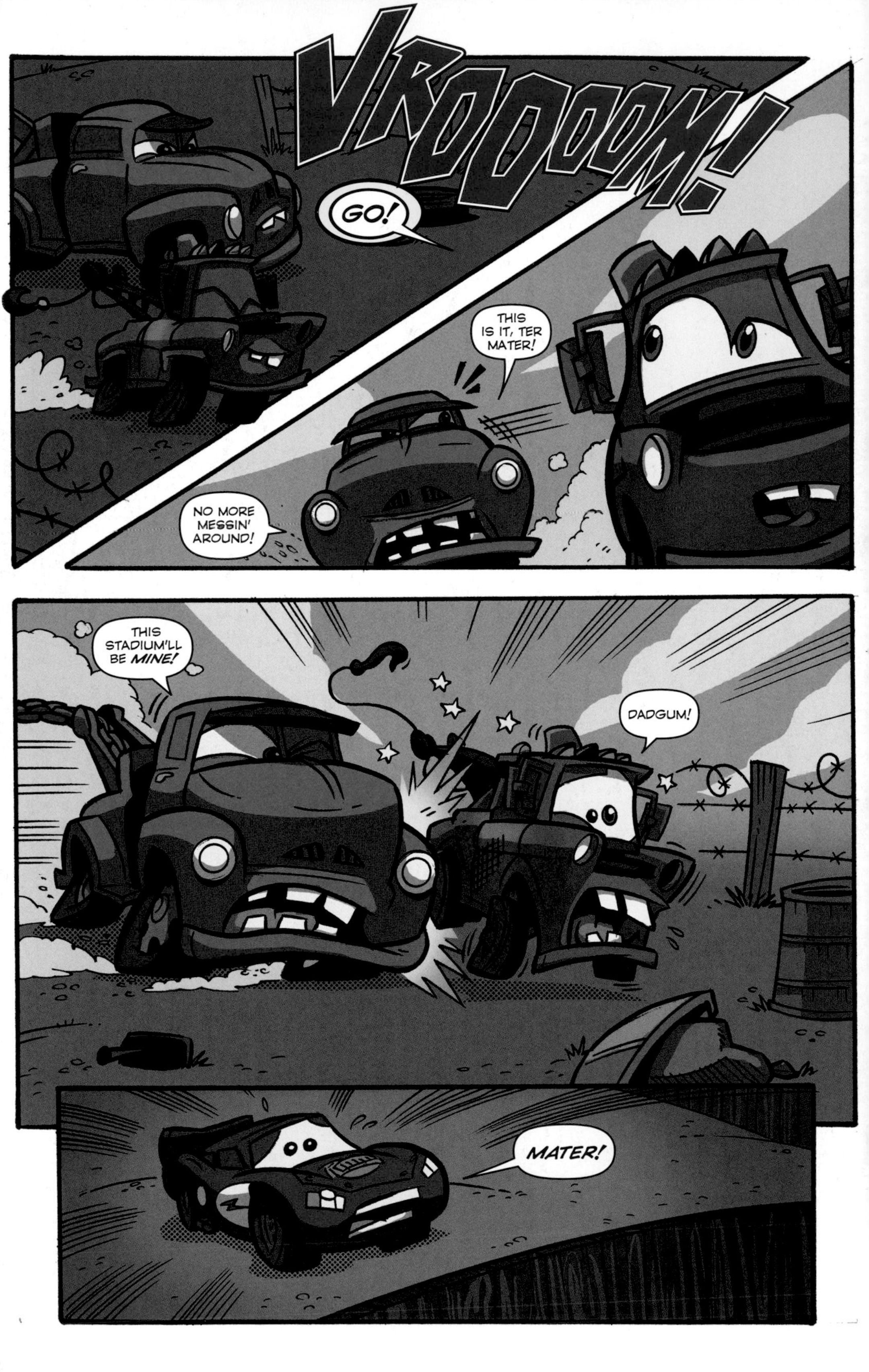
VROOOOOM!
GO!
THIS IS IT, TER MATER!
NO MORE MESSIN' AROUND!
THIS STADIUM'LL BE *MINE!*
DADGUM!
MATER!

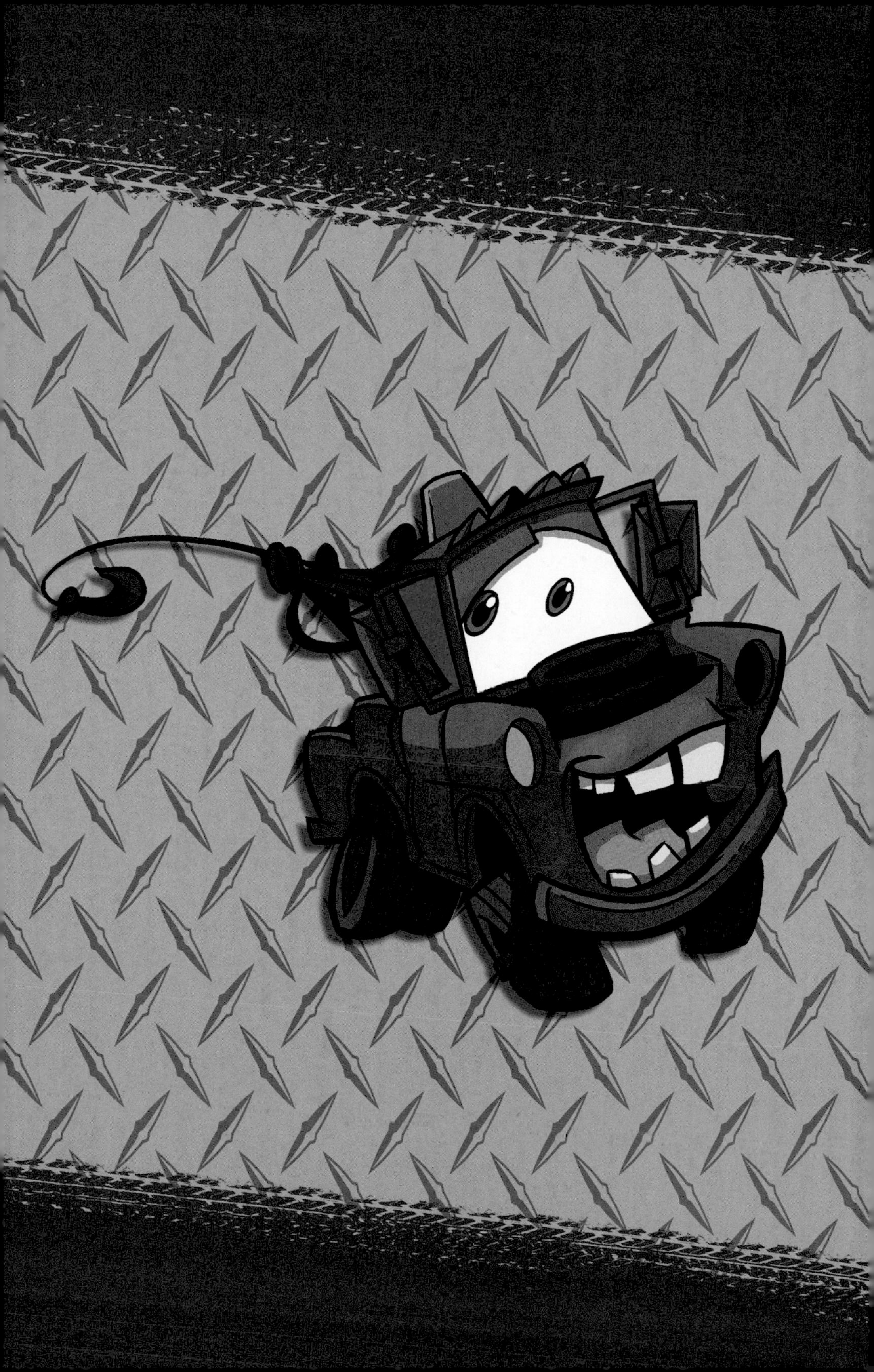

Chapter Four

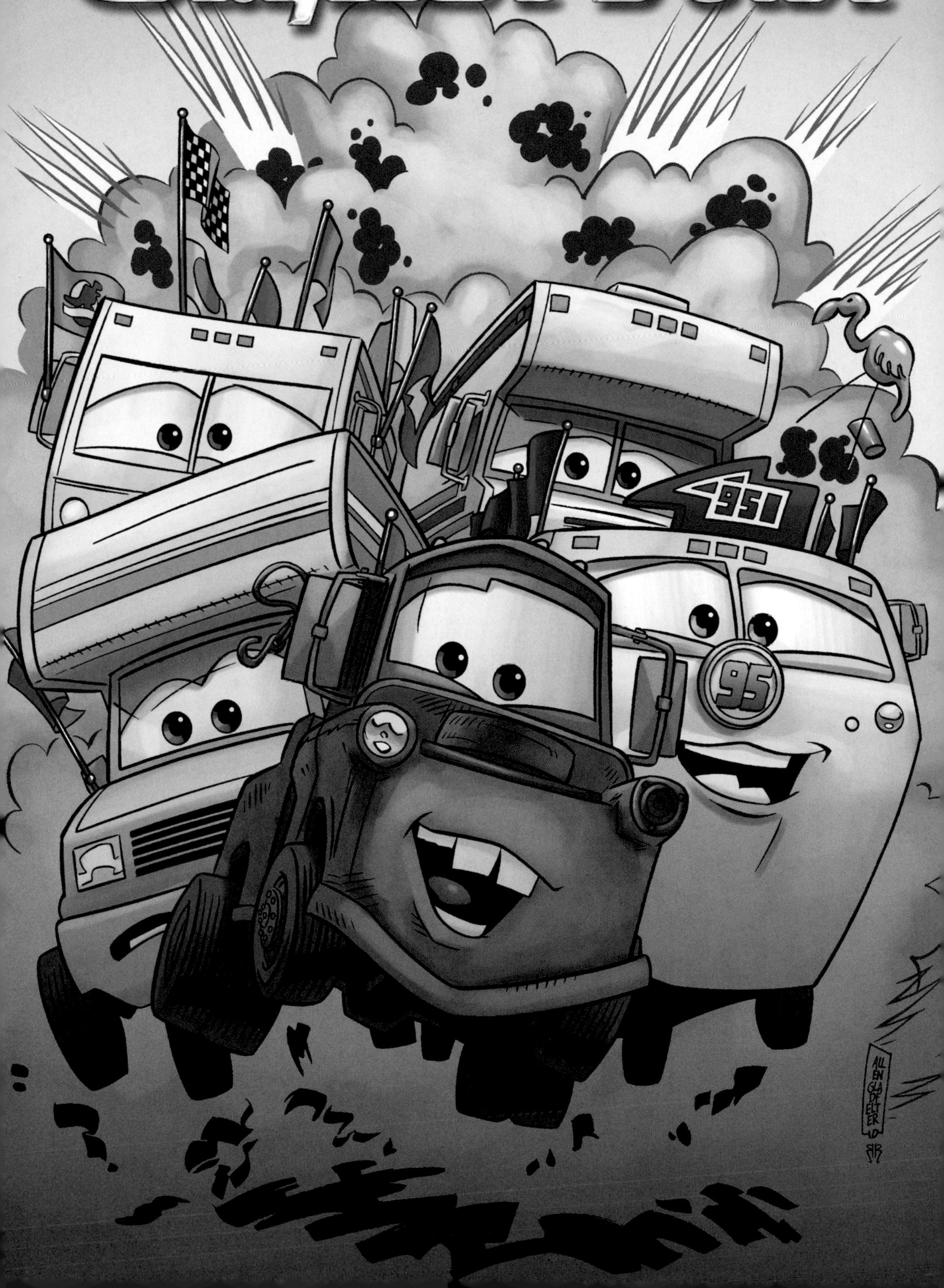
95
95

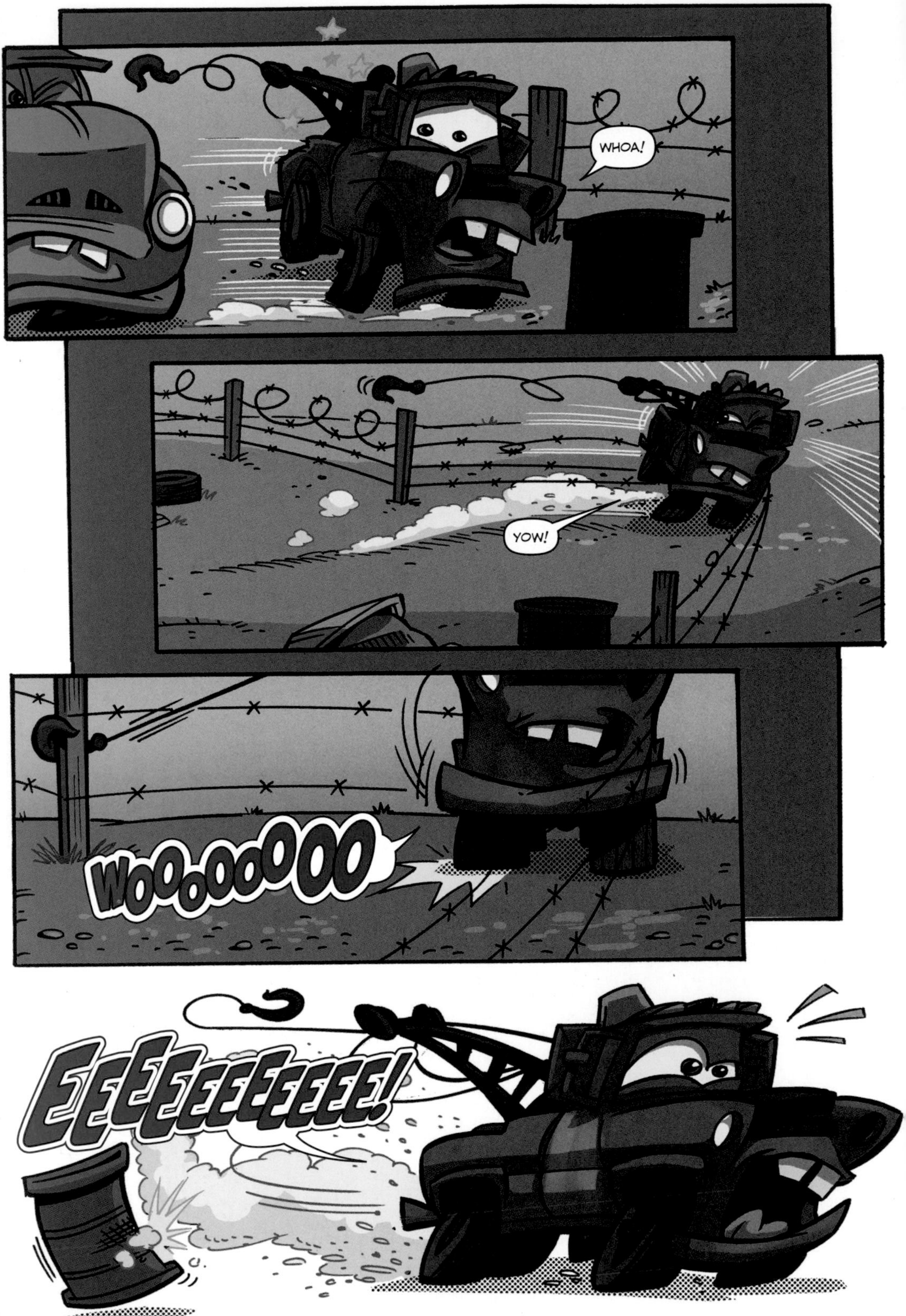
WHOA!
YOW!
WOOoooOOO
EEEEEEEEEEEE!

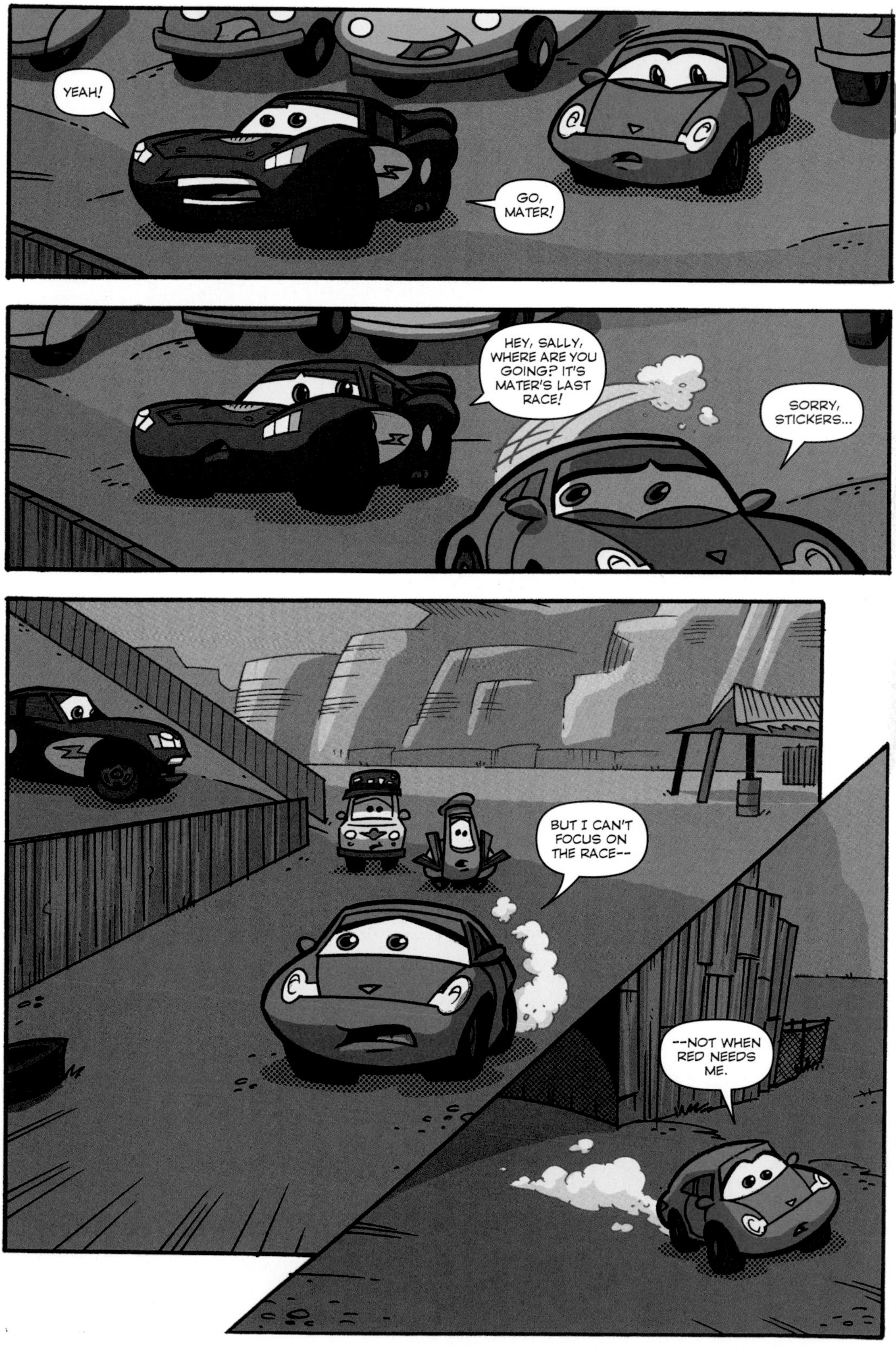
YEAH!
GO, MATER!
HEY, SALLY, WHERE ARE YOU GOING? IT'S MATER'S LAST RACE!
SORRY, STICKERS...
BUT I CAN'T FOCUS ON THE RACE--
--NOT WHEN RED NEEDS ME.

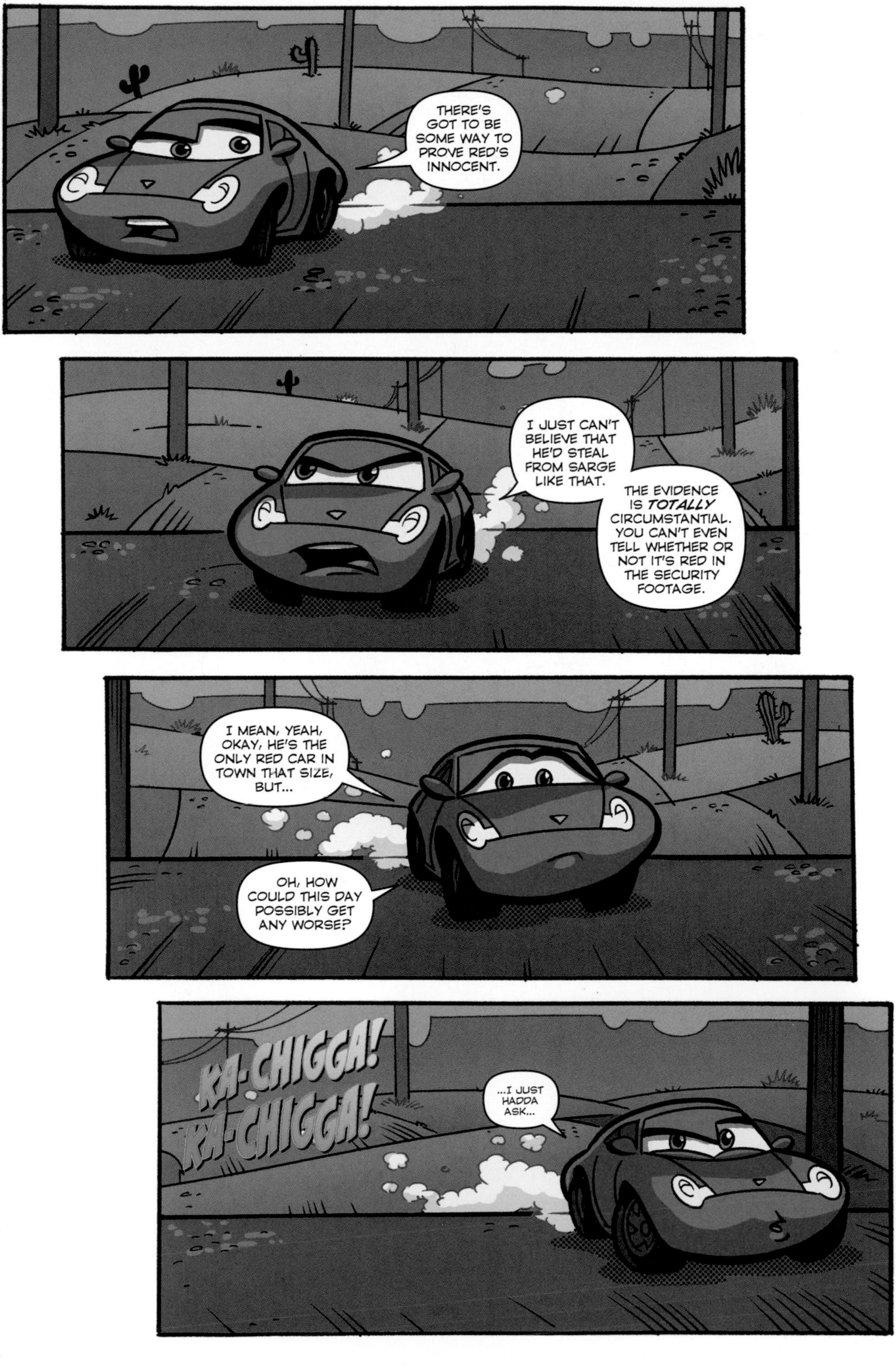
THERE'S GOT TO BE SOME WAY TO PROVE RED'S INNOCENT.
I JUST CAN'T BELIEVE THAT HE'D STEAL FROM SARGE LIKE THAT.
THE EVIDENCE IS *TOTALLY* CIRCUMSTANTIAL. YOU CAN'T EVEN TELL WHETHER OR NOT IT'S RED IN THE SECURITY FOOTAGE.
I MEAN, YEAH, OKAY, HE'S THE ONLY RED CAR IN TOWN THAT SIZE, BUT...
OH, HOW COULD THIS DAY POSSIBLY GET ANY WORSE?
KA-CHIGGA! KA-CHIGGA!
...I JUST HADDA ASK...

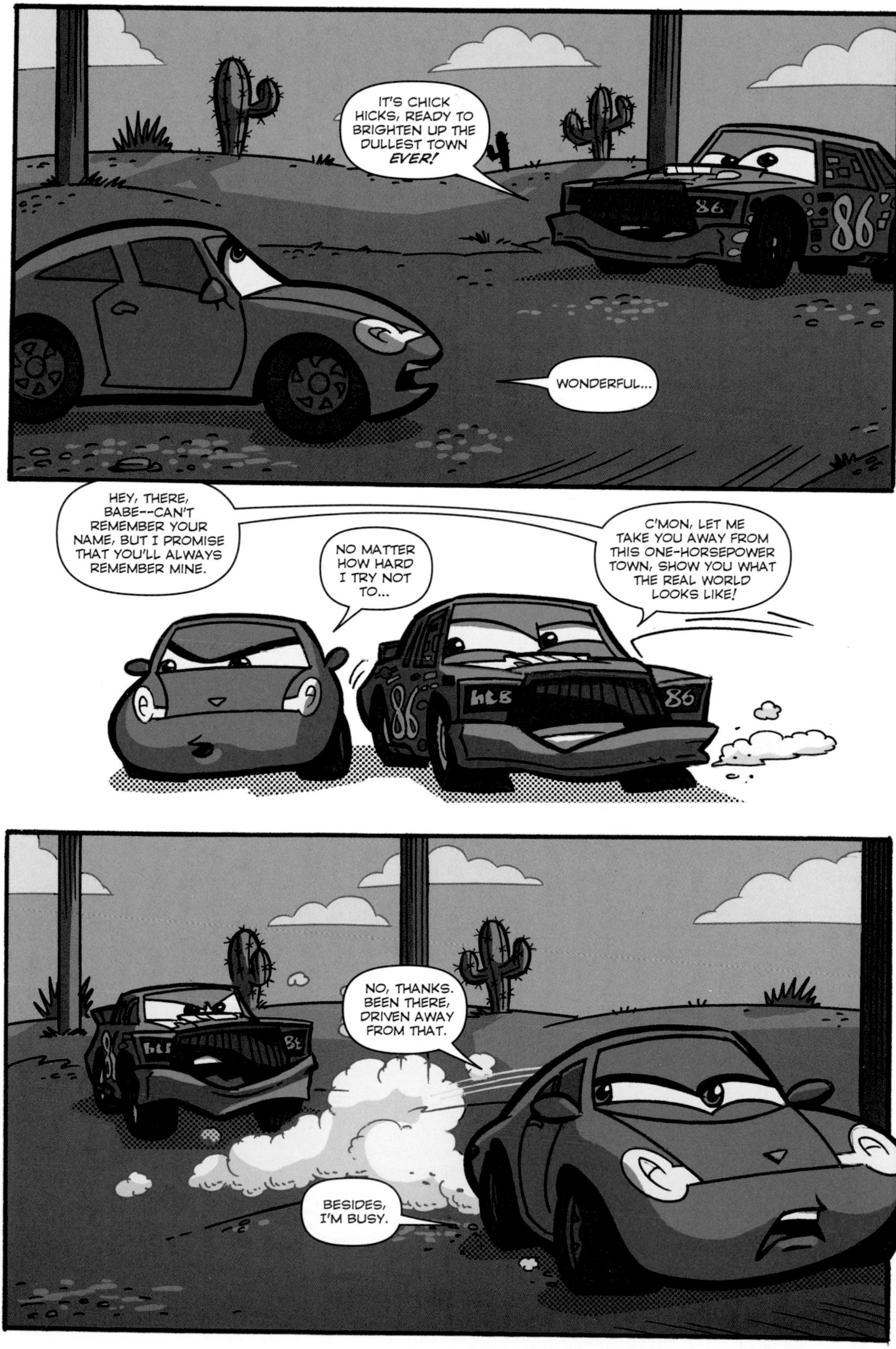
IT'S CHICK HICKS, READY TO BRIGHTEN UP THE DULLEST TOWN *EVER!*
WONDERFUL...
HEY, THERE, BABE--CAN'T REMEMBER YOUR NAME, BUT I PROMISE THAT YOU'LL ALWAYS REMEMBER MINE.
NO MATTER HOW HARD I TRY NOT TO...
C'MON, LET ME TAKE YOU AWAY FROM THIS ONE-HORSEPOWER TOWN, SHOW YOU WHAT THE REAL WORLD LOOKS LIKE!
NO, THANKS. BEEN THERE, DRIVEN AWAY FROM THAT.
BESIDES, I'M BUSY.

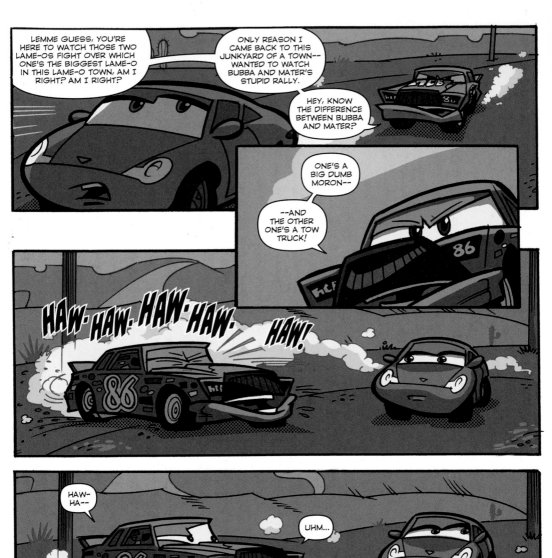

LEMME GUESS, YOU'RE HERE TO WATCH THOSE TWO LAME-OS FIGHT OVER WHICH ONE'S THE BIGGEST LAME-O IN THIS LAME-O TOWN, AM I RIGHT? AM I RIGHT?

ONLY REASON I CAME BACK TO THIS JUNKYARD OF A TOWN-- WANTED TO WATCH BUBBA AND MATER'S STUPID RALLY.

HEY, KNOW THE DIFFERENCE BETWEEN BUBBA AND MATER?

ONE'S A BIG DUMB MORON--

--AND THE OTHER ONE'S A TOW TRUCK!

HAW-HAW-HAW-HAW-HAW!

HAW-HA--

UHM...

SEE, THE JOKE IS THAT THEY'RE *BOTH* BIG DUMB MORONS AND THEY'RE *BOTH* TOW--

YEAH, I *GOT* IT.

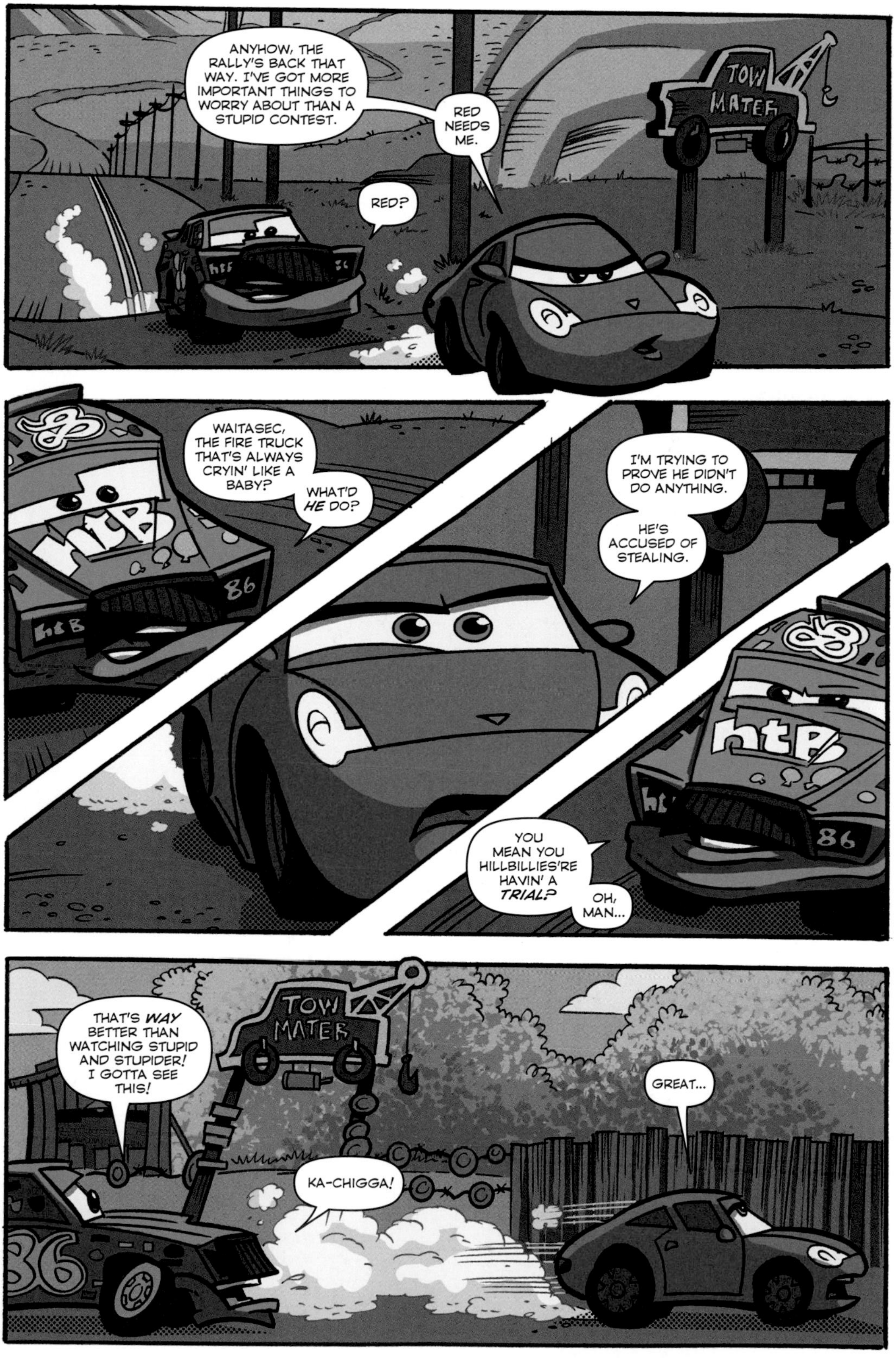
ANYHOW, THE RALLY'S BACK THAT WAY. I'VE GOT MORE IMPORTANT THINGS TO WORRY ABOUT THAN A STUPID CONTEST.
RED NEEDS ME.
RED?
TOW MATER
WAITASEC, THE FIRE TRUCK THAT'S ALWAYS CRYIN' LIKE A BABY?
WHAT'D *HE* DO?
I'M TRYING TO PROVE HE DIDN'T DO ANYTHING.
HE'S ACCUSED OF STEALING.
YOU MEAN YOU HILLBILLIES'RE HAVIN' A *TRIAL?*
OH, MAN...
TOW MATER
THAT'S *WAY* BETTER THAN WATCHING STUPID AND STUPIDER! I GOTTA SEE THIS!
GREAT...
KA-CHIGGA!

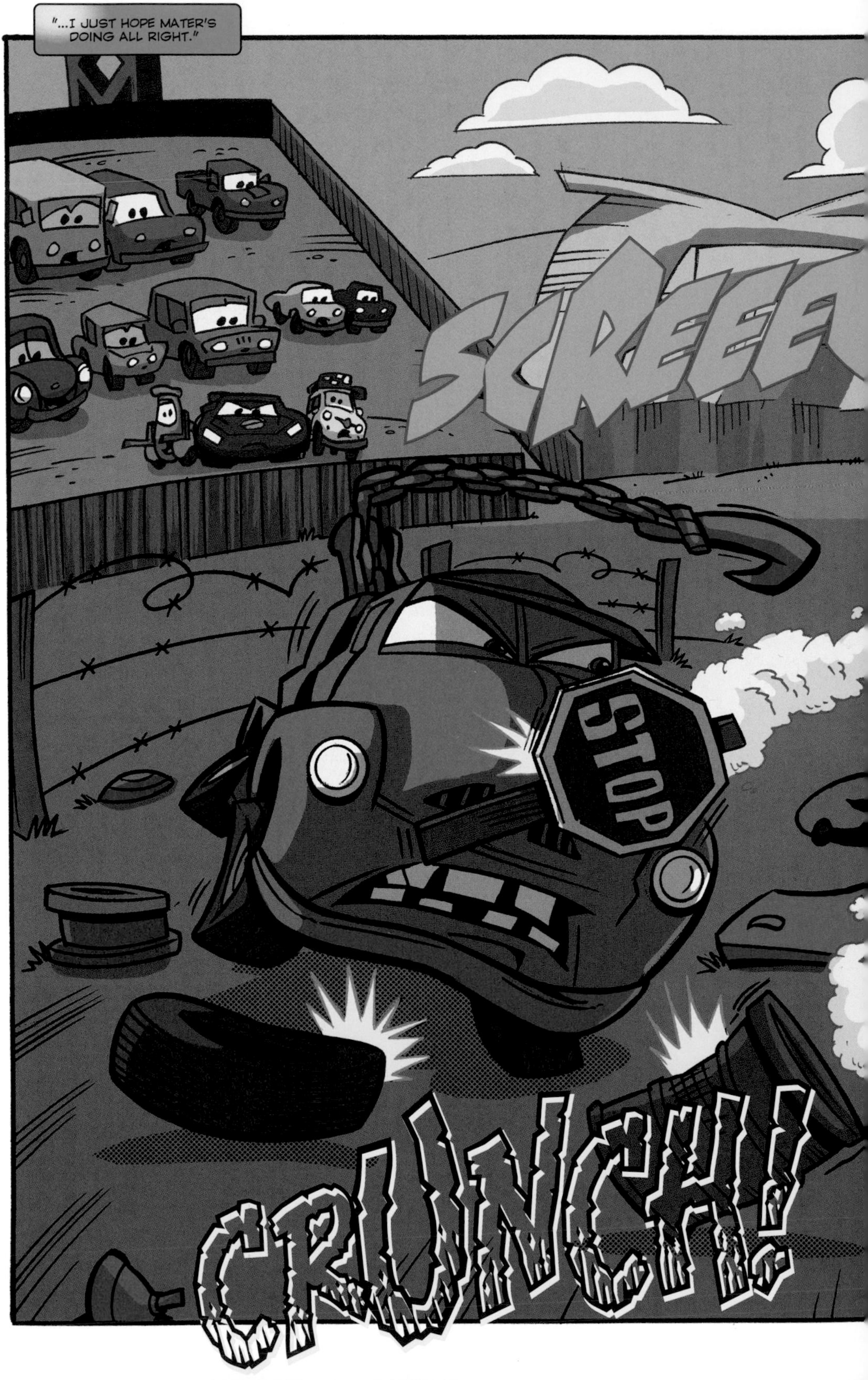
"...I JUST HOPE MATER'S DOING ALL RIGHT."
SCREEE
STOP
CRUNCH!

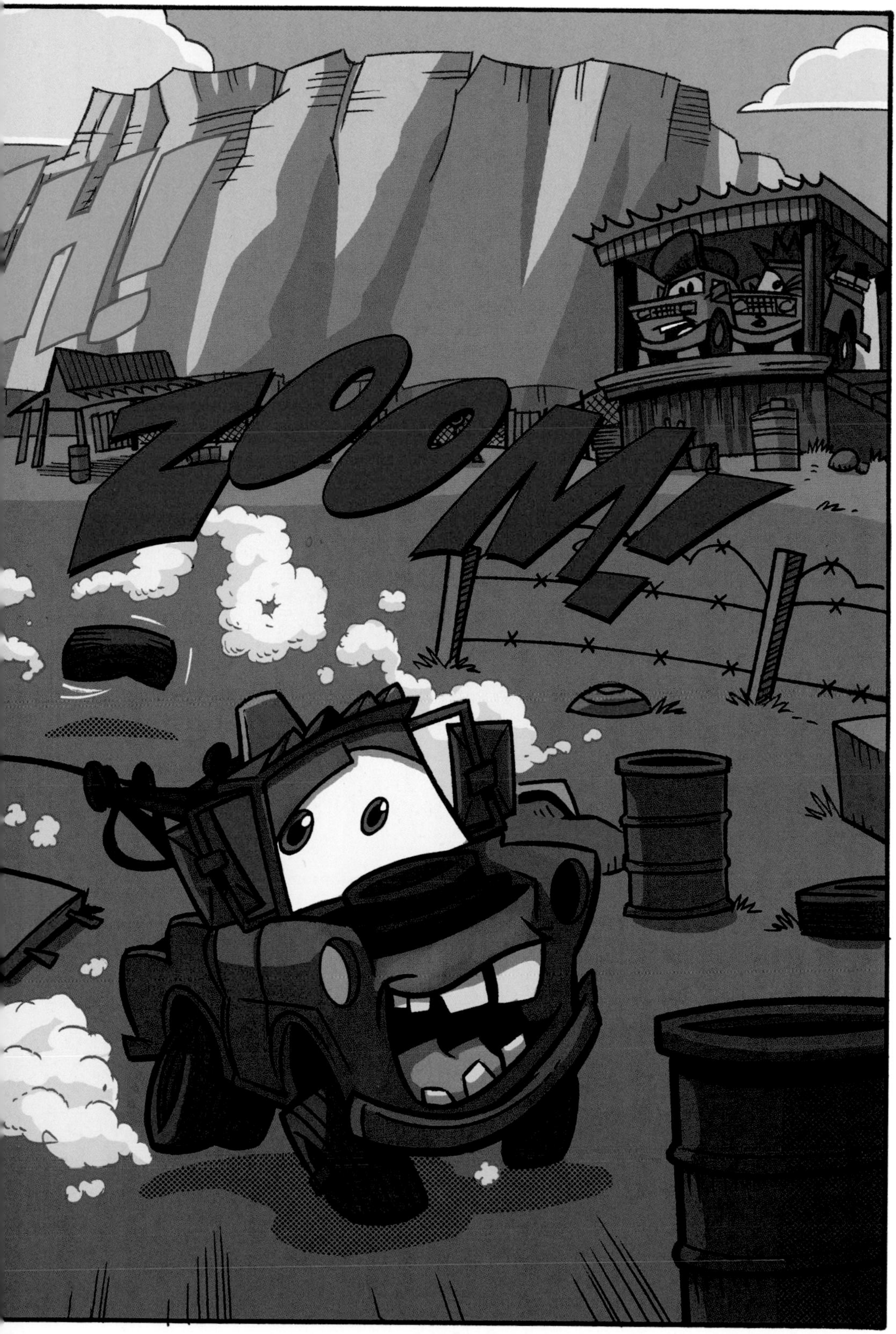
ZOOM!

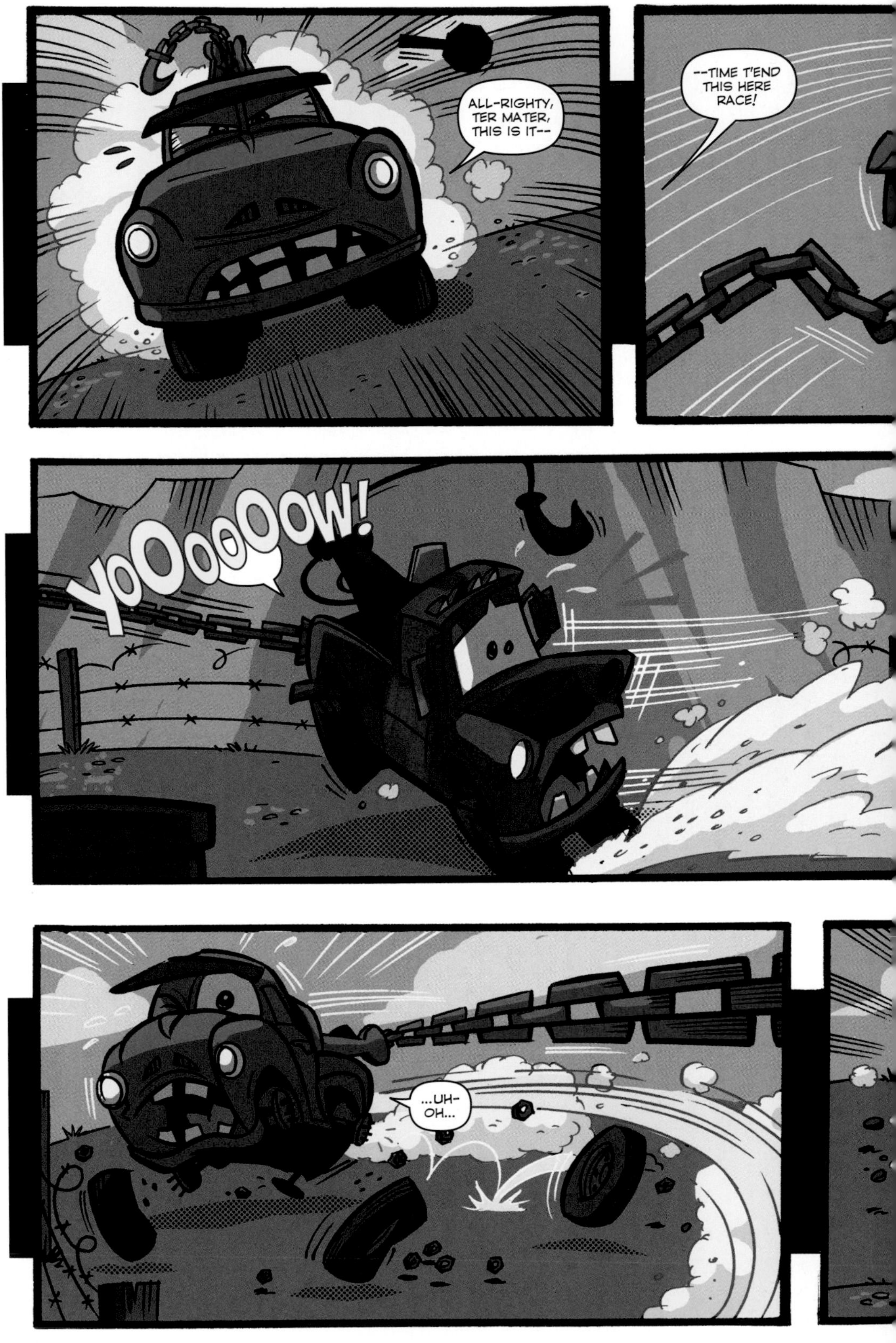
ALL-RIGHTY, TER MATER, THIS IS IT--
--TIME T'END THIS HERE RACE!
YOOOOOOW!
...UH-OH...

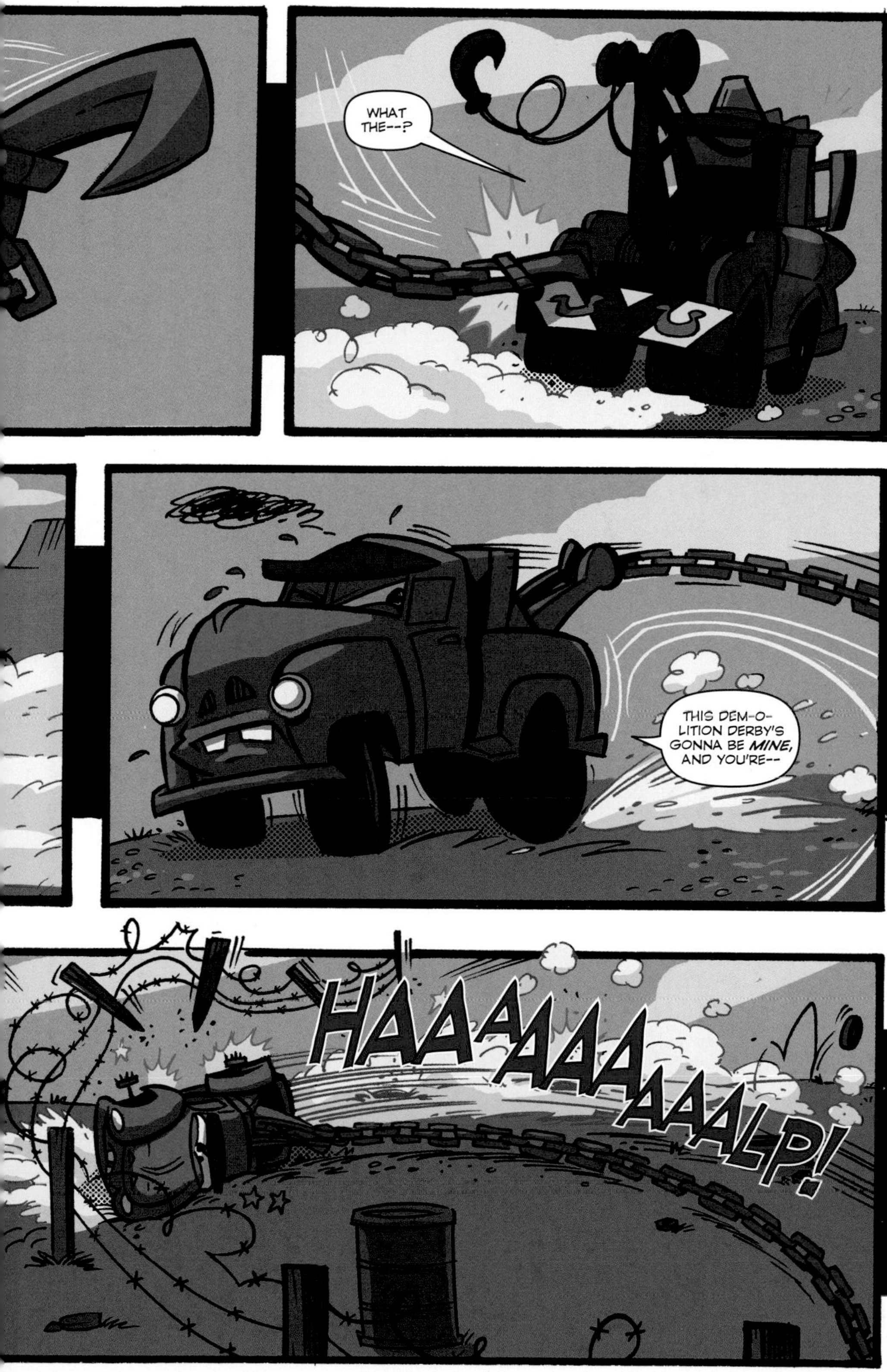
WHAT THE--?
THIS DEM-O-LITION DERBY'S GONNA BE *MINE*, AND YOU'RE--
HAAAAAAAAALP!

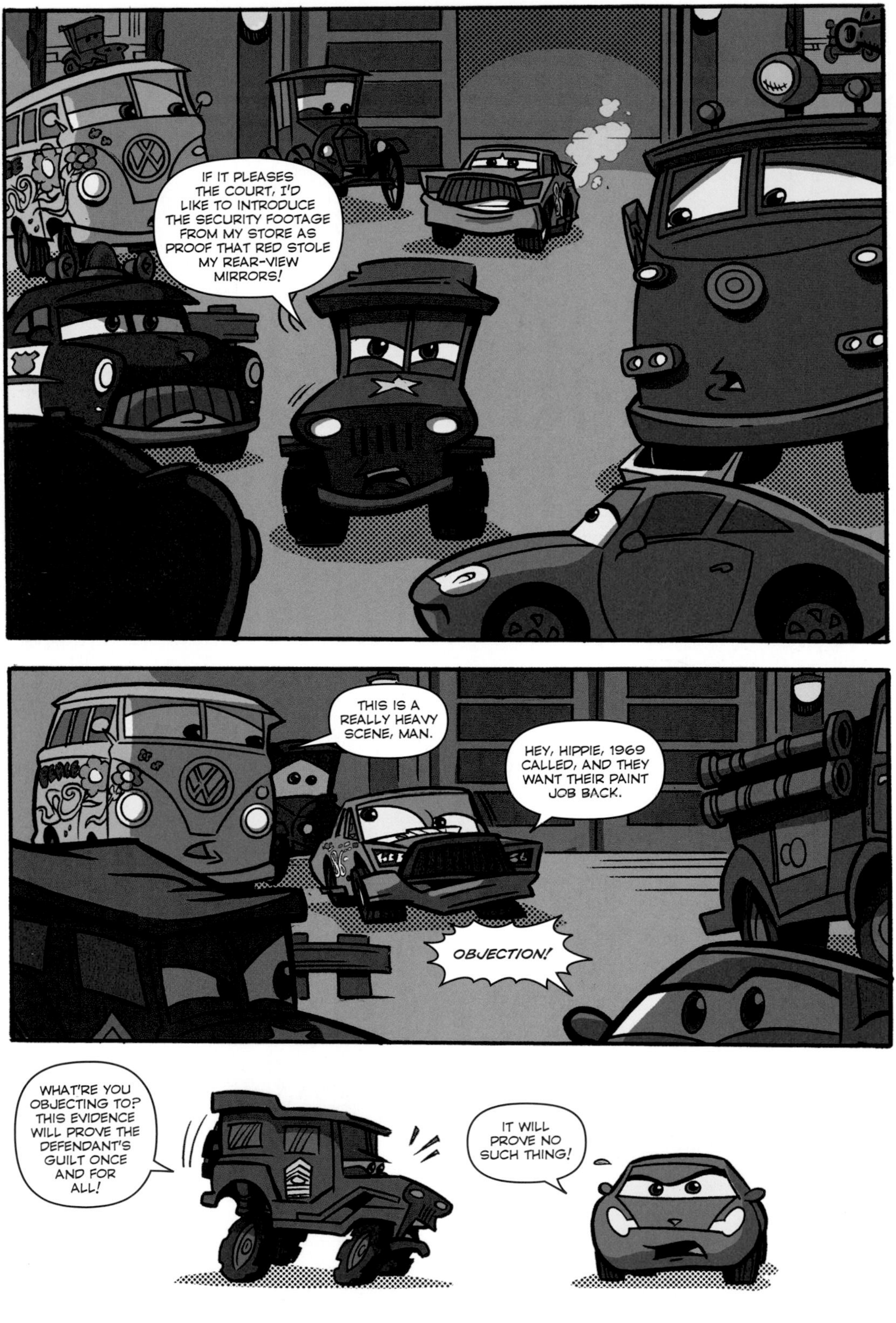
IF IT PLEASES THE COURT, I'D LIKE TO INTRODUCE THE SECURITY FOOTAGE FROM MY STORE AS PROOF THAT RED STOLE MY REAR-VIEW MIRRORS!
THIS IS A REALLY HEAVY SCENE, MAN.
HEY, HIPPIE, 1969 CALLED, AND THEY WANT THEIR PAINT JOB BACK.
OBJECTION!
WHAT'RE YOU OBJECTING TO? THIS EVIDENCE WILL PROVE THE DEFENDANT'S GUILT ONCE AND FOR ALL!
IT WILL PROVE NO SUCH THING!

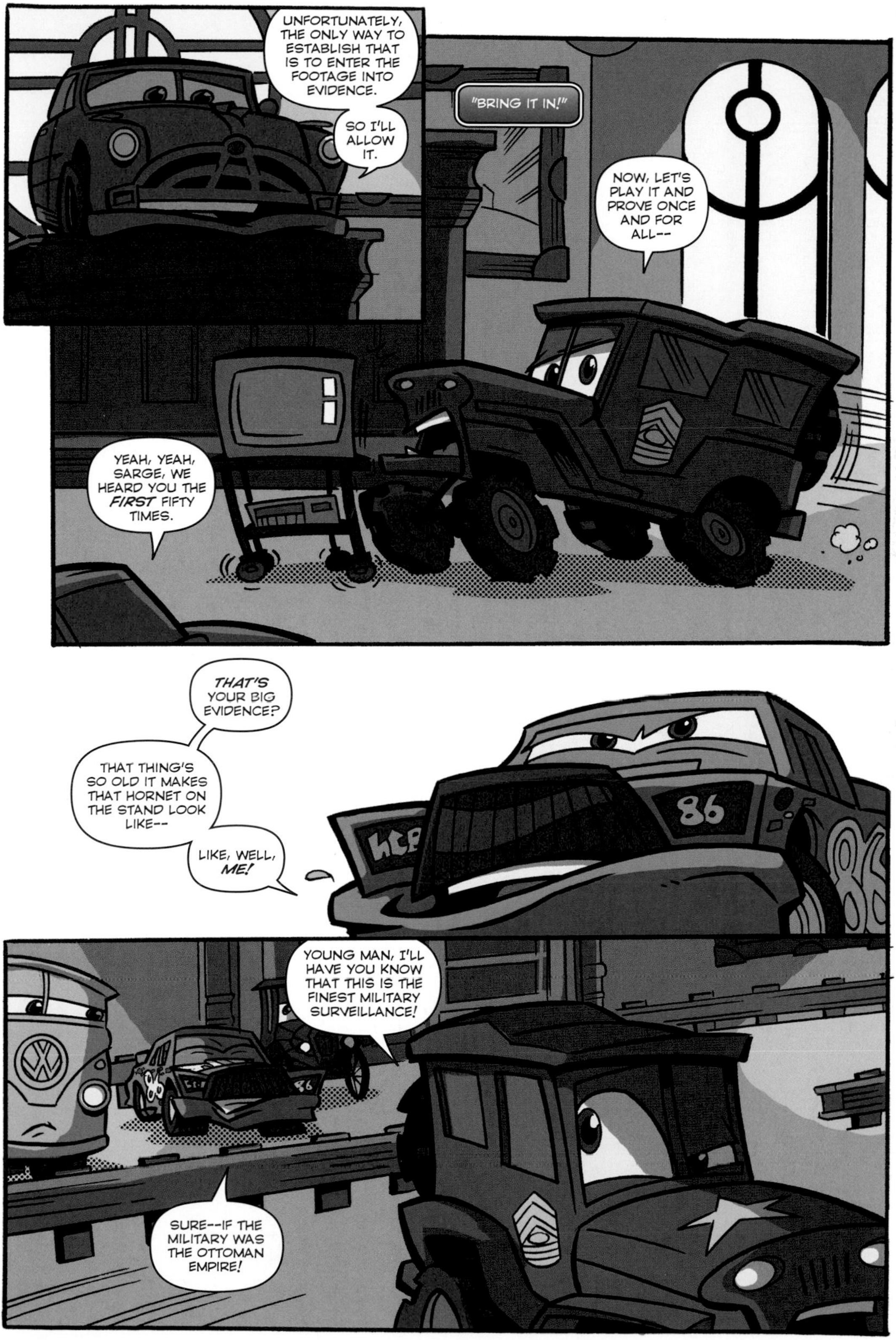
UNFORTUNATELY, THE ONLY WAY TO ESTABLISH THAT IS TO ENTER THE FOOTAGE INTO EVIDENCE.
SO I'LL ALLOW IT.
"BRING IT IN!"
NOW, LET'S PLAY IT AND PROVE ONCE AND FOR ALL--
YEAH, YEAH, SARGE, WE HEARD YOU THE *FIRST* FIFTY TIMES.
THAT'S YOUR BIG EVIDENCE?
THAT THING'S SO OLD IT MAKES THAT HORNET ON THE STAND LOOK LIKE--
LIKE, WELL, *ME!*
86
YOUNG MAN, I'LL HAVE YOU KNOW THAT THIS IS THE FINEST MILITARY SURVEILLANCE!
SURE--IF THE MILITARY WAS THE OTTOMAN EMPIRE!

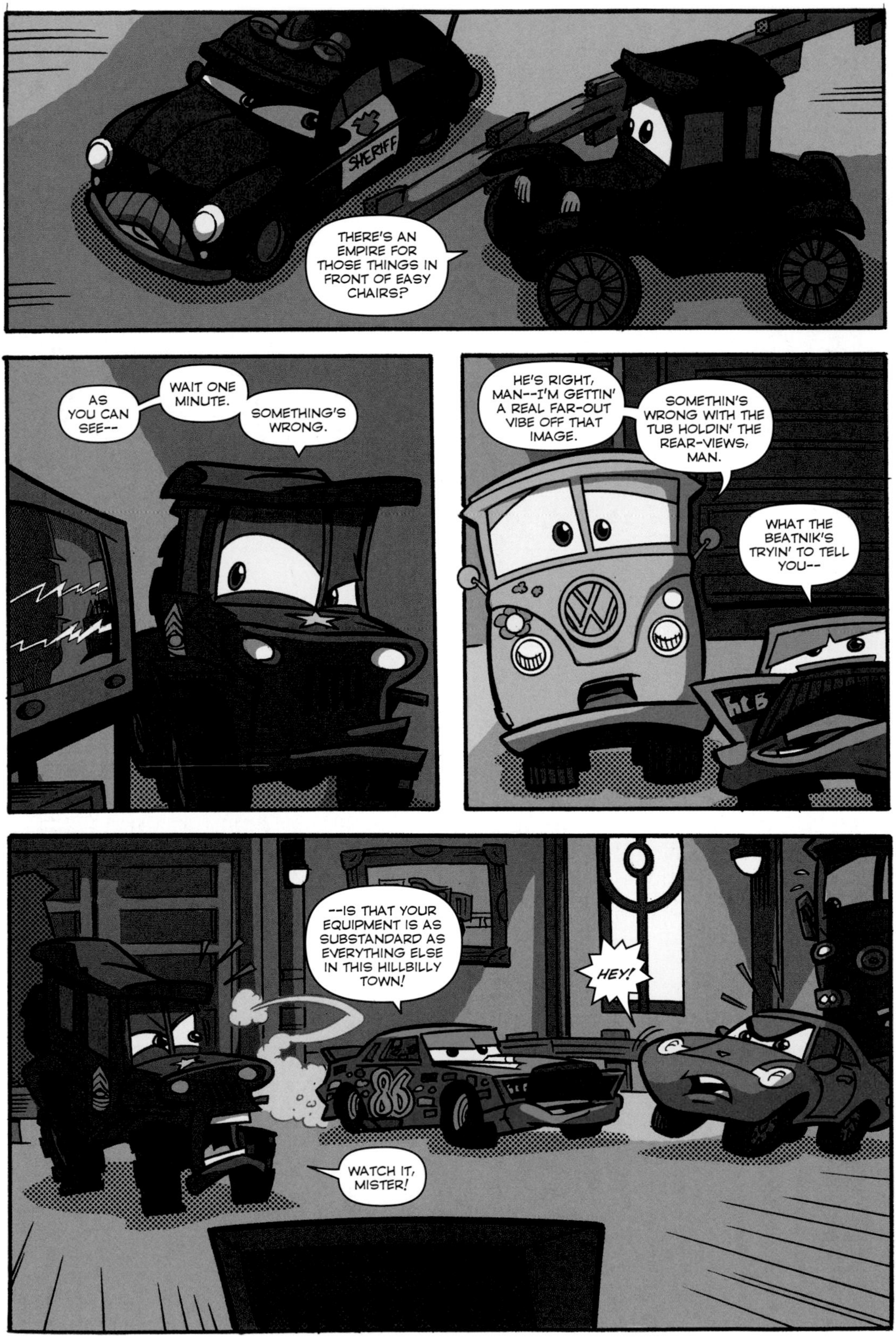
THERE'S AN EMPIRE FOR THOSE THINGS IN FRONT OF EASY CHAIRS?
SHERIFF
AS YOU CAN SEE--
WAIT ONE MINUTE.
SOMETHING'S WRONG.
HE'S RIGHT, MAN--I'M GETTIN' A REAL FAR-OUT VIBE OFF THAT IMAGE.
SOMETHIN'S WRONG WITH THE TUB HOLDIN' THE REAR-VIEWS, MAN.
WHAT THE BEATNIK'S TRYIN' TO TELL YOU--
--IS THAT YOUR EQUIPMENT IS AS SUBSTANDARD AS EVERYTHING ELSE IN THIS HILLBILLY TOWN!
HEY!
WATCH IT, MISTER!

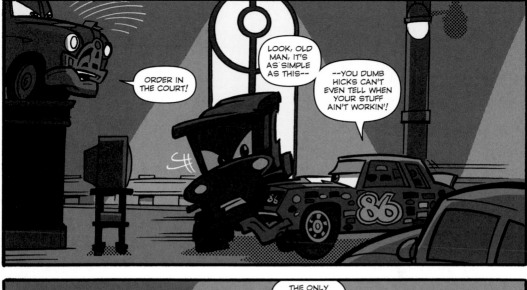

ORDER IN THE COURT!

LOOK, OLD MAN, IT'S AS SIMPLE AS THIS--

--YOU DUMB HICKS CAN'T EVEN TELL WHEN YOUR STUFF AIN'T WORKIN'!

THE ONLY "DUMB HICKS" HERE IS *YOU*, BUSTER!

OH, HARDY-HAR-HAR!

CONGRATS, YOU'RE THE 9000TH PERSON TO MAKE THAT JOKE!

WHAT YOU GOT HERE IS A BAD ADJUSTMENT TO THE COLORS.

BUT IF YOU CHANGE THE CONTRAST A BIT...

YEAH, THAT'S IT!

THE TUB IS TAN, MAN, NOT BROWN!

SO IT *ISN'T* A RED VEHICLE--

--WHICH MEANS RED IS INNOCENT!

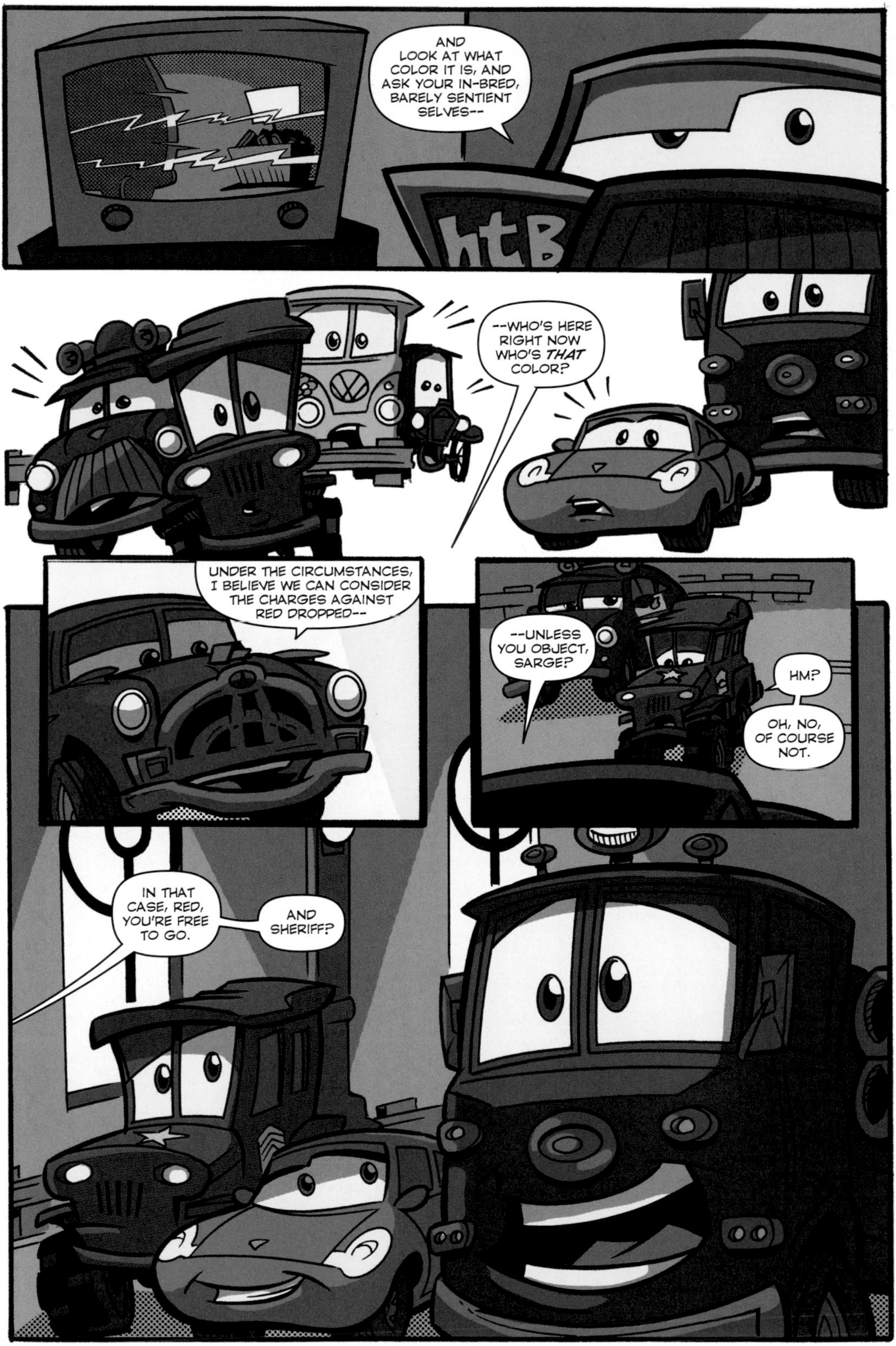
AND LOOK AT WHAT COLOR IT IS, AND ASK YOUR IN-BRED, BARELY SENTIENT SELVES--
--WHO'S HERE RIGHT NOW WHO'S *THAT* COLOR?
UNDER THE CIRCUMSTANCES, I BELIEVE WE CAN CONSIDER THE CHARGES AGAINST RED DROPPED--
--UNLESS YOU OBJECT, SARGE?
HM?
OH, NO, OF COURSE NOT.
IN THAT CASE, RED, YOU'RE FREE TO GO.
AND SHERIFF?

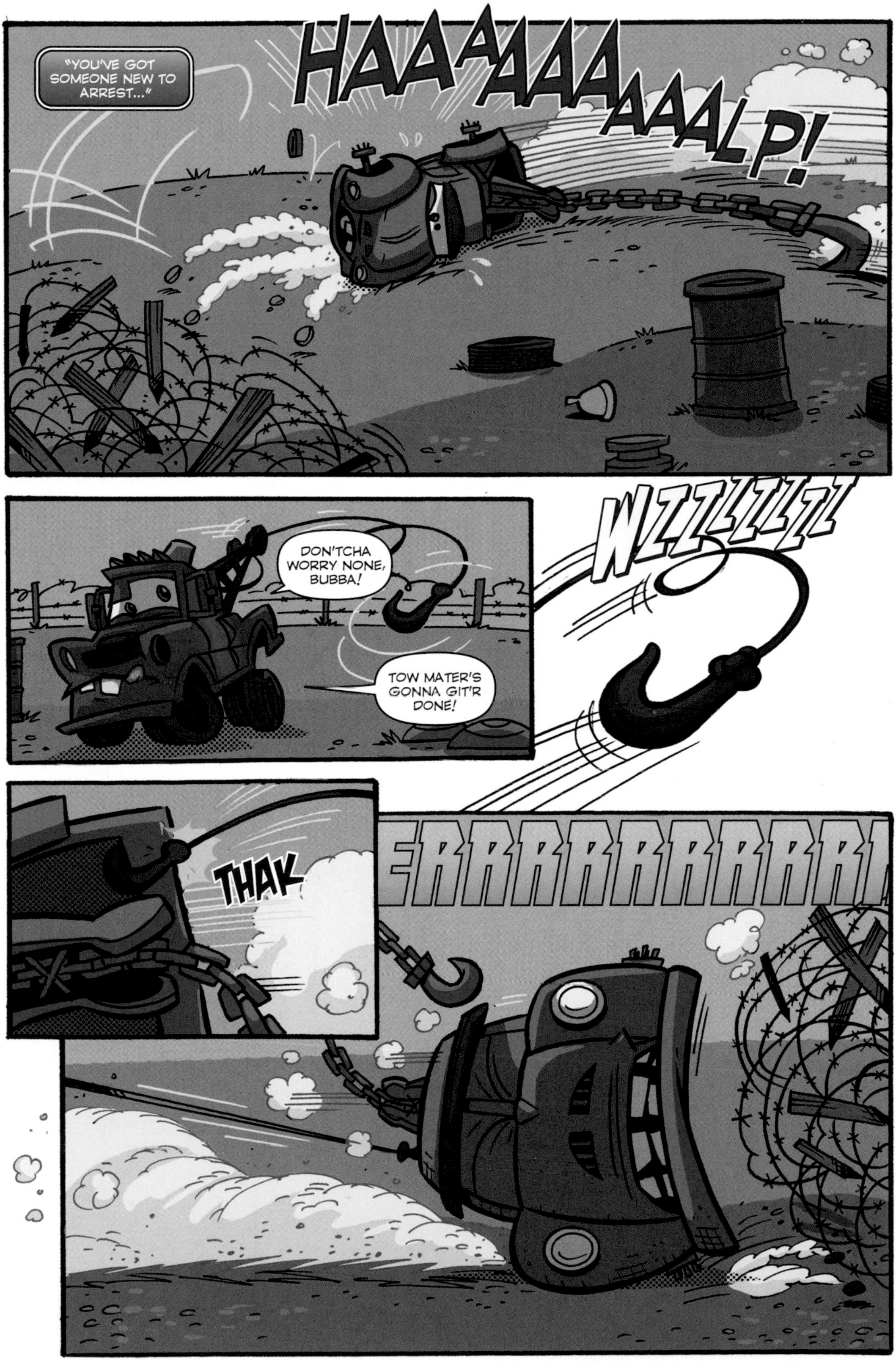
"YOU'VE GOT SOMEONE NEW TO ARREST..."
HAAAAAAAAAALP!
DON'TCHA WORRY NONE, BUBBA!
TOW MATER'S GONNA GIT'R DONE!
WZZZZZZZ
THAK
ERRRRRRRRRRR

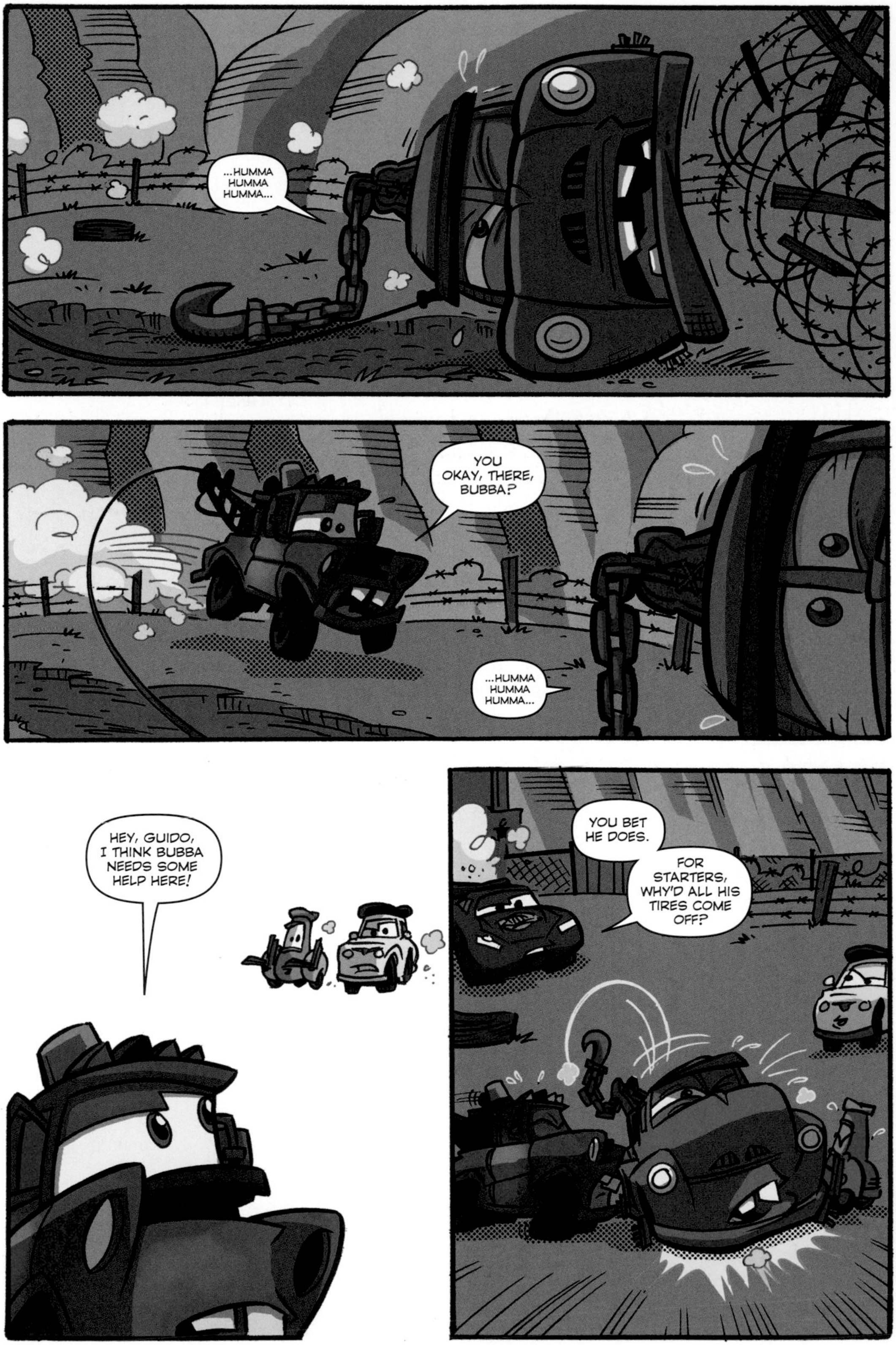
...HUMMA HUMMA HUMMA...
YOU OKAY, THERE, BUBBA?
...HUMMA HUMMA HUMMA...
HEY, GUIDO, I THINK BUBBA NEEDS SOME HELP HERE!
YOU BET HE DOES.
FOR STARTERS, WHY'D ALL HIS TIRES COME OFF?

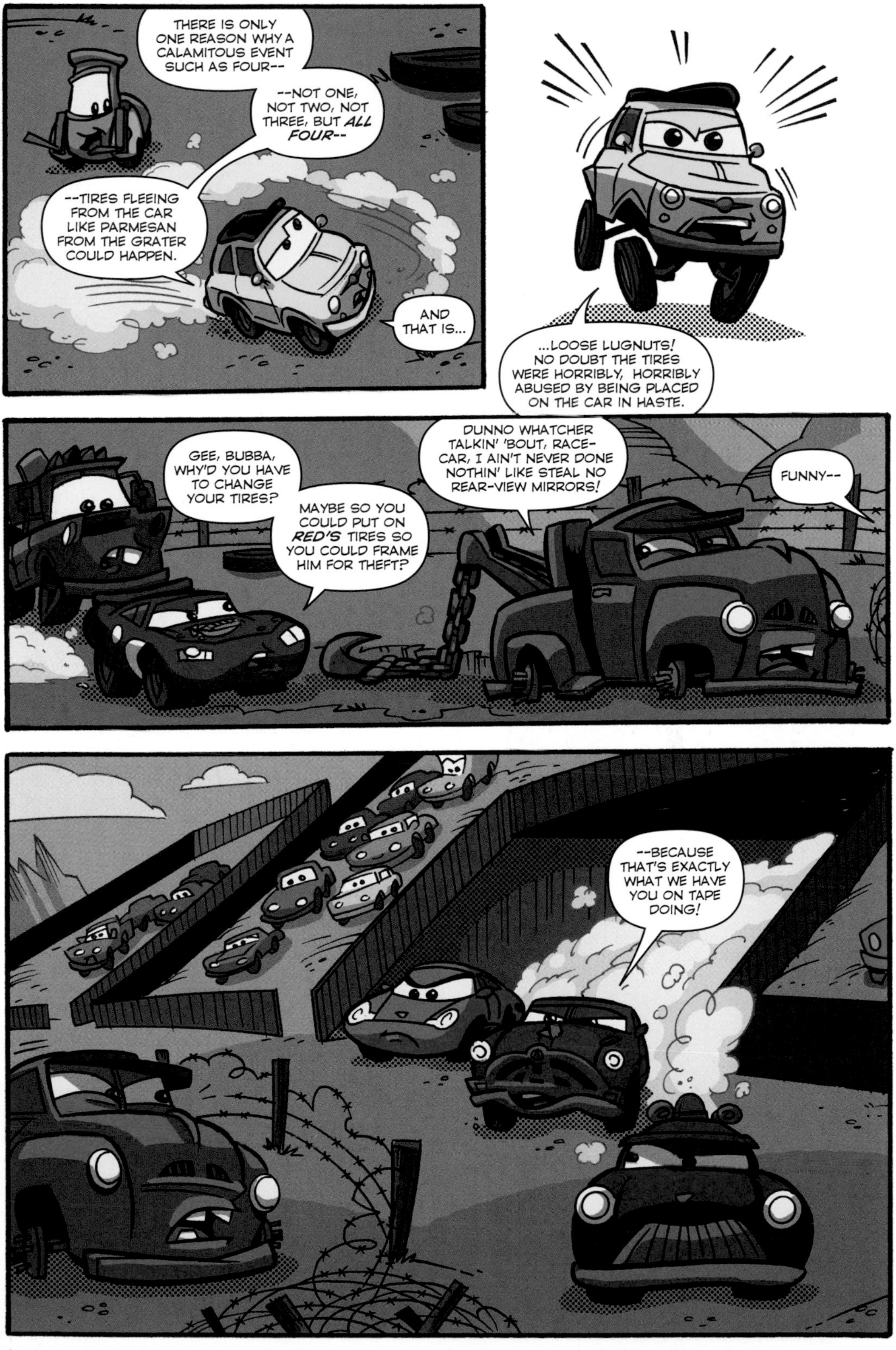
THERE IS ONLY ONE REASON WHY A CALAMITOUS EVENT SUCH AS FOUR--
--NOT ONE, NOT TWO, NOT THREE, BUT *ALL FOUR*--
--TIRES FLEEING FROM THE CAR LIKE PARMESAN FROM THE GRATER COULD HAPPEN.
AND THAT IS...
...LOOSE LUGNUTS! NO DOUBT THE TIRES WERE HORRIBLY, HORRIBLY ABUSED BY BEING PLACED ON THE CAR IN HASTE.
GEE, BUBBA, WHY'D YOU HAVE TO CHANGE YOUR TIRES?
MAYBE SO YOU COULD PUT ON *RED'S* TIRES SO YOU COULD FRAME HIM FOR THEFT?
DUNNO WHATCHER TALKIN' 'BOUT, RACE-CAR, I AIN'T NEVER DONE NOTHIN' LIKE STEAL NO REAR-VIEW MIRRORS!
FUNNY--
--BECAUSE THAT'S EXACTLY WHAT WE HAVE YOU ON TAPE DOING!

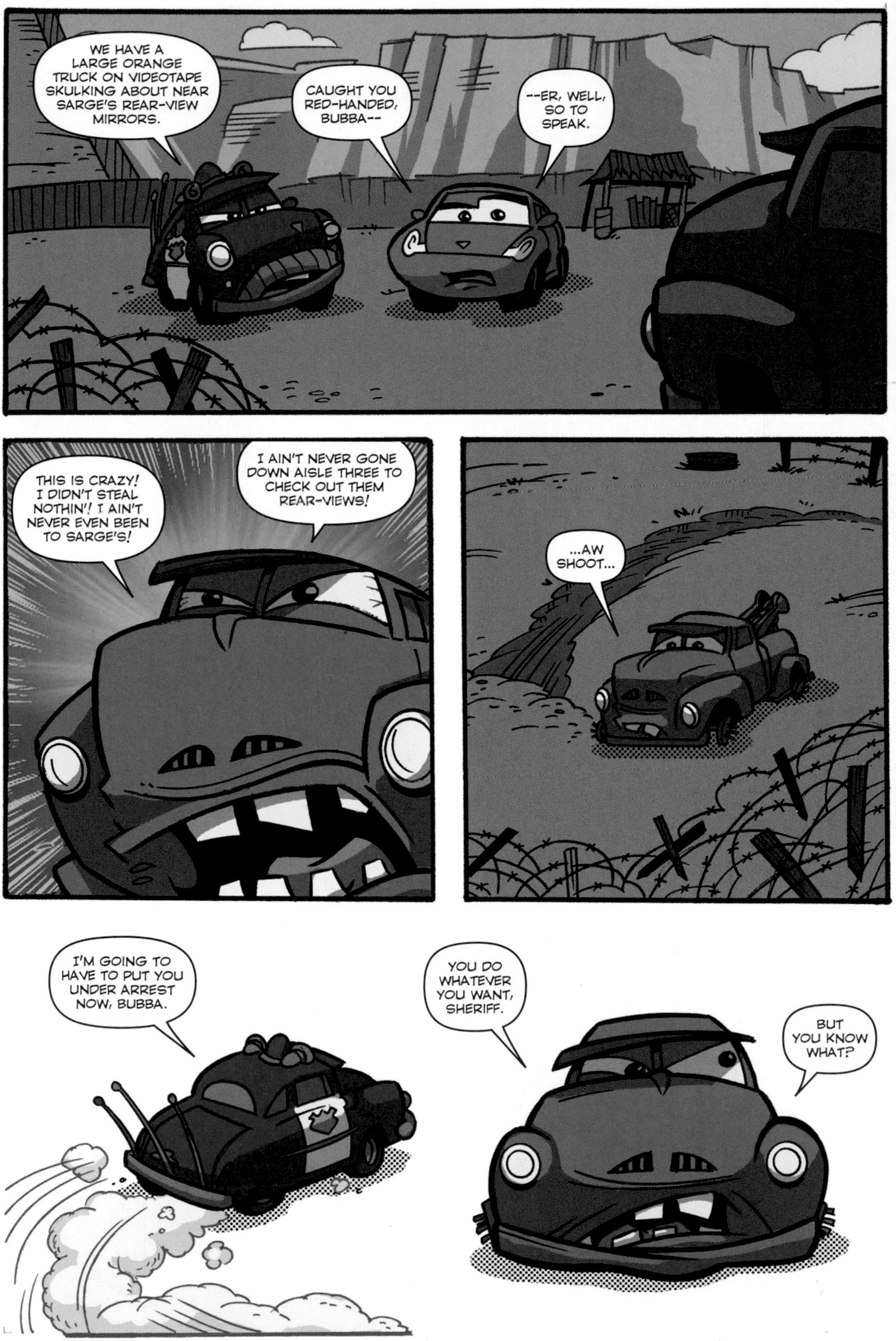
WE HAVE A LARGE ORANGE TRUCK ON VIDEOTAPE SKULKING ABOUT NEAR SARGE'S REAR-VIEW MIRRORS.
CAUGHT YOU RED-HANDED, BUBBA--
--ER, WELL, SO TO SPEAK.
THIS IS CRAZY! I DIDN'T STEAL NOTHIN'! I AIN'T NEVER EVEN BEEN TO SARGE'S!
I AIN'T NEVER GONE DOWN AISLE THREE TO CHECK OUT THEM REAR-VIEWS!
...AW SHOOT...
I'M GOING TO HAVE TO PUT YOU UNDER ARREST NOW, BUBBA.
YOU DO WHATEVER YOU WANT, SHERIFF.
BUT YOU KNOW WHAT?

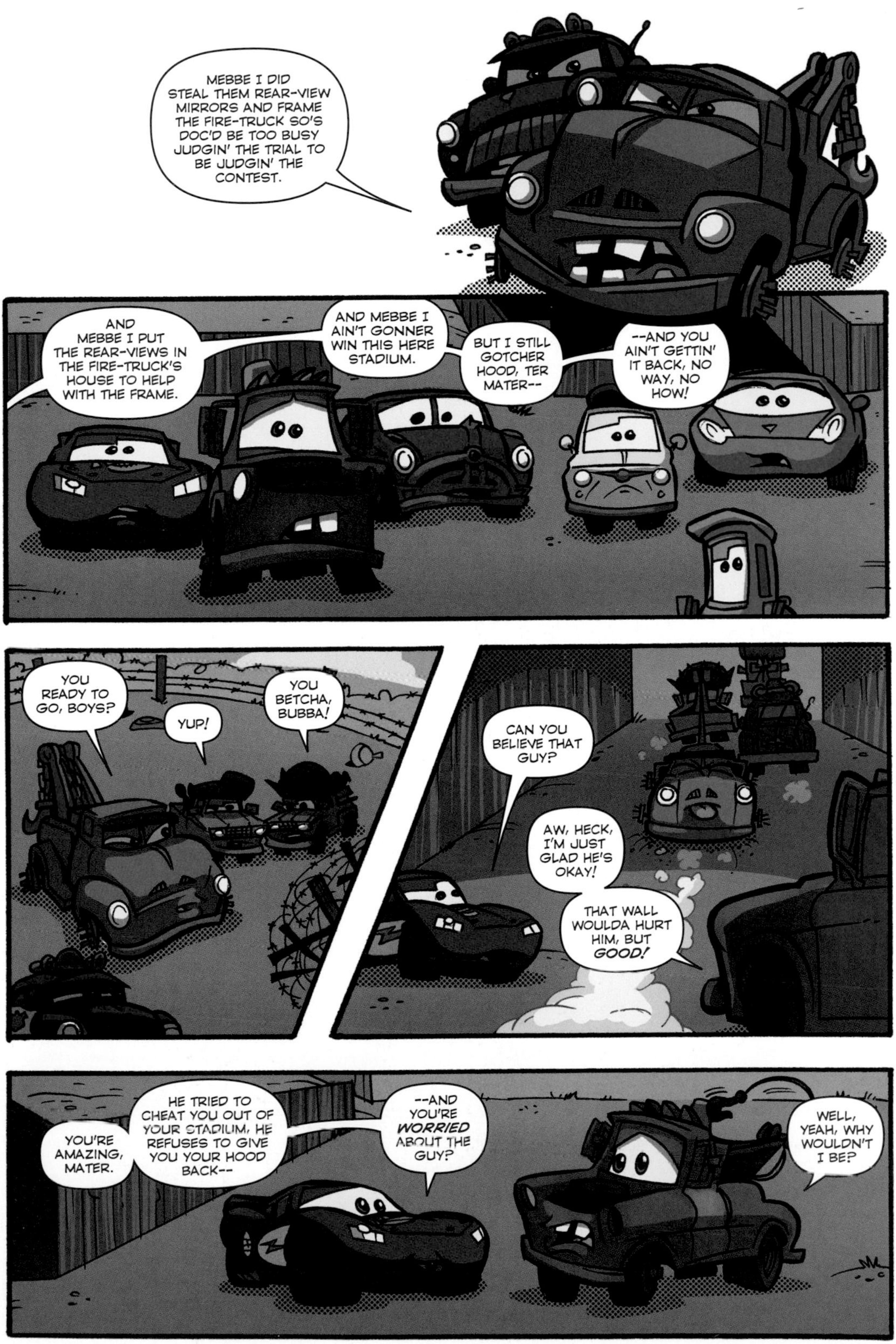
MEBBE I DID STEAL THEM REAR-VIEW MIRRORS AND FRAME THE FIRE-TRUCK SO'S DOC'D BE TOO BUSY JUDGIN' THE TRIAL TO BE JUDGIN' THE CONTEST.
AND MEBBE I PUT THE REAR-VIEWS IN THE FIRE-TRUCK'S HOUSE TO HELP WITH THE FRAME.
AND MEBBE I AIN'T GONNER WIN THIS HERE STADIUM.
BUT I STILL GOTCHER HOOD, TER MATER--
--AND YOU AIN'T GETTIN' IT BACK, NO WAY, NO HOW!
YOU READY TO GO, BOYS?
YUP!
YOU BETCHA, BUBBA!
CAN YOU BELIEVE THAT GUY?
AW, HECK, I'M JUST GLAD HE'S OKAY!
THAT WALL WOULDA HURT HIM, BUT GOOD!
YOU'RE AMAZING, MATER.
HE TRIED TO CHEAT YOU OUT OF YOUR STADIUM, HE REFUSES TO GIVE YOU YOUR HOOD BACK--
--AND YOU'RE WORRIED ABOUT THE GUY?
WELL, YEAH, WHY WOULDN'T I BE?

DON'T EVER CHANGE, MATER.
REALLY? BUT WHAT ABOUT MY OIL? IF'N I DON'T CHANGE THAT, I MIGHT GET ALL--
NEVER MIND...
SO I GUESS IT TURNED OUT OKAY, HUH?
YEAH--I JUST WISH WE DIDN'T HAVE TO THANK CHICK HICKS.
CHICK WAS HERE???
YUP. AND HE WAS THE ONE WHO REALIZED THAT THE CONTRAST WAS OFF ON SARGE'S MONITOR.
HEY, MAN, I WAS THE ONE WHO SPIED THE TUB OF A DIFFERENT COLOR, MAN...
THAT'S TRUE, FILLMORE.
BUT NOW, AS THE BARD, WINDSHIELD SHAKESPEARE, ONCE SAID, "ALL'S WELL THAT ENDS WELL."
SO RED, OL' BUDDY, HOW'S IT FEEL TO BE A FREEEEEEEEEEEE MAN AGAIN, HUH?
BUUUUH- HUH-HUH HUH
COULDN'T'A SAID IT BETTER, M'SELF, BUDDY!
WOOOO-EEEE!
THE END

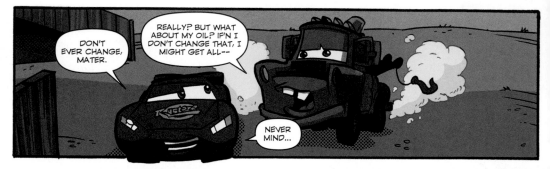

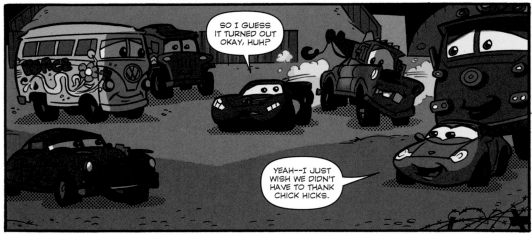

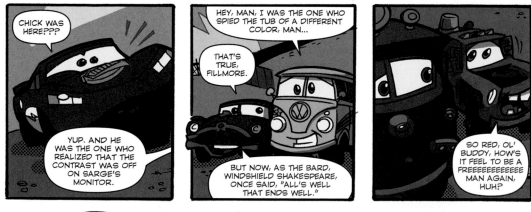

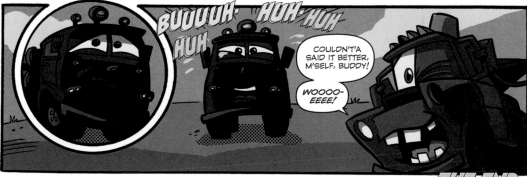

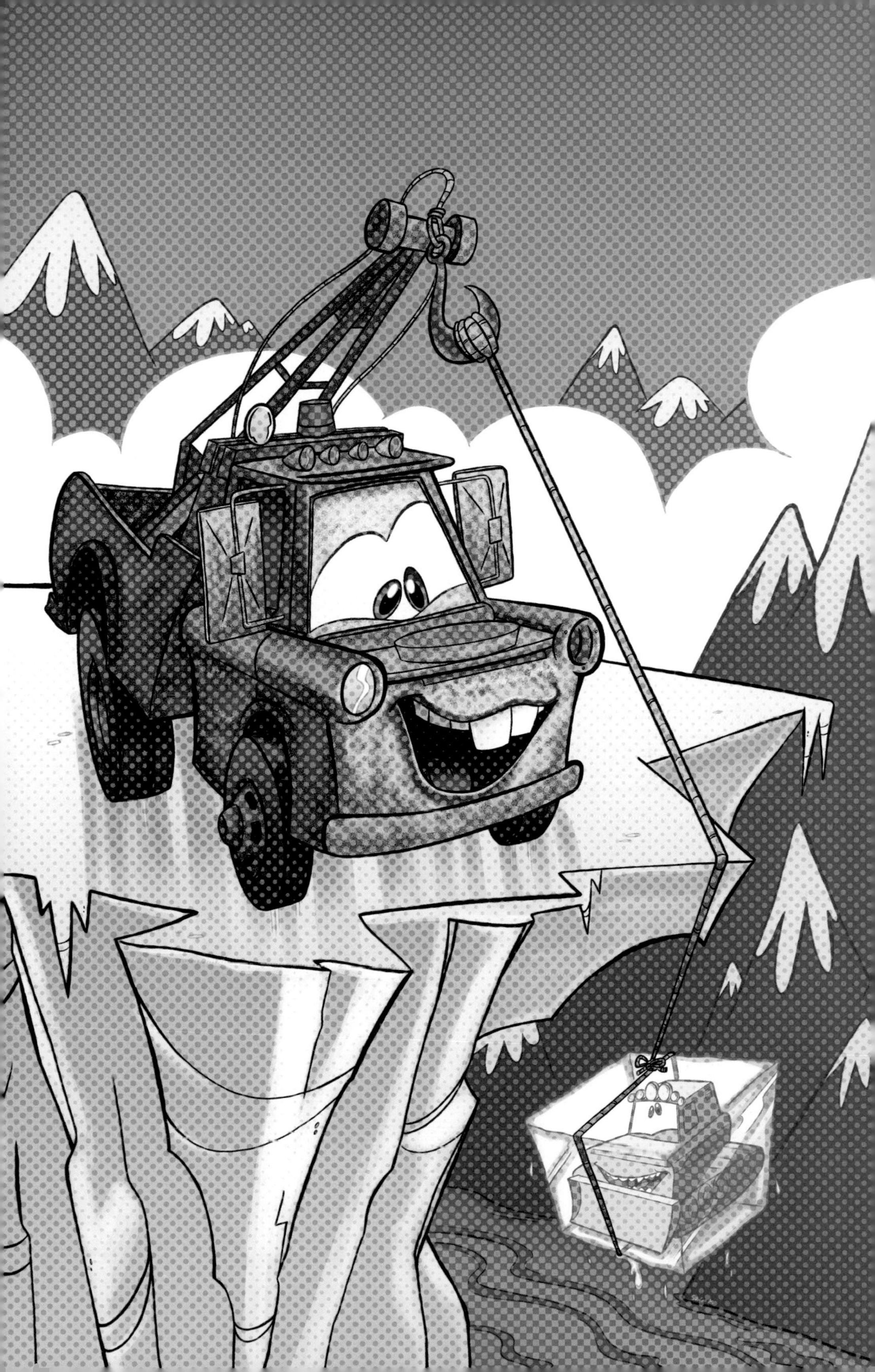

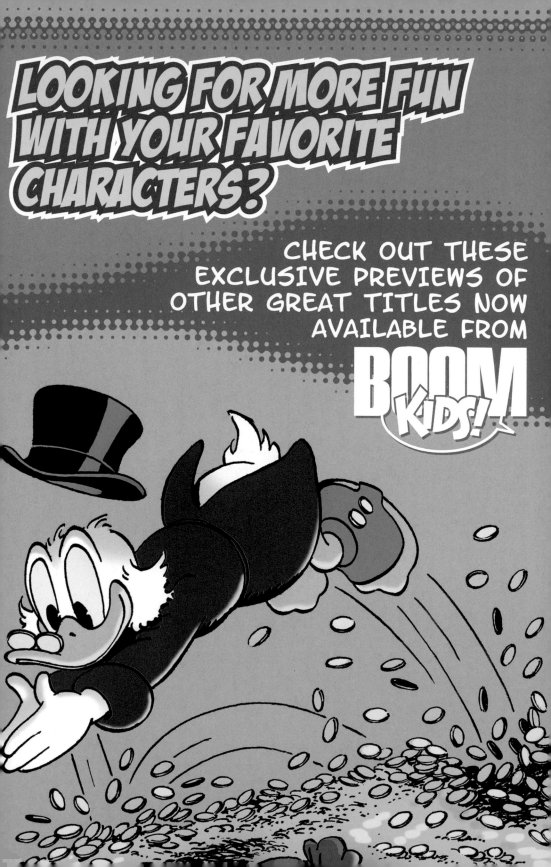

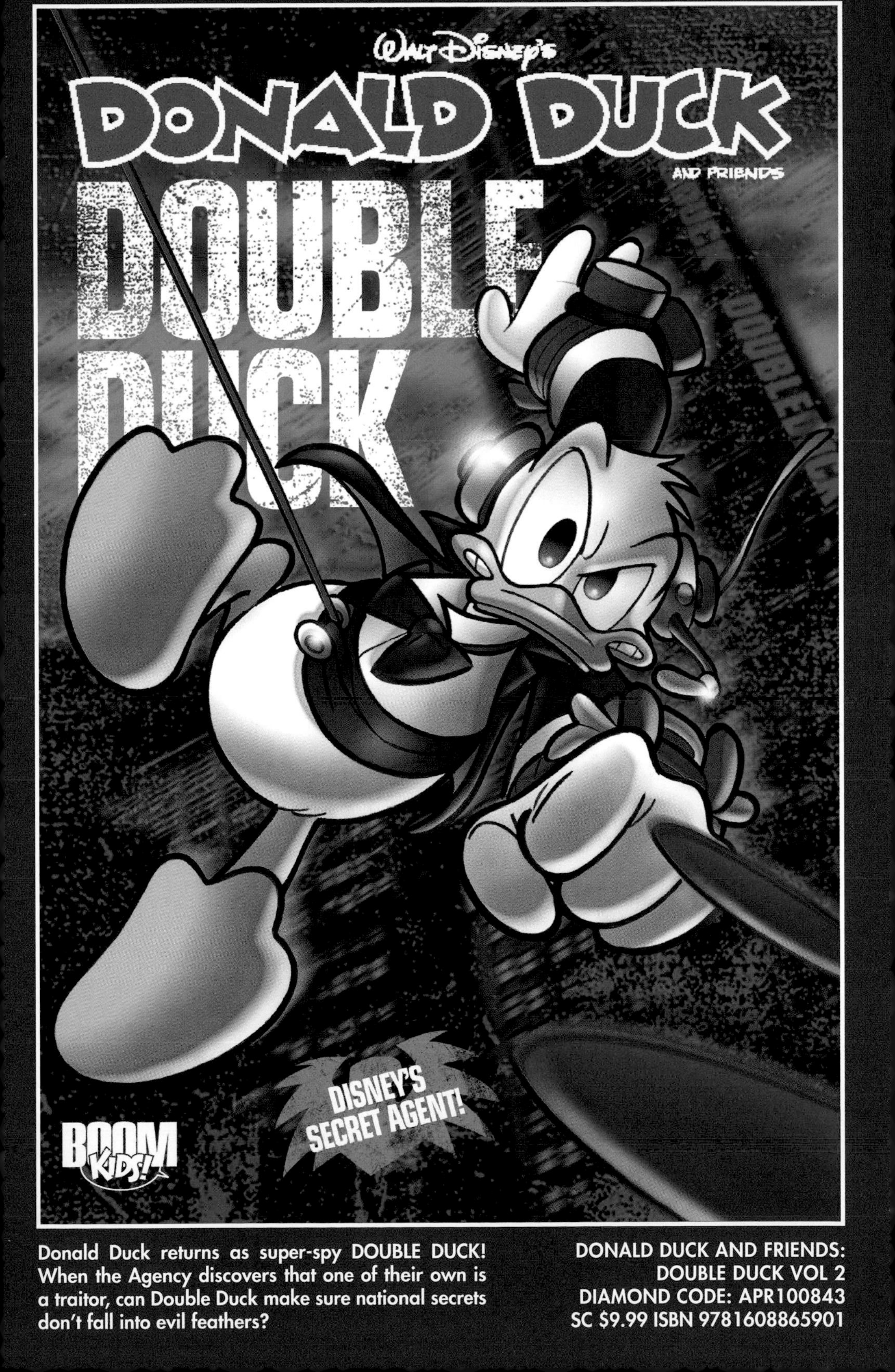
Walt Disney's
DONALD DUCK
AND FRIENDS
DOUBLE DUCK
DISNEY'S SECRET AGENT!
BOOM KIDS!

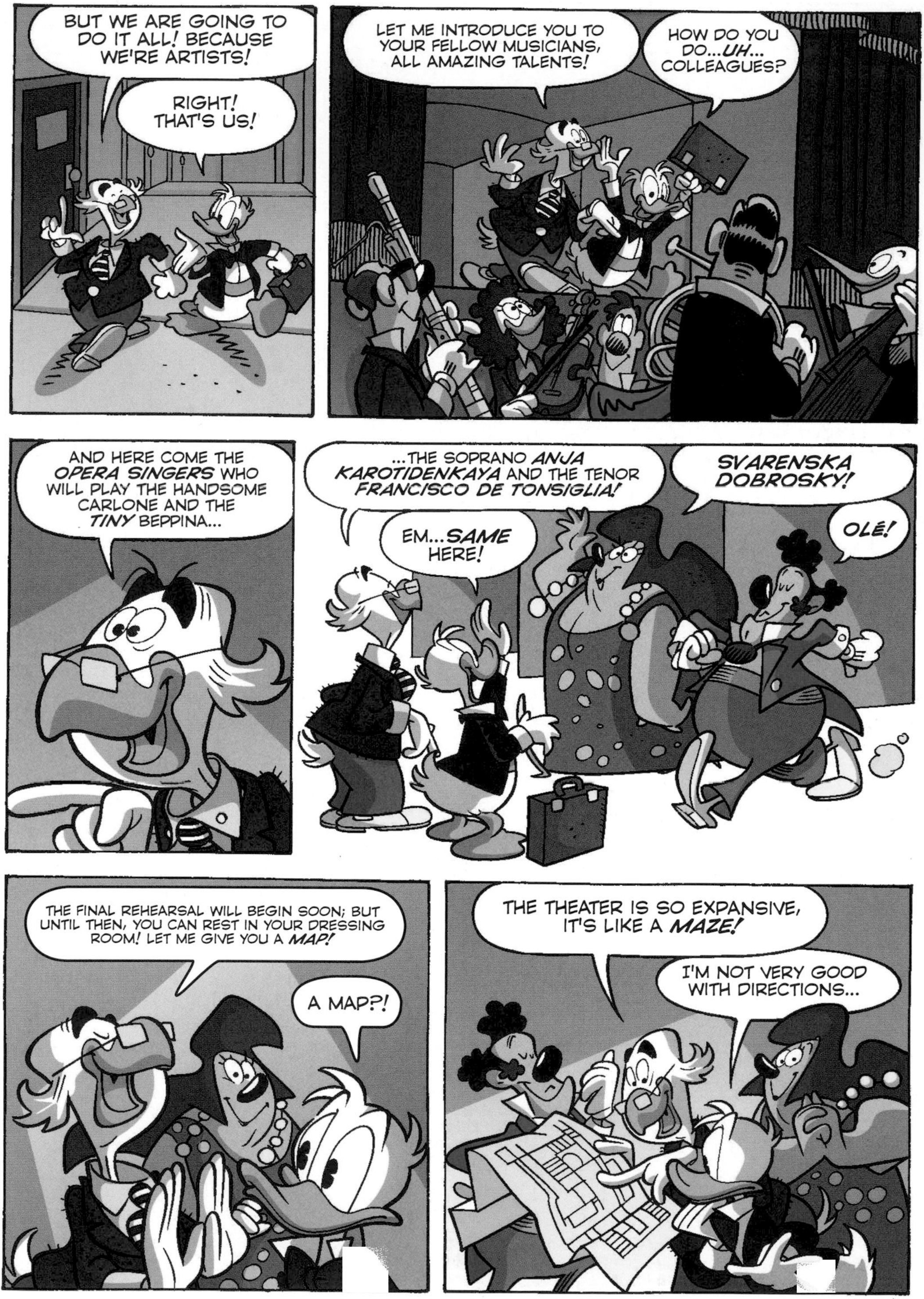
BUT WE ARE GOING TO DO IT ALL! BECAUSE WE'RE ARTISTS!
RIGHT! THAT'S US!
LET ME INTRODUCE YOU TO YOUR FELLOW MUSICIANS, ALL AMAZING TALENTS!
HOW DO YOU DO...UH... COLLEAGUES?
AND HERE COME THE OPERA SINGERS WHO WILL PLAY THE HANDSOME CARLONE AND THE TINY BEPPINA...
...THE SOPRANO ANJA KAROTIDENKAYA AND THE TENOR FRANCISCO DE TONSIGLIA!
EM...SAME HERE!
SVARENSKA DOBROSKY!
OLÉ!
THE FINAL REHEARSAL WILL BEGIN SOON; BUT UNTIL THEN, YOU CAN REST IN YOUR DRESSING ROOM! LET ME GIVE YOU A MAP!
A MAP?!
THE THEATER IS SO EXPANSIVE, IT'S LIKE A MAZE!
I'M NOT VERY GOOD WITH DIRECTIONS...

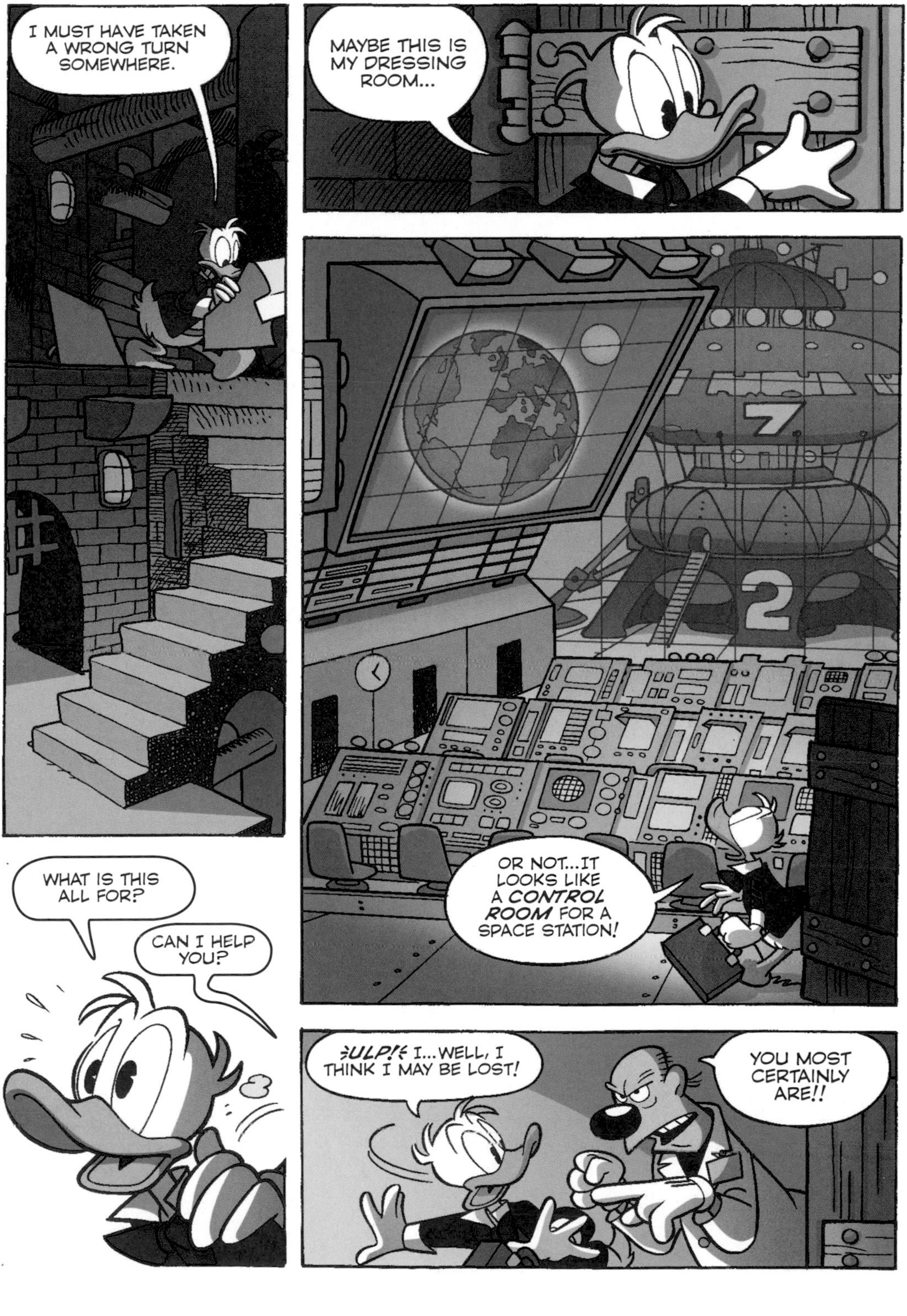
I MUST HAVE TAKEN A WRONG TURN SOMEWHERE.
MAYBE THIS IS MY DRESSING ROOM...
7
2
OR NOT...IT LOOKS LIKE A **CONTROL ROOM** FOR A SPACE STATION!
WHAT IS THIS ALL FOR?
CAN I HELP YOU?
ULP! I...WELL, I THINK I MAY BE LOST!
YOU MOST CERTAINLY ARE!!

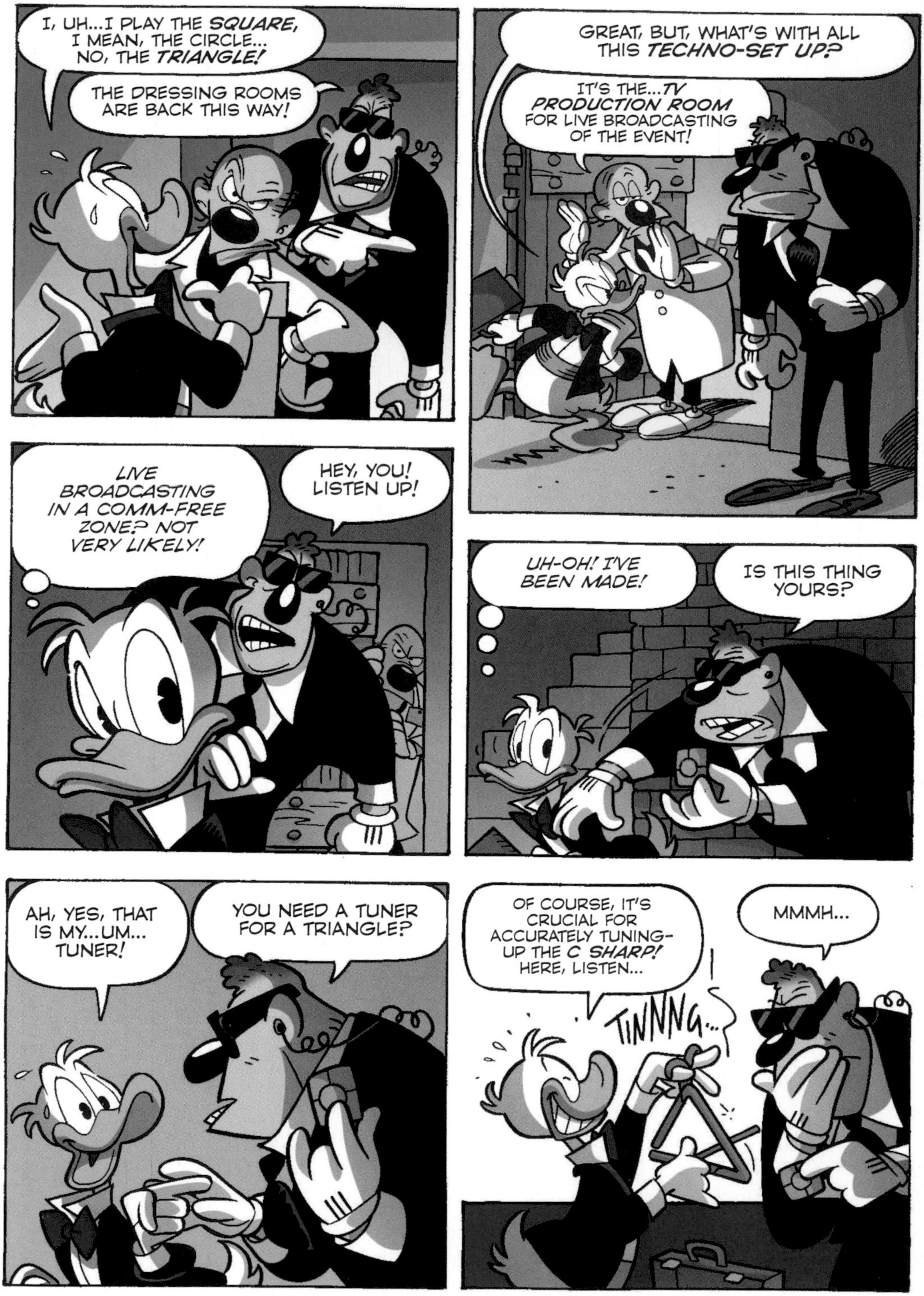

I, UH...I PLAY THE SQUARE, I MEAN, THE CIRCLE... NO, THE TRIANGLE!
THE DRESSING ROOMS ARE BACK THIS WAY!
GREAT, BUT, WHAT'S WITH ALL THIS TECHNO-SET UP?
IT'S THE...TV PRODUCTION ROOM FOR LIVE BROADCASTING OF THE EVENT!
LIVE BROADCASTING IN A COMM-FREE ZONE? NOT VERY LIKELY!
HEY, YOU! LISTEN UP!
UH-OH! I'VE BEEN MADE!
IS THIS THING YOURS?
AH, YES, THAT IS MY...UM... TUNER!
YOU NEED A TUNER FOR A TRIANGLE?
OF COURSE, IT'S CRUCIAL FOR ACCURATELY TUNING-UP THE C SHARP! HERE, LISTEN...
MMMH...
TINNNG...

DISNEY · PIXAR

THE INCREDIBLES

SECRETS & LIES

When the Eiffel Tower explodes, only Mrs. Incredible can save the day! Meanwhile, Mr. Incredible, Dash and Violet track down a mysterious thief — and uncover a secret that could tear the family apart!

THE INCREDIBLES: SECRETS AND LIES
DIAMOND CODE: MAY100883
SC $9.99 ISBN 9781608865833

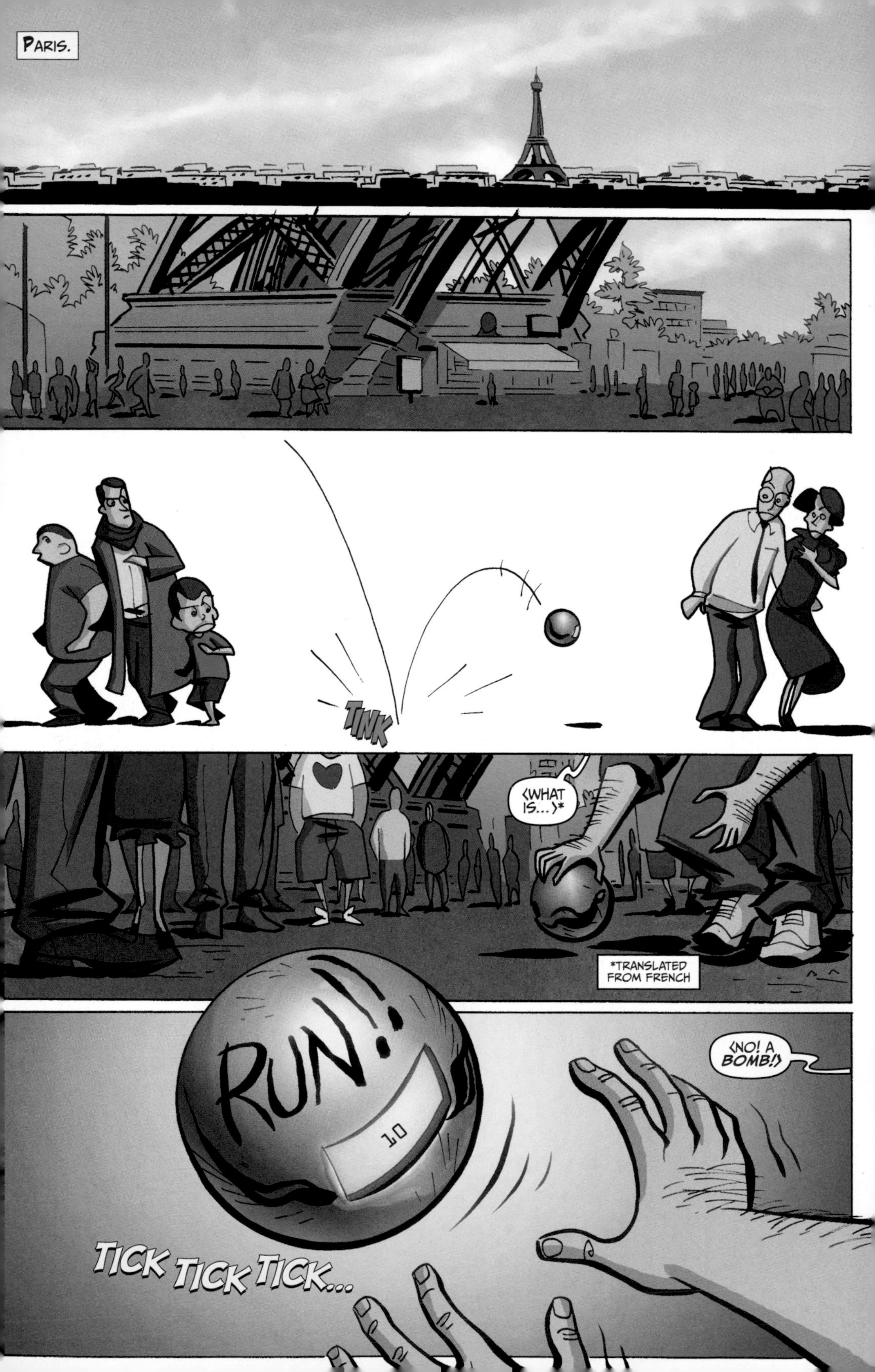
PARIS.
TINK
⟨WHAT IS...⟩*
*TRANSLATED FROM FRENCH
RUN!!
10
⟨NO! A BOMB!⟩
TICK TICK TICK...

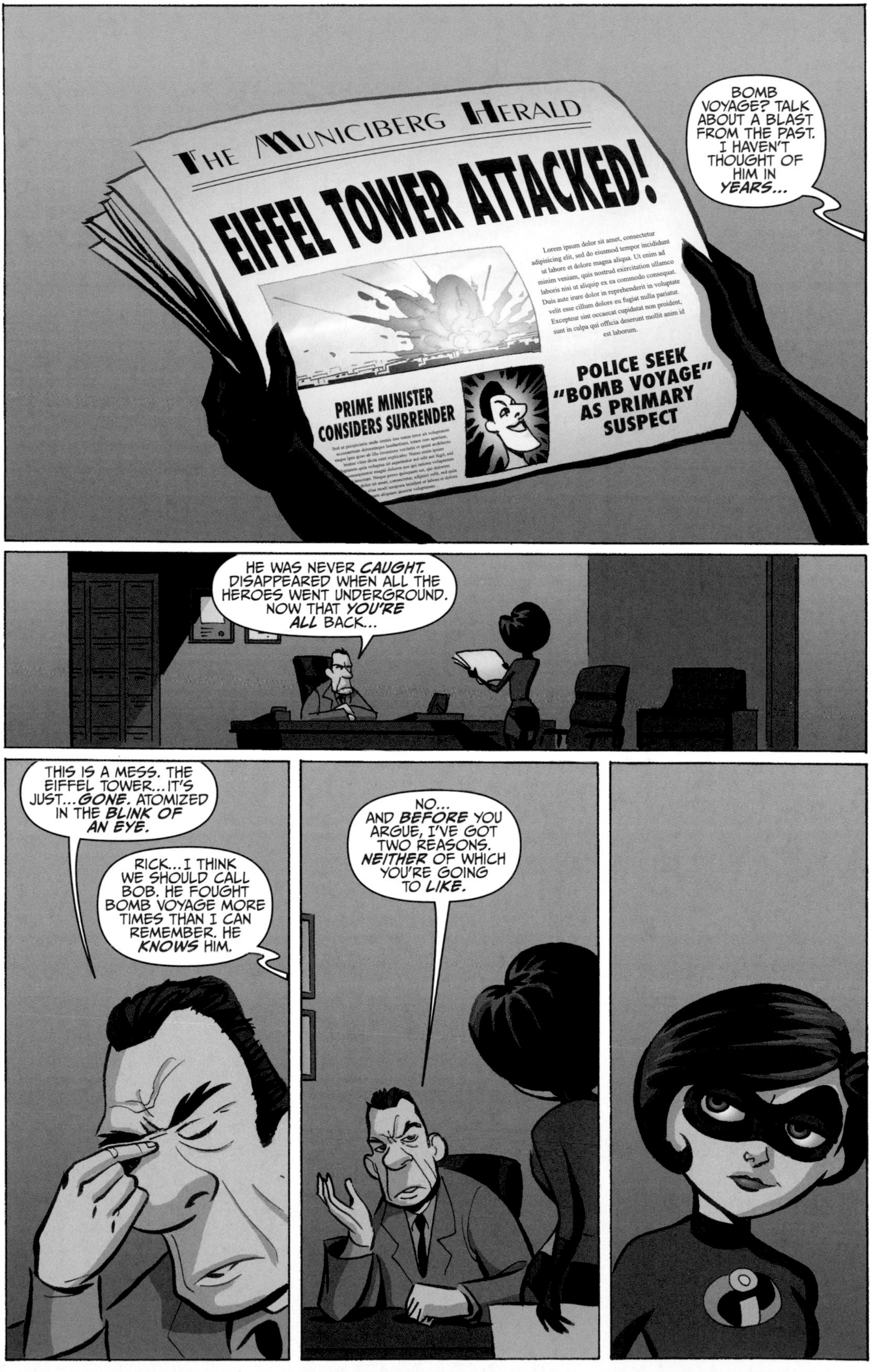
THE MUNICIBERG HERALD
EIFFEL TOWER ATTACKED!
PRIME MINISTER CONSIDERS SURRENDER
POLICE SEEK "BOMB VOYAGE" AS PRIMARY SUSPECT
BOMB VOYAGE? TALK ABOUT A BLAST FROM THE PAST. I HAVEN'T THOUGHT OF HIM IN YEARS...
HE WAS NEVER CAUGHT. DISAPPEARED WHEN ALL THE HEROES WENT UNDERGROUND. NOW THAT YOU'RE ALL BACK...
THIS IS A MESS. THE EIFFEL TOWER...IT'S JUST...GONE. ATOMIZED IN THE BLINK OF AN EYE.
RICK...I THINK WE SHOULD CALL BOB. HE FOUGHT BOMB VOYAGE MORE TIMES THAN I CAN REMEMBER. HE KNOWS HIM.
NO... AND BEFORE YOU ARGUE, I'VE GOT TWO REASONS. NEITHER OF WHICH YOU'RE GOING TO LIKE.

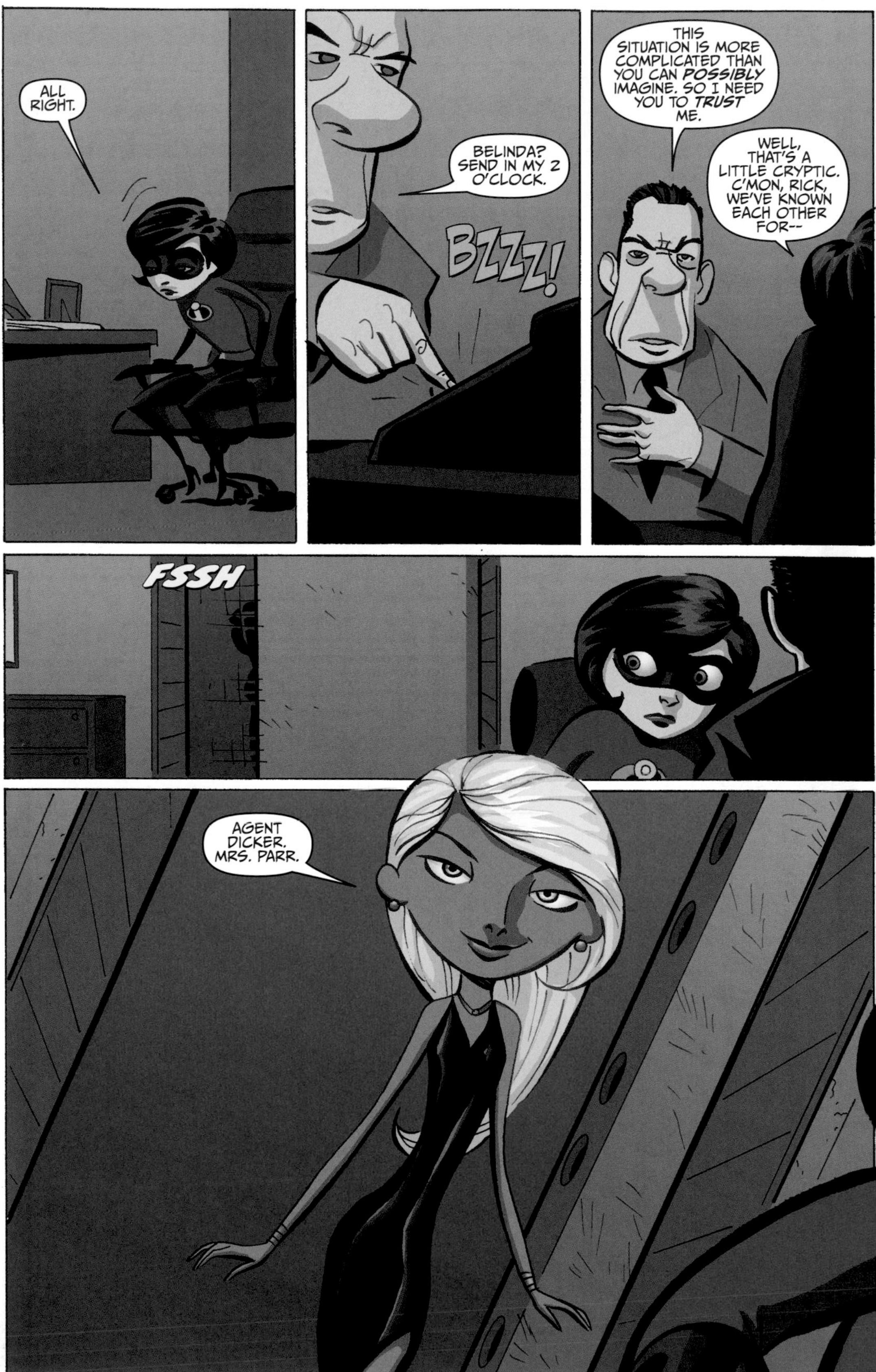
ALL RIGHT.
BELINDA? SEND IN MY 2 O'CLOCK.
BZZZ!
THIS SITUATION IS MORE COMPLICATED THAN YOU CAN POSSIBLY IMAGINE. SO I NEED YOU TO TRUST ME.
WELL, THAT'S A LITTLE CRYPTIC. C'MON, RICK, WE'VE KNOWN EACH OTHER FOR--
FSSH
AGENT DICKER. MRS. PARR.

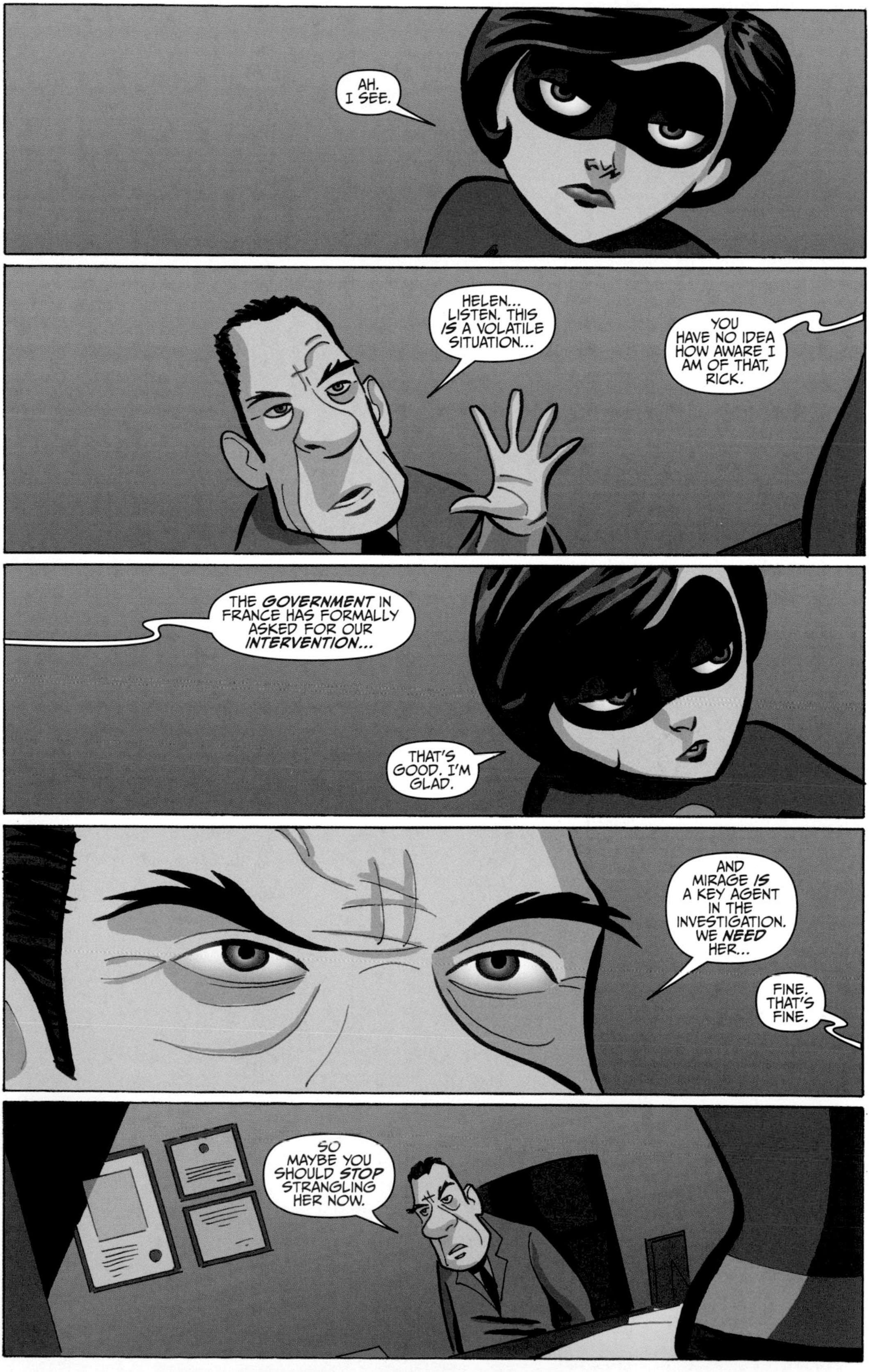
AH. I SEE.
HELEN... LISTEN. THIS *IS* A VOLATILE SITUATION...
YOU HAVE NO IDEA HOW AWARE I AM OF THAT, RICK.
THE *GOVERNMENT* IN FRANCE HAS FORMALLY ASKED FOR OUR *INTERVENTION*...
THAT'S GOOD. I'M GLAD.
AND MIRAGE *IS* A KEY AGENT IN THE INVESTIGATION. WE *NEED* HER...
FINE. THAT'S FINE.
SO MAYBE YOU SHOULD *STOP* STRANGLING HER NOW.

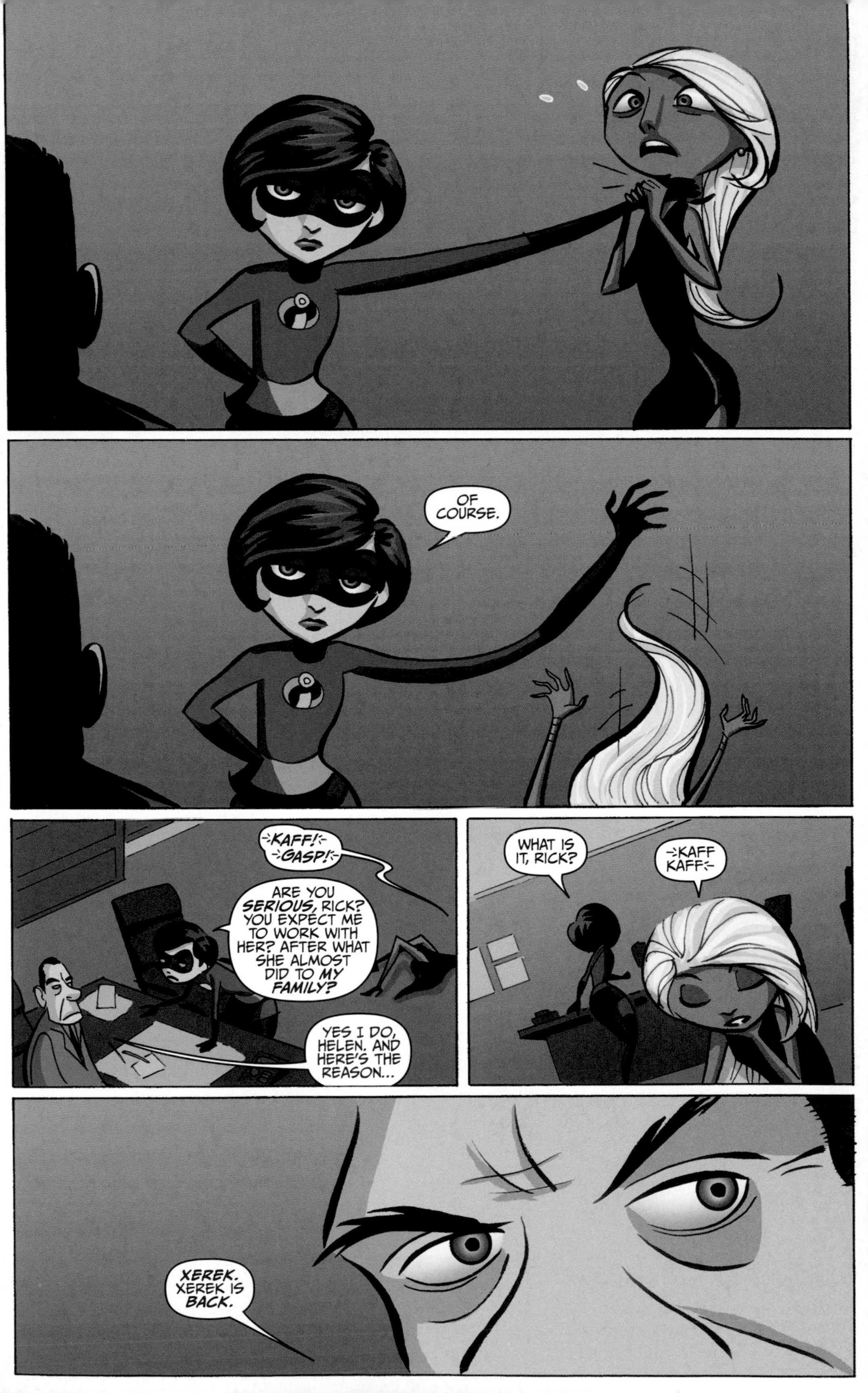
OF COURSE.
-KAFF!- -GASP!-
ARE YOU SERIOUS, RICK? YOU EXPECT ME TO WORK WITH HER? AFTER WHAT SHE ALMOST DID TO MY FAMILY?
YES I DO, HELEN. AND HERE'S THE REASON...
WHAT IS IT, RICK?
-KAFF KAFF-
XEREK. XEREK IS BACK.

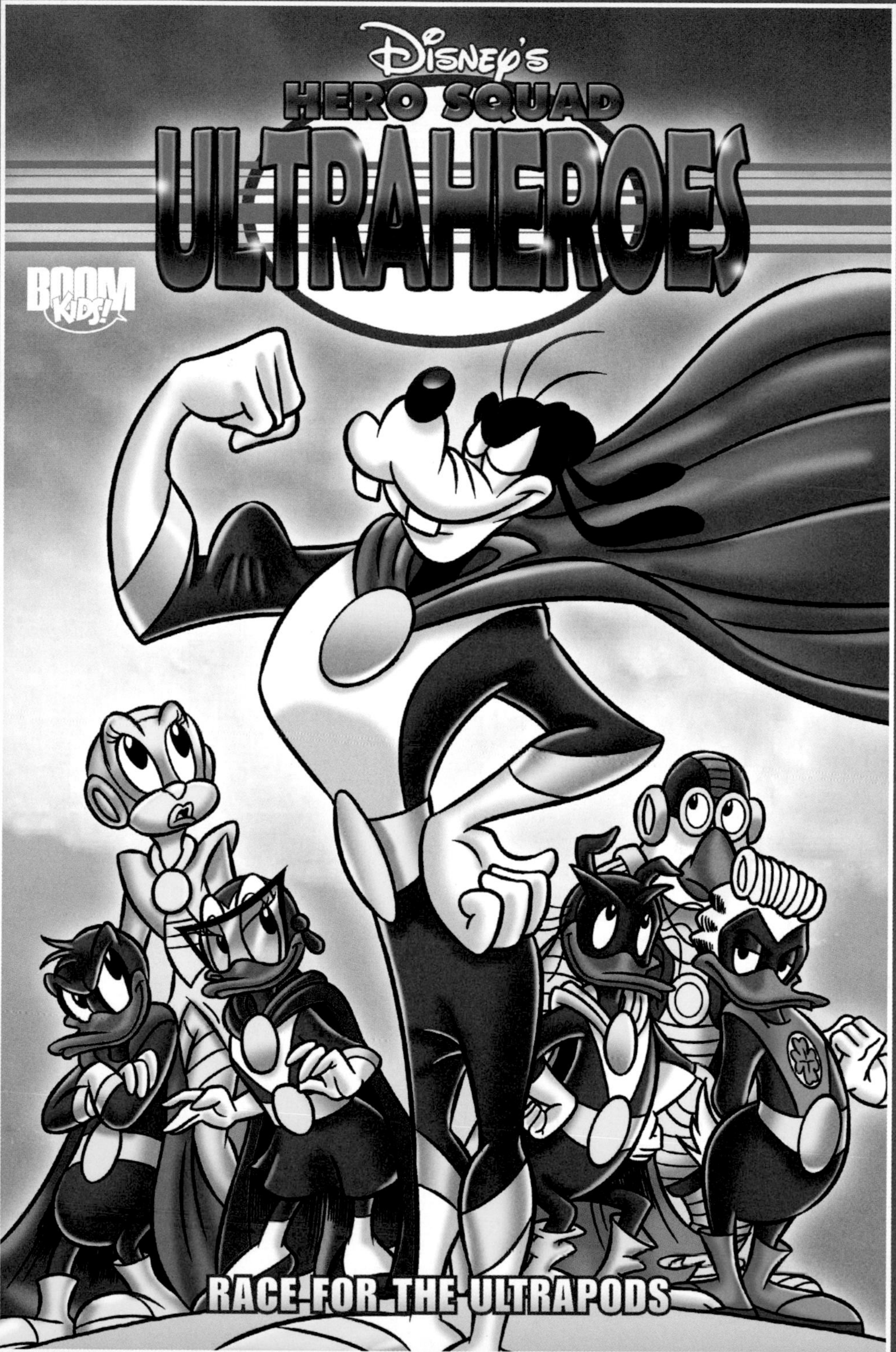
DISNEY'S
HERO SQUAD
ULTRAHEROES
BOOM KIDS!
RACE FOR THE ULTRAPODS

The greatest team of Disney super-heroes ever assembled combats Emil Eagle and the Sinister 7! It's a tremendous tug-of-war for control over the earth-shattering Ultramachine!

DISNEY'S HERO SQUAD: ULTRAHEROES VOL. 2:
RACE FOR THE ULTRAPODS
DIAMOND CODE: MAR100809
SC $9.99 ISBN 9781608865604

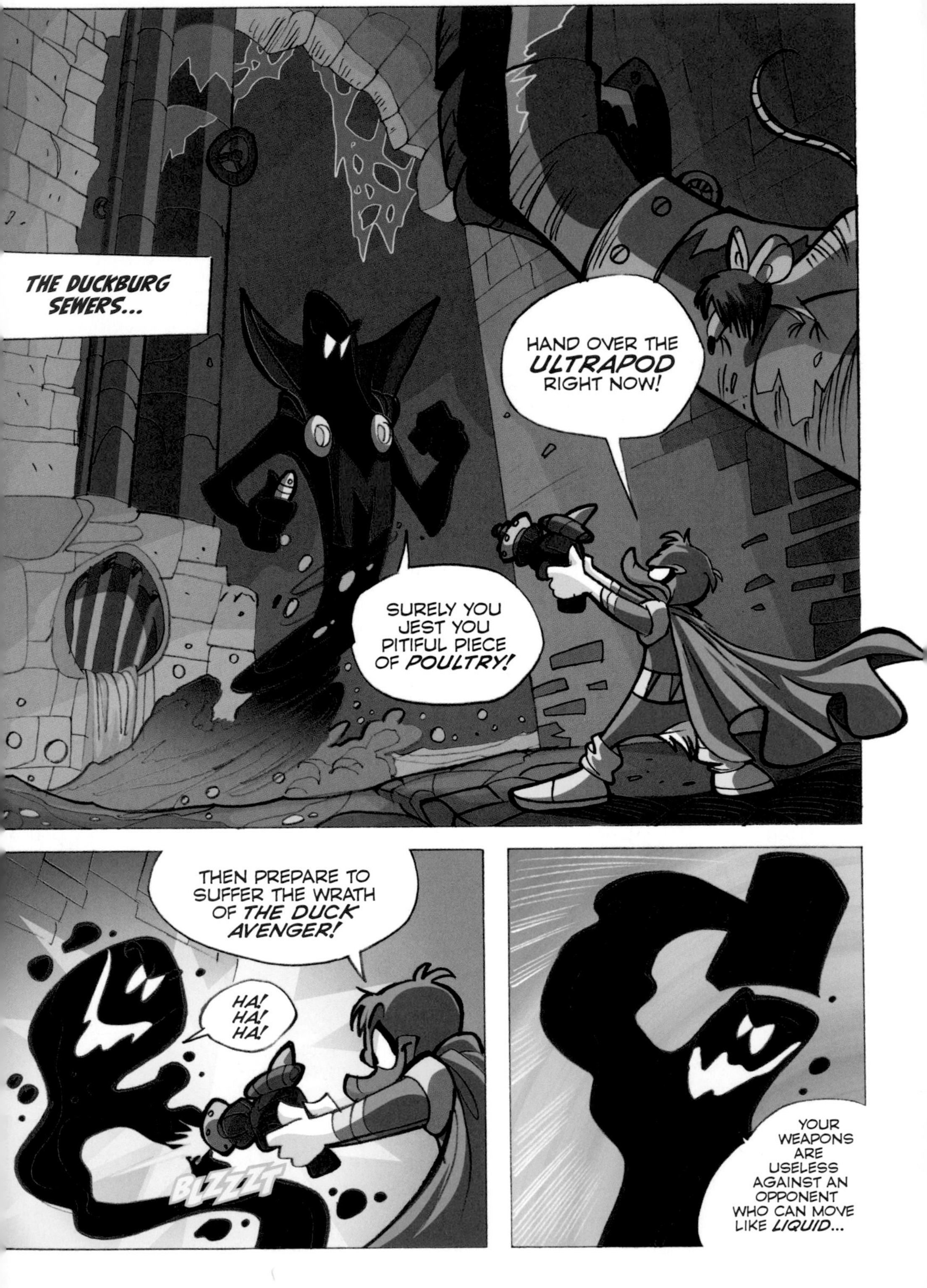
THE DUCKBURG SEWERS...
HAND OVER THE ULTRAPOD RIGHT NOW!
SURELY YOU JEST YOU PITIFUL PIECE OF POULTRY!
THEN PREPARE TO SUFFER THE WRATH OF THE DUCK AVENGER!
HA! HA! HA!
BLZZZT
YOUR WEAPONS ARE USELESS AGAINST AN OPPONENT WHO CAN MOVE LIKE LIQUID...

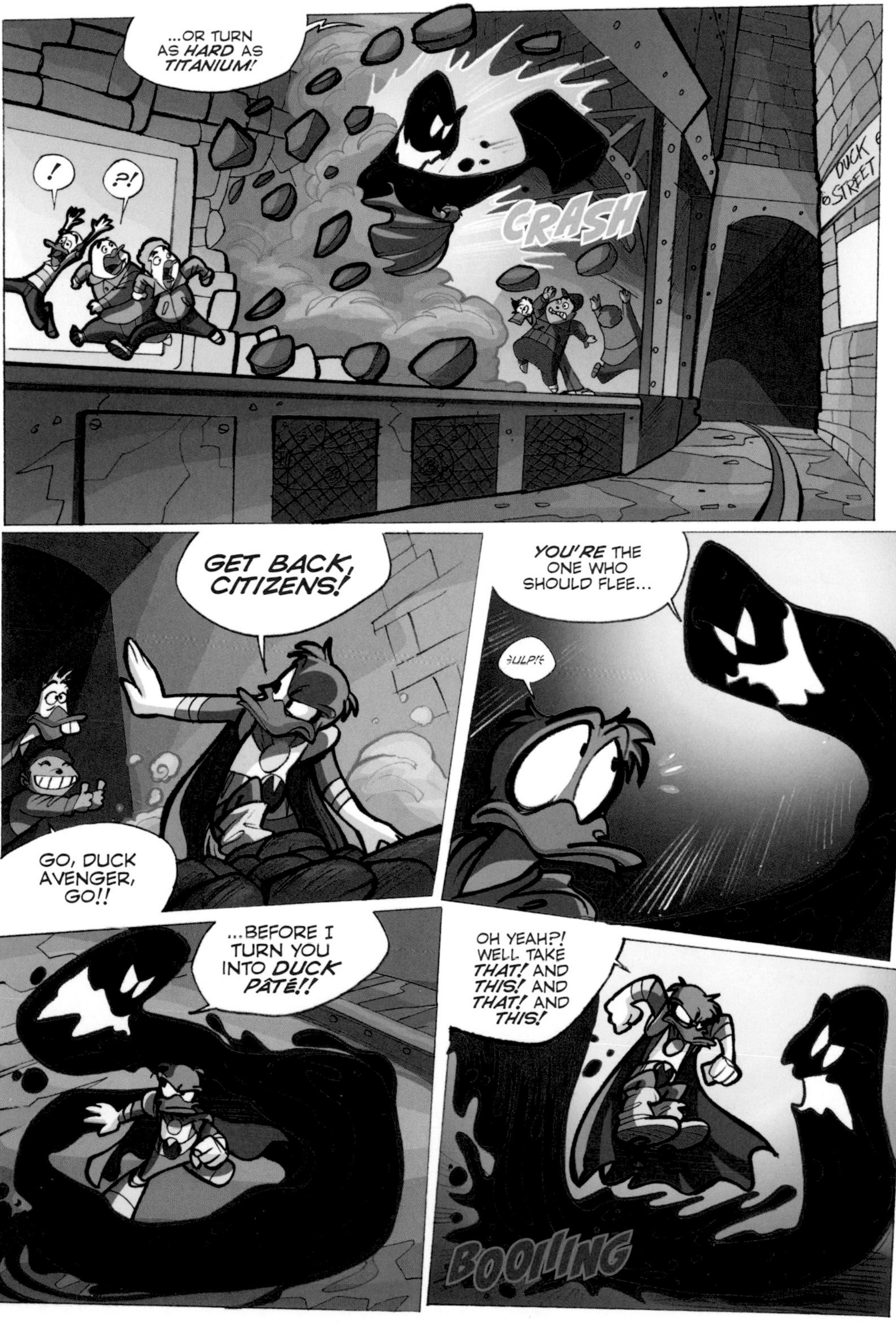
...OR TURN AS HARD AS TITANIUM!
!
?!
CRASH
DUCK STREET
GET BACK, CITIZENS!
GO, DUCK AVENGER, GO!!
YOU'RE THE ONE WHO SHOULD FLEE...
GULP!
...BEFORE I TURN YOU INTO DUCK PÂTÉ!!
OH YEAH?! WELL TAKE THAT! AND THIS! AND THAT! AND THIS!
BOOIING

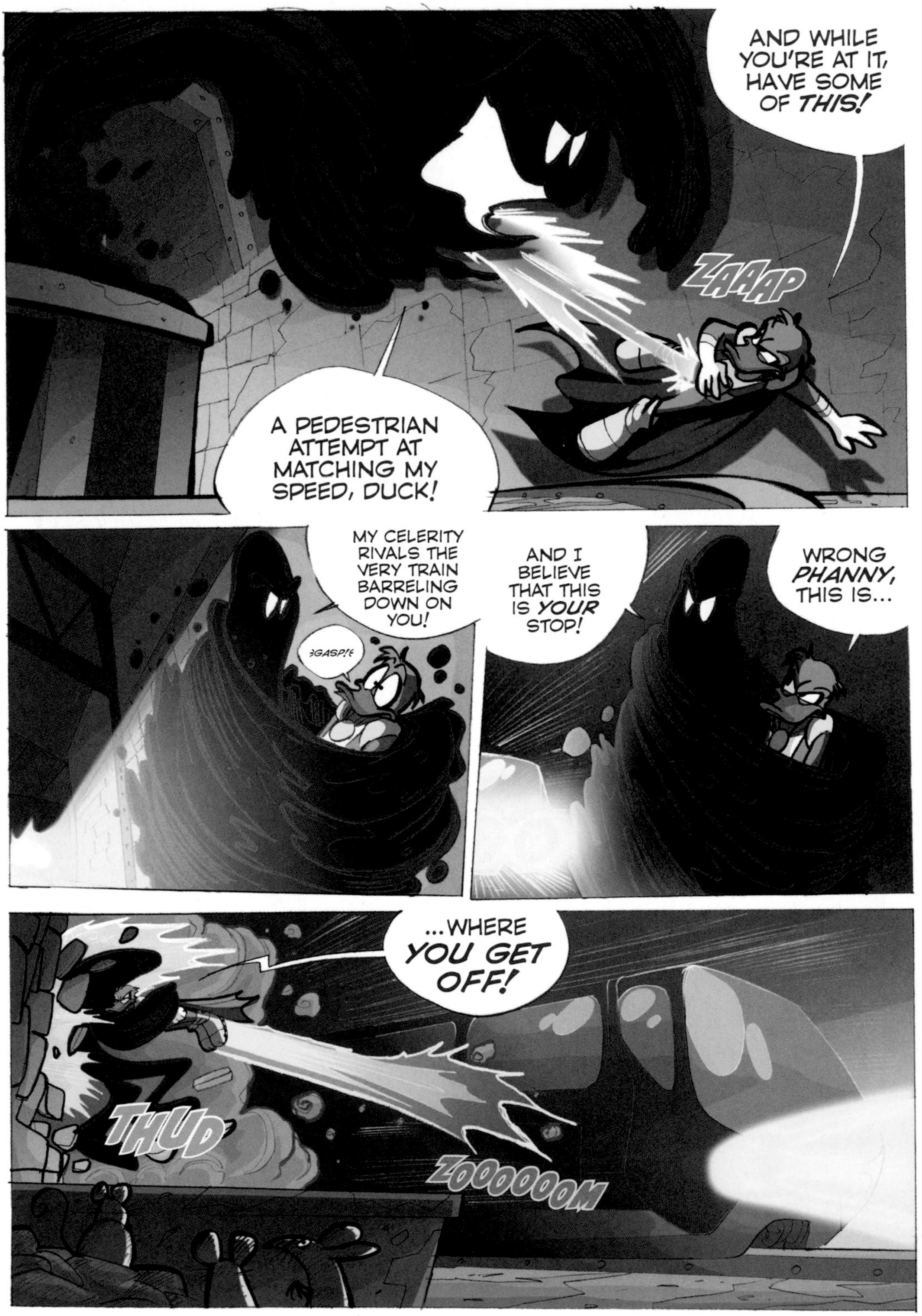
AND WHILE YOU'RE AT IT, HAVE SOME OF *THIS!*
ZAAAP
A PEDESTRIAN ATTEMPT AT MATCHING MY SPEED, DUCK!
MY CELERITY RIVALS THE VERY TRAIN BARRELING DOWN ON YOU!
GASP!
AND I BELIEVE THAT THIS IS *YOUR* STOP!
WRONG *PHANNY,* THIS IS...
...WHERE *YOU GET OFF!*
THUD
ZOOOOOOM

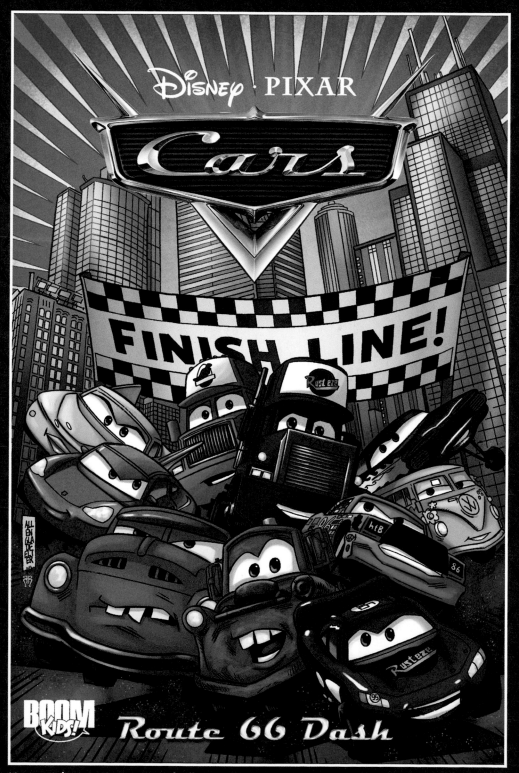

DISNEY · PIXAR

Cars

FINISH LINE!

BOOM KIDS!

Route 66 Dash

Mater, Lightning McQueen and all your CARS pals take to the interstate for a pair-on-pair racing adventure! Who will be the first to downtown Chi-Car-Go? It's anyone's race!

CARS: ROUTE 66 DASH
DIAMOND CODE: MAY100871
SC $9.99 ISBN 9781608865857

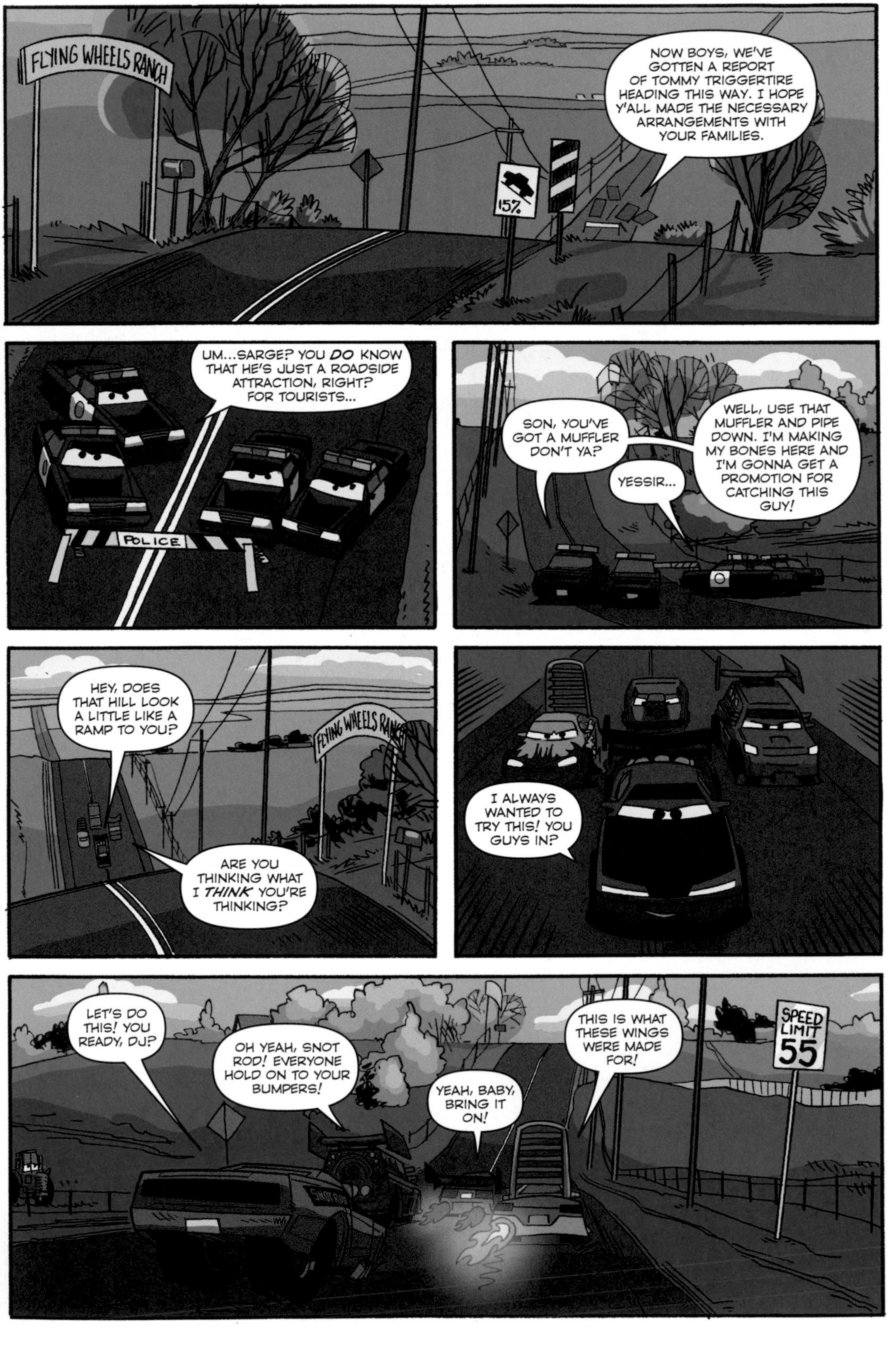
FLYING WHEELS RANCH
15%
NOW BOYS, WE'VE GOTTEN A REPORT OF TOMMY TRIGGERTIRE HEADING THIS WAY. I HOPE Y'ALL MADE THE NECESSARY ARRANGEMENTS WITH YOUR FAMILIES.
UM...SARGE? YOU DO KNOW THAT HE'S JUST A ROADSIDE ATTRACTION, RIGHT? FOR TOURISTS...
POLICE
SON, YOU'VE GOT A MUFFLER DON'T YA?
YESSIR...
WELL, USE THAT MUFFLER AND PIPE DOWN. I'M MAKING MY BONES HERE AND I'M GONNA GET A PROMOTION FOR CATCHING THIS GUY!
HEY, DOES THAT HILL LOOK A LITTLE LIKE A RAMP TO YOU?
FLYING WHEELS RANCH
ARE YOU THINKING WHAT I THINK YOU'RE THINKING?
I ALWAYS WANTED TO TRY THIS! YOU GUYS IN?
LET'S DO THIS! YOU READY, DJ?
OH YEAH, SNOT ROD! EVERYONE HOLD ON TO YOUR BUMPERS!
YEAH, BABY, BRING IT ON!
THIS IS WHAT THESE WINGS WERE MADE FOR!
SPEED LIMIT 55

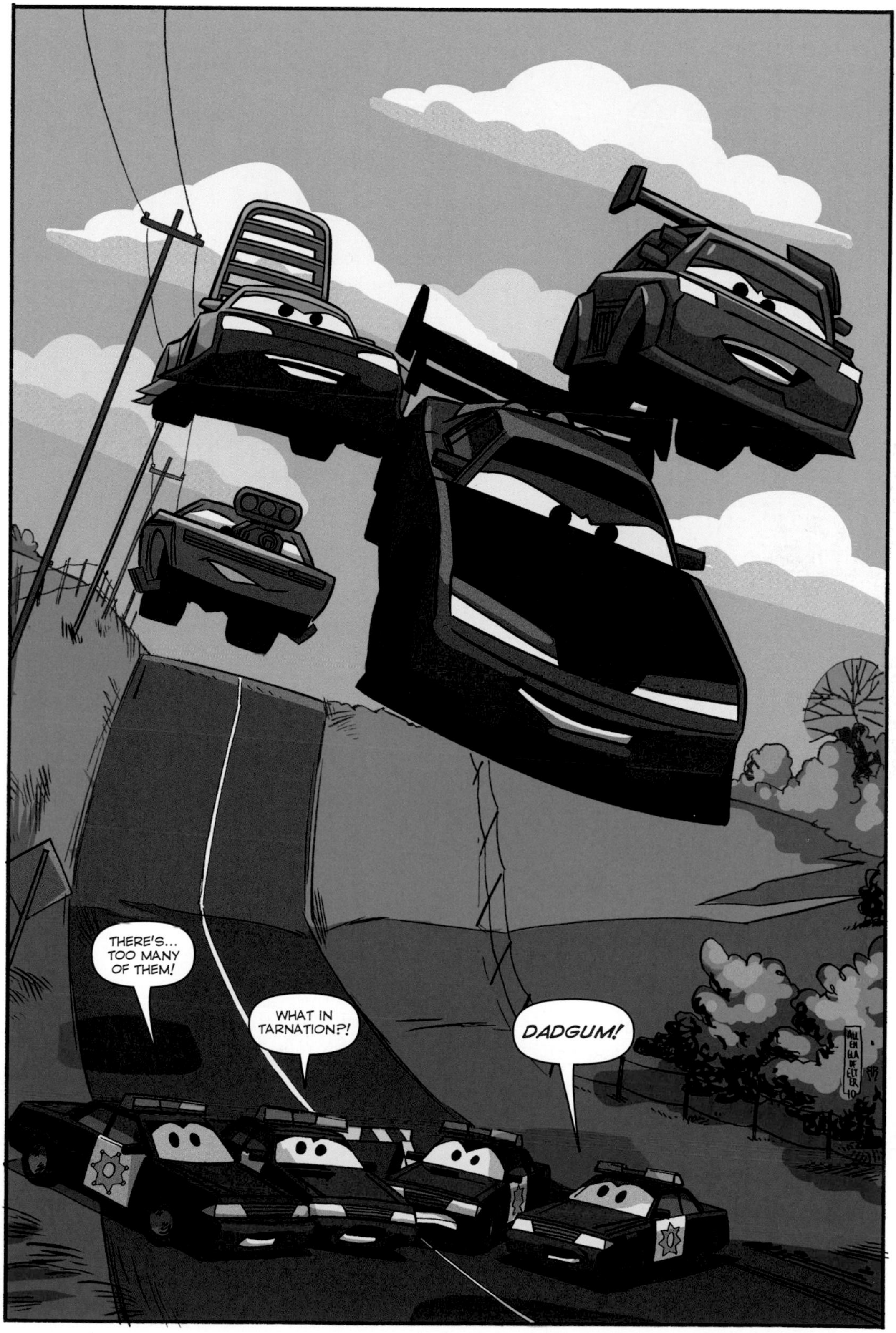
THERE'S... TOO MANY OF THEM!
WHAT IN TARNATION?!
DADGUM!

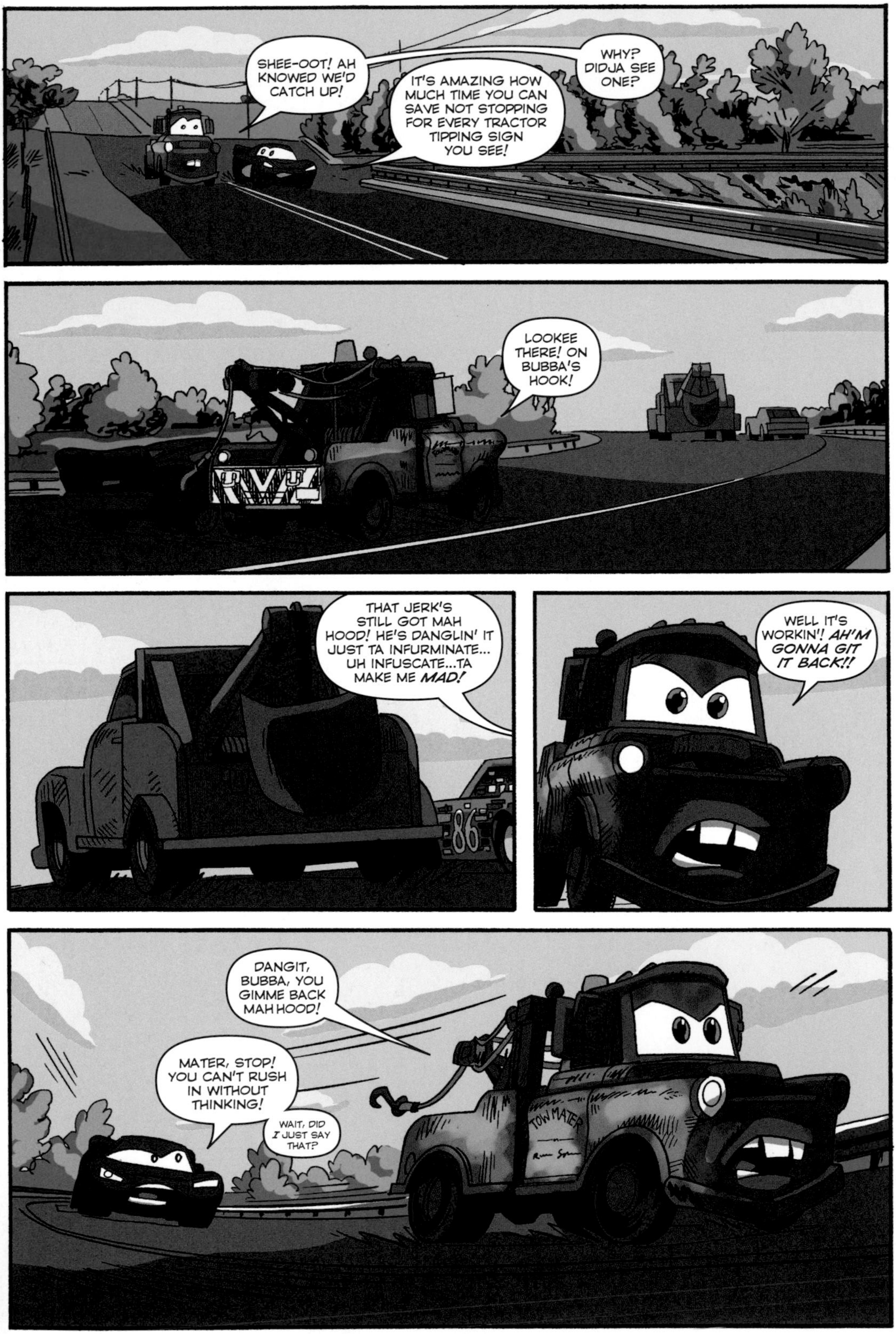
SHEE-OOT! AH KNOWED WE'D CATCH UP!
IT'S AMAZING HOW MUCH TIME YOU CAN SAVE NOT STOPPING FOR EVERY TRACTOR TIPPING SIGN YOU SEE!
WHY? DIDJA SEE ONE?
LOOKEE THERE! ON BUBBA'S HOOK!
THAT JERK'S STILL GOT MAH HOOD! HE'S DANGLIN' IT JUST TA INFURMINATE... UH INFUSCATE...TA MAKE ME MAD!
86
WELL IT'S WORKIN'! AH'M GONNA GIT IT BACK!!
DANGIT, BUBBA, YOU GIMME BACK MAH HOOD!
MATER, STOP! YOU CAN'T RUSH IN WITHOUT THINKING!
WAIT, DID I JUST SAY THAT?
TOW MATER

When their ship sinks in a storm, Mickey Mouse, Minnie, Goofy and the gang find themselves marooned on the mysterious Quandomai Island, where dinosaurs still roam the earth, and nothing is as it seems!

MICKEY MOUSE ON QUANDOMAI ISLAND
DIAMOND CODE: SEP100907
SC $9.99 ISBN 9781608865994

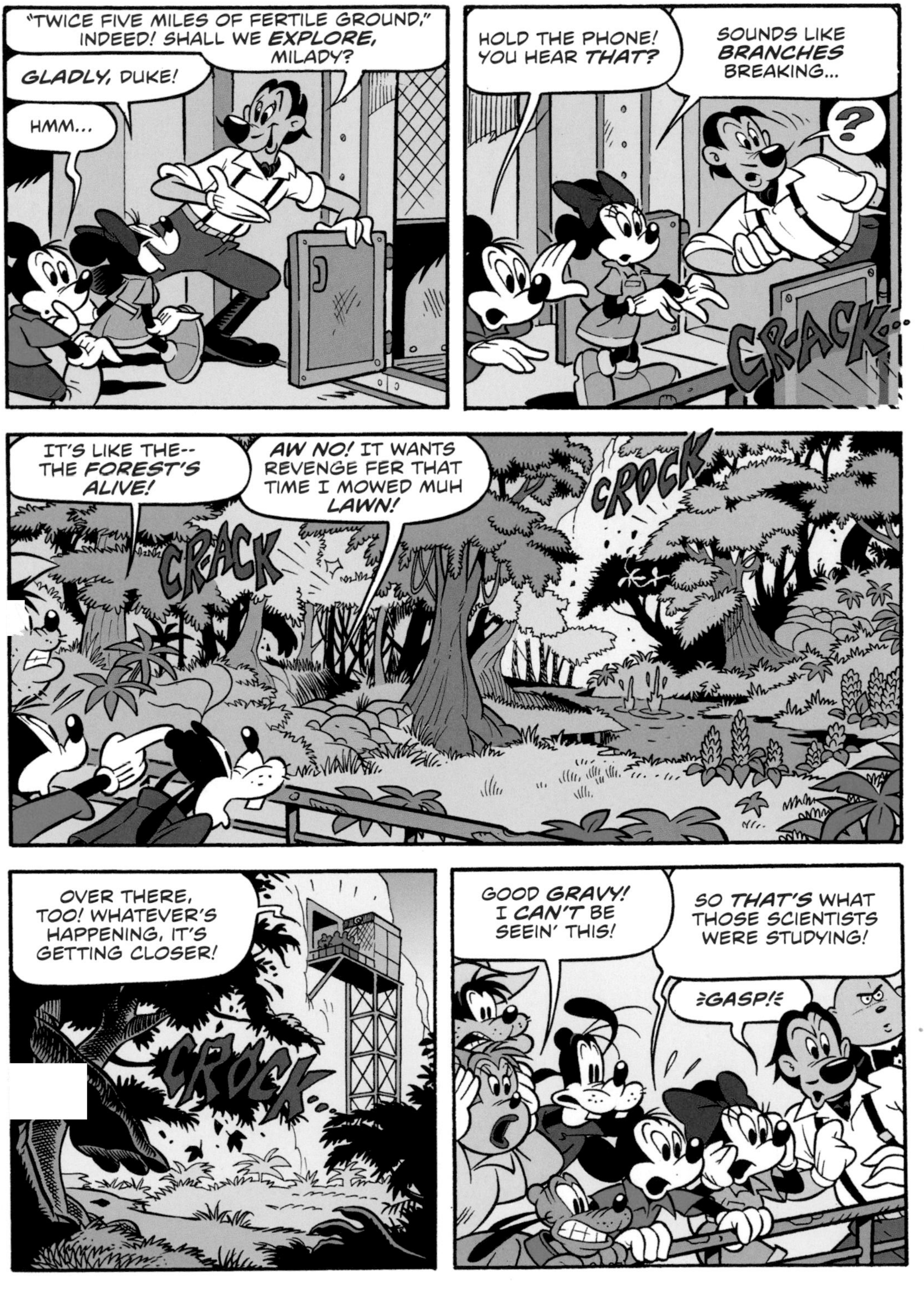

"TWICE FIVE MILES OF FERTILE GROUND," INDEED! SHALL WE EXPLORE, MILADY?
GLADLY, DUKE!
HMM...
HOLD THE PHONE! YOU HEAR THAT?
SOUNDS LIKE BRANCHES BREAKING...
?
CR-ACK...
IT'S LIKE THE-- THE FOREST'S ALIVE!
AW NO! IT WANTS REVENGE FER THAT TIME I MOWED MUH LAWN!
CR-ACK
CROCK
OVER THERE, TOO! WHATEVER'S HAPPENING, IT'S GETTING CLOSER!
CROCK...
GOOD GRAVY! I CAN'T BE SEEIN' THIS!
SO THAT'S WHAT THOSE SCIENTISTS WERE STUDYING!
GASP!

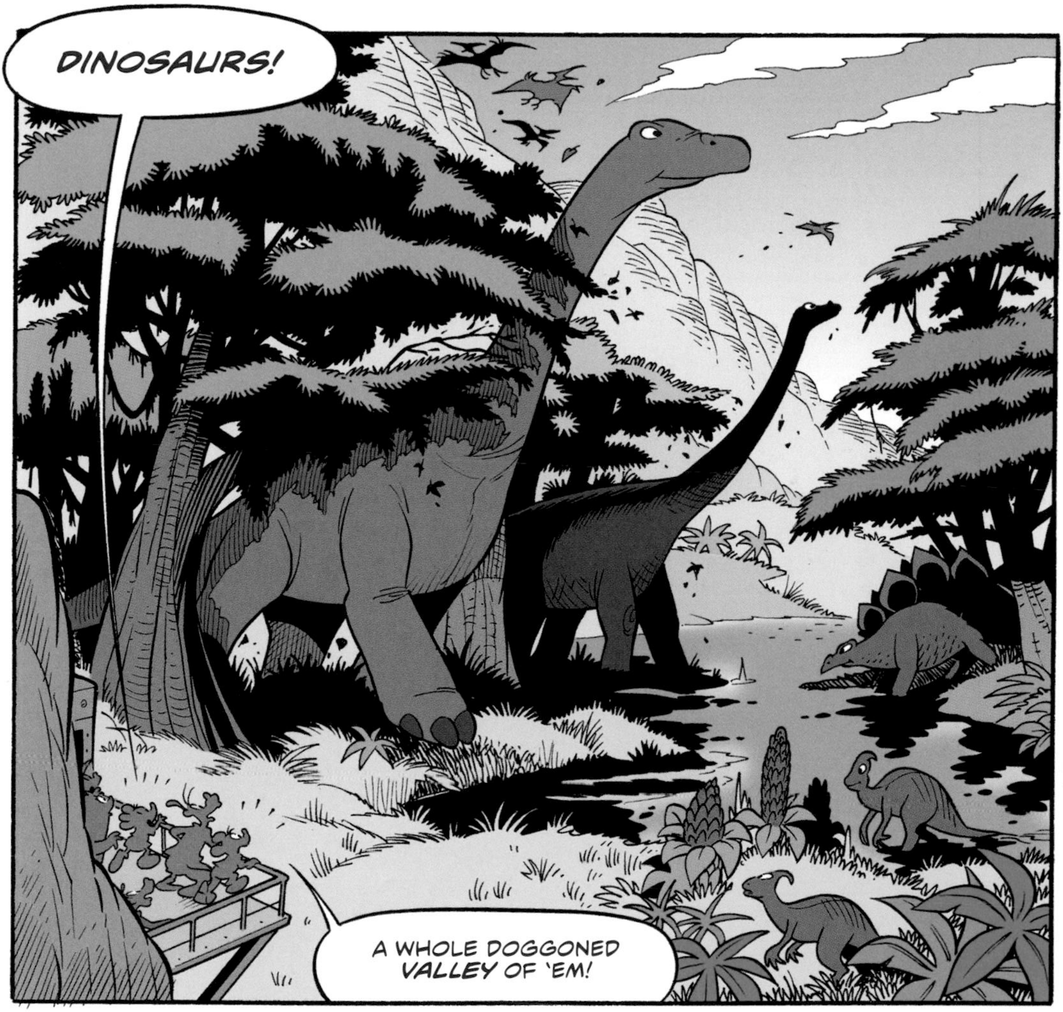
DINOSAURS!
A WHOLE DOGGONED VALLEY OF 'EM!

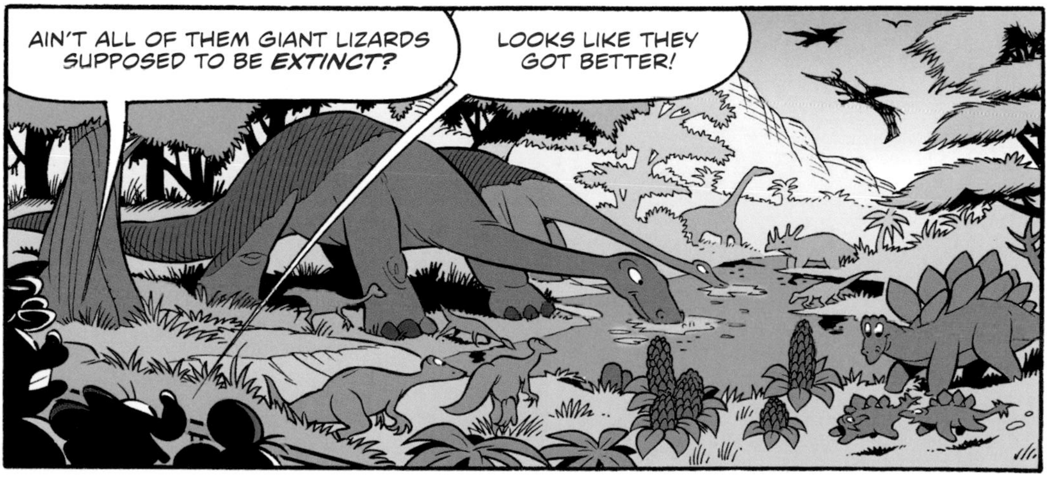
AIN'T ALL OF THEM GIANT LIZARDS SUPPOSED TO BE EXTINCT?
LOOKS LIKE THEY GOT BETTER!

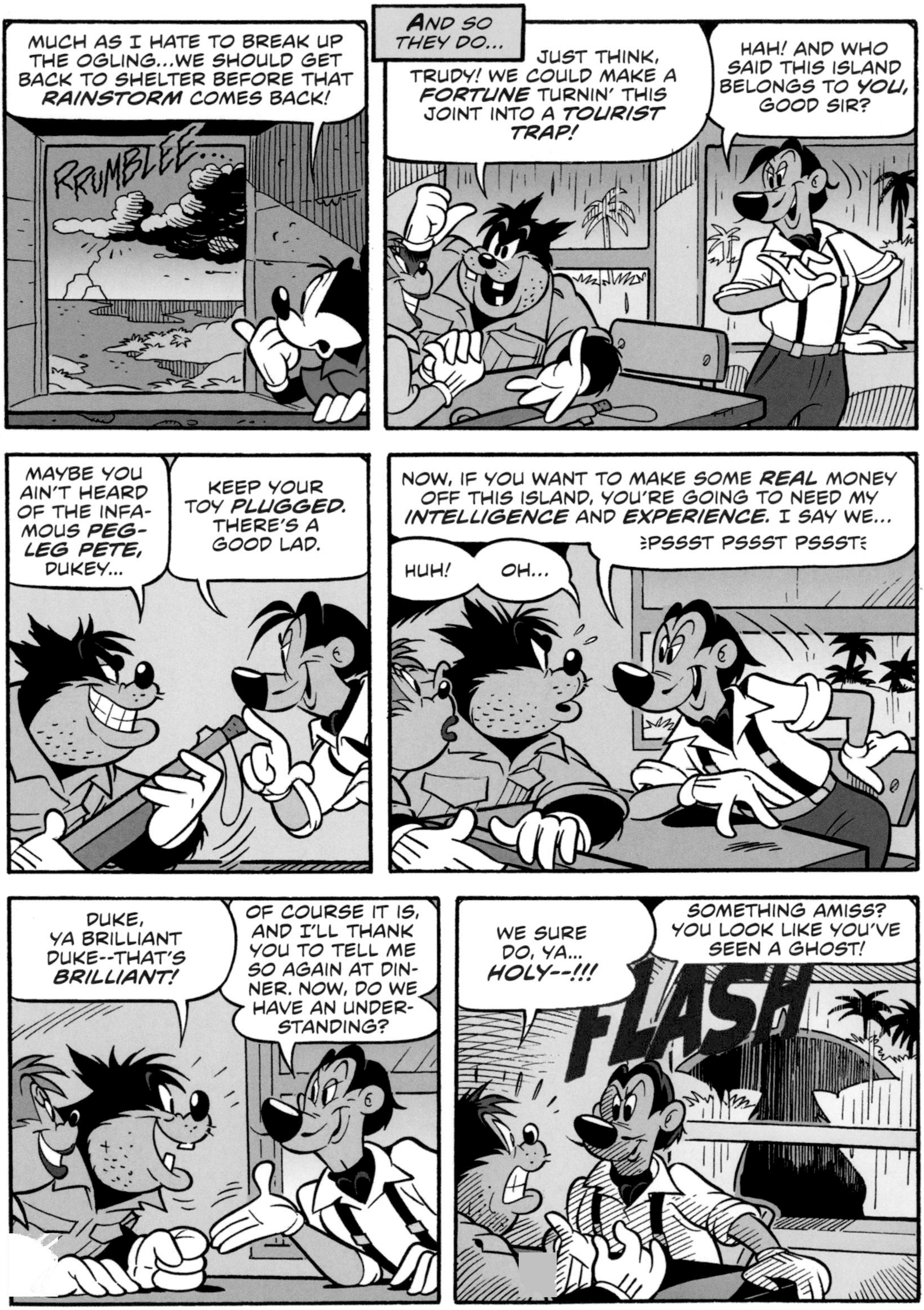
MUCH AS I HATE TO BREAK UP THE OGLING...WE SHOULD GET BACK TO SHELTER BEFORE THAT RAINSTORM COMES BACK!
RRUMBLEE...
AND SO THEY DO...
JUST THINK, TRUDY! WE COULD MAKE A FORTUNE TURNIN' THIS JOINT INTO A TOURIST TRAP!
HAH! AND WHO SAID THIS ISLAND BELONGS TO YOU, GOOD SIR?
MAYBE YOU AIN'T HEARD OF THE INFAMOUS PEG-LEG PETE, DUKEY...
KEEP YOUR TOY PLUGGED. THERE'S A GOOD LAD.
NOW, IF YOU WANT TO MAKE SOME REAL MONEY OFF THIS ISLAND, YOU'RE GOING TO NEED MY INTELLIGENCE AND EXPERIENCE. I SAY WE...
PSSST PSSST PSSST
HUH!
OH...
DUKE, YA BRILLIANT DUKE--THAT'S BRILLIANT!
OF COURSE IT IS, AND I'LL THANK YOU TO TELL ME SO AGAIN AT DINNER. NOW, DO WE HAVE AN UNDERSTANDING?
WE SURE DO, YA... HOLY--!!!
SOMETHING AMISS? YOU LOOK LIKE YOU'VE SEEN A GHOST!
FLASH

GRAPHIC NOVELS AVAILABLE NOW!

BOOM KIDS!

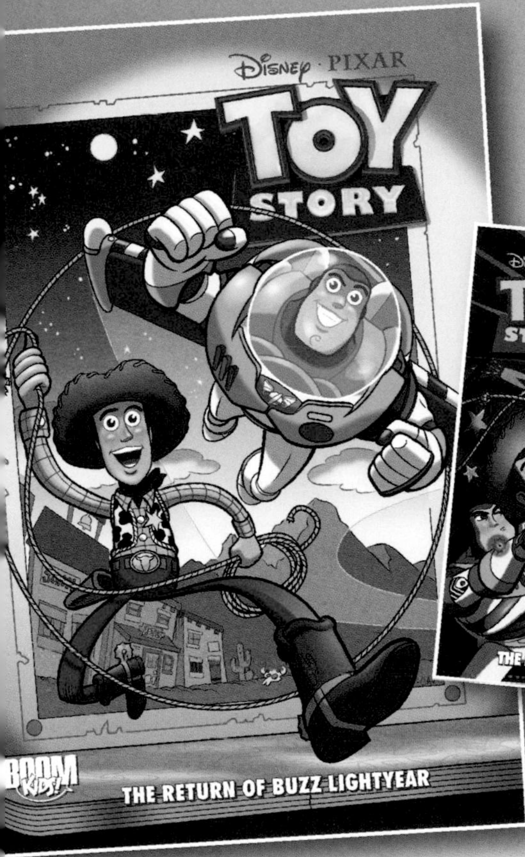

DISNEY · PIXAR
TOY STORY
BOOM KIDS!
THE RETURN OF BUZZ LIGHTYEAR

TOY STORY: THE RETURN OF BUZZ LIGHTYEAR

When Andy is given a surprise gift, no one is more surprised than the toys in his room...it's a second Buzz Lightyear! The stage is set for a Star Command showdown when only one Buzz can stay!

SC $9.99 ISBN 9781608865574
HC $24.99 ISBN 9781608865581

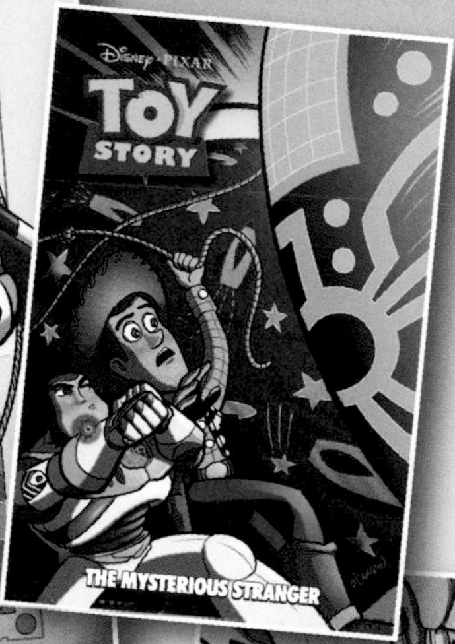

DISNEY · PIXAR
TOY STORY
THE MYSTERIOUS STRANGER

TOY STORY: THE MYSTERIOUS STRANGER

Andy has a new addition to his room—a circuit-laden egg. Is this new gizmo a friend or foe? This adventure kicks off the first of four self-contained stories featuring all your favorite characters from the TOY STORY movies – Woody, Buzz and the gang!

SC $9.99 ISBN 9781934506912
HC $24.99 ISBN 9781608865239

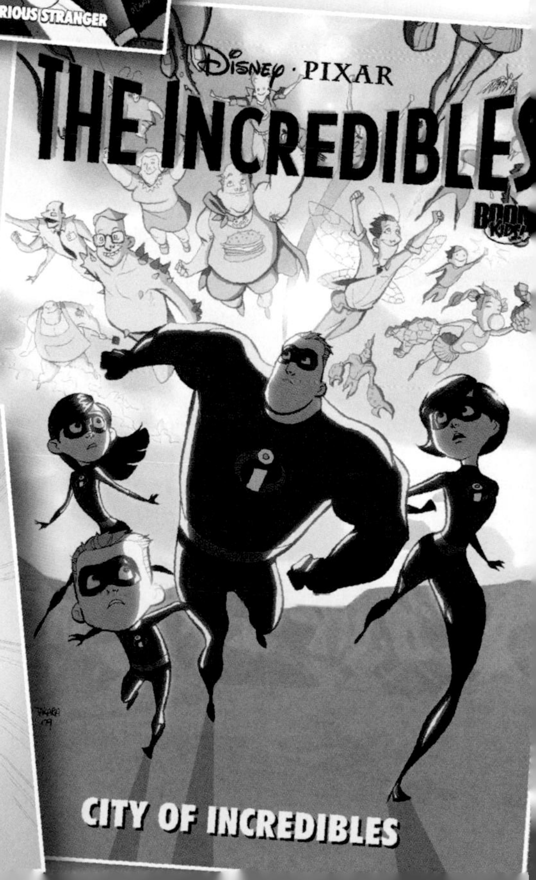

DISNEY · PIXAR
THE INCREDIBLES
BOOM KIDS!
CITY OF INCREDIBLES

THE INCREDIBLES: CITY OF INCREDIBLES

Baby Jack-Jack, everyone's favorite super-powered toddler, battles...a nasty cold! Hopefully the rest of the Parr family can stay healthy, because the henchmen of super villains are rapidly starting to exhibit superpowers!

SC $9.99 ISBN 9781608865031
HC $24.99 ISBN 9781608865291

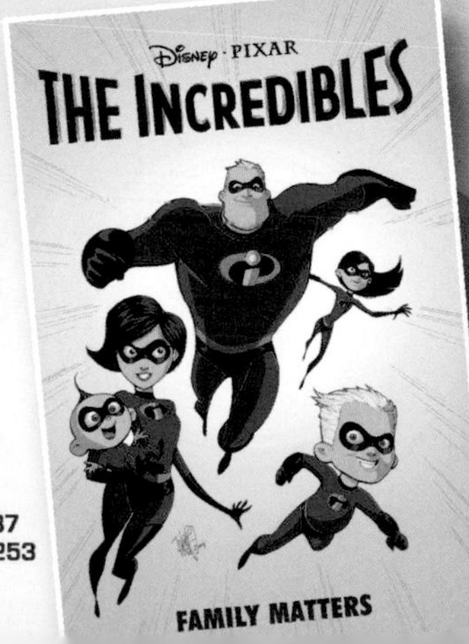

DISNEY · PIXAR
THE INCREDIBLES
FAMILY MATTERS

THE INCREDIBLES: FAMILY MATTERS

Acclaimed scribe Mark Waid has written the perfect INCREDIBLES story! What happens when Mr. Incredible's super-abilities start to wane...and how long can he keep his powerlessness a secret from his wife and kids?

SC $9.99 ISBN 9781934506837
HC $24.99 ISBN 9781608865253

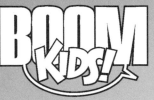

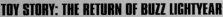

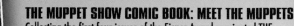

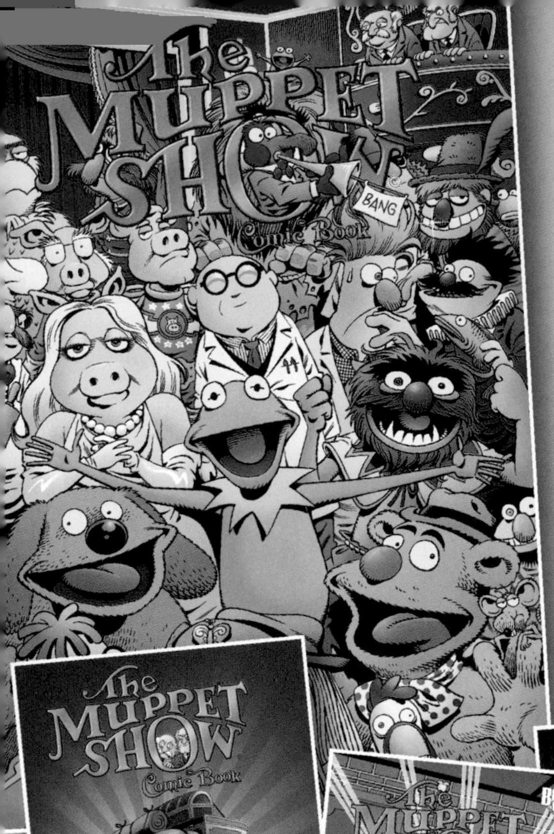
The Muppet Show
Comic Book
BANG

THE MUPPET SHOW COMIC BOOK: MEET THE MUPPETS

Collecting the first four issues of the Eisner Award-nominated THE MUPPET SHOW COMIC BOOK, written and drawn by the incomparable Roger Langridge! Packed full of madcap skits and gags, this trade is certain to please old and new fans alike!

SC $9.99 ISBN 9781934506851
HC $24.99 ISBN 9781608865277

THE MUPPET SHOW COMIC BOOK: THE TREASURE OF PEG-LEG WILSON

Scooter discovers old documents which reveal that a cache of treasure is hidden somewhere within the Muppet Theater...and when Rizzo the Rat overhears this, the news spreads like wildfire! Can Kermit keep everyone from tearing the theater apart?

SC $9.99 ISBN 9781608865048
HC $24.99 ISBN 9781608865307

THE MUPPET SHOW COMIC BOOK: ON THE ROAD

With the Muppet Theater destroyed, the Muppets take their act on the road...but with two very familiar hecklers in every town, will the show be a hit, or will our Muppet minstrels be run out of town in tar and feathers? Also: PIGS IN SPACE!

SC $9.99 ISBN 9781608865161

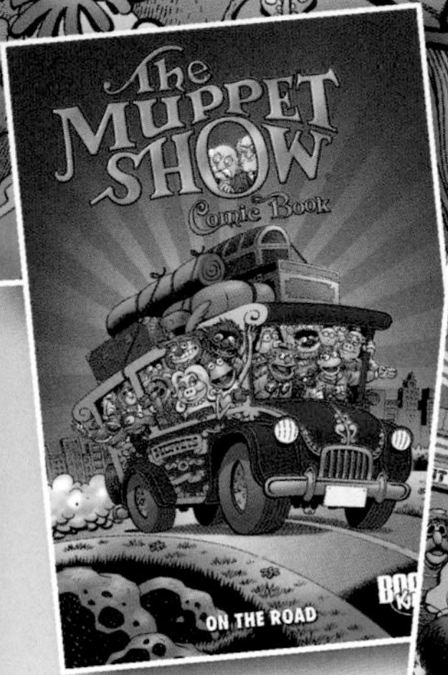
The Muppet Show
Comic Book
ON THE ROAD

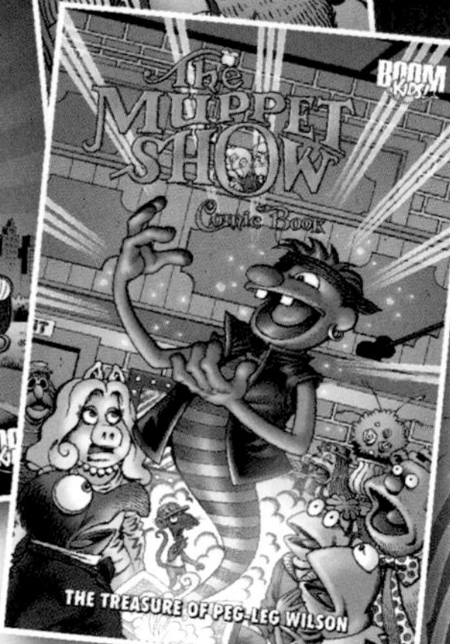
The Muppet Show
Comic Book
BOOM! KIDS!
THE TREASURE OF PEG-LEG WILSON

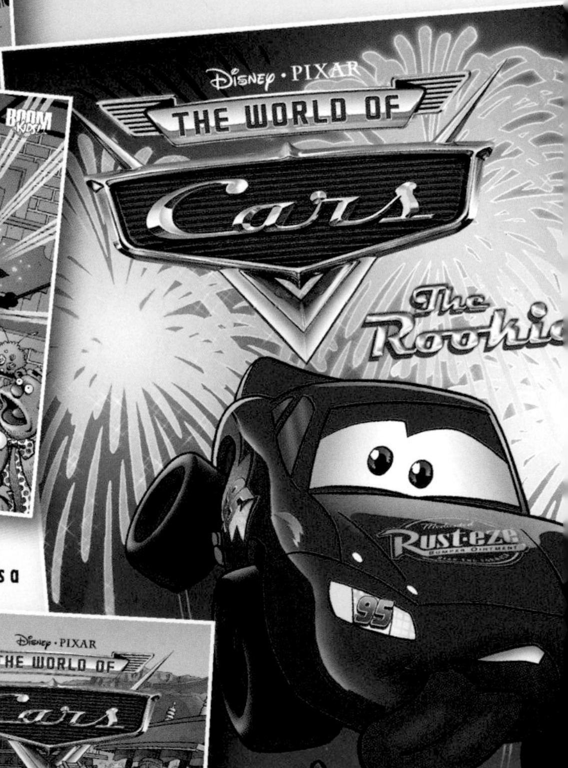
Disney · PIXAR
THE WORLD OF
Cars
The Rookie
Rust-eze
95

CARS: THE ROOKIE

See how Lightning McQueen became a Piston Cup sensation! CARS: THE ROOKIE reveals Lightning McQueen's scrappy origins as a local short track racer who dreams of the big time... and recklessly plows his way through the competition to get there!

SC $9.99 ISBN 9781934506844
HC $24.99 ISBN 9781608865222

CARS: RADIATOR SPRINGS

Lightning McQueen is hanging out with his friends at Flo's V8 Café when he realizes that everyone knows his story...but he doesn't know anyone else's! Lightning wants to know how his friends ended up in Radiator Springs...and more importantly, why they decided to stay!

SC $9.99 ISBN 9781608865024
HC $24.99 ISBN 9781608865284

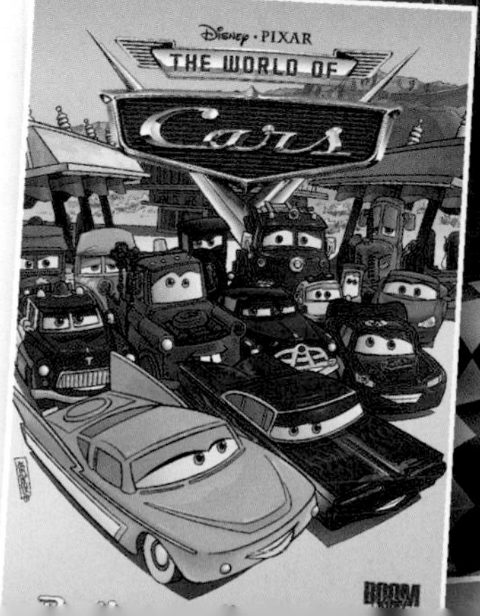
Disney · PIXAR
THE WORLD OF
Cars

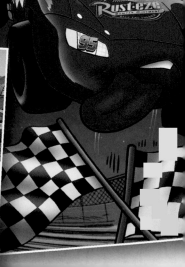

WALL•E: RECHARGE

Before WALL•E becomes the hardworking robot we know and love, he lets the few remaining robots take care of the trash compacting while he collects interesting junk. But when these robots start breaking down, WALL•E must adjust his priorities...or else Earth is doomed!

SC $9.99 ISBN 9781608865123
HC $24.99 ISBN 9781608865543

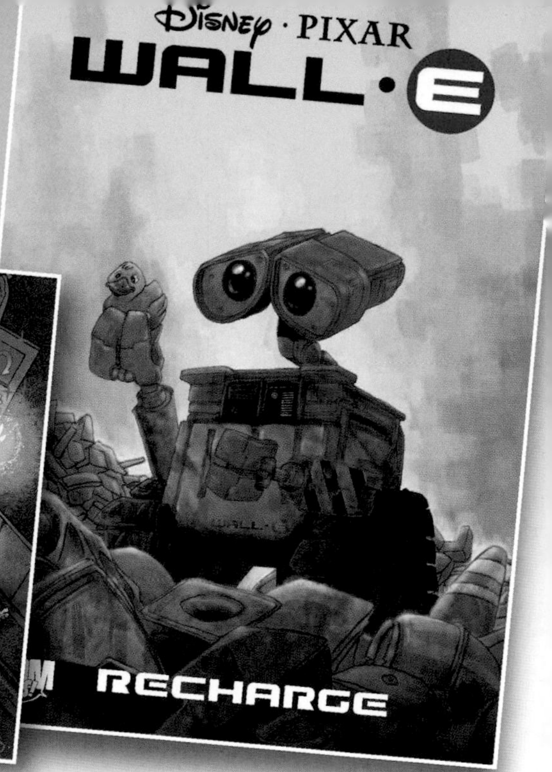

DISNEY · PIXAR
WALL·E
RECHARGE

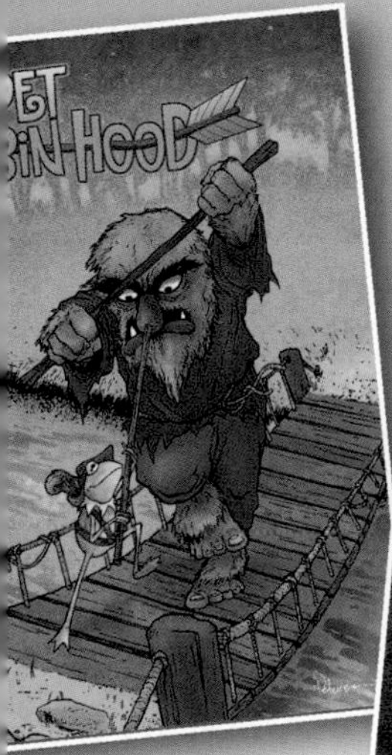

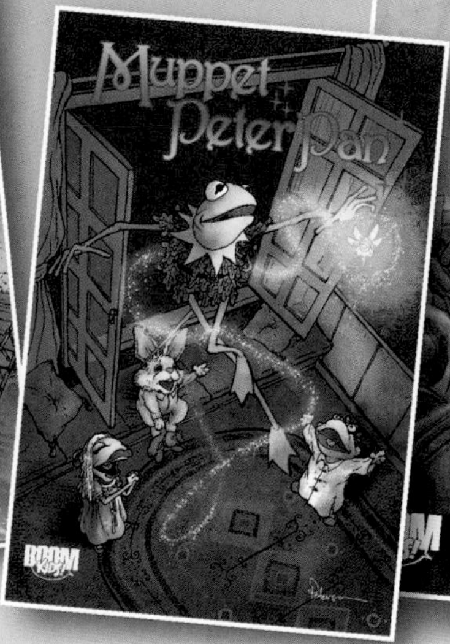

Muppet Peter Pan

MUPPET ROBIN HOOD

The Muppets tell the Robin Hood legend for laughs, and it's the reader who will be merry! Robin Hood (Kermit the Frog) joins with the Merry Men, Sherwood Forest's infamous gang of misfit outlaws, to take on the Sheriff of Nottingham (Sam the Eagle)!

SC $9.99 ISBN 9781934506790
HC $24.99 ISBN 9781608865260

MUPPET PETER PAN

When Peter Pan (Kermit) whisks Wendy (Janice) and her brothers to Neverswamp, the adventure begins! With Captain Hook (Gonzo) out for revenge for the loss of his hand, can even the magic of Piggytink (Miss Piggy) save Wendy and her brothers?

SC $9.99 ISBN 9781608865079
HC $24.99 ISBN 9781608865314

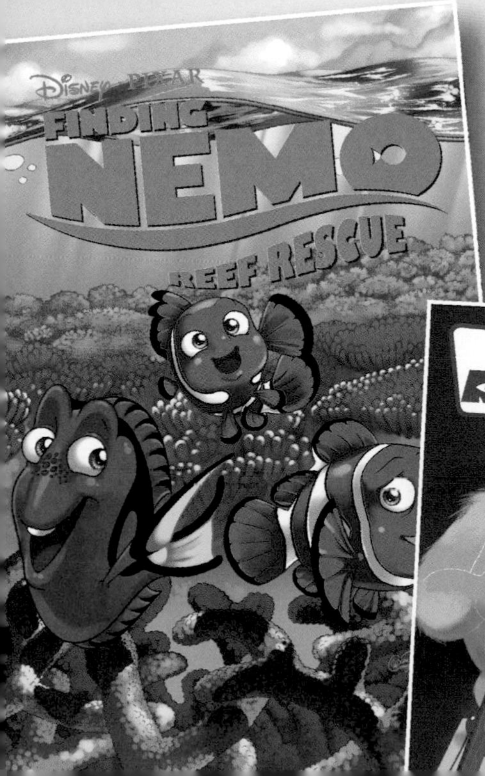

FINDING NEMO
REEF RESCUE

FINDING NEMO: REEF RESCUE

Nemo, Dory and Marlin have become local heroes, and are recruited to embark on an all-new adventure in this exciting collection! The reef is mysteriously dying and no one knows why. So Nemo and his friends must travel the great blue sea to save their home!

SC $9.99 ISBN 9781934506882
HC $24.99 ISBN 9781608865246

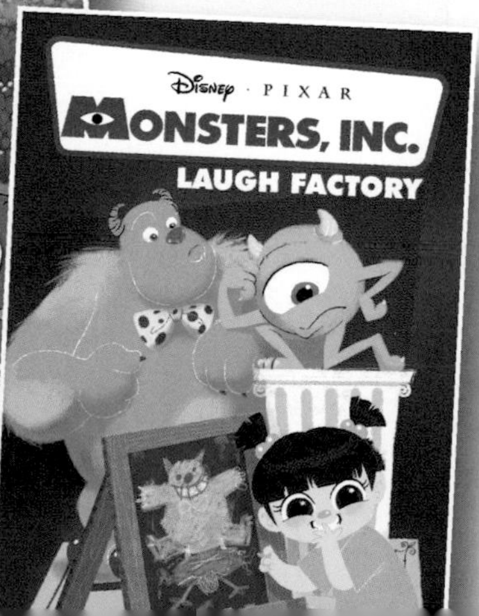

DISNEY · PIXAR
MONSTERS, INC.
LAUGH FACTORY

MONSTERS, INC.: LAUGH FACTORY

Someone is stealing comedy props from the other employees, making it difficult for them to harvest the laughter they need to power Monstropolis...and all evidence points to Sulley's best friend Mike Wazowski!

SC $9.99 ISBN 9781608865086
HC $24.99 ISBN 9781608865338

DISNEY'S HERO SQUAD: ULTRAHEROES VOL. 1: SAVE THE WORLD

It's an all-star cast of your favorite Disney characters, as you have never seen them before. Join Donald Duck, Goofy, Daisy, and even Mickey himself as they defend the fate of the planet as the one and only Ultraheroes!

SC $9.99 ISBN 9781608865437
HC $24.99 ISBN 9781608865529

UNCLE SCROOGE: THE HUNT FOR THE OLD NUMBER ONE

Join Donald Duck's favorite penny-pinching Uncle Scrooge as he, Donald himself and Huey, Dewey, and Louie embark on a globe-spanning trek to recover treasure and save Scrooge's "number one dime" from the treacherous Magica De Spell.

SC $9.99 ISBN 9781608865475
HC $24.99 ISBN 9781608865536

WIZARDS OF MICKEY VOL. 1: MOUSE MAGIC

Your favorite Disney characters star in this magical fantasy epic! Student of the great wizard Nereus, Mickey allies himself with Donald and teammate Goofy, in a quest to find a magical crown that will give him mastery over all spells!

SC $9.99 ISBN 9781608865413
HC $24.99 ISBN 9781608865505

DONALD DUCK AND FRIENDS: DOUBLE DUCK VOL. 1

Donald Duck as a secret agent? Villainous fiends beware as the world of super sleuthing and espionage will never be the same! This is Donald Duck like you've never seen him!

SC $9.99 ISBN 9781608865451
HC $24.99 ISBN 9781608865512

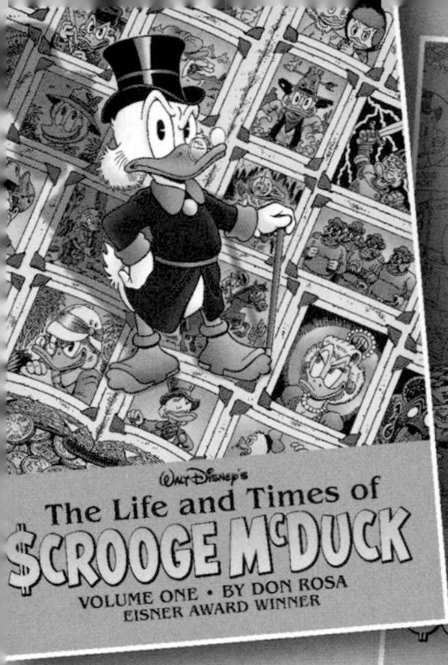
Walt Disney's
The Life and Times of
$CROOGE McDUCK
VOLUME ONE • BY DON ROSA
EISNER AWARD WINNER

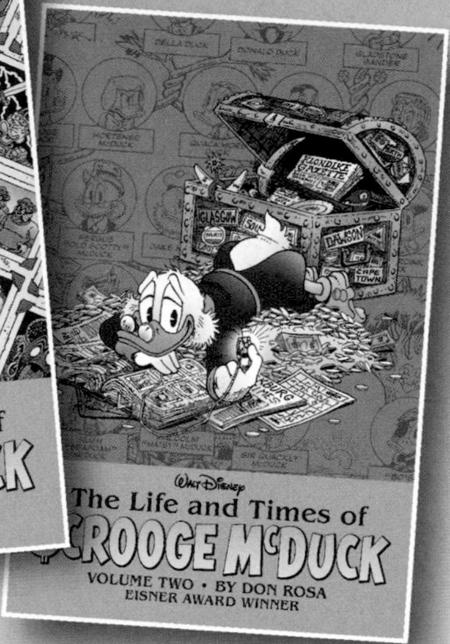
Walt Disney
The Life and Times of
$CROOGE McDUCK
VOLUME TWO • BY DON ROSA
EISNER AWARD WINNER

THE LIFE AND TIMES OF SCROOGE McDUCK VOL. 1

BOOM Kids! proudly collects the first half of THE LIFE AND TIMES OF SCROOGE MCDUCK in a gorgeous hardcover collection – featuring smyth sewn binding, a gold-on-gold foil-stamped case wrap, and a bookmark ribbon! These stories, written and drawn by legendary cartoonist Don Rosa, chronicle Scrooge McDuck's fascinating life.

HC $24.99 ISBN 9781608865383

THE LIFE AND TIMES OF SCROOGE McDUCK VOL. 2

BOOM Kids! proudly presents volume two of THE LIFE AND TIMES OF SCROOGE MCDUCK in a gorgeous hardcover collection in a beautiful, deluxe package featuring smyth sewn binding and a foil-stamped case wrap! These stories, written and drawn by legendary cartoonist Don Rosa, chronicle Scrooge McDuck's fascinating life.

HC $24.99 ISBN 9781608865420

MICKEY MOUSE CLASSICS: MOUSE TAILS

See Mickey Mouse as he was meant to be seen! Solving mysteries, fighting off pirates, and generally saving the day! These classic stories comprise a "Greatest Hits" series for the mouse, including a story produced by seminal Disney creator Carl Barks!

HC $24.99 ISBN 9781608865390

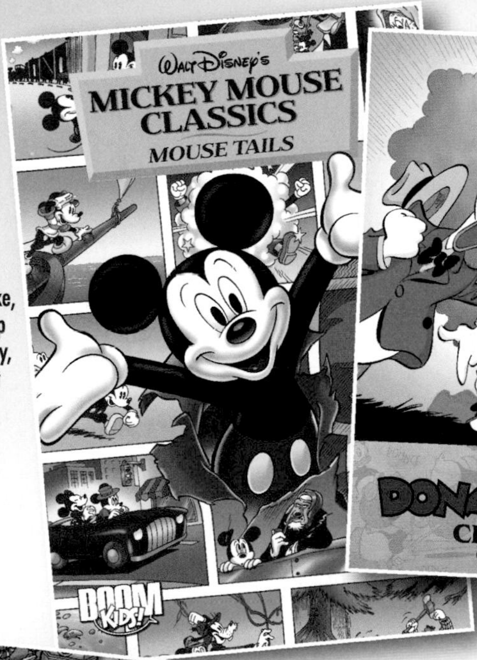
Walt Disney's
MICKEY MOUSE CLASSICS
MOUSE TAILS
BOOM KIDS!

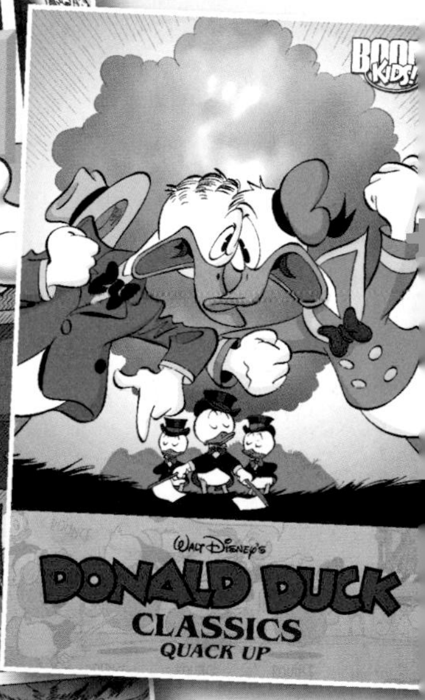
BOOM KIDS!
Walt Disney's
DONALD DUCK
CLASSICS
QUACK UP

DONALD DUCK CLASSICS: QUACK UP

Whether it's finding gold, journeying to the Klondike, or fighting ghosts, Donald will always have the help of his much more prepared nephews – Huey, Dewey, and Louie – by his side. Featuring some of the best Donald Duck stories Carl Barks ever produced!

HC $24.99 ISBN 9781608865406

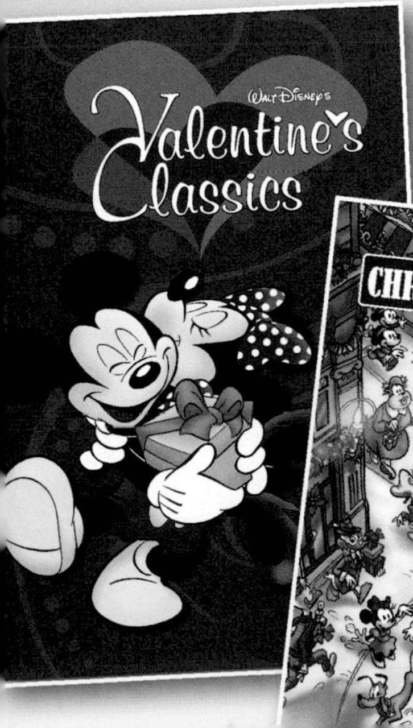
Walt Disney's
Valentine's
Classics

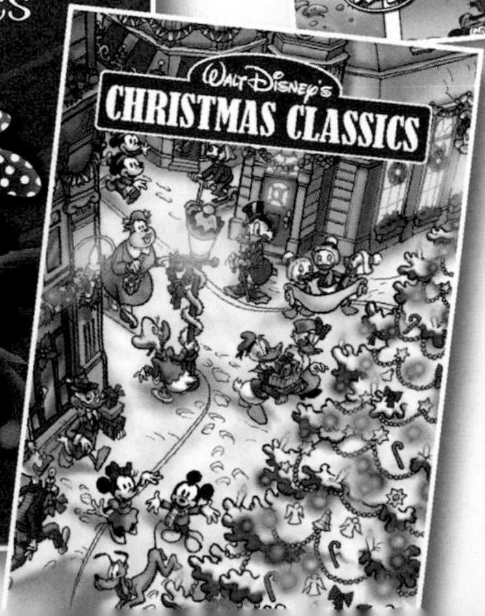
Walt Disney's
CHRISTMAS CLASSICS

WALT DISNEY'S VALENTINE'S CLASSICS

Love is in the air for Mickey Mouse, Donald Duck and the rest of the gang. But will Cupid's arrows cause happiness or heartache? Find out in this collection of classic stories featuring work by Carl Barks, Floyd Gottfredson, Daan Jippes, Romano Scarpa and Al Taliaferro.

HC $24.99 ISBN 9781608865499

WALT DISNEY'S CHRISTMAS CLASSICS

BOOM Kids! has raided the Disney publishing archives and searched every nook and cranny to find the best and the greatest Christmas stories from Disney's vast comic book publishing history for this "best of" compilation.

HC $24.99 ISBN 9781608865482

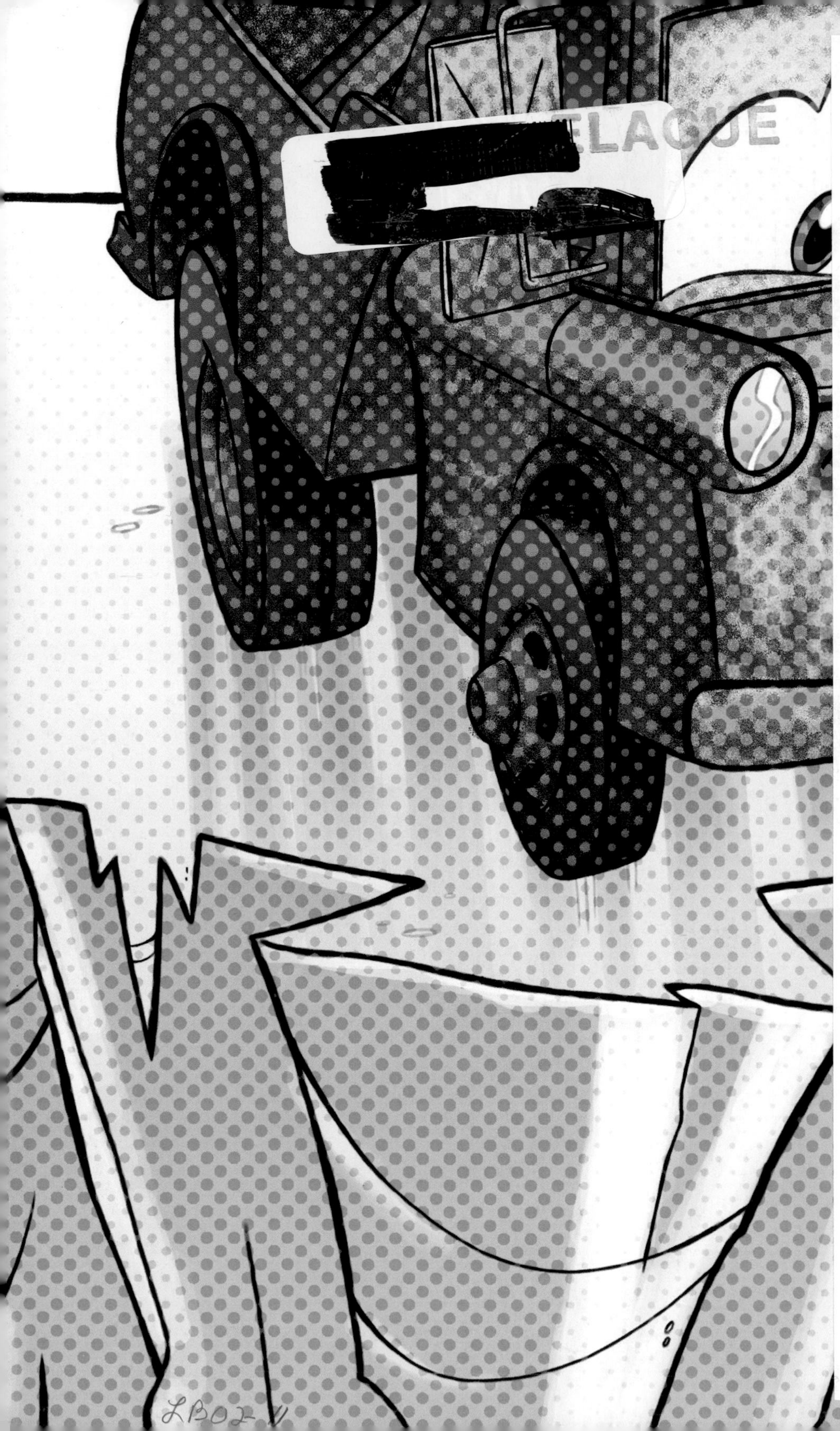